THE IRONCLAD PROPHECY

THEY HALTED AT the jungle edge. When Mathers *looked* there was nothing, but he knew they were there. The fumes from the tank allowed him to *see* their breathing; slight yellow eddies in the air around the undergrowth.

Through the protective eye slits of his splash mask, he caught a movement from the tree line. A group of urmen stepped out from under cover. One came forwards hesitantly.

Mathers braced himself. You could never be quite sure of the reaction, but he heard the great six pounders coming to bear behind him, and Clegg running up the engine so it sounded like a throaty growl. That usually did the trick. Behind his chainmail mask, Mathers smiled. He enjoyed this next bit.

The warrior stopped, his eyes wide with fear and, while still a full twenty yards away from the ironclad, gave a great cry, threw up his arms and dropped to his knees, genuflecting until his forehead touched the ground. Behind him, his fellows did the same, hardly daring to look upon them.

Then from his position of supplication, he spoke. "We have been expecting you. Your coming has been foretold."

Mathers hadn't expected that.

An Abaddon Books™ Publication
www.abaddonbooks.com
abaddon@rebellion.co.uk

First published in 2011 by Abaddon Books™, Rebellion
Intellectual Property Limited, Riverside House, Osney Mead,
Oxford, OX2 0ES, UK.

10 9 8 7 6 5 4 3 2 1

Editors: Jenni Hill & David Moore
Cover Art: Pye Parr
Design: Simon Parr & Luke Preece
Marketing and PR: Michael Molcher
Creative Director and CEO: Jason Kingsley
Chief Technical Officer: Chris Kingsley
No Man's Wolrd™ created by Pat Kelleher

UK ISBN: 978-1-907992-15-5
US ISBN: 978-1-907992-16-2

Printed in the US

To Jonathan

NO MAN'S WORLD

THE IRONCLAD PROPHECY

PAT KELLEHER

Best Wishes

Pat K

ABADDON
BOOKS

WWW.ABADDONBOOKS.COM

*"When sorrows come, they come not single spies
But in battalions."*

– *Hamlet*, Act 4, Scene 5,
William Shakespeare

ACKNOWLEDGEMENTS

I would like to thank Stephen Maugham and the Broughtonthwaite Historical Society for their continuing support. I am grateful to Faye Joy for her dedication in undertaking research and tracking down French newspaper reports and primary documents concerning the Harcourt Event and the subsequent Lefeuvre Find. I am also grateful to the estate of the late Arthur Cooke for continued access to his collection. I should also like to thank Ellie McDonald at the Broughtonthwaite Museum, who brought to my attention some of their more recent acquisitions concerning the Fusiliers. I am indebted to Bill Crinson at the British Library archive of British Periodicals, for his encyclopaedic knowledge on the history of British magazines of the period, invaluable help in tracking down issues of *Great War Science Stories* and for providing information on the works of Harold G. Cargill. Special thanks must go to all those people who have kindly contacted the publishers and offered me access to private family documents and photographs in my continuing research. Once more, I must thank my wife, Penny, for her continuing support and dedicated work in transcribing interviews.

13th BATTALION PENNINE FUSILIERS: COMPANY PERSONNEL

Battalion HQ.
C.O.:   2nd Lieutenant J. C. Everson
2C.O.:   Company Sergeant Major Ernest Nelson
Company Quartermaster Sergeant Archibald Slacke
Pte. Henry *'Half Pint'* Nicholls (batman)

Royal Army Chaplain: Father Arthur Rand
(CF4) ('Captain')

War Office Kinematographer Oliver Hepton

'C' Company

No 1 Platoon
C.O.:   Lieutenant Morgan

No. 2 Platoon
C.O.:   2nd Lieutenant Palmer
2C.O.:   Platoon Sergeant Herbert Gerald Hobson

1 Section
I.C.:   Lance Corporal Thomas *'Only'* Atkins
Pte. Harold *'Gutsy'* Blood
Pte. Peter *'Nobby'* Clark
Pte. Wilfred Joseph *'Mercy'* Evans
Pte. Bernard *'Prof'* Gates
Pte. George *'Porgy'* Hopkiss
Pte. Leonard *'Pot-Shot'* Jellicoe
Pte. David Samuel *'Gazette'* Otterthwaite
Pte. Eric *'Chalky'* White

RAMC
Regimental Aid Post
RMO: Captain Grenville Lippett

Red Cross Nurses
      Sister Betty Fenton
      Sister Edith Bell

      Driver Nellie Abbott
      (First Aid Nursing Yeomanry)

Orderlies
      Pte. Edgar Stanton
      Pte. Edward Thompkins

Machine Gun Corps (Heavy Section) 'I' Company
I-5 HMLS Ivanhoe
C.O.: 2nd Lieutenant Arthur Alexander Mathers
      Pte. Wally Clegg (Driver)
      Pte. Frank Nichols (Gearsman)
      Pte. Alfred Perkins (Gearsman)
      Pte. Norman Bainbridge (Gunner)
      Pte. Jack Tanner (Gunner)
      Pte. Reginald Lloyd (Loader/ Machine Gunner)
      Pte. Cecil Nesbit (Loader / Machine Gunner)

D Flight 70 Squadron: Sopwith 1 ½ Strutter
      Lieutenant James Robert Tulliver (Pilot)
      Corporal Jack Maddocks (Observer)

For Niall and Niamh

PREFACE

"It's a Long, Long Way to Tipperary..."

THE MYSTERY OF the Harcourt Crater galvanised a generation when, in 1916, nine hundred men of the 13th Battalion of the Pennine Fusiliers vanished from the Somme. Ten years afterwards, a find in a French field revealed silent film footage, letters and journals, describing the Fusiliers' existence on another planet, only for it to be declared a hoax and forgotten as time passed.

Almost a hundred years later, the publication of *No Man's World: Black Hand Gang* revived interest in the case of the missing Pennine Fusiliers. Since then, members of the public have contacted the publisher with claims of new evidence, of unseen documents and letters that have lain in ordinary boxes and in dusty attics for decades, unregarded.

This volume, continuing the account of the Pennine Fusiliers' fate, has been able to include this new information, where appropriate, with the permission of the families, in order to shed light on one of the biggest military cover-ups of the last century.

It must be remembered, however, that it was not just the 13th Battalion of the Pennine Fusiliers that vanished that day. The *HMLS Ivanhoe*, one of Britain's secret weapons, the new-fangled 'tanks,' also disappeared, along with its eight-man crew.

While the mystery of the Pennines inspired lurid pulp tales in magazines such as *Great War Science Stories*, and featured in adventures like *The Curse of the 13th Battalion*; *The Golem of No Man's Land*; *Zeppelin from Another World* and *Crater of the Somme-bies*, the *Ivanhoe* appeared in only a small number of tales published during 1928. They were written by Harold G. Cargill who, the publication's editors sensationally suggested, was an eyewitness survivor of the Fusiliers, returned from the planet.

While there was no evidence to suggest that Cargill was ever a member of the Pennine Fusiliers, his name not appearing in any official war records, nor indeed in a list of the missing, it is clear from his personal correspondence that he knew more than he was telling, or perhaps was *allowed* to tell.

The *Ivanhoe* and its crew were portrayed in those tales as cheery, jingoistic modern day knights-in-armour, riding out across a strange planet on colourful, rip-roaring quests.

The truth, however, is more inauspicious.

Military records show that the *Ivanhoe*, with five other tanks from I Company, Machine Gun Corp, Heavy Section, was ordered into battle on 1st November 1916 to support an assault on Harcourt Wood by the Pennines. Of those tanks, three broke down before they reached the front line. I4, the female tank *Igraine*, was mired in mud and abandoned. Wreckage of I3, the *Invicta*, was found at the bottom of the Harcourt Crater itself. It is assumed that it drove blindly over the edge, moments after the crater's appearance, killing all on board.

All of the major events in this account are drawn, where possible, from primary sources, including fragments of the *Ivanhoe's* tank diary. Scribbled in faded pencil and almost indecipherable in places, they were found among the papers of Arthur Cooke, author of *The Harcourt Crater: Hoax or Horror?* While incomplete, the fragments do give some clues to the apparent fate of the *Ivanhoe* and its crew, a fate that is firmly entrenched in that of the Pennine Fusiliers.

And it is uplifting to discover from these sources that while the Pennines were fighting for their existence in a place that was, most definitely, a long, long way from Tipperary, throughout the travails and terrors they had to endure their hearts did, indeed, remain right here.

Pat Kelleher
Broughtonshaw
December, 2010

PENNINE FUSILIERS

PROLOGUE

"Here Comes The British Navy,
Sailing On The Land..."

Elveden, Suffolk, May 1916

THE GREAT ARMOURED beast stood passively, like a great destrier waiting to be ridden into battle.

Lieutenant Arthur Mathers tried to hold his nerve in front of his men but, despite his efforts, the muscle beneath his right eye began to twitch uncontrollably. His palms began to sweat and he started to hyperventilate. He could feel his heart pounding in his chest.

To his men beside him, this thing was a magnificent brute. They crowded around it admiringly, patting its flanks and inspecting it like a prize thoroughbred.

"Bleedin' hell, it's a sight, isn't it, sir?" Wally Clegg, the small, thin-haired cockney beside Mathers, beamed with a joy the officer couldn't feel.

"Yes, Clegg. Yes it is," said Mathers, trying to temper his rising fear.

Reginald Lloyd looked over at the small man with the weary air of one given to correcting those less educated than himself. "It's not an *it*, Wally. Tanks are a *he* or a *she*." Reggie had been a butler to minor aristocracy, but had joined up to 'do his bit,' a duty he seemed to interpret as trying to instil some manners into his crewmates.

"Well, begging your pardon, Reggie, but I ain't no vet. How do you tell them apart?"

"Most of us, Wally, paid attention on the course, but for your benefit, both types have front and rear machine guns, but females have smaller sponsons either side with two Hotchkiss machine guns in each, while the males, like this one here, have bigger sponsons, each with a six-pounder gun and a Hotchkiss."

"By God, the Hun'll pay now," said Wally, with evident glee. He was a chipper bloke, Wally. A motor omnibus driver before the war, he had a wife and eight kids. Loved his family, he did, and talked about them at the drop of a hat. It was a pity that they were all dead, having died in a Zeppelin raid on the East End.

Norman Bainbridge smacked his hand on the barrel of the six-pounder. "Aye, the Hun'll be running scared all right, but only because of your driving!" Norman had been in the music hall, as he was never shy of reminding people, although often so far down the bill you needed spectacles to see his name. Life and soul he was; wherever there was a pianola, there he was leading the singing.

Frank Nichols, an electrical engineer, answered a cryptic advert placed in *The Motor Cycle* magazine by the War Office and ended up here. He walked around, inspecting the huge caterpillar tracks. "I tell you what; I certainly wouldn't like to see this bugger coming at me, Alfie."

Alfie Perkins, his fellow gearsman, was checking out the one-and-a-half-ton hydraulic steering tail, with its iron wheels, at the rear of the tank. He'd joined the Motor Machine Gun Service to be a motorcycle machine gunner, before volunteering for the new Heavy Section. "Me neither. I wouldn't want to be the Hun when we get over there."

The fearsome metal beast before him was a Mark I tank. At thirty-two feet long and eight feet high, with its distinctive rhomboid shape, the ironclad land ship weighed twenty-eight tons. This was Britain's new secret weapon. It was going to help turn the tide of the war and break the deadlock on the

Somme. And put the wind up Fritz. More than that, this one, designated I5, was theirs.

The tank had been tuned, the guns cleaned, and Cecil Nesbitt had just put the finishing touches to the name, now painted on the side of the front track horn. Cecil was the youngest crewmember. An orphan and a truculent sod, he'd been signed up by his Platoon Commander, who just wanted shot of him, and he had found a real home. He looked to big Jack Tanner, who nodded with satisfaction. Jack used to be a boxer in a travelling fair until he joined up. His brother was in the Royal Navy and had been killed at the battle of Jutland. He thought joining the 'Land Navy' a fitting tribute to him.

They stood back and looked at it with pride. HMLS *Ivanhoe*.

Outside of the top-secret camp at Elveden, very few people had seen a tank, let alone knew what one was, and that was no surprise. The project was so secret that most men applied without any real idea of what they were applying for. They just knew the pay was slightly better. Three separate perimeters surrounded the camp. No one could get in or out, and it was impossible to get hold of passes for leave. Should they actually manage to see anyone from outside, there was a one hundred pound fine, or six months' imprisonment, if they disclosed anything about what went on in there. No wonder they were nicknamed the Hush Hush Crowd.

Then there were the months of training, without any hint of what it was they were training for. There was lots of drill and training on Vickers machine guns, but with no reasons why. It was months before they even saw a real tank.

And the tank before them wasn't just any tank. This was *their* tank. They were learning to drive it. It wasn't easy. It took four people just to steer it.

Today was merely battle practice, that was all, but Mathers was nervous.

He had a secret phobia of enclosed spaces, but he would master his fear. He would master this brute machine and make it his.

"Right" he said, as his crew crowded about the sponson hatch. "Top brass will be watching today. I've even heard a rumour that the King himself might be coming to watch. So, let's show them and the rest of I Company what the *Ivanhoe* can do, eh?"

His crew were in a jocular mood and gave a rowdy cheer.

"That shower in the *Igraine* reckon they can reach the 'enemy trenches' before we can," continued Mathers. "I've got five guineas in the Officer's Mess that says we'll beat them."

It may have been just a training exercise, but now there was money on it, it was serious. This meant war. They entered through the hatches at the rear of the sponsons. At barely four foot high they were a bit of a squeeze, and you had to watch your head, too.

Inside, the compartment was barely five feet high. They couldn't stand up straight without cracking their heads on the low roof. The Daimler engine almost reached the roof. With a small wooden platform behind it, it sat squarely in the middle of the white-painted compartment, taking up most of the space. Two wooden gangways, less than two feet across and eight feet long, ran down either side.

These opened out into the sponsons, the turrets projecting out either side of the tank, where the six-pounder guns sat, manoeuvred by the sheer strength of the gunner alone. Behind them were the belt-fed Hotchkiss machine guns. To the rear of each sponson was a small entrance hatch.

At the back of the engine was the large starting handle. It took four men to turn it in order to start the engine up.

Either side of that, each caterpillar track had its own gear system, each operated by a gearsman. Privates Alfie Perkins and Frank Nichols manned the independent gears, one for each track.

At the front, in a slightly raised cockpit, Private Wally Clegg, the small bantam cockney, sat in the right-hand driver's seat, and the tank commander, Lieutenant Mathers, in the left seat, next to him, to operate the steering brakes.

Once the hatches clanged shut, sealing the men in, Mathers felt the panic rising in him. Wally ran the engine up. Frank and Alfie stood by their track gears at the back. The *Ivanhoe* set off across the training ground.

The tank commander, using steering brakes for each track, could only make slight turns along with the driver, using the wheel that controlled the steering tail. Large swinging manoeuvres took four men.

The engine was too loud for verbal instructions, so Mathers had to get the attention of the gearsmen by banging a wrench on a pipe. He gave a signal with his hand to swing right. He stopped the tank and locked the differential gear. Alfie put his track gear into neutral, stopping the right hand track, while Frank pushed the left track gear into first speed, swinging the tank to the right. The tank had to stop again, while Mathers re-engaged the main gears, and Alfie took the right track out of neutral. It was a long and laborious process.

Obstacles filled the training ground: earthwork ramps, trenches, craters, barbed wire entanglements and deep ditches, all to test the prowess of the tank crews. The noise of the engines filled the training area, as six tanks of 2 Section, I Company set off over the course, the guns blazing away at targets. The *Igraine* got itself ditched in a crater. The *Illustrious* threw a track.

The *Ivanhoe* advanced on a large crater, teetering on the lip until the front track horns tilted, and the tank crashed down. The tracks caught the ground in the trough and began to haul the ironclad up the far side.

With the engine running, the temperature inside was becoming almost unbearable, and the compartment soon filled with petrol vapour and cordite fumes.

Mathers was beginning to sweat. He could feel his chest tighten and his breathing become shallower. The sooner he could finish this, the sooner he could get out. Hardly caring now, he pushed the machine to its limits.

The last obstacle of the course was a steep bank about forty yards long. The other tanks nosed cautiously over the edge, and descended gingerly.

The *Ivanhoe* raced over the top of the rise, and dashed down the slope at a terrific pace, sparks flying from its tracks. Despite having no suspension, it bounced as it crashed to the bottom of the slope.

Inside, the manoeuvre threw the crew about roughly. Cecil cracked his head on the gun breech; Norman slammed against the engine block, burning his arm. Thrown into the steering column, Wally had the wind knocked out of him. All of them were cursing, except Reggie, who managed a heartfelt, "Dash it all!" They fell out of the sponson hatches, badly shaken, coughing and retching.

Mathers staggered from the tank, gasping for breath, relieved to be in the open air again. The Company commander greeted him with enthusiasm. "Great Scott, Arthur. I was wrong about you. I've seen some devilish driving in my time, but that's the kind of gumption we need if we're going to stick it to the Hun! It's always the quiet ones, eh?"

"You know what," said Frank, catching his breath and jerking his chin towards where Mathers was talking with the other officers. "I'll tell you this for nothing. He'll either win us medals for getting to Germany first, or he'll be the bloody death of us all."

Signal from the HMLS Ivanhoe,
1st November 1916*

"C" Form (Original)				Army Form C 2121
MESSAGES AND SIGNALS.				No. of message

Prefix	Code	Words	Received From *Cpl*	Sent, or sent out	Office Stamp
Charges to collect	£ s. d.		By *Knott*	At _____ m	
Service Instructions: *Pigeon Priority*				To _____	
Handed in at _____			Office *7-48 a.m.*	By _____ Received *8-24 a* m	

TO	*Divn HQ*

Sender's Number	Day of Month *1-11-16*	In reply to Number	A A A

Tanks	*I-1*	*I-2*	*and*	
I-6	*broken*	*down*	*en route*	
from	*ST. GERMAINE*	*to*	*starting*	
Point	*tanks* *I-5*	*I-3*	*and*	
I-4	*proceeding*	*on*	*to*	
primary	*objectives*			

FROM	*Lt. Mather*	*HMLS I-5*
PLACE & TIME	*Hancourt Sector*	*7-20 a*

Wt 1753. A.W. & Co. 40,000 Pads 6/15

*Sent by carrier pigeon, this was the last message ever received before HMLS *Ivanhoe* and the 13th Battalion of the Pennine Fusiliers vanished.

CHAPTER ONE

"Let the Great Big World Keep Turning..."

Four months later...

"RUN!"

Lance Corporal Thomas Atkins of the Pennine Fusiliers could hear the terrifying rhythmic chittering noise behind him, even over the measured thud of his hobnailed boots on the crimson alien soil.

Ahead of them lay the vast expanse of the tube grass veldt and, too far away across it, the Pennines' encampment.

Atkins and the rest of 1 Section urged and cajoled the ragtag band of urmen, the primitive humans who inhabited this planet, through the shoulder-high tube grass. Bewildered young children shrieked as desperate parents dragged them along.

Naparandwe ran up alongside him. The middle-aged native guide had been the first urman they had encountered on this world and his help had been invaluable. The men, however, called him 'Napoo,' army slang for 'all gone,' after his initial habit of finishing everyone's food when they first met. Like most urmen, he wore a combination of animal skins and insect shell armour. His usually cheerful face was drawn, his tanned forehead creased with concern. "Atkins, they cannot keep this pace up," he said. "They are tired, hungry, terrified."

"They don't have a choice, Napoo. Not if they want to live. We've got to keep moving." He stopped and waved past a few urman warriors armed with short swords and spears. "Come on, come on!" They, in turn, herded and encouraged their distressed families.

"Ruined my soddin' day, this has," said Gutsy as he jogged past with a young lad on his back. Too exhausted to cry any more, the lad just clung to the brawny butcher's shoulders, his small chest heaving with dry sobs.

"Saved mine," said Mercy, the section's inveterate scrounger, with a grin. "Nobby was just about to start telling jokes. He's only got three and they're all bloody rubbish."

"Look at this, nearly took me bloody leg off!" said Pot Shot.

Mercy glanced down at the lanky soldier's charred calf-wrapping as he trotted alongside. He shook his head and grinned. "Just be thankful it's your puttee that kaput-ee, and not you, you grousing sod."

The incorrigible Porgy, and Gazette, the best sharp shooter they had, trotted along with several new replacements. Prof, Nobby and Chalky had brought the section up to strength. The other new addition, Shiner, had died three weeks earlier when, on patrol, he'd stopped to take a leak. He peed on something in the undergrowth that took exception to the act. Atkins winced whenever he thought of it.

An explosion of shrieks and feathers erupted to their right – Gazette wheeled around with his rifle to meet the threat. A flock of grubbing bird-things, startled by their passing, took to the air with raucous cries.

Atkins watched an urman woman clutching a baby to her breast as she ran, a wild desperation in her eyes. He thought of Flora, his missing brother's fiancée, now pregnant with his own child. He had only found that out here, after discovering that Ketch, his old corporal, had spitefully withheld her letter from him. She was his Flora, now. Not William's. Not his brother's. *His* sweetheart, waiting for him on Earth. *His* child, growing up fatherless. Or it soon would be. He'd kept count. Flora would be seven months gone by now. And he was stuck here on this benighted world.

He felt more alone now than ever. More than once, he thought about confiding in Porgy, but stopped himself. That someone else would take your wife or sweetheart while you were fighting at the front was every soldier's worst nightmare. He doubted he'd find much sympathy, and he feared the friendships he'd lose.

He would do whatever it took to return home to Flora, to his child. He wouldn't rest until she was in his arms again. But to do that he had to survive the day.

To do that he had to run.

SINCE THEIR ARRIVAL on this God-forsaken planet, Padre Rand, the army chaplain, had watched the Pennine Fusiliers re-dig the parallel lines of Somme trenches into a defensible stronghold, encircling the area of Somme that had come with them, protecting all they had left of Earth.

Without the distraction of constant Hun artillery bombardment, they were able to dig deep dugouts, after the German fashion, with the time to construct them properly, dry and strong and deep.

Now linked by radial communications trenches, three concentric circles of defensive trenches ringed the ground at the centre, now home to a parade ground and assorted tents and crude wooden hutments. Lewis and Vickers machine gun emplacements strengthened the perimeter.

Above it all, in the centre of the small parade ground, the torn, tattered Union Jack hung lifelessly from its makeshift flagpole.

It should be snapping in the wind, the Padre thought, proud and glorious, filling the men with hope and pride. Instead, it seemed limp and forlorn, unable to instil anything in anyone. It looked the way he felt.

It had been three months since Jeffries had conducted the obscene occult ritual that had apparently condemned them all to this place. The Padre had a hard time dealing with that one. That someone as evil as him could have access to such supernatural power as to bring them here while he, with his prayers and his Almighty, barely seemed to accomplish a thing. He felt insignificant in comparison. It challenged his faith in a way the war itself never had, and he felt unequal to the task now before him, caring for the souls of these castaway men.

The men had embellished the tale of their arrival, until Jeffries had glowing red eyes and magic bolts coming out of his fingers. As a result, his Church Parades were better attended now than they had been on the Somme, but it gave him little comfort.

He watched a wiring party at work beyond the front line trench. It was dangerous work, as was everything on this world. Barbed wire was in limited supply, but they had found a lethally barbed creeper they called wire weed that made a living substitute. The men, wearing old sniper's armour for protection, weren't so much laying it as cutting back the writhing vines, training it over wooden x-frame knife rests to fill gaps in the barbed wire entanglement in front of the fire trenches.

Walking over a small footbridge across the support trench, the Padre wrinkled his nose. The sweaty feet, cordite and corpse stench of the Somme had long since faded, to be replaced by the acrid tang of animal dung. Gathered from the veldt, huge tarpaulin-covered heaps of it had been left to rot down. They told him it was a saltpetre experiment, an attempt to make their own gunpowder. That, however, was still some months off yet, if they succeeded at all.

The sun, that was not their sun, was just rising above the valley sides and beginning to take the chill off the morning air, and the poppies were beginning to open.

He had been surprised to see the poppies when they first appeared. They all had. Their seeds, long buried in the Somme mud, had somehow survived. In the warm climes offered by this foreign world, they had germinated and flowered, dispersing their seeds on the wind so that now a carpet of red flowed across the scorched cordon sanitaire around them and onto the alien veldt beyond in an invasion all of their own. The poppies spread out, like the red of the British Empire across the maps of the world in his old atlas. To the men, they were a cheering sight. A sign of hope. It was as if God had sent a message to say he had not abandoned them after all.

Poppies hadn't been the only things to appear. Potatoes had sprouted too: after all, before the war, before the trenches, the Somme was rich farming ground. They cleared some land beyond the encampment for agriculture. They planted the potatoes there and some native vegetables. It all went well until the alien weeds came and the new plants had literally fought each other for dominance until the entire area had to be razed.

It had put him in mind of the Old Testament story of Joseph and the Pharaoh's dream, of seven thin and shrivelled ears of wheat swallowing up the ripe ones. That unsettled him deeply, reminding him of his own vision, the terrifying hallucination brought on by the Khungarrii in a heathen ritual he had been forced to undergo, along with Jeffries. The vision itself had faded as the drugs had left his system; he had tried remembering it, but he could not. He was left with an unsettling sense of terror and despair. Recently, he had begun waking with night terrors, things that receded and vanished from memory as he awoke in a sweat. Things that made him afraid. He was terrified his vision was coming back to haunt him.

He was shaken from his thoughts by Sergeant Dixon across the parade ground, barking out instructions to a platoon of heathen urmen. Nicknamed 'Fred Karno's Army,' after a popular song, they were dressed in skins and customised pieces of armour shaped from the chitinous shells of various creatures. They were drilling with spears instead of rifles, much to the amusement of the Tommies on work parties nearby, who had stopped to watch the entertainment.

The NCO was teaching them the rudiments of drill, forging into shape a ragtag army of urmen refugees who, displaced by recent Khungarrii attacks, had sought sanctuary here. For the urmen, it would give them the tools they needed to defend themselves against the Ones. It also served to bolster the numbers of the Pennines themselves.

On one side of the parade ground stood the single-storey log building that was the small hospital. Huddled around it, groups of tents served as wards and surgical theatres. A group of soldiers stood waiting to be seen by the MO.

Across the small parade ground, in isolation, was a barbed wire compound, 'the Bird-Cage,' where those poor souls suffering emotional shock from the Somme, or from finding themselves here, could be kept safe. Some shook uncontrollably, and others rocked themselves incessantly, or cried or howled in torment. A few sought to hide themselves, however they could.

The Padre said a silent prayer for them, trotted down into the reserve trench and headed for Lieutenant Everson's dugout.

Approaching the gas curtain, he heard a woman's voice tinged with exasperation. He knew the voice well. Only three women had the misfortune to accompany them to this place. Edith Bell had been one of those kidnapped with him and taken to the Khungarrii edifice. She, Corporal Atkins and Lieutenant Everson had confronted Jeffries, who then gutted the Khungarrii edifice and destroyed their sacred library, setting them all even more at odds with the creatures that ruled this world than they had been before.

Lieutenant Everson sounded just as frustrated. "Nurse Bell, I'm sorry, but I have over five hundred men under my command. It is becoming clearer day by day that we cannot depend on being returned by whatever forces brought us here. If we are to return, then it will have to be under our own cognisance. That map of his you saw. You said yourself he went to a lot of trouble to get it. It's obviously important. The sketch you gave us was helpful, but short on detail. Anything else you can give me, anything at all, will be most valuable."

Bell sighed heavily. "I know that, Lieutenant, and I have tried. I have wracked my brains. And I can assure you, if I remember the slightest thing you'll be the first to know."

"I'd appreciate that."

"Then give me more aid for the shell-shock patients," she asked. "Captain Lippett has no time for them. He believes they're nothing but shirkers and malingerers. They're ill. You can't keep them in the Bird Cage, like prisoners! You just can't!"

"Nurse Bell, Captain Lippett is the Medical Officer here. I don't think he'd appreciate you going over his head. Please do try and stick to the proper channels," said Everson with a sigh. "Do I have to tell Sister Fenton?"

Padre Rand coughed politely outside the rubberised canvas flap that formed the dugout's door.

"Enter!"

He stepped inside. Everson was at his desk. Scattered in front of him was Jeffries' coded occult journal and various maps and papers they had taken from his dugout. Sat opposite, Nurse Bell took the opportunity to end her interview. She stood up, brushed down her nurse's apron over her part-worn khaki trousers and bobbed a slight curtsey to Rand as she passed him. "Padre," she said curtly, pulling the canvas door aside and stepping out into the light.

Everson looked up from behind his desk, sweeping a hand across the papers and journal before him.

"No matter how many times I look at this stuff, I come up with nothing. Nothing but that damn Croatoan symbol with which Jeffries seemed to be obsessed. The rest I can't make head or tails of, even after three months."

The Padre felt for him. Lieutenant Everson was a good officer, respected by the men, but where the blame for bad decisions might be passed back up the line to Battalion HQ or the General Staff, here the buck stopped with him. He was the highest-ranking infantry officer left. Whatever credit he had with the men was running out. He had turned more and more frequently to the scattered papers looking for answers, as another might turn to the bible or the bottle.

Everson gave him a weary smile. "Tea, Padre? Nichols!"

The man called Half Pint clumped into the room from an office beyond. He was twenty four, but looked twice that age. He'd lost his right leg below the knee at Khungarr. Unfit for duty, Everson had taken him on as his batman.

"What do you think, Padre?" he said with a grin, thrusting out his new peg leg. "Mercy – Private Evans, that is – carved it out of a lump of wood he found. Mind you, hurts like the blazes. Rubs something awful on me stump, it does. Me wife were the same about her new teeth when I bought her the highland clearances for a wedding present. Serves me right, I suppose. What goes around, comes around she'd say."

Everson cleared his throat.

"Sorry, sir. Tea, was it? Right away, sir," said Half Pint, hobbling off.

The Padre looked down at the scattered papers littering the desk. "There's a whole world out there, Lieutenant. He could be dead by now. But somehow I doubt it. Man has the luck of the devil."

"You can say that again."

"If he's alive, a man like him won't stay hidden for long. He needs to show off. He wants people to know what he's up to, how clever he is. He only has us who would understand. We'll hear from him again, you take my word."

"I hope you're right, Padre. Sending men out to find his trail is becoming too costly. Sending the tank has become the only choice. It's practically impervious to anything this place throws at it."

"Running a risk, though, isn't it?"

"So Sergeant Hobson keeps telling me. The Khungarrii are still afraid of us. Well, of the tank, really. So they seem to be taking it out on the urmen, stepping up reprisal raids against them. You told me they'd a mind to cull us and, after Jeffries betrayed them, it's probably no more than I'd expect. I just hope it doesn't come to that."

SPURRED ON BY the incessant rhythm behind them, Atkins ran, pushing his men on through the tube grass, harassing and chivvying the urmen onward. The day had started out so well, too, at least for this place...

"Take your black hand gang eve-ward out round the edge of the veldt," Lieutenant Everson had said. "Napoo informs me that there's an enclave of urmen out there this time of year. Try to convince them to side with us. The more influence we have, the better our chances of dealing with the Khungarrii."

That and "keep an eye out for Jeffries," an order repeated so often that it was now becoming a standing joke amongst the men.

It had seemed simple enough. They'd left the encampment that morning on routine patrol with the new replacements. Everson had ordered that every patrol have an urman guide, and now Napoo led the way down into a small valley through a wood of tall jelleph trees, with their smooth, bulbous trunks and broad, flat damson-coloured fronds.

Behind him, Gutsy and Porgy were talking in low voices. Every so often, a snort of laughter would burst from them only to be stifled as Atkins glanced back. Time was, as a private, when he'd be in on the joke.

Porgy ambled up to him trying to suppress a smirk. "Here, Only, I want you to meet Chalky. He's a big admirer of yours. Hey, Chalky!" he yelled.

The eager young private came running up the file, "Here, sir!" he said with a salute.

Atkins sighed. "It's just Corporal, Private. I'm not an officer."

Chalky looked at Atkins in awe.

"What?" he asked irritably.

"It's just, the stories? Are they true, Corp?"

Atkins shook his head in exasperation. The stories around his and Everson's confrontation with Jeffries had started shortly after they returned from the Khungarr raid. They spread like latrine rumours, embroidered with each retelling until men were swearing it was true, as true as the Angel of Mons.

Right now, he was up there with St. George or the Phantom Bowmen. Christ, in some quarters you'd think he'd tricked the very devil himself. But it didn't happen like that.

That was why Atkins liked it out on patrol, away from the curious stares of those who believed the stories, those who sneered at them and those who resented him, thinking he'd spread them himself for his own glory. In truth, he didn't know who had started them, but he wished they hadn't.

He scowled at Porgy and shook his head in disappointment.

Porgy beamed, having got just the reaction he wanted, and steered Chalky away. "Later, Chalky, later."

Atkins saw a faint smudge in the air ahead, above the trees. "Gazette?"

Gazette had the sharpest eyes in the section. They narrowed. "Smoke. That'll be the urman enclave Napoo told us about."

Through the damson-coloured foliage came a scream. At first, they hesitated. Men had gone charging off in aid of a human-like scream before only to end up gored to death. Then a second and a third pierced the leaden air.

"Stand to!" said Atkins.

The screams continued, mingled with inarticulate shouts of rage. Atkins began to trot along the forest path, keeping parallel to the valley floor. He wanted to try and see what they were up against before they went charging in. A creek roared and tumbled below them, as if to drown the screams, but the urgent notes rose above it. Great wet fronds of saltha weed slapped at them as they passed and small creatures, startled by their passing, crashed away through the undergrowth.

The strains of battle now reached them. Through gaps in the trees they caught the familiar blue flash of Khungarrii bioelectrical lances. Atkins held up his hand and the section came to a halt.

"Load," said Atkins hoarsely, fishing a fresh magazine from his webbing. He slotted the magazine home, flicked open the magazine cut-off and pulled the bolt, cycling a bullet into the chamber. From the noises around him, the rest of the section did the same, finishing the routine drill within split seconds of each other. They only had twenty rounds and one Mills bomb apiece.

Beyond that, they each had a bayonet; seventeen inches of cold British steel. Some had constructed trench clubs, brutal wooden clubs with hobnails or other protrusions. And Gutsy, Gutsy had his best butcher's cleaver, Little Bertha.

As the vegetation thinned and the camp below became visible, the source of the screams and blue flashes proved to be a circle of a dozen crude huts, several of the thatched roofs ablaze as the Khungarrii scentirrii attacked.

They were hard to miss. The arthropod soldiers were the size of a man, but thickly built and heavily armoured with a natural chitinous shell covered with sharp spines. Their face shells were broad, flat and ugly with small antler nubs, and long antennae sprouted from the tops of their facial shells. In their abdominal section, they had the two vestigial claw-like limbs common to all chatts. They moved quickly on legs which were jointed so their knees faced backwards, giving them a powerful leap.

Twelve urmen were under attack from three times their number. They fought back with swords and spears, putting up a valiant fight, but they were losing and the encircling scentirrii were closing in.

Atkins motioned to Gazette, who came and crouched down beside him.

"Chatt scentirrii, all right. About thirty of them. Not good odds," Gazette offered.

"Trench fighting, no. But we've got these," Atkins said, slapping the palm of his hand against his Enfield. "We'll even the odds a little first before we go down. Gazette, you stay up here with Nobby, Chalky and Prof. Cover us. Go for the head, stop 'em giving off an alarm scent. We'll make for the huts."

Gazette grunted an acknowledgement. Atkins and the others scrambled down through the trees to the rear of the huts, huddling themselves against the wattle-and-daub walls. Atkins peered round into the centre of the enclave.

It was a massacre. The crackling blue arcs of the electrical lances threw men into spasms. Chatts with curved swords and some sort of thorny halberd spat acid from their mouthparts between their mandibles. Urmen screamed as the burning liquid caught their faces or arms.

"Shit," said Atkins. "Gas masks! They've got spitters."

The men fumbled at the canvas bags on their chests and pulled their PH hoods on over their heads. They were a bugger to fight in for any length of time, but they were invaluable against the acid-spitting chatts, as the scorch marks on several of them attested.

Atkins indicated to Gutsy that he and the others should circle around the huts to flank the Khungarrii within.

He lifted his gas hood, took a whistle out of his top pocket and blew. A rapid fusillade of bullets rang out as 1 Section poured their fire into the settlement. Cracks of sniper fire rang across the open ground as Gazette and the others picked off chatts from the hillside.

A dozen fell before the others knew what had happened.

The Tommies let out blood-curdling, if muffled, roars and charged into the fray with bayonets glinting.

Atkins sank his bayonet blade into the thorax of the nearest scentirrii and twisted it, before stomping forward with his boot to drive it off the point.

He swung the butt of the rifle against the head of another. A dark eye burst as it went down, its mandibles opened in surprise, its small abdominal limbs twitching uselessly as it fell. Atkins stepped over the body.

The air was filled with crunching carapaces and agitated chitters as he moved on his next target, a chatt with a clay battery pack and bioelectrical lance. Somehow, these inhuman creatures were able to store and amplify a natural electrical discharge in these devices. The lance spat out a jolt of blue fire, convulsing an urman before he fell to the ground.

He stepped up behind the chatt, staving in the battery pack with the shoulder stock of his Enfield rifle. As the chatt turned, he thrust the bayonet into the soft unprotected innards of its abdomen and tore it to one side, disembowelling it, ripping delicate organs from its body. It dropped to the ground, where it clawed feebly before Atkins stamped on its head.

Napoo's attacks were as economical as they were devastating, thrusting at weak joints in the chatts' chitinous armour.

Gutsy swung his butcher's cleaver down through the skull of another, splitting the head in half.

Mercy, stabbing and parrying with the bayonet and bludgeoning with the shoulder's stock, whirled the Enfield around through chatt after chatt with a dexterity that bewildered Atkins. All Mercy had ever said was that someone in the Chink Labour Battalions had owed him a favour. This, apparently, was it.

Atkins wheeled about looking for his next target and found none. Chatts lay strewn on the ground, dead or dying. He pulled off his gas hood.

"That's the last of 'em," said Porgy, jabbing his bayonet into a twitching chatt to still it.

Atkins looked around, catching his breath. Napoo was calmly wiping his sword with a saltha leaf.

The huts were ablaze, the dry crackles of the flames mingling with the wailing of women and children as the surviving warriors sought out their families, and those who found no comforting reunion realised their loss and wailed all the louder.

As 1 Section regrouped, Napoo sought out the Clan elder. They gripped each other by the forearms in greeting and talked in low voices, all the time casting glances at the Tommies.

Wanting to secure his position, Atkins called Gutsy over. "Take Gazette and Nobby. Go for a look-see. Check downwind. Make sure nothing's picked up any alarm scent these things might have got off. I don't want any more surprises."

The three men shouldered their rifles and moved off.

Napoo and the Clan elder came over to Atkins.

"This urman is Haradwe," said Napoo.

The urman Clan elder grinned in hospitality, white teeth beaming out of his weathered face, but his eyes betrayed his sorrow and pain. Atkins held out his hand only for the man to reach out and clasp his forearms.

The elder shook his head. "I have heard tales of your Clan, the Tohmii; the Urmen who challenge the Ones and who have Skarra fighting by their side. Naparandwe says you will protect us."

"If you'll accompany us back to the encampment, to our enclave, and add your number to ours. Gather your people together and we'll take you now. Mercy, help them round things up, just what they can carry – and don't nick anything."

He saw Nobby running back down towards him through the trees. "Only! Corp! Gutsy told me to tell you he's found something for you."

"What is it?"

"It's a surprise, Gutsy said."

Atkins mouthed an obscenity and followed Nobby as he trotted out of the trees and up a small hillock. Gutsy and Gazette were lying just below the crest. Atkins crawled the last few yards to keep out of sight.

He was aware of an insistent thrumming. "What's that bloody noise? Sounds like something crunching with its teeth."

"I think we've got a problem, Only."

"We wouldn't be the bloody Pennines if we didn't," said Atkins bitterly.

Gutsy thrust his chin towards the summit. "See for yourself."

Enfield cradled in the crooks of his arms, Atkins crawled up the crest on his elbows, lifted his head cautiously above the lip and peered out across the open veldt.

"Fuck!"

He slid back down a few feet in shock and looked back at Gutsy, who gave him an apologetic shrug.

Atkins crawled back to the top again. Not taking his eyes from the plain in front of him, he thrust his right hand back, feeling blindly in the air until Gutsy put a pair of binoculars into it. He peered through them.

There, far across the veldt, he saw chatts. Khungarrii. Thousands of them, column after column of a vast army on the march. Great caterpillar-like beasts writhed along in front, clearing a path through the tube grass, followed by massed ranks of Khungarrii scentirrii, their rear-most ranks lost in the dust cloud of the vanguard.

The rhythmic thrumming he heard was the marching step of the chatts muted by the distance, as they banged swords, spears and electric lances against their thorax plates.

They were marching on the British encampment.

PENNINE FUSILIERS

CHAPTER TWO
"All Our Might and Main..."

THEY RAN.

Atkins and his men half-jogged, half-walked, sure they were hidden from sight of the approaching army, but cajoling the weary and frightened urmen on anyway. The speed of their initial flight had gained them some ground, but now the logistics of moving families slowed them down.

They briefly stopped to let the last of the stragglers catch up, an urman urging on an old woman, and casting anxious glances behind them.

The Khungarrii were in no hurry to reach the Tommies' stronghold. Their pace was steady and persistent and their chanting and clicking relentless and pervasive.

Chalky mumbled something. Gutsy bent his ear to listen.

"Nah, don't you pay it no heed, boy. That racket there, it's meant to frit you. Don't you let it get to you. Bloody hell, Jerry's done worse than that. They're just chatts out there. No artillery, no trench mortars. Once we're back in the trenches they can't touch you, so buck up, lad."

Atkins was reminded of the Old Contemptibles' tales of the Battle of Mons, as the BEF retreated across Belgium before an advancing German army. He'd seen photographs in the newspapers and war news magazines of fleeing Belgian peasants, on the move with nothing more than they could carry. Then, the British had turned up and made a stand. And they would here, too. But right now they still had a way to go.

Atkins scanned the sky, hoping Tulliver might be up there in his aeroplane, but he realised he hadn't heard the insistent drone of its engine all day. Tulliver would have spotted the chatts' movements in plenty of time. These days, however, Everson didn't allow Tulliver to go up except for urgent missions. His machine may have been a marvel of modern mechanics but it was made from spit, string and paper and there were things here that would tear it out of the sky in an instant.

Nobby stumbled and fell, and Prof picked him up.

"Not now, there's a good chap," he rasped. "Be terribly inconvenient."

The clumsy private dusted himself off and mumbled an apology.

Gutsy rolled his eyes at Atkins. He shrugged his shoulders in return. Nobby suffered from a natural-born clumsiness and was the bane of many an NCO's life, which was how he ended up in Atkins' section as a replacement. Atkins wondered how he managed to fall over in the first place since he never raised his eyes from his feet.

"Going to be one hell of a scrap," said Gazette, cradling his rifle.

"Aye," admitted Atkins.

"First decent one we've had since we got here, if you don't count the trench raid on Khungarr. I hope we've not got soft and flabby. The Lieutenant's a good man, but I think the troops may be getting away from him a bit."

"Aye. He needs something to bring 'em along. This may just be it," said Atkins. Inside, he felt the familiar pull in his stomach as the tide of fear sucked at his soul with its insidious undertow. "Or it may be his undoing."

"Holy Mary, mother of God!" yelped Gutsy, snatching his foot back from a large crimson growth almost the colour of the soil. It shrank back into itself. "It moved! The damn stuff moved!"

"What the hell is it?" Atkins asked Napoo.

"Urluf, good djaja," replied the urman with an eating mime.

Some of the urmen quickly harvested the mass, tearing chunks off and eating it on the run, passing the lumps around young and old until it had all been consumed.

Gazette nudged Gutsy with his elbow as he jogged past. "You know that stuff the mongey wallahs have been putting in the broth to pad it out, that you thought was bully beef?"

"Uh huh."

"That's it."

Gutsy gave a dry retch. "And I thought onions in me tea was disgusting enough."

"Well the MO said it was fit to eat."

"What does he know? He'd give a number nine pill to cure the shits."

ATKINS PUSHED HIS men and their wards on as hard as he dared, driven by the awful, insistent gnashing and drumming. Ahead of them across the plain Atkins could see the hills start to rise as they ran towards the valley. From their current position, the stronghold was still out of sight, beyond the spur.

"Who's the replacement that knows iddy umpty?"

Mercy smirked. "That'll be Chalky."

Atkins hung his head. "Bloody hell."

Chalky was summoned.

"I want you to get your mirror out and send a message to the hill-top OP. Warn the dozy buggers, if they haven't already seen them, that there's an entire chatt army headed their way. I reckon we're only an half an hour or so ahead of the bastards, if that."

"Yes, Corporal!" he said snapping a salute and turning smartly to carry out his orders.

Atkins groaned. "Blood and sand, anyone'd think I'd just gazetted him."

He felt a tug at his leg. Tearing his gaze from the ominous dust across the veldt, he looked down to see a young urman child pulling at his trousers. He looked around for a parent. His eyes met those of a fair-haired Urman woman, who beckoned the child away from him. It was only when he looked again, as the child threw himself round her legs, that he noticed the roundness of her belly. She was with child. A desperate longing filled him, an ache he could not ease.

THE HILLS GREW larger, although much more slowly than Atkins would have liked. At last, they rounded the foothill and came to the valley mouth. He heard the faint, reassuring sound of a bugle on the wind.

Prof slapped Nobby on the back and they began marching with renewed vigour towards the mouth of the valley. "There you go, lad. Home soon."

Atkins stopped and counted his men past, along with forty-three urmen.

"Come on! Get a move on. We haven't got all day," he urged.

The party made for the encampment at the double, while the noise behind them droned on incessantly until he wanted to stop his ears up.

They reached one of the main paths radiating out from the stronghold, trampled down by the passing of many feet. Through the tube grass, the odd blood-red poppy bloom caught his eye, until they found themselves walking through a drift of poppies populating the charred cordon sanitaire.

Atkins could see frantic activity now as, beyond the wire entanglements, platoons moved up communications trenches to man the fire trench. All along the front line, barrels of guns and tips of bayonets flashed cold in the light as the NCOs bellowed orders.

Over to his left, he heard the impatient putter of the aeroplane's motor as it ran up. At each new sight, each new sound, his optimism that they could hold the line grew.

The clashing beat of the massed Khungarrii army's approach began to echo off the valley sides, amplifying it and momentarily dousing his confidence.

He had to stop and get his bearings.

"Well, don't just stand there, Corporal!" bellowed a familiar voice. Sergeant Hobson beckoned from the trench parapet beyond the wire weed entanglement. He pointed to a section some hundred yards along to his right.

Wire weed had been trained over a small wooden tunnel to provide a temporary sally port under a ten-yard-deep stretch of entanglement. The wire weed writhed lethargically as Atkins ushered the urmen through. They had to crawl on their hands and knees through the tunnel. For every urman that stopped, getting clothes or skin caught on the spreading weeds, for every child that had to be bawled at and pushed through the barbed thorns, the Khungarrii came closer. At length, the last of the urmen were through and were being escorted back to the safety of the trenches and the encampment beyond. He glanced back over his shoulder to see the Khungarrii army stretching to fill the entire valley mouth.

Without warning, the wooden tunnel collapsed, the wire weed falling to the ground on top of it. Some nervous private, whether through fear or incompetence, had yanked the shoring struts that held up the tunnel. Their way back to the trenches was blocked.

1 Section were stranded in No Man's Land, between their own front line and the approaching Khungarrii army.

BACK BEHIND THE lines, in one of the tented Casualty Clearing Stations, Nurse Edith Bell and Nellie Abbott, the FANY, prepared for the first waves of wounded to come in, setting out trays of clean field dressings commandeered from soldier's kits and bandages made from boiling old ones and cutting up the flannel shirts of the deceased.

"So how are you and Alfie the tanker getting on?" asked Edith casually.

Nellie scowled at the insinuation. "That's Mister Perkins to you. We're good pals we are, and don't you go getting other ideas," she protested, before confiding, "but he is nice, isn't he? And I do worry about him so. The *Ivanhoe* was due back yesterday. It only has a range of twenty-three miles on full tanks of petrol, and –"

"Goodness, Nellie, if only you could hear yourself. You sound like a man. It isn't feminine to talk about things like that. No one will thank you for it."

"Perkins will."

"But you can do better than that, Nellie."

"What if I don't want to?"

"Well, on your head be it."

"I ain't too worried, though. He's in the safest place, isn't he? Nothing can get to him in there. That's why Everson sends 'em out, ain't it?"

An orderly thrust his head into the tent.

"Nurse Bell, it's the shell-shock patients. They've got the wind up, well, more than usual. I can't do nuffin' with them. They'll respond to you."

Edith glanced at Nellie. They both looked over at Captain Lippett, the Medical Officer, who was deep in conversation with Sister Fenton.

"You'd better watch it, Edi. You know how Lippy feels about the poor souls."

Edith shot him a disapproving glance. "Oh, I've been well apprised of his feelings towards them on several occasions. He may not care for them, but someone has to."

Lippett was dismissive of the shell-shock victims. It was all down to low morale, as far as he was concerned. Even the urmen gave them a wide berth, believing them possessed by malign spirits. She didn't agree. She'd been through her own traumas; the thought of Jeffries still made her shudder. She bore the mental scars and empathised with those whose minds crumpled under the weight of their experiences.

"Go," Nellie said, with a brief smile and a nod. "We can cope for the moment, but be quick. If you're not here when the wounded start coming in you'll be for the high jump. If Lippett asks I'll tell him you've gone to an Aid Post." She turned to the hovering orderly. "Stanton, get in here and help me, then."

Edith put down her tray and stepped smartly out of the tent.

The rhythmic noise of the Khungarrii chittering gave her chills and she kept her head down, not daring to look as she walked briskly across to the barbed wire compound. Nicknamed the Bird Cage, it had been constructed as a temporary solution along the same specifications as a large POW compound, but was still in use months later, much to Edith's chagrin. There always seemed to be more important things to do. Still, at least now there was a crude wooden hut at one end, rather than tents to provide shelter, and some little comfort to those that would use it. Others preferred the familiarity of the dugout at the other end.

In here, thirty-odd men had been abandoned by the meagre medical staff at the moment they needed help most, unable to cope. Some were trying to hide under blankets. Others flung themselves at the barbed wire in an attempt to escape. Others just sat weeping and howling, covering their ears, or jerking and twitching uncontrollably. Some had arrived on the planet like this, the bombardments of the Somme proving too much. Others had joined them here since, the shock of their predicament proving too much for their already fragile minds.

Lieutenant Everson had often asked her to stop them howling and wailing as it was distracting the men. It made them uncomfortable; the Bird Cage was a visible reminder of their frailties and fears, failure as men under horrific conditions. But it was not failure, not as she saw it, and it certainly wasn't cowardice.

A number of new cases had been referred to her, unable to cope with the strangeness and violence of the new world around them. One of the triggers for shell-shock had been the unrelenting artillery barrages, the sustained bombardment and the inability to do anything about it. Here, there were no minniewerfers or five-nines, but when the very landscape around you proffered a sustained barrage of unpleasant and painful experiences, when any plant or creature might try to kill you and, more often than not, succeed, to some it was much the same. Those that weathered the Hun artillery with chirpy good humour or dogged willpower could crumble here, the sight of the alien sky above them sending them into the most fearful funks.

Entrance was gained though a single gate set into the barbed wire fence. Everson had allowed the posting of a single sentry. "You!" Edith called him as she approached. "Help me get them into the hut. And be gentle."

A few allowed themselves to be herded towards the hut. Others were too physically incapable of moving by themselves, too paralysed by fear.

She dropped on her haunches by Private Miller. He was trying to claw a hole in the ground to hide, his fingers now raw and bloody as he scraped away at the hard earth, heedless of the pain and driven by a desperate desire to flee. She grasped his wrists gently.

"Shhh. It's all right. You're safe. Safe. Come with me."

He looked up at her with a vague recognition. Her window of opportunity was slim, before he slipped back into whatever nightmare he'd been trapped in. "Come on," she said, lifting him up. He acquiesced calmly, but she could feel the tremors through his arms. She led him towards the hut, distracting him every time he flinched or his eyes flicked towards the front line, muttering comforting maternal words as she led him step by step towards the relative safety of the hut, away from the clamour of the oncoming battle.

From the fire trench, Lieutenant Everson scanned the alien army in his binoculars, chewing his lip. Every so often, the purple black of the huge slow larval beasts blotted out his view for a moment only for the advancing scentirrii to appear, as he continued his sweep, gnashing their mandibles and striking their chitinous thorax plates with their weapons.

The men called those great beasts 'battlepillars.' They were twice as high as an elephant and twenty to thirty yards long, making up the vanguard of the chatt army. Purple and black in colour, with fearsome-looking yellow markings on their faces, their bodies were covered with chitinous sections covered with defensive spines. A rider stood behind each head in a howdah-type affair, a canopied box, reins running down to the battlepillars' head and fixed in some manner to their mandibles. Along the beasts' lengths were slung long boat-cradles carrying yet more Khungarrii scentirrii armed with electric lances. They may not have had tanks, but these beasts weren't far off.

And speaking of the tank, where the bloody hell was it? The Khungarrii thought it was some great demon or god of the dead or something. If the tank had been here they wouldn't have dared attack. Or perhaps that was the point. Maybe they were attacking because it wasn't here. Which meant they must have been watching all this time.

Everson realised that there was the very real danger that the chatts would try to flank and surround the encampment. He would have to hit them hard and fast to dissuade them.

He was depending on his machine guns. Normally that wouldn't have been a problem – the field of fire from their emplacements covered the entire valley mouth – but their ammunition supplies were severely limited. He'd only have one good shot at this.

Since the dwindling ammunitions reserves were rationed, and even he daren't cross Company Quartermaster Sergeant Slacke, he had taken to wearing the dress sword that his father had bought for him. Although only ever meant for ceremonial use, it was, nonetheless, a real sword. He wasn't looking forward to the day he would have to use it. He hoped it wouldn't be today.

CAUGHT IN THE poppy field, Atkins ordered his men to take up positions in front of the wire weed entanglements and find hasty cover, if they could.

The Khungarrii battlepillars began to advance, crunching their way over tube grass. Behind the great warbeasts marched the first wave of the Khungarrii assault. Thankfully, they didn't seem to possess any long-range weapons of any kind. Atkins and his section had their guns, but they'd been on patrol and in a skirmish.

"Bugger!" muttered Mercy. "I've only got a magazine left."

Gazette glanced over and smiled grimly. "Better not miss, then."

Here they were again. Same old same old. It never changed. Atkins nodded back and shifted his attention to the great battlepillars that lumbered towards them.

The wire weed behind them, he thought, was going to present as little problem to these creatures as Hun barbed wire did to their own tanks. In the pit of his stomach Atkins felt the same fear that the Huns must have felt when the tanks first came crawling out of the Somme mud towards them, crushing everything in their path.

Behind them, he could see the first ranks of Khungarrii scentirrii begin to charge, their mandibles open.

He felt his bowels churn.

"This is it, lads," he said gravely. "Pick your targets."

He could hear Nobby whimper and Prof's soothing tone trying to calm the boy. He briefly remembered Ginger. That seemed a lifetime ago. He focused on the wave of advancing chatts marching across the poppy field towards them.

As they marched through the flowers, the closed ranks of disciplined scentirrii began stumbling about. They lost their measured step. The line broke. They began to mill about in confusion as though blinded, like chlorine gas victims.

"What's happening to them?" asked Prof.

"No idea," replied Mercy. "But it looks like they're funking it."

Gazette sneered. "That makes 'em easier to pick off."

Others had the same idea. In answer, a volley of NCOs' orders rang out along the outer front line trench. The air filled with the crackle of gunfire and the reassuring smell of cordite and the chatts began to fall.

A jubilant cheer went up from the trenches behind them,

"The chatts are funking it. We've got 'em, lads. We've got 'em!"

Whatever was affecting the scentirrii, it didn't seem to be affecting the battlepillars. Atkins' stomach shrank to a hard knot in his belly as one of the beasts, its great mandibles scything through the tube grass, advanced implacably towards them.

EVERSON WATCHED THE centre of the Khungarrii attack collapse. On the flanks, the chatts broke into a charge. The Lewis machine gun emplacements raked a line across the first wave and the advance faltered.

Tulliver's Sopwith 1½ Strutter roared low overhead, sweeping along the Khungarrii advance, his machine guns stuttering, enfilading the enemy.

Then, in answer to some unheard, unseen chemical scent command, what was left of the ranks of chatt scentirrii began to withdraw, all except those in the poppy field, who still staggered round as if in a stupor, unable to obey.

Panning his binoculars across the mass of the Khungarrii army waiting in reserve, Everson caught sight of what he presumed was their general. It watched from the howdah of a large battlepillar that had reared up, its head and front legs resting atop a copse of trees, affording a better view as his mount scissored idly at the foliage with large mandibles.

And he knew he'd met this chatt before, deep in the nurseries of Khungarr. He almost felt like saluting him, as he had once done with a German officer who appeared above the Hun parapets one morning.

That felt like an age away.

GAZETTE TOOK MEASURED shots at the electric lancers in the battlepillar's passenger cradles. Three chatts collapsed, and one fell backwards out of the cradle to land on the ground with a crack. Its companions in the adjacent cradles now turned their attention towards Gazette. Blue streams of electric fire arced from the cradles towards the ground but fell short, incinerating the trampled tube grass.

Gutsy picked the rider off. It fell back, caught awkwardly on the howdah's side by the reins.

Atkins reached into his webbing for a Mills bomb. "Cover me!"

Porgy looked at him. "What the bloody hell are you going to do?"

Atkins grinned and patted Porgy's cap as he got up. "Something stupid."

He dashed off, running in a crouch though the poppies, zigzagging towards another oncoming battlepillar.

Crackling ribbons of blue-white fire arced down around him from the electric lancers.

He pulled the pin from the Mills bomb and threw it. It skittered to a halt in front of the battlepillar.

He didn't wait to see the great armoured larval beast, unperturbed, continue its relentless progress over it. He darted back to his section, where they laid down covering fire.

The grenade exploded beneath the beast, red-hot shrapnel shards slicing up through its vitals. It reared up, exposing a huge wet gaping wound in its soft underbelly, hot organs slopping out as it toppled over to the side. The huge beast crashed down, twitching.

Some of its riders lay crushed beneath its huge bulk. Others though, scrambled to get away from it. Gazette and the others rushed forward through the trampled poppies to mop up those chatts still left alive.

Around the other side of the battlepillar, thrown yards from its monstrous cracked head, Atkins found the shattered howdah. The contorted body of one chatt lay on the ground, tangled in a snapped cradle rope and reins.

The howdah's torn silken covering had come adrift from the splintered canopy. There was a rasp of movement from beneath the sheet.

Atkins nodded and he and Gutsy edged towards the cloth.

An ivory chitinous arm clawed out from under the breeze-ruffled sheet. Gutsy stepped forward, ready to thrust his bayonet down though the fabric, but Atkins shook his head.

"I don't think it's scentirrii."

He inched towards it. He nodded at Gutsy who drew up his rifle to his shoulder and fixed the shape in his sights.

Atkins caught the cloth and pulled it back with the tip of his bayonet.

The chatt tried to scuttle away on its back. It wore a white silk sash with knotted tassels and its antennae were broken, but they seemed like old injuries. Its vestigial mid-limbs at its abdomen were scissoring frantically. Atkins had been right. It was not a scentirrii, a chatt soldier. It was smaller, its carapace a smoother, off-white colour, its head-shell smooth and ovoid. It drew in a deep breath and forced it out through its four finger-like mouth palps as if weaving the air into a crude approximation of human speech.

"This One is Dhuyumirrii. This One does not fight. This One watches, observes."

Atkins frowned, but didn't let down his guard. Something about it was familiar. Chatts all looked the same, true, but the broken antennae?

"I... know you," he said. "The edifice. Jeffries. You were there. I saved you from the gas. You called yourself..." But the name evaded his memory.

"This One is called Chandar," said the chatt.

Gutsy turned, bayoneted and shot a charging scentirrii. "Only, this is no place for a reunion," he warned.

Chatts began to swarm around them. The section fell on the confused Khungarrii with bayonets and clubs and succeeded in driving them back.

"Better give us a hand then," said Atkins, helping Chandar up. "'Cause we've just got ourselves a prisoner."

An arc of blue fire earthed by Gutsy's feet, and he turned and fired. A chatt fell dead.

"He'd better be bloody important," he said.

There was a sporadic ripple of jubilant cheers from the trenches behind them. The main Khungarrii force was withdrawing, but the confused chatts stumbling around 1 Section in the poppy field still posed a threat.

He heard Sergeant Hobson's voice cut through the cheers.

"Atkins, get out of there. Make for the farmhouse!" he ordered.

Atkins looked along the length of wire entanglement behind them. Over to the right he saw the front of the old Poulet farmhouse flanked by the wire entanglements. Heavily shelled on the Somme, it was now a forward observation post. The ground floor had been converted into a machine gun emplacement, while the first floor acted as an observation platform. It might be their only chance.

One of the milling scentirrii rushed Atkins with a long, barbed spear. Confused they might be, but they still recognised an enemy. Atkins thrust Chandar back towards Gutsy, ducked under the spear thrust and brought his bayonet up, burying it deep between the chatt's mandibles.

Running at a crouch, the section made for the farmhouse.

Behind them, he heard the soldiers in the trench open fire at the crowd of dazed, stumbling chatts.

Atkins could see the muzzle of a Vickers machine gun poking out of the window of the farmhouse. Past it, he saw angled wooden doors leading down to the old fruit cellar.

"Lance Corporal Atkins, 1 Section 2 Platoon, C Company!" he called out to the machine gun section inside. "We've got a prisoner. We're coming in through the cellar. Cover us!"

"Stoppage!"

"Well get it cleared, man, you know the drill!"

Bloody Nora, the day just gets better, Atkins thought as he shot the bolt and flung open the cellar doors.

"In," he yelled. "Make for the sap at the rear of the house!"

Prof, Chalky, Nobby, Pot Shot, Gazette, Mercy and Porgy tumbled into the dark hole.

Gutsy pushed Chandar down into the cellar and Atkins followed.

A shadow fell over him as he hit the floor. He turned, rifle at the ready, as a scentirrii sprung through the cellar opening at him. It was dead before it fell on his bayonet, a bullet hole through its horned flat facial plate. Gazette was covering them from the cellar door across the low room.

Gutsy ushered Chandar through.

Another scentirrii appeared at the cellar opening. Crouching, spider-like, it let out a challenging hiss. Atkins pulled his trigger but his magazine was empty.

Gazette fired again, sending it spinning out of sight.

"We need to get these doors shut," Atkins said.

A third chatt sought to clamber in. Gazette killed that, too, and a fourth crawled over the bodies of its comrades to reach them. That, too, fell. No more attempted to come through.

Atkins steeled himself, reached out and pulled the cellar doors shut, jamming them closed with the handle of a broom that he found stood in the corner.

Above, he heard the machine gun stutter start up again.

"About bloody time!" he spat. He clapped Gazette on the shoulder. "Thanks."

He staggered up the worn stone cellar steps and out of the house, following his men down the sap trench towards the front line.

Alarmed by the appearance of Chandar in the fire trench, several Tommies swung their Enfields in the chatt's direction as 1 Section emerged from the sap.

"It's all right, he's with us," said Atkins. He looked around and saw a private with a runner's brassard. "You. Tell Lieutenant Everson that we have someone he'll want to meet."

PENNINE FUSILIERS

CHAPTER THREE

"For God's Sake Don't Send Me..."

THE HEAVILY SANDBAGGED command post looked out over the lines of trenches, breastworks and earthworks now crawling with Pennine Fusiliers as they dispatched straggling and retreating chatts. Linseed lancers of the RAMC scuttled about with stretchers, collecting the wounded and carrying them back to the aid posts and hospital, while flocks of carrion creatures were already circling and descending on the bodies. Frustrated 'hell hounds,' smelling the blood, could be heard howling across the valley.

Lieutenant Everson looked out through a loophole with his binoculars, across the wire weed entanglements and the bodies that hung on them, already being ensnared and sapped of their life by the slow-moving thorny creepers tightening around them. His gaze didn't rest there, but was drawn out across the veldt where he watched the Khungarrii retreat.

They had repulsed them, but only because of their guns, and their ammunition was rapidly running out. Of course, the chatts didn't know that, but at some point, the Khungarrii would attack again. No doubt they could hold off several such attacks. His counterpart was exceedingly clumsy, tactically. With their short-range weapons, the alien scentirrii seemed to be much more proficient in small police actions, defending their edifice and the like, but the growing confidence evident in recent raids on urmen enclaves showed his nemesis was a fast learner and damned if he wasn't learning it all from the Pennines.

The observation posts on the valley hilltops had reported no sign of a support column. They must have been foraging food along the way. Nor were there any signs of siege machines. So they didn't see this action lasting very long. A short brutal engagement, then, to stamp out their enemies.

However, if the chatts were to lay siege to the stronghold and this turned into another war of attrition, then God help them. They had barely held their own against the Hun on the Somme. This time, without reinforcements, without logistical support, they couldn't hope to hold out against such a superior force. Everson gave them a fortnight at best, a month at the outside. The Pennines' own foraging parties had to range further and further to find food and wood. Even with the help of the refugee urmen, feeding this many men was becoming a nightmare without some degree of successful agriculture. He couldn't allow a siege to happen. He needed to deliver a swift, decisive blow. Something that would have the Khungarrii give them a wide berth in future. To do that, he needed to know more about them, and he recognised that the captured chatt represented a slim opportunity.

"Is this absolutely necessary?" asked Padre Rand nervously, from the other side of the sandbagged room. He'd asked the Padre here because he'd had dealings with them in Khungarr.

"Yes, Padre, I'm afraid it is. But don't worry. You're only here to observe. It won't touch you. I've taken precautions."

The Padre, though, seemed little mollified by this.

Sergeant Hobson appeared in the doorway. "The prisoner is here, sir."

Everson turned from the unsettling sight of the chatt army regrouping out on the veldt. "Show him in, Hobson."

Atkins, accompanied by a grim Napoo, escorted the captured chatt into the dugout. It hobbled into the room with a lopsided gait that suggested old injuries and new pains. Everson felt a cold shock of recognition. Most chatts looked the same to him, even now after all this time, but this one, even with its featureless white facial plate, was unmistakable. Its worn stumps of antennae moved with feeble jerks like a broken clockwork toy. This was no mere chatt soldier. This was the chatt that Jeffries had held hostage in Khungarr. Everson remembered that the damn thing had refused to help them when they were trying to find a way out of the labyrinthine tunnels. But there was so much information it might give them, not least about Jeffries' last movements and intentions. If it would talk. But every moment it was here it could be gathering information about them; numbers, layout, weapons.

Atkins stood smartly to attention, by the prisoner. Sergeant Hobson brought up the rear of the escort party and stood, stiff and formal, behind the chatt, his eyes never leaving it. In the far corner was Padre Rand, backed against the sandbagged wall, his hands clutching his bible to his chest as though it were a shield, his lips moving silently in prayer, his eyes following the chatt warily as it looked around. Even captured, its curiosity seemed insatiable.

"Your herd is truly different from that of other urmen," it said, in its breathless, monotone way. "They build their flimsy dwellings on the ground. I had heard reports from raiding scentirrii that Tohmii dwellings and burrowings imitate those of the Ones. This structure is crude, but strange and wondrous nonetheless."

Everson stepped toward the arthropod and held out a hand.

"I'm Lieutenant James Charles Everson, Acting Commanding Officer of the 13th Battalion of the Pennine Fusiliers. We've met," he added pointedly.

The chatt finished surveying the room before answering. "Yes. This One is Chandar, gon-dhuyumirrii, olfactotum to Sirigar, liya-dhuyumirrii of the Khungarrii Shura." It appeared to swallow air and force it out, as if having to shape words with organs not meant for human speech. "In gratitude this One offers you a blessing in the name of GarSuleth," it said, opening its arms, tilting its head back and opening its mandibles.

There was a loud click as Sergeant Hobson cocked a Webley revolver and pointed it at the back of the chatt's head.

"I've read the reports," said Everson. "Attempt to spray

anything – acid, a soporific mist – and Sergeant Hobson here will shoot you. Is that understood?"

The creature lowered its head, relaxed its mouthparts and sank down on its legs in a submissive posture. "This One intended no threat."

Everson offered it a seat. The Khungarrii looked at the wooden chair incomprehensibly. He shrugged, then sat down behind his desk. "I suppose a cup of tea is out of the question, then?" He gave a nod of dismissal in the Lance Corporal's direction. "Thank you, Atkins."

Atkins looked at the Sergeant for confirmation.

"Off you go, lad."

"Sir." Atkins saluted and snapped his heels together.

There was a strangled gasp as the chatt abandoned its half-hearted attempt to sit, and regurgitated air. Its mouth palps seemed to knit the human words laboriously. "This urman stays."

"I beg your pardon?" said Everson.

"The urman stays," insisted Chandar, rearing up.

Recognising the aggressive stance, Napoo drew his short sword and took a step towards the chatt. Everson held up a palm to stop him. Napoo relented, but remained tensed, ready to spring.

"Why?" asked Everson of the creature. "Why him?"

"That urman saved this One from the mandibles of Skarra when your Jeffries would have me wrapped in clay and rolled into the underworld. This spinning, this same urman spared this One again. These acts are of significance to this One. They are acts of Kurda, a basic tenet of colonyhood."

If it made the damn thing more predisposed to talk, then that was fine with him. "Very well," said Everson. He waved his hand and indicated that Atkins should stay. "At ease, Lance Corporal."

"Sir." Atkins looked uncomfortable as he stood at rest. He glanced at Hobson, who just shrugged.

Its request acceded to, Chandar relaxed its stance.

"Now, see here," Everson began. "We will not surrender to you. You will not take us prisoners to be mesmerised as slaves in your colony. We will not bow to any tyrant's yoke."

"It is too late for that," said Chandar. "Not since the days of Wuljungur has Khungarr been invaded. Now, in retribution, Sirigar has chemically decreed that you and any wild urmen caught within our sovereign burri are to be expelled. Failing that, you are to be culled to preserve the sanctity and safety of Khungarr. Those are your choices."

There was no choice at all and Everson knew it. They could not leave this stronghold, this circle of the Somme earth that came with them. It was all they had left of Earth. It seemed they had their backs against the wall.

"We forewarned your emissary Jeffries of these eventualities," continued the chatt.

Everson shifted forward in his chair. Atkins, too, stared at the chatt. Only Hobson remained unperturbed.

"Jeffries?"

"He promised to deliver the Tohmii, your herd, to us. You would have been accepted into our colony, given food, shelter, purpose, treated as our own. It is Kurda."

"He had no damn right to speak on our behalf," replied Everson with measured fury. "No damn right at all. Man was a snake in our midst. He's not one of us. He's –" he searched for a word the arthropod might understand.

"Outcast," offered Napoo gruffly.

"Outcast," repeated Everson, with a degree of satisfaction at the sound of the word.

"Nonetheless, an agreement was made and breached," said Chandar.

"But at what price? What was it that Jeffries wanted from you? What was worth so much to him that he was willing to sell the rest of us into slavery?"

The chatt's posture seemed to slump. "An old heresy thought long forgotten," it wheezed.

"Croatoan," suggested Everson.

"Yes."

He put his elbows on his desk and leant forward, hands clasped. "Tell me about this Croatoan."

The chatt's mandible parted as it hissed, its mouth palps flapping like windsocks in the brief rush of air. "The urman Jeffries asked the same thing before committing the most unforgivable transgression in destroying our sacred repository. Therein lay the basis of our laws, our beliefs. Ancient aromas that bottled the wisdom of generations. Tunnels can be rebuilt, chambers repaired, but the Tohmii have left us dispossessed. Robbed. The Redolence of Spiras gone forever."

The chatt ran out of air, its human vocabulary tumbling into the incoherent chittering of its own tongue. It seemed to Everson that the thing was cursing.

"That's right. Jeffries. Not us. Jeffries tried to kill us, too. You were there in that chamber. You saw."

"Yes. The fact that this One owes its life to this urman is one of the few mitigating circumstances in your favour."

"Yes, Kurda. You said." Everson looked to Atkins standing beside the creature. Their eyes met briefly. Atkins' face flushed and he shuffled uncomfortably. Everson felt a glimmer of almost paternal pride. He had been right about Atkins. But to think that their salvation might hinge on that single act of altruism, well, that was a very slender thread indeed.

Chandar took another hoarse breath. "There is yet another reason Sirigar wants you wiped out. Khungarr is mired in tradition. The coming of the Tohmii has ignited an old debate, long feared and unsought by some. The Unguent of Huyurarr warns against the coming of a Great Corruption. When you made your camp on our burri, the Breath of GarSuleth heralded your arrival with the stench of death and putrescence. Sirigar feared that this was the fulfilment of the long-held prophecy. We sought to discover your intentions. You resisted the will of the Ones unlike any other urman herd we had encountered. Then by your actions you declared yourself a threat to Khungarr and your fate was sealed. Now, through your own actions, we are compelled to seek your destruction. This is regrettable."

"We won't surrender, you know. This is our land and we will defend it to the last man."

"You cannot hope to defeat the massed army of Khungarr," said Chandar.

Scraping his chair back, Everson stood now. "You're not up against savages here. You're up against a battalion of His Majesty King George's army. We've faced the worst that Kaiser Bill could throw at us and survived. And you forget," he added. "We are protected by Skarra, your god of the dead." That the Khungarrii had mistaken the appearance of His Majesty's Land Ship *Ivanhoe* as their god of the underworld was a work of providence and one he had been quite willing to take advantage of at the time, but how long could they keep up the pretence?

"Then where is he?" said Chandar looking around and gesturing to the empty air. "Why does Skarra not come to your aid? The army of Khungarr has retreated. They are waiting to see if he appears. If he does not then they will attack again and carry out the will of GarSuleth as set forth by Sirigar."

"Thank you, Chandar. You've been quite candid. Sergeant, take the prisoner to the guardhouse. Keep to the trenches. Make sure it doesn't see more than it has to."

He watched as Hobson, Atkins and Napoo marshalled the prisoner and escorted it from the dugout. He was surprised to see the Padre shaking, as if the chatt had stirred deep, unwelcome memories of his incarceration.

"Padre, go. We'll talk later."

The Padre smiled thankfully with an anxious nod, not trusting himself to speak, and hurried from the post.

So it was war, then. And where *was* that bloody tank? It seemed to Everson that Chandar was not entirely convinced of their claim regarding the tank but was unwilling to question the sanctity of Skarra without further proof. If only he had it. The *Ivanhoe* should have been back days ago. He pulled out a packet of Woodbines from his pocket and was dismayed to see only two battered cigarettes left. Once they were gone, they were gone. He had no more left. He doubted the men did either, except the hoarders. Evans, his platoon's best scrounger, could probably lay his hands on some. Maybe he should ask.

He pulled one out, tamped it on the desk, lit it and took a long luxurious drag before exhaling, staring absently at the haze of blue smoke, momentarily lost in thought.

Their arrival had set off ripples across this world, and those ripples were still spreading with unforeseen consequences. The Pennines, it seemed, had spent a good deal of time on this world unwittingly digging a deeper and deeper hole for themselves. Everson hoped it didn't turn out to be their grave.

AMID THE CHAOS of the Aid Post, Edith was trying to hold down and calm a wounded young soldier. He seemed about sixteen years old, barely older than her younger brother and almost certainly not old enough to join up. He lay writhing and whimpering on the mat before her. Nellie had just finished bathing and bandaging the eyes of a lad caught out by an acid spit, and Edith caught her attention. "Nellie!"

They unbuttoned his tunic and ripped open the blood-soaked shirt. The spear must have been barbed. It went in cleanly enough but ripped his guts out on the withdrawal. His belly was a mess. Nellie applied pressure to the wound with a field bandage, but he wouldn't lie still. He thrashed about in pain, sobbing openly. Blood pulsed up and soaked the field bandage; in moments it was sopping. She discarded it in a tray and pressed another to the wound.

He needed surgery, but there were several other surgical cases backed up ahead of him and it was unlikely this boy would survive long enough to make it to the table.

"Mother!" he cried, through snivelling sobs. "I don't want to die. I don't want to die."

"Shush now," said Edith, taking hold of his hand and trying to look him in the eye, but he kept throwing his head from side to side. "Look at me," she said firmly. "Look at me." He turned his face to hers but he no longer saw her.

"Charlotte, is that you?" he said with relief, spluttering through the blood.

Edith clasped his hand more firmly so that he would know someone was there.

"Yes," she said. "I'm here."

"I love you," he muttered.

"I love you, too," said Edith.

He started to smile but the life left him before he could complete it.

Edith felt the corners of her eyes begin to sting with tears. She blinked them away fiercely. It always got to her, the little white lie. The one nurses always told the dying. In her time she had been mothers, sisters, wives, sweethearts, anyone, so long as they eased the passing. Edith slipped his hand from hers and placed it across his chest. There were no words left to say. Just a job to do.

NELLIE CLEARED UP the blood-soaked bandages and left Edith to lay out the body, before summoning the orderlies to remove it to where the Padre would give it the Last Rites as they cleared the space for the next poor soul. Nellie stepped outside to where a brazier burned, tipped the bloodied pads into the fire and returned to the aid tent.

Nellie was looking for her next patient when Half Pint hobbled into the hospital tent on his peg leg, clutching the thigh above it, his face ashen as he looked wildly around. His gaze latched on Nellie.

"Gawd help me, it's my leg!" he cried, limping towards her.

"Private Nicholls, you'll have to wait. There are more urgent cases," she said, only half listening as she glanced around, looking for assistance. Poilus, an urman of Napoo's clan, was helping to bring more wounded in, some walking, others carried in on blood-soaked stretchers.

"But the pain, nurse. Shooting pains right up me thigh. Sharp they are, like bloody red hot needles," he griped.

His forehead was beaded with sweat. He gritted his teeth and a grunt escaped his lips as his hand clutched his thigh. He lost his balance and collapsed into her.

"A little help here!" she called as she staggered under his weight.

Edi and Poilus came to her rescue. By now Half Pint's breath was coming in ragged pants and his eyelids fluttered as he struggled to keep them open, his head lolling back.

Nellie directed the pair to an empty straw mat, where they laid him down. She put a hand on his forehead and tutted. "He has a fever. The stump is probably infected. I told him not to wear that peg leg of his for more than an hour or so at a time, but he was so bloomin' proud of it. Said the pain would give him something to grouse about."

"Well let's get it off him," said Edith as she began to cut his trouser leg away to reveal the stump. She clapped a hand to her mouth. "Oh, dear Lord!"

Pale roots sprouted from the inert black wood of the carved peg leg, reaching up and entwining themselves around the pink stump before sinking into the flesh of Half Pint's thigh.

"Bloomin' hell!" said Nellie. "It's growing into him!"

"Corpsewood," said Poilus.

"What?"

"It is corpsewood. It feeds on dead or rotting flesh, but will eat living things if it can. We must get it off him. It will kill him."

Nellie knelt and, with shaking hands, unbuckled the leather straps that kept the false leg in place. Gingerly she waggled the peg leg loose, attached now only by the roots that fed deep into Half Pint's thigh.

Edith made to cut them with a scalpel in order to remove the wooden leg.

"No!" said Poilus. "We must withdraw every root cleanly, unbroken. You cannot leave any part of it in him or it will continue to grow." He pressed his thumb against the flesh of the upper leg, feeling for the roots, finding how far they had penetrated. "We are lucky. It has not grown in too far yet. We may still save him. We must ease the roots from his legs, slowly. Do not let them break."

Edith placed a strip of old leather belt in Half Pint's mouth for him to bite on and save his tongue, then leant herself across

Half Pint's torso that he might not witness the operation and to hold him down should he struggle. She nodded at Poilus. He used the discarded length of puttee, wrapped it around the peg leg to avoid touching it, and took a grip. He applied a steady pressure, drawing it back. Half Pint twisted and grunted as he bit down on the leather, hard enough to leave teeth marks.

Nellie's nimble fingers eased out each of the dozen or so long thin roots in turn as Polius continued to pull. Eventually, the last thin tendril-like tips were pulled free, writhing weakly as they sought flesh to burrow into. She nodded, and Poilus took the corpsewood peg leg, dangling six inches of bloody roots, their tips writhing feebly. Like some kind of changeling child from a fairy tale, Nellie thought with a shudder. She watched as he strode outside and dropped the thing into the brazier. The flames expanded to greet it, burning a blue-green colour. The corpsewood gave off a high-pitched noise, as if it was squealing in pain.

It was only after that she thought perhaps she should have preserved the specimen for Captain Lippett, who was striving to catalogue this world's flora and fauna, but it was too late now.

Poilus returned and sank down on his haunches beside Nellie and gave the feverish Half Pint a long, appraising look. "He was lucky. It was old wood. We got it out of him in time. He should live. I will get one of our women to make up a poultice for his leg to stop the fever, though what fool thought to use it in such a manner I cannot think. Even the smallest piece can sprout roots and begin to grow again if it finds a living source. Strapping it to someone is as good as killing them." He shook his head slowly. "I wonder how you Tohmii are all still alive? You treat us as if we are the children, yet it is you who need your hands holding." He stood up, still shaking his head to himself as he left the tent.

There was another influx of walking wounded. Edith stood up and walked over to them.

Half Pint grasped Nellie's hand. "You wouldn't be a good girl and fetch me my lucky harmonica from by the typewriter, would you?" he said, his voice faint and hoarse. "And tell the Loot – tell him... I'm sorry but I think I'll be a little late with dinner tonight."

It was nearly an hour later before Nellie was able to beg a fag break from Sister Fenton and slip away to let the Lieutenant know what had happened to his batman.

In the days that followed, she often wished Sister Fenton had kept her back.

SERGEANT HOBSON ENTERED the command post. Everson looked up from his desk.

"The chatts are still just sat there, sir. They don't seem to be doing anything."

"They're waiting for a 'sign,' Sergeant, and I bloody well wish we had one to give them."

"The tank, sir?"

"As you so rightly say, Hobson, the tank." He tapped his pencil on the desk and came to a decision. "I want to see Lance Corporal Atkins. I've got a job for him and his black hand gang."

"Very good, sir. I'll send him along directly." The sergeant turned sharply and left.

Everson was about to take another look at Jeffries' journal when there was a polite knock on the doorjamb.

"Come."

Nellie Abbott stepped inside, saluted and stood to attention. Unlike the Nurses, the FANYs were run along military lines.

"Yes, Miss Abbott, what can I do for you?"

"Begging your pardon, Lieutenant, it's about Half Pint – I mean Private Nicholls, sir."

"Well, if you're looking for him, I don't know where the devil he is," said Everson, vaguely frustrated.

"Sir, he's in the aid post."

Everson was a little shocked. "He's not injured, is he?"

"It's his leg, sir.

"Oh, Christ, the poor bloke. Not both now?"

"Oh. Oh, no, sir. No, the other one, the peg leg, sir. It tried to eat him."

Everson wasn't sure he heard right. "I beg your pardon?"

"It tried to eat him, it did, sir, but he's all right now. He's resting. But he won't be stomping around like Long John Silver for a while, sir. Said to tell you that dinner would be a little late and could I fetch him his lucky harmonica? Said he left it on his desk, sir."

Everson slumped back in his chair with a sigh and waved her in the direction of the small clerk's office. She gave a little curtsey and went through.

Everson ran a hand through his hair. There was another knock. "Come."

Sergeant Hopkins and Lance Corporal Atkins entered.

"You wanted to see me, sir?" said Atkins.

"Yes, Atkins. Got a job for you. I wouldn't ask, but our backs are against the wall on this one."

"Aren't they always, sir?"

"Hmm. The fact is, Atkins, the tank is overdue. The *Ivanhoe* should have been back several days ago. And frankly if it had, we might not be in this mess with those bloody chatts camped on our doorstep. The *Ivanhoe* has a limited speed and a limited range and, by all accounts, it should have returned yesterday. Now, either it's in trouble or it's broken down or the crew are injured or dead..."

There was an audible gasp from the back of the room. Nellie Abbott stood in the small doorframe to the next room, a harmonica in her hand. She leant against the doorframe.

"Miss Abbott, I'm sorry," said Everson. "I didn't realise you were still there."

"Injured?" she said. "Then let me go, too, sir. I can help."

"You, Abbott? No, sorry. Out of the question. If nothing else, Sister Fenton would certainly have something to say about it."

"But you said yourself they might be injured, sir," she said in earnest. "I've got first aid training. And I can drive, sir. I ain't afraid of what's out there. Sister can spare me. There's the orderlies and the vets, sir. I won't hardly be missed."

Damn the girl, but she had a point. The tank crew were the only ones who could drive the blasted thing. If they were injured... And she could drive ambulances, so she might be able to help if the crew were down. Damn it. Why did they have to be so bloody logical? "Very well," he said reluctantly. "But only if Sister Fenton agrees."

"Thank you, sir! You won't regret it."

"But, sir –" protested Atkins. "I don't want to be responsible for a woman, sir."

"Do as the Lieutenant, says, son," said Hobson, leaning in with a stage whisper.

"'Only' Atkins, how dare you!" retorted Nellie. "I can do anything you can. Don't treat me like no porcelain doll, then. I'm responsible for myself. Or do you just want me to stay here and cook meals, wash uniforms and tend wounds, is that it? "

"No!" said Atkins defensively. "That's not what I meant. It's just that –"

Everson coughed. "It's done, Atkins. She goes with you. I need you to find the tank and its crew, both in one piece, and get them back here. We can hang on for a few days, a week maybe. The chatts think it's their god of the dead; it may be the only thing that can save us. I'm relying on you."

Atkins recovered his composure while Nellie fixed him with a belligerent stare.

"If the tank can be found sir, we'll find it. Leaves a trail a blind man could follow, so we should be able to track it. And we'll bring it back if we have to push it all the way."

The tank weighed twenty-eight tons, so that was highly unlikely, but Everson appreciated the sentiment. "And take Napoo, because Christ knows what you'll find out there and I don't want to lose another patrol.

"And take that chatt, Chandar, with you. He seems well disposed to you. We can't keep him here and we can't send him back. I have some surprises for his friends and I don't want to take the chance that he's spying."

"But sir –" began Atkins.

"It's done, Atkins. Find that bloody tank. And keep an eye out for Jeffries."

INTERLUDE TWO
Letter from Private Thomas Atkins
to Flora Mullins

17th February 1917

My Dearest Flora,
  Sometime I feel daft sitting here and writing letters that I don't know you'll ever get, but I feel like if I stop writing you'll just drift away and I'll lose you forever. Maybe it would be better not to torment myself, to lay down this burden, to forget that you and Blighty exist at all. Some blokes already have, like so many Hun souvenirs that chaps carry round with them from posting to posting until one day they just become too heavy and they chuck them.
  You may never read these, but while I write them, I feel like I'm talking to you, like I'm close to you. If I ever stop writing, then not only have I lost you but will have lost part of myself, too, so here I sit, carrying on.
  The days have settled into a routine here, although we are having a spot of bother with some of the locals. I don't think they like what we've done with the place. Mind you, if you saw it you'd hardly recognise it yourself. Lovely new trenches. Dry warm dugouts. It's like the Ritz.
  The new lads in the section seem grand. I do wish Chalky would lay off, though. Not strictly his fault. The others egg him on a bit. I don't know, you do one thing and people go on and on about it. But that's what it's like around here.
  We've got orders to go and find the tank. You can't put anything down around here without it disappearing. Most people blame Mercy when that happens. To be fair, if anything has gone missing he's usually had a hand in it. I don't think they can pin the tank on him this time, though. It's all a bit of puzzle. They should have been back yesterday. Things might

have been a lot easier if they had, but there you go, C'est la guerre, as Gutsy says. Still, how hard can it be to find?

Ever yours
Thomas.

CHAPTER FOUR
"A Wilderness of Ruin..."

Two days earlier...

THE CANYON HADN'T been carved by turbulent river waters. It was a brutal crack, a rift torn suddenly in the skin of this world by some groundquake that sundered the land in ages past. The walls rose almost vertically for hundreds of feet and only in the heat of the day did the alien sun penetrate the bottom-most depths, where great blocks of stone lay strewn where they fell.

The only scraps of vegetation to be seen were large patches of blue-green matter, scattered over the rock-face like lichen, attached to the rock and formed of small blisters of varying sizes that seemed to pulse in direct sunlight, as if breathing. The ones in shadow remained inert, as if asleep. The rocks were pockmarked with shallow circular depressions, where acid from long-vanished blooms had eaten into the surface.

An unremitting rumble filled the rock-strewn canyon, echoing off the walls like some imminent, but never delivered, avalanche as His Majesty's Land Ship *Ivanhoe* crawled along, pitilessly shattering small rocks caught under its tracks into dust. Grey smoke billowed from the roof exhaust to be snatched up by the breeze and dispersed behind it as the armoured behemoth crept and clanked through the rocky terrain as if sniffing out a trail.

Not that the crew could see much from inside, where the heat and fumes were a microcosm of hell. Progress was slow.

With no suspension, the tank had reduced its speed to a crawl, not wanting to belly or throw a track.

The machine gunners, Norman and Cecil, squinted through the machine gun loopholes for threats as the rocky walls, partially obscured by dust thrown up by the tracks, rolled by with mesmerising slowness, without incident or interest apart from the blue-green pulsating growths. Cecil took a brief shot at them with the Hotchkiss to see if they'd burst. The rattle of machine gun fire reverberated through the canyon, causing Lieutenant Mathers to turn in his seat and glare at him.

It also earned him a clip round the back of the head from Jack Tanner, the ex-prize-fighting gunner. It smacked his forehead into the handles of the gun barrel. "Quit that, you dozy mare. You're wasting ammunition," he bellowed above the engine's roar.

For the moment they were riding with hatches open to try and cool the interior. At least without the Hun firing machine guns at them there was no need to wear the stifling splash-masks and bruise helmets, and in the baking heat of the great iron oven, most of them had unbuttoned the coveralls they wore over the trousers, puttees and flannel shirts of their service dress, and undoing the shirts, too.

At the back of the compartment, by the starboard secondary gears, Alfie wiped the sweat from his forehead and tried to keep his focus on the back of the driver's chair from where, every now and again, hand signals for gear changes would come. When he wasn't doing that, he was putting grease on the gears every thirty minutes or so. He caught a glimpse of a small love heart on the engine casing in front of him, drawn by Nellie Abbot's oily finger. He smiled. That was one thing he hadn't bargained on. One of many; this bleeding planet being one of them. But Nellie, what a find she was. She was different. He remembered the first time he met her, here on this world. They had been celebrating their first fresh food and the Fusiliers' commander, Captain Grantham, God rest his soul, had given permission for a bit of a bash.

The tank crew hadn't really socialised with the Fusiliers since they found themselves on this world. They were trained to act as an independent unit and that was the way they liked it. It was part of the attraction of the Machine Gun Corps. They bivvied beside the *Ivanhoe*. It rarely left their sight. But that night he'd gone for a walk amongst the campfires. A couple of rowdy bloody infantry had tried to engage him in conversation, but on hearing his accent they began to jeer and josh him. So he'd wandered off and took a piss over a parapet into one of their trenches. Cocky northern bastards. He was on his way back to the tank when he was accosted by a young girl in a long brown skirt and jacket, who took his arm, linking hers through his, and talked as if they were old friends.

"Cor blimey, what a night. I just got the old 'eave-'o from my mate. She's over there talking to that NCO with the crutch. Well, I can tell when I'm not wanted. Mind you, she needs a bit of perkin' up, bless her heart. Then I saw you in your coveralls. And I thought aye-aye, you're from the tank, ain'tcha? I ain't never seen one up real close. Don't they look funny, like a huge great iron slug? What kind of engine has she got? I bet she's a beaut. Can I see it?"

He could tell from her accent she wasn't a northerner, but Lord Almighty, she never stopped talking, and he let her talk, because she spoke of gears and pistons and carburettors and, quite frankly, he'd never met a girl like her. He'd come all this way from one world to another and there she was, large as life and twice as brassy. Nellie bleedin' Abbott. And he'd shook his head in wonder. She'd spent time in the FANYs driving ambulances and knew how to strip an engine. Had to. No bugger else to do it for her, half the time. She'd ridden a motorcycle once or twice. They talked of the country rides they might take together if they got back, but she wouldn't have it, not in a sidecar at any rate. Oh no. Not her. She wanted a motorcycle of her own. That was when he fell in love with her. Right there. Alfie's face split into an involuntary grin at the memory.

The rest of the crew were wary of her. They were used to their secrets, their own company. They didn't welcome outsiders. They wouldn't let her in the tank. Crew only, they said. But he'd snuck her in anyway. Once he'd had to shove her out of one sponson door as Jack squeezed in the other.

The crew had been despondent at the time. It looked like their fuel would run out, and without petrol, the tank was just so much scrap. Without the tank they would be transferred into the battalion to be Poor Bloody Infantry again.

But then one of the Tommies had brewed some evil alcoholic concoction that killed a couple of men daft enough to drink it. Unfit for human consumption, they said. But it gave them a new fuel. It ran a little better than the petrol they were used to, but then that was nearly all 'flogged' inferior stuff anyway. This new stuff had been distilled from what they now called petrol fruit. They were back in the game.

That was when everything changed.

They had been breathing the fumes for a week or so before they noticed. At first they felt keener, their senses seemed more acute. Colours were brighter, crisper. Sounds were clearer and smells sharper and more distinct.

"It's the clean air here," Reggie informed them. "Clears out the tubes!" he said, thumping his chest. He couldn't have been more wrong. Even Lieutenant Mathers seemed to relax now. Before, he had been a bundle of nerves in the tank, always on the verge of funking it, but now he seemed to relish driving it. Then again, they all did. Mind you, it helped when you were not being constantly shelled by Fritz artillery or hammered with machine gun fire. It was quite like the old days driving round Elveden as if it were a fairground ride. The days when they weren't in it were fraught with tension and short tempers. Even the engine, after some initial troubles, seemed to run smoother.

It was the fuel itself. They'd heard stories of how the Tommies that had drunk it saw things, hallucinated. That's why it was declared unfit for human consumption. But they weren't drinking it. They didn't have to. Fumes from the engine filled the small confined space. Ordinary petrol fumes would give them carbon monoxide poisoning. They'd end up with vicious headaches, convulsions and, in extreme cases, delirium or psychosis. They'd stagger from the tank and vomit. The petrol vapour would sting their skin and give them itching rashes and impetigo.

This new fuel had different side effects. Once they discovered the effects of petrol fruit fumes, they vowed amongst themselves to keep it quiet. It gave them a sense of euphoria, changed their vision. Under its influence they began to see the bright little whirls and eddies of indigo as the vapour swirled lazily about the cabin. The white painted iron plate surrounding them throbbed green with the vibration of the engine. Alfie soon found he could identify the state of the engine by the colour it gave off. But most of all he liked looking at Nellie. Great gaseous expanses of soft yellows billowed gently from her like silk sheets in the wind and oh, how she shone. If only he could tell her how beautiful she was. She thought herself rather plain. But he doubted anybody had ever seen her the way he had.

He hated leaving her now. Before, all he had was the crew of the *Ivanhoe*. Now, there was her.

He recalled the last time he saw Nellie, a day ago now, just before they left, but it seemed an age away when he wasn't in her company. They'd received orders to move out on another seek and find patrol. He'd spent half the night checking and tuning the engine, oiling it, having to use rendered down fats as grease. The rest of Ivanhoe's crew were full of pep and up for it, knowing they'd be able to partake of the intoxicating fumes again.

The only other person who might have an inkling of the effects was Tulliver, the RFC chap. He used the same petrol fruit liquor to fuel his aeroplane. But he wasn't confined in a dark, airless cabin with it. The wind would soon whip away any fumes he might inhale.

As the others stocked up on supplies, carefully watched by Company Quartermaster Sergeant Slacke, Alfie had wandered off to say goodbye to Nellie. He found her trying to haul a large pan of some sort of edible, well, stew, for want of a better word.

"Alfie. Can't give us a hand, can you, m'duck?"

"Sorry, Nellie. Moving out. Another one of the infantry's explore and patrol missions."

"Oh aye. And keep an eye out for –"

"– Jeffries, yes," he finished. They laughed together.

He peered into the pot. "Cor. What have the mongey wallahs come up with this time? It looks disgusting."

"Yes, well, it isn't for you. It's for them poor beggars in the Bird Cage," she said, nodding her head towards the barbed wire enclosure where the shell-shocked men were housed.

Lieutenant Mathers had climbed the steps out of the communications trench that led to the battalion HQ, his shoulders hunched and a sullen look on his gaunt, pasty face.

"Perkins. Don't dally. We've got to shove off." He sniffed the air and homed in on the cauldron. "Mmm, what's that?" He reached in and pulled out a lump of something, put it in his mouth and chewed experimentally.

"Oi!" Nellie slapped his hand. "This is for the poor shell-shock victims, not the likes of you, sir."

The rebuke caught Mathers off guard. He looked towards the enclosure at the shuffling, jerking scraps of manhood within and at least had the manners to look guilty. He coughed in embarrassment. "Yes. Right." He wagged the rest of the handful at her. "Still, not bad," he said and strode away. "Come on, Perkins. Work to do."

Alfie had shrugged an apology, "Must dash," and he'd followed his commanding officer. The last he saw of Nellie was her lugging the pan towards the Bird Cage...

BRIGHT GREEN RIPPLES burst from the floor of the compartment as the tank lurched and Alfie cracked his head on an overhead pipe.

"Watch where you're driving!" Alfie bellowed at Wally's back.

"Plenty of room up bloody top if you're not bleedin' happy with it!" Wally retorted.

"Got a real bee in his bonnet about that bounder Jeffries hasn't he, that Lieutenant Everson?" Norman was yelling above the noise of the engine. "I mean this is the fifth time he's sent us out on patrol to try and pick up his trail, and have we? Have we, billy-o. Not a sign. One of the promising directions picked out by Tulliver? Bollocks. I bet everything looks promising from a thousand feet up. Oh, and here's a map what a nurse saw. Sorry it's mostly empty, would you chaps mind filling in the blank bits as you go?"

"We could run right over Jeffries in *Ivanhoe* and not even notice," Cecil yelled back.

Norman nodded in agreement. "Wild goose chase is what it is. Waste of time."

"Not at all, dear chap," Reggie chipped in. "Travel broadens the mind, you know."

"In a place like this, Hell's back yard? Loosens the bowels, more like. Thank God I've got armour plating between me and it, is all I can say."

"Well, I'm all for these little trips of Everson's. Very nice of him. Don't care if we never find this Jeffries," said Reggie.

Frank spat on the gangway. "Jeffries, my arse."

"Frank! Please."

"Yeah, mind your language," scolded Norman. "Has Reggie taught you nothing?"

"Yeah, I holds me pinky up when I use me canteen now," Frank said, demonstrating to wild laughter. "Besides, if he ain't got a boojum like us then frankly he's probably dead meat. Why else d'you think they send us out here? 'Cause every bugger else gets eaten, that's why."

"Just makes us tinned bully beef," said Norman with a grin.

"Quite frankly I don't care if we never find the bleeder. Don't need the blighter mucking up the sweet little deal we've got going here."

"Well I don't feel too happy about that," Alfie shouted across the engine. "It doesn't seem right, somehow. Doesn't it bother the rest of you? Maybe we should discuss it again, that's all I'm saying."

Frank reached out, grabbed Alfie's coveralls and pulled him towards him under the starting handle. "And all I'm saying, Alfie, is you need to back off a little, mate. We're getting fed up with your holier-than-thou attitude. It was the Sub's idea. If our plans make you breezy, why don't you just do one and take up with your long-haired chum back with the mud sloggers?"

"Why? Because we're tankers. I'm maybe not so crazy about this idea, but I'd take a bullet for any single one of you, you know that, right?"

"Do we, Alfie? Do we? We don't even know if we can trust you." Frank thrust Alfie away from him with a snort of derision as the others looked on.

Alfie shook his head in despair. Their devotion to Mathers, who had seen them through, who had kept them supplied with the petrol fruit fuels and kept them safe and alive inside their shell of iron, was slipping into the fanatical and tinged with paranoia. Even Mathers' moods seemed to fluctuate between insanity and lucidity. Their world had shrunk and they no longer noticed nor cared. But his? His world had been expanded. He saw beyond the horizons of armoured plate and rivets. His world was illuminated by Nellie, a moon whose tidal influence was pulling him slowly from their orbit.

There was a hollow *krunng*. And another, accompanied by brilliant green migraine flashes radiating from the roof of the compartment.

"Rockfall?"

The tank lurched to a halt, and the engine died to an idle. Alfie held his breath, straining to listen above the chug of the engine. If it was a rockfall, they had no chance of getting out of there in a hurry. Their top speed was barely above walking pace.

Norman stuck his head out of the rear sponson hatch. A rock smashed into the sponson, just missing him.

"Bloody hell, we're under attack!" he yelped, ducking back in and slamming the hatch shut behind him. "It's an ambush. Place is lousy with 'em. Buggers are throwing rocks at us. Reminds me of a show at the Leeds Empire. Bloody hell, they were a hard audience that night."

The others did likewise, shutting the other hatches, their only illumination now the small electric festoon lamps.

"*Language*, Norman," warned Reggie.

There was another round of bangs as more rocks rained down on the hull.

Jack and Norman manned their six pounders and peered out of the vertical gun port slits, looking for a target. Cecil and Reggie loaded the breaches then readied their machine guns, threading fresh belts into the mechanism.

"Where are they?" said Reggie, peering through a pistol port. "I can't see anything. Where the deuce are they?"

"Above us."

"Well, we can't sit here," said Mathers. "Carry on, Clegg. They can't harm us."

"Sir."

The engine roared into life again and the *Ivanhoe* rumbled forwards for a minute before Wally raised his right fist. At the signal, Alfie threw his left track gear into neutral, disengaging his track. Frank pushed the right track gear into first speed. The tank began to swing right to avoid a large boulder the size of a terraced house before jerking to a halt. Another signal from Wally. Alfie pushed his gear into first speed too and the tank lurched straight ahead for another ten yards as it passed the boulder.

"I can't see anything. Just rocks!" said Reggie, becoming agitated, his face pressed to a loophole.

They heard a succession of softer thuds on the roof followed by a scratching clatter above them.

"They're on the roof."

Another signal from Wally and Frank slipped his track gear into neutral while Alfie pushed his into first speed. *Ivanhoe* swung sharply to the left. There was a thud on the sponson and Reggie lurched back as something chitinous blocked the light.

"It's outside!"

"Well, bloody shoot it!"

Reggie squeezed the Hotchkiss' trigger and the belt feed zipped through a few feet, firing a hail of bullets. There was an anguished squeal and light flooded in from the pistol port again.

"Damn it!" Mathers stood up and squeezed back down the port

gangway past Norman and Reggie, drew his pistol and opened the manhole hatch in the roof above the rear of the engine.

There were three Yredetti on top of the tank. Ugly buggers, reminiscent of beetles, with mottled green chitinous armour. They walked upright, like chatts, but they had better developed powerful middle limbs that they used for gripping, and were just as comfortable and fast on on all sixes. They were primitives, a race of carnivorous hunters. They had no weapons and didn't need them. Their large saw-toothed mandibles were capable of decapitating a man. One was trying to wrench off the exhaust covers. Mathers fired, and it fell over the side with a squeal. Another turned and lunged at him. He got off a second shot, which raked down the carapace and sent it spinning from the roof to bounce off the starboard sponson.

More were emerging now from behind boulders and closing in on the tank.

They charged the *Ivanhoe*. One was crushed beneath the track, and a second was cut down by Wally with a burst from the forward facing machine gun. Half out of the hatch, Mathers wrestled with the creature. A third Yrredetti was using its mandibles to slice through the ropes holding the drums of spare fuel to the rear of the tank. There was a hearting-rending *thung* and a drum fell loose and bounced off the tank's steering tail and back along the canyon, coming to rest against a couple of small rocks.

Mathers fired at the creature again. It hissed and he ducked down and grabbed the hatch, partially shutting it after him, and bellowed down into the cabin.

"Clegg, for Christ's sake stop the tank. We've lost the spare fuel!"

The tank lurched to a halt, the engine still idling. Mathers thrust himself up, slamming the opening hatch into the facial carapace of the creature, crushing a mandible. He fired point blank into the stunned creature's face and paused momentarily to watch the head explode in a myriad of colours, creating a rainbow of mist in the air. He looked back over the roof of the tank to where the fuel drum had come to rest. Several

Yrredetti were gathered around it and were pounding it with stones. He boosted himself up onto the roof, ran down the rear of the track, leapt off the back and charged towards the insect-creatures, waving his pistol and bawling like a maniac.

"Bloody hell, the Sub's blood is up," said Jack as he followed the thumping footfalls over the roof and peered out of the sponson door loophole. "Better give him a hand, lads. Stick close to me, Cecil. Norman, Frank? Keep me covered. Wally, stay with *Ivanhoe*. You too, Reggie."

"Really? Don't mind if I do," said Reggie with relief. "Most kind."

Jack glanced dismissively at Alfie as he opened the sponson hatch and clambered down. It was a deliberate snub. They didn't need him. They didn't want him. Cecil followed Jack out, cocking his pistol as he went.

"Bloody hell!" Alfie muttered, clambering out and joining Cecil by the rear starboard track horn anyway.

A cry from high up on the canyon side preceded another boulder, bouncing down the rocky face, dislodging a tumble of smaller scree that chased it down the slope, like ragamuffins chasing an ice-cream cart. It bounced wide. Norman aimed his revolver and fired. The small figure of an Yrredetti tumbled forwards from its rocky perch to fall into a patch of the blue-green blisterous growths which burst under its impact.

By now Mathers had reached the drum and had shot the three Yrredetti beating it. He inspected the drum. There were several alarming dents, but it was still intact, thank God. Another group of Yrredetti shuffled warily nearby. Mathers roared at them. They scuttled back. Jack reached the drum, Cecil panting in his wake.

Jack nodded at the drum. "Better get this back on the *Ivanhoe*, sir."

"What?" said Mathers, shaking his head and looking around as if suddenly realising where he was. He glanced around the canyon walls. More Yrredetti were beginning to rear their heads from behind boulders and were crawling down the scree slope towards them.

"Hmm? Yes, you're right. Can you manage it, Tanner?"

"I can, sir."

Mathers strode back to the tank, reloading his revolver from his belt pouch as he went. Frank and Alfie crouched by the tank, using the rear track horns and the steering tail as cover, keeping an eye on the creatures that seemed to be getting bolder by the minute, or more desperate.

Mathers thought he heard whispering. He scowled at Frank. "What did you say?"

Frank looked at him, startled. "Nothing, sir. Didn't say a word."

"Hmm." Mathers held his gaze for a moment, then shook his head.

Jack rolled the drum back towards the *Ivanhoe*. Cecil, now dangerously exposed, was edging back towards the tank, revolver raised, wavering, switching targets indecisively. "I got you, Jack."

"Get it stowed, quickly," said Mathers, boarding through the port sponson hatch.

On the roof, Frank helped haul the drum into position on top of the other one while Jack, standing on the steering tail, strained as he lifted the drum above his head.

One Yrredetti flung a stone, cracking the retreating Cecil on the back of the skull. The lad stumbled and went down, clutching his head, and his revolver skittered away from him. From the cover of a nearby boulder a couple of Yrredetti darted forwards, urged on by the calls of others. A claw snapped down on Cecil's foot and dragged him back towards the shelter of the rock.

"Cecil's down!" Alfie fired his revolver. The round ricocheted off the boulder,

"Oh Jesus, help me, for Christ's sake!" screamed Cecil as he was dragged towards the boulder.

Alfie ran towards it. Time seemed to slow. Around him the air shifted in whorls of effervescent vermillion, parting as he ran and, in the periphery of his vision, orange auras blazed among the rocks indicating the position of the creatures hidden in the rocks around and above him, his fear swamped by an exhilaration.

He scrambled up the side of the large boulder even as Cecil disappeared round the back. Stood on the top, he saw three arthropods huddled behind the rock, arguing over Cecil.

A blue-green blister throbbed on a small rock, the size of a football, near Alfie's feet. He shouted. They looked up and he kicked the rock down, hitting one of them in the head, blisters bursting and drenching the creature's face, burning it. Its scream was bright orange, fading quickly to red as it reflected off the canyon walls, before dissipating as it died.

Alfie leapt down, landing on the arm that held the screaming Cecil. He felt the chitinous armour crunch beneath his boots as he fired his revolver point blank into the face of the second. The third tried to scuttle back to the safety of the scree slope, but Jack appeared, caught it by the leg and swung it against the boulder. Alfie heard its carapace crack and Jack let it fall limply to the ground, leaving a dark sticky stain on the rock.

Alfie pulled Cecil to his feet, ducked under his armpit, took his weight and helped him back to the tank. Jack stood his ground before backing towards the tank, picking up Cecil's fallen revolver and guarding their retreat. The gathering creatures hissed and clicked their mandibles, but kept their distance.

By now the fuel drum had been re-secured, and Alfie could hear Wally running up the engine in readiness to move off. He passed Cecil to Frank, who hauled him in through the sponson hatch.

"Come on, Jack," Alfie called, one foot on the starboard hatch lip as he prepared to step through. Jack danced backwards towards the tank, his eyes never leaving the rocks.

"Natives are still restless," he said, ducking as a fist-sized stone hit the tank's metal track.

"All aboard," called Reggie, banging cheerfully on a pipe with a wrench.

The ironclad moved off.

Frustrated, the Yrredetti howled and a rain of rocks clattered down against the tank, setting off a rainbow of percussion inside.

"Looks like they're trying a final attempt to ditch us," said Frank, peering through his pistol port. Mathers peered through the pistol port in the side of the driver cabin. Damn things were trying to prise a boulder loose and start an avalanche.

"Put your foot down, Clegg. We don't want to get caught in this canyon." The tank lurched as it picked up what speed it could.

Several more Yrredetti were helping to lever the boulder free as the tank started to pass beneath it.

Reggie loaded a shell into the breech of the port gun. Norman took a deep breath, gritted his teeth and pushed down with all his weight, levering the gun up so that it was pointed up towards the canyon wall. He targeted the boulder as best he could in the moving tank, and fired. The boulder and the Yrredetti disappeared in a plume of fire and dirt. A cloud of dust rolled down the canyon side, enveloping the tank. A rain of clinker and debris pattered down on the hull, sending verdant ripples through the compartment.

"Yes! Got the blighters. Thank you and goodnight! That'll teach 'em to mess with old *Ivanhoe*!" whooped Norman.

Rubble rattled down the canyon sides to be crushed beneath the tracks of the *Ivanhoe* as, oblivious, it continued on its halting way towards the mouth of the canyon.

Behind it, a lone wail of frustration echoed round the walls of the canyon, before being picked up and amplified by other Yrredetti.

As the dust cloud settled, the blue-green blisters, stilled in the fleeting darkness of the cloud, began to pulse in the rays of the sun once more. On the canyon side, where the shell had exploded, something cold and metallic glinted through the shattered rock in the dust-filtered daylight.

CHAPTER FIVE
"The Outlook isn't Healthy..."

LIEUTENANT MATHERS, OPERATING the steering brake levers, peered out of the front visor at the small rectangle of world he could see before him, a world that see-sawed violently as the landship crashed up and down on the swell of ground beneath them. As they nosed up over obstacles, the bright rectangle of sky was snatched away with vertiginous speed to be replaced with lurching glimpses of soil and rock, before he was teased with a horizon line of vermillion-hued vegetation that vanished again abruptly.

Again, Mathers heard the whispering. He glanced at Clegg beside him, the bantam cockney's wiry arms tense on the driving levers.

"Blimey," the driver shouted over the noise of the engine behind them. "This place has got more pot holes than Oxford Street."

Mathers shook his head. He could barely hear Clegg speak, let alone whisper. It must be some resonant engine note he'd not noticed before.

As they left the canyon behind them, the blue-green rock blisters gave way to a cinnamon-coloured soil. Ahead of them lay a rocky plateau scored with haphazard cracks and stress marks from the same geological event that caused the canyon. Cracks and gullies splintered the landscape like crazy paving; some rocky plates tilting, some sunken, some thrust up. Some gullies were too wide for the tank to cross, even though the weight of its hydraulic steering tail was designed as a counter-balance to cross trenches of up to nine feet.

They had to find a way to safely cross the labyrinthine field. As tank commander, that job fell to Mathers, and quite frankly he was glad of it. He was the tallest man in the crew, a real legs eleven. Sat in the small cockpit on the hard chair being jolted and jarred had given him a stomach cramp. Even now he hated being cooped up in the tank for long periods and he found himself tensing, clenching his stomach muscles against the unexpected drops, jolts and bangs.

He had cramp. And a headache. Maybe the fresh air would help. He tapped Clegg on the shoulder.

"I'll walk on ahead, guide you through."

It was a common procedure in tanks. When going became difficult it was the commander's unenviable task to negotiate paths round shell-hole-pocked roads, and he'd done his fair share during night manoeuvres and under fire. There were times when he almost preferred that to being cooped up in an iron coffin. At least here, there was no chance of Fritz sniping at you, and that brought a great deal of relief. On the other hand, you never knew here what you were going to encounter next.

He walked ahead of the tank, checking the ground, searching for narrow enough gullies for them to cross. He could hear things moving about in the bottom of them, slithering and snuffling. He peered over the edge of one, but some form of bruised purple vegetation obscured the gully bed. In a way, he was relieved. He indicated to Clegg to swing right over a gap narrow enough for the *Ivanhoe* to bridge.

In this manner, the tank crew progressed slowly across the broken plain, having to go out of their way to find a route passable enough to be of little concern to the great metal behemoth. From then on, progress was faster and the jungle loomed ahead. A short sort of crimson brambly plant became more prevalent, its thorns scratching the leather of his calf-length boots.

One caught his ankle and sent him tumbling into a gully; he

slipped to the bottom. An accompanying land slither sent dirt and soil raining down onto him. For a moment, disorientated, unable to move, the old panic rose in him again.

Mathers had been an officer in the infantry, on the front lines, until one day he found himself under heavy bombardment for days. The dugout he was in had collapsed under shellfire. There was a large bang, and then darkness. And silence. He couldn't move. He was buried, pinned under the body of an orderly, Hammond, that lay across him, staring at him with lifeless eyes for what seemed like hours, but must have been a lot less. His ears were ringing. Muffled by the dirt, the sandbags and joists, he could hear the barrage going on around him, the shriek of whizz-bangs and, in the breeze that blew gently through the collapsed dugout, a hint of gas. He could barely hear his own voice as he called for help. He knew he mustn't be seen to funk it in front of the men he could hear digging for him. He had enough gumption about him not to scream, fighting off the urge by biting his own hand while, in his head, he pleaded with a god he barely believed in to let him get out. He promised anything, everything.

When they finally dragged him from under Hammond's corpse and carried him by stretcher to the aid post, he was found to have no serious injuries. Hammond's body had cushioned him. He was lucky. But his scars couldn't be seen.

He was still shaking the next day. The tremors made it difficult to walk, so he was forced to remain in bed by stern matrons.

Commotional distress, they said. Perfectly understandable. Several weeks behind the lines helped him recover. Except that it didn't. Back at the front, it didn't take long for his nerves to fray. He noticed the tremors, the rising panic, and the tic under his eye, whenever he had to go into a dugout. He could hardly sleep. Alcohol helped, initially. Eventually they sent him back to Blighty to recuperate.

That was when he met Major Parkhurst. Damn Major Parkhurst. Man had the bloody temerity to call himself an MO. Bloody croaker, more like. The man didn't believe in neuralgia. You were either a coward or you weren't. Mathers insisted he wasn't, which was all Parkhurst wanted to hear to declare him fit for duty. The trouble was, Mathers no longer knew for sure. He had to prove it to himself one way or the other. Kill or cure, he thought.

The Machine Gun Corps' new Heavy Section was looking for officers and men. It would be a fresh start away from his old battalion. He applied, hiding the true extent of his condition. He hadn't realised what was involved until he'd arrived at Elveden. But you couldn't show fear in front of the men. You were an officer. To do so was to invite a court martial. Every time he entered the tank he could feel the pressure building inside him, like a pot that threatened to boil over, but he managed to control it, tensing his stomach and legs so that he wouldn't jump at unexpected noises or lurches. Thankfully, it seemed everyone in the tanks was ill from the fumes and the working conditions at one time or another and he found he could disguise the worse of his nervous debility. Here, on this world, however, the tank provided its own medication. The fuel fumes seemed to have a beneficial effect on him, making him less jumpy. He wondered what was in it to make him feel this way, but only briefly. Mostly he was just glad. Even that infernal tic under his left eye, that would fire uncontrollably in bursts, like a machine gun, had stopped recently.

He put it to the back of his mind and breathed deeply.

He realized he wasn't buried. The cloth of his jacket had just caught fast on the bramble. He tore his arm free, ripping the serge. He heard something in the damp shadows slithering towards him along the gully bed, under the cover of the creeping plant, and he scrambled back up the side of the gully.

As he clawed his way to the lip, he heard a sound over the noise of the tank, and he saw an apparent cluster of boulders a hundred yards away lift itself up, limbs unfolding from beneath it. He had seen one of these things before in a forest, on the way to rescue captured Tommies from Khungarr. They had only survived then by good fortune. A stone beetle, about the size of the *Ivanhoe*.

Cautiously, it stretched and unrolled itself, watching the tank warily. Clegg tried to turn the *Ivanhoe* so that it faced their foe; Mathers urged them on silently. The stone beetle was quicker and scuttled round the tank, as if looking for weaknesses. In order to turn more quickly Clegg had kept both tracks running, one in reverse. It would strip the differential if he kept that up and they'd be buggered out in the middle of nowhere with no tankodrome or machine shops. Mathers was sure Perkins would be scolding him.

The beetle crouched low on its limbs, its head down, mandibles scything, all the while watching the tank.

The tank halted, its engine growling. Mathers urged it to do something. It seemed an eternity before the tank began to lurch backwards away from the beast. The huge rock beetle advanced, keeping pace with it. It then tried scuttling round to the right as if to flank it. A burst of machine gun fire spitting across the ground soon stopped that.

Mathers watched, helpless, as the tank tried to fix the thing in its sights, but it was altogether faster and more agile than the cumbersome armoured machine. Mathers threw himself to the ground as a spray of bullets zipped over his head.

"Nesbit!" he roared, the admonition all but drowned by the noise of the tank.

The giant beetle, having abandoned its flanking manoeuvre, now sought to charge the trespasser. Head down, swaying, its great stone stag horns wove through the air. It scuttled forwards again in short, abrupt bursts, the brief spatter from the forwards facing Hotchkiss ricocheting off its carapace, merely giving it pause for thought. It was almost with reluctance that the stone beetle then backed away. It regarded the ironclad hesitantly before slinking away and slithering down into a large gully.

Mathers breathed a sigh of relief. When he picked himself off the ground, a sharp pain in his abdomen almost doubled him over. He frowned and sucked air in through gritted teeth until the sensation passed.

He felt inside his tunic, pulled out his hip flask and took a quick slug of the distilled petrol fruit. Its fumes alone weren't enough to dull the pain. More recently, he needed something stronger.

The tank slewed round blindly, trying to find its vanished foe. Mathers approached the tank and stood in front of it. He could make out Clegg's face through the driver's open visor plate, and waved him on. The tank began to clank obediently towards him as he continued to scout ahead. The crevices and gullies were becoming fewer and narrower, but he didn't want to take any chances. He hadn't gone fifty yards when he heard a pistol go off. He turned to see someone fire from one of the tank's pistol ports.

This stone beetle creature was obviously more cunning than its forest cousin was. It had used the cover of the gullies to come round behind the tank and surprise its rival.

"Swing to port!" Mathers yelled, waving his arms to his right as if he could speed up the tank's turn by the action. "For Christ's sake, swing to port!"

INSIDE THE TANK, peering out of the sponson door pistol port, Frank saw a flash of stone carapace and fired his revolver.

"Bugger's back!" he yelled. Faces peered out of the other pistol ports, searching for the creature.

"Where?"

"It's behind us," said Cecil, peering out of the pistol port in the rear door by the radiator.

"Wally, about face, ninety degrees!" yelled Alfie. He nodded to Frank and when Wally gave the signal from his driving seat, they changed gears. The tank began to turn almost on the spot.

"Where is it? I can't see it!" said Wally, peering though his visor plate. They peered out of pistol ports and gun slits, checking off their positions.

"Not here," called Jack, swinging the gun round through a hundred and twenty degrees and peering through the gun slit.

"Nor here," said Cecil.

"Can't see it," said Norman.

"Then where the bloody hell is it?"

As if in answer, there was a heavy thud accompanied by an oppressive green synesthetic flash as the creature landed on top of the tank. A noise like nails on a blackboard pierced the bass rumble of the engine as the creature's feet sought purchase. Blocked by the belly of the creature above, exhaust fumes began to belch back into the compartment, filling the space with a choking black smoke.

Alfie began coughing until spots burst before his eyes.

Reggie took the commander's seat next to Wally.

"No free rides on this 'bus!" he said, pulling on the brake lever. The *Ivanhoe* jerked to a halt. Unable to get a firm grip, the stone beetle slithered off the front.

"That'll teach it," said Wally with a self-satisfied sneer. "Go on, clear off, you great bleedin' cockroach."

It skittered off round out of his limited field of view. Back in the compartment, the crew flung themselves at the pistol ports again. It was too fast for the gunners to get a bead on it.

The back end of the tank tilted up as the creature shoved its horns beneath the steering tail and tried to lever it up. The tank crashed down again as it failed. It tried again.

"Oi!" Wally drove the tank forwards.

"Cecil, take a peek and see what the bleeder's trying to do, will you."

Cecil peered out of the rear loophole. "Lawks, it's coming after us again!"

The tank juddered once more as the back end tilted up and crashed down again.

"We can't take much more of this."

There was a brief stillness. Alfie held his breath.

Then Cecil piped up, jerking back from the pistol port in the rear door. "It's trying for the roof again."

Alfie found himself looking up at the roof, from where the noise, and jagged green spikes, of scrambling issued. Between them, Wally, Alfie and Frank tried to swing the tank and throw it off, but it clung tenaciously to the roof.

"What the hell do we do now?"

"Aaaugh. Shit!" yelled Cecil stumbling back over the differential. "It's trying to get in!" After several attempts, a thin exoskeletal tube about two feet long appeared through the pistol port. He reared back and cocked his revolver at it. He watched, open-mouthed, as the end opened and something wet and glistening, like a tentacle, protruded from the chitinous casing.

"It, it's a whatsit, a prob-sis? It's trying to suck us out!"

"I don't think so, son." Jack edged past Alfie, put a hand on Cecil's wrist and forced him to lower the weapon. "Don't shoot in here, Ces. The bullet'll ricochet."

"Fellas," said Norman, warily.

The tank began to rock as the beetle creature above them sought purchase. The rocking became more rhythmic. The tentacle, if that's what it was, began to throb.

A vile thought took hold as Alfie watched. "That's not a bloody tentacle, or a proboscis. It's a bleedin' short arm!"

Reggie blanched. "A what?"

The rocking became more urgent and the occupants of the tank were being shunted backwards and forwards with every thrust. Expressions of horror and disgust dawned on their faces as they realised what was going on.

"It's not trying to kill us. It's after a bon time," said Norman. Only Cecil still looked blank.

"It thinks we're a lady friend?" Frank suggested.

Cecil frowned. "But this is a male tank."

Alfie braced his hands against the roof as another enthusiastic thrust rocked the tank. "I *really* don't think it cares."

"Jesus! Well don't just stand there," bellowed Wally.

Cecil looked at them. "What do we do?"

Moral indignation flooded Jack's face. "Well, I'll tell you what I'm bloody well not going to do and that's lie back and think of bloody England." He grabbed a wrench and took a swing at the now tumescent and dripping appendage. "D'you know, Ces," he said, "after this, I can see me and you is going to need a long talk about... country matters."

Frank leered. "After this, I don't think he'll need one."

*   *   *

MATHERS WATCHED AS the giant beetle attempted to mount the *Ivanhoe,* using its mandibles to try to bite and hold the tank's roof, its legs scrambling for leverage as it began to grind against the rear of the tank. All thought of its own safety washed away in a primal urge too strong to ignore.

The tank juddered forward, but the beetle was determined not to lose its mount and tottered forwards with it, almost comically, still attached.

Mathers felt a hint of shame that the ironclad should be misused so shamefully, as if it had been a faithful beast unwillingly put out to stud. He picked up a rock and hurled it at the creature, but it bounced off. He picked up another one and edged closer, this time aiming at its face. It bounced off a mandible. He felt light-headed, but didn't stop. Whatever he was feeling, it wasn't fear; it was... exhilaration. He picked up another rock and, yelling incoherently, he charged. He ran at the tank and, using his momentum, and the starboard gun barrel, in one swift move he scrambled onto the *Ivanhoe* and began smashing at the beetle's legs, which seemed to be the most vulnerable part. Smoke began billowing out from the smothered exhaust vents beneath the beetle. He was about to leap on its back in an attempt to stove its head in when a sheering screech ripped the sky.

A shadow flicked overhead.

Mathers looked up. A large creature like a manta ray swooped down over the rutting beetle. It had a long neck and small head, with a deceptively wide mouth and sharp teeth. The beetle, locked as it was in congress with the tank, neither knew nor cared.

The flying creature Mathers recognised; the men called it a jabberwock. They preyed on the herds of tripodgiraffes that roamed the veldt. It wheeled round and extended its hind legs and sharp talons, like a hawk's. Mathers, unperturbed, threw the rock at it, less of a defence and more of a challenge. He stood on the beetle's back as it humped and roared at the jabberwock in defiance. So close to death and he had never felt so alive.

By now, the beetle was hastily trying to dismount the tank but seemed to be having difficulty withdrawing.

The jabberwock screeched again as it dived towards the unnatural pairing. Mathers, stood atop the mating beetle, was prepared to meet the thing head on, though with what he had no idea and didn't care. The struggling stone beetle freed itself and slipped clumsily off the back of the tank, tipping Mathers from its back. He put out a hand but found no hold and fell from the creature onto the starboard tank track before tumbling heavily to the ground by the sponson. His graceless dismount saved his life, as talons tore through empty air above him.

Winded and dazed, he shuffled back on his buttocks away from the tracks, for fear the tank should start up again and crush him. Shrieking in frustration, the jabberwock banked sharply and, talons first, slammed down onto the disorientated and satiated stone beetle. Using its great manta wings to stabilise itself, the jabberwock sought gaps that its sharp curved claws could lock under, while its head sought similar weaknesses on its prey's back.

The beetle flailed pointlessly, unable to grasp anything of its attacker with its mandibles. Turning this way and that like a dog chasing its tail, desperate to dislodge its assailant from its back, it slammed into the tank, shunting it sideways. Mathers watched as the vehicle slid several feet towards him. He could only see the flapping of the great wings and hear the cries of the jabberwock, hidden from view by the tank.

His face and back began to prickle with drying sweat, he felt a wave of nausea rise up, and he vomited on the ground. What the hell did he think he was doing? His hands began to shake. Thinking of himself up on the tank beating that damn thing with a rock made him heave again. Jesus. His head began to pound.

There was a screech of triumph as the jabberwock rose from the ground, talons locked tightly onto the beetle. The stone beetle's legs thrashed weakly, defenceless. The pair rose higher and higher as Mathers scrambled to his feet. Trembling, feeling faint and clammy, he staggered towards the tank.

The jabberwock cawed loudly and released the beetle, which dropped like a dead weight. There was a wet cracking sound as the beetle slammed down onto the tank's roof. It clawed feebly. Triumphant, the jabberwock flew down and began to prise at the cracked carapace with a taloned foot. Its long neck and hooked beak began ripping at the innards, tearing its soft wet organs.

Thirty feet away, Mathers made to creep towards the sponson hatch, but the gimlet-eyed predator spotted him. For a moment, he thought it was going to attack, but it just extended its neck, screeched in his direction, warning him off, and went back to tearing at the beetle carcass.

The jabberwock kept one eye on him, jealously guarding its kill as it ripped and tore, throwing back its head to swallow lumps of offal. He needed to get the thing and its meal off the tank. Slowly, still trembling, he edged round to the front of the tank and ducked round the starboard track horn, and over the pervasive rumble of the engine shouted into the driver's cockpit.

"Clegg, the beetle thing is lying on the starboard track. If you drive forwards the track might run it off the front of the tank."

Clegg nodded his comprehension through the driver's visor. Mathers saw him turn back in the tank and yell something. Her ran up the engine and the tank jerked into life, then began, clanking track plate by track plate, to inch forwards. The beetle carcass moved. The jabberwock didn't notice at first, but when its kill was tugged away from it, it looked around for the unseen rival.

Mathers backed off and watched the progress of the dead beetle as it ground slowly forward. The jabberwock, furious that its meal was being snatched, put one clawed foot on the body to hold it. The tracks ground on inexorably, shredding the underside of the carcass and leaving viscous blue stains on the track plates. The weight of the jabberwock was holding it back.

Mathers would have to do something. Picking up a rock, he threw it at the jabberwock to draw its attention. The first one hit its body; it turned and hissed at him. The second hit its neck. It roared in his direction. A third had it rearing up over its kill and spreading its huge wings. But Mathers now felt no fear. He grinned to himself. His crew had better be ready for this.

"Come on!" he yelled at the beast, waving his arms. "Come on! You great ugly trout! Over here!" Ugly trout? Really? Was that the best he could do? Never mind. It seemed to do the trick. The jabberwock flapped its wings and took off, shrieking at him all the while. Mathers backed off even further, trying to draw the creature away from the tank. He glanced behind him. There were several boulders that might provide cover, if he could reach them.

Without the weight of the jabberwock, the beetle carcass began moving as the *Ivanhoe* advanced, and flopped limply off the front track horns, where it fell to the ground. The tank rolled over it, crushing it and staining the ground blue.

The jabberwock advanced on Mathers in short agile hops. Mathers wasn't a serious threat to it, no more than an annoyance.

Now would be a good time, thought Mathers as he backed away, facing the creature.

A burst of machine gun fire from the driver's position raked the jabberwock, perforating a bloody line across its wingspan. The jabberwock turned on the new threat. The landship lumbered towards it. There was another burst of machine gun fire and the jabberwock's head vanished in an explosion of bloody vapour. The body staggered on another few yards under its own momentum before collapsing, also to be crushed under the tracks of the advancing *Ivanhoe*.

Mathers collapsed against the boulder, his breath coming in great heaving pants, sweat trickling down his back. He could feel his heart banging in his chest and waited for it to settle down.

The tank halted and Clegg called out through the driver's visor. "Lieutenant, are you all right?" Mathers nodded and waved his hand to brush off his driver's concern, his mouth too dry to speak.

From the back of the tank, he could hear the sponson hatches clang open and the crew staggering out into the fresh air, a tangle of voices, to survey the bodies.

Perkins ignored the dead creature, turning his attention to the tank. Mathers watched him. He walked along its length checking the tracks and track plates, tapping rivets. Eventually he was satisfied.

"Damage?" asked Mathers, remembering his position, straightening himself up, and striding purposefully towards Perkins.

"We were lucky, a couple of buckled plates, but they should be all right. The track tension will need adjusting soon, but we're all tickety-boo, sir."

"Good man," he said, patting him on the shoulder and walking off towards the tank.

"Sir?" asked Perkins.

Mathers turned. "What is it, Perkins?"

"I was just wondering, sir, shouldn't we be heading back to camp? We've come far enough. We've found no sign of Jeffries so far and we're reaching the limits of our range. Our fuel *is* limited, we should think about returning. I mean, they'll be expecting us back, sir."

"But we're all right for now?"

"Yes, sir, but –"

Mathers stepped closer and fixed Perkins with a stare, aware that his eye had started to twitch again. "Any complaints?"

If Perkins noticed it, he didn't say anything. "Complaints, sir? No sir."

"Then we'll carry on. As you were, Perkins."

THE *IVANHOE* HEADED off, leaving the corpses behind to be picked over by whatever scavengers found them. They made for the forest a couple of miles off.

Mathers was still walking in front of the tank, only now he carried a large suitably gnarled wooden staff tied to the top of which was a PH gas hood, looking like some desiccated head. He wore his 'turtle shell' helmet and splash mask, even though he was outside. It afforded him some meagre protection at least. But more than that, right now it served to accompany his rain cape, daubed as it was with hand prints and strange arcane symbols, or at least what the crew had decided passed for magical signs: spirals, stars, lightning flashes and unblinking eyes. Mathers fancied himself the subject of some fantastical Arthur Rackham illustration. He looked for all the world like a tribal shaman leading some great, tamed antediluvian beast.

Which was exactly how it was supposed to look.

Behind him, the *Ivanhoe* squeaked, clanked and growled its way closer to the jungle, its periscopes up, looking like eye-stalks or antennae.

Mathers could hear the whispering again. This time it was more insistent. This time he thought he could detect words in the tinny susurration. It was coming from behind him, from the *Ivanhoe*. It *was* the *Ivanhoe*. No, not the *Ivanhoe*. It was Skarra.

Mathers walked on. And listened.

THEY HALTED AT the jungle edge. When Mathers *looked* there was nothing, but he knew they were there. The fumes from the tank allowed him to *see* their breathing; slight yellow eddies in the air around the undergrowth.

Through the protective eye slits of his splash mask, he caught a movement from the tree line. A group of urmen stepped out from under cover. One came forwards hesitantly.

Mathers braced himself. You could never be quite sure of the reaction, but he heard the great six pounders coming to bear behind him, and Clegg running up the engine so it sounded like a throaty growl. That usually did the trick. Behind his chainmail mask, Mathers smiled. He enjoyed this next bit.

The warrior stopped, his eyes wide with fear and, while still a full twenty yards away from the ironclad, gave a great cry, threw up his arms and dropped to his knees, genuflecting until his forehead touched the ground. Behind him, his fellows did the same, hardly daring to look upon them.

Then from his position of supplication, he spoke. "We have been expecting you. Your coming has been foretold."

Mathers hadn't expected that.

PENNINE FUSILIERS

CHAPTER SIX
"Here Comes the Bogey Man..."

THEY WERE RUNNING with hatches and pistol ports shut now. Inside the tank, it was stifling, with only the four small festoon lights illuminating the compartment. The stench of sweating bodies, engine oil and rendered animal fats filled the small space, along with the ever-present hallucinogenic fumes from the engine. The men breathed deeply of it, oblivious to all but the petrol fruit fumes; each lost, momentarily, in their own little internal worlds. They might have been in an opium den but for the noise and the infernal juddering as the tank lumbered along the uneven ground. With his visor shut, Clegg had to use his look-stick in order to drive.

"What's going on? Have the natives bought it?" asked Norman.

"Yeah," he said. "Now pipe down 'til the Loot gives us the signal."

Norman winked. "Looks like we've got another performance coming up, boys."

"Good, we haven't had any decent scran for ages. I wasn't going to eat that fungus muck they was dishing out before we left. God, what I wouldn't give for a nice bit o' mutton."

"Speak for yourself," barked Reggie. "Give me a nice fillet steak any day."

At the back, by the starboard gear levers, Alfie watched small close-knit ripples of red emanating from the vibrating engine and saw each man glowing with a faint aura. He shook his head to disperse the sight as he had tried many times before. The coloured patterns remained drifting in his vision like the stubborn after-images of a star shell. He didn't like much about this stunt. Everything in his gut told him they shouldn't be doing this, but do it they did, each time more brazenly and more confidently than the last.

On their first encounter with an urmen enclave the natives, thinking the tank was Skarra, this world's god of the underworld, prostrated themselves before it and treated the crew as holy men. The crew went along with it in a bemused manner, because it suited their purpose. They rather liked the idea. Too much, it seemed. After months of subsisting on half rations and whatever vile local stew the mongey wallahs came up with, it was a relief to be feted for a change.

Reinforced by the euphoria and confidence imparted by the constant inhalation of the fumes, they were soon exaggerating and expanding the act until it was like a carnival sideshow. Norman, the ex-music hall actor, painted their rain capes with magic symbols and did a few conjuring tricks. At first it was just a jolly, but as the weeks went on their attitudes were tempered by the fumes, and as their side effects took hold, they began to half-believe the act themselves.

Alfie felt a sharp rap on his turtle shell. Jack was staring at him. He looked around to find Frank, Cecil and Norman staring across the engine at him.

Norman stepped up to him and put his mouth close to his ear in order to yell over the sound of the engine.

"I'll say this once. We've got a chance to be something here, to be someone. Don't you dare muck this up for us." He poked Alfie in the shoulder to emphasise his point.

Alfie was a little taken aback. He glanced at each of his crewmates in turn. They looked at him with expectation. They wanted his compliance. Alfie, disappointed in his mates but more so in himself, gave a reluctant nod.

Norman held his gaze a little longer, pointed to his own eyes and then at Alfie, "I'm watching you," before turning back to his gun.

OUTSIDE, MATHERS TURNED around and, with an expansive gesture, held his staff aloft, like Moses before the burning bush, and bowed low before the tank. The ironclad wavered gently in his vision, an effect of the fuel fumes, although it seemed to him that the tank was breathing, its sides expanding and contracting, a fact he now accepted as quite natural.

He wheeled smartly to face the front, his rain cape whipping around him as he turned. He had them in the palm of his hand. He raised his staff like a Regimental Sergeant Major on a parade ground and nodded at the urman. "Lead on. Skarra, god of the underworld, will follow."

The urman backed slowly away on his knees before getting to his feet and walking back into the jungle with his companions, casting fearful glances behind them. The warriors before him slipped into the undergrowth and vanished from sight, only to re-emerge tens of yards further on.

BEHIND HIS MASK, Mathers took a deep breath and began to march imperiously behind them, ushering the way for his god. Behind him, the armoured juggernaut kept up a stately pace as they entered the jungle.

The undergrowth closed in about them, the shrubbery and saplings groaned and snapped, giving way under the rolling plates of the *Ivanhoe*. Mathers was aware of shapes in the undergrowth surrounding them. Quick, fleeting, almost insubstantial. More urmen. He pretended not to notice, keeping his steady pace.

The noise of the oncoming tank quelled the chatters and whoops of unseen beasts and the high boughs shook as creatures, startled by the unworldly noise beneath, took flight through the canopy.

The tank took no heed. An air of death, of lifelessness, surrounded it, striking trees and ploughing over stricken trunks as if gorging itself on the life that fell before it. That life should flee it or be crushed beneath it seemed only right and something the urmen expected from a god of the underworld. No wonder they melted into the undergrowth, reappearing only to offer a brief benediction and a direction, unwilling to approach for fear of their very lives being sucked from them.

All the time as he walked, Mathers could hear the tank muttering to him in its mechanical growl, whispering encouragements and dark truths, pattering out half-perceived homilies, making promises, soothing with words of power. It filled his head with such concepts that it began to pound, luring him with talk of other spaces, other realms. Ideas so profound that he couldn't hold them in his mind and they slipped from his consciousness, leaving only a vague sense of loss and shame as though he had somehow disappointed it.

So rapt was he by this communication that he scarcely noticed the slavering creature with matted fur and great long limbs, all angles and joints, as it swung screeching down towards him, teeth bared. He felt nothing. No fear, no anger, just a complete disinterest. Then his god, Skarra, the god of the underworld, spoke, its words a brief staccato chant of death. The gangly beast, its momentum stilled in mid-air by the abrupt invocation, dropped to the jungle floor, dead.

His primitive escorts froze as the machine gun burst ripped through the air, but seeing the beast die they bowed and bobbed towards the *Ivanhoe* before moving off, emboldened by the protection now offered by the crawling god.

Mathers looked down at the body, its long limbs twisted and snapped beneath it. He cricked his neck, cleared his throat, gathered himself and walked on for what seemed like hours, but he had no way of telling. Time seemed to expand and contract. The only constants he had were the jungle and the iron murmurs of Skarra.

An excited muttering rippled between their urmen escorts.

Mathers saw the reason for it. A totem. The mouldering body of an urman lashed to a carved post by liana vines, his chest split open, its soft tissues eaten long ago, leaving only a mummified husk. Echoing the hollow-eyed stare of the PH helmet on the top of his staff, its eye sockets were empty but for shadows and its jaw hung slackly as if in an eternal scream. Was it a sacrifice, a warning, a boundary marker or all three? It didn't funk the urmen. If anything, they seemed relieved to pass it. It no doubt marked the edge of their territory.

Transfixed by it, Mathers watched as darkness seemed to seep from the skull's sockets with a malicious intent, threatening to drown him in the rising shadows. Yet he could not take his eyes from it.

A voice reached out to him and he used it to pull his attention away from the deepening shadows about him.

"A sacrifice."

"I'm sorry, what?"

"A sacrifice," said his urman guide. "He was *jundurru*. Now he's a warning to other bad spirits that come to tempt or trick the Gilderra Clan. They will face the same fate. Jarak's magic is strong. You will see."

Mathers swallowed dryly, his tongue rasping against the roof of his mouth. He caught the tortured thing out of the corner of his eyes as he walked past it. If there was a chance to turn back, this was it. But now he felt no fear, no guilt. After all, he thought, why should he? Was he not under the aegis of the god of the underworld? Urged on by its whisperings in his mind, he took the first defiant step beyond the grisly totem. That broke the spell, and from thereon his fate was sealed.

The *Ivanhoe* rumbled past it, oblivious to its petty magics. The ground shuddered under its passing and the totem trembled in the wake of its iron tread.

As THE TREES thinned, Mathers saw the urmen escort waiting expectantly on their edge. Beyond, a great wall of living bark rose up before them. Great thick sheets of it spanned the spaces between rising tree trunks, forming a stockade. They were not cut and hewn by crude tools, but grafted by some esoteric form of arboriculture from the very trees themselves, shaping and training the living wood so that planes of thick rough bark, some twenty or thirty feet high, grew from one tree to the next to form a natural living barricade, supported and strengthened by pleached boughs. Roots thrust out from the base of the living bark wall like natural buttresses. In spite of himself, and anything he expected to find on this world, Mathers was impressed. This was obviously a much older enclave than they had visited before. Established, less nomadic than those of their previous encounters. The gnarled and cracked bark fortification told of decades of growth, if not a century or more. This looked promising.

The jungle had been cleared from around the stockade and overhanging boughs cut back, right up to the canopy, which spanned out high above to become a natural vault.

Their urman escort called out with a yodelling cry towards the bark-walled enclave. A single great crack echoed around the clearing, followed by a succession of dry creaks. Two large gates of bark opened, revealing the compound within. Stood in the open gateway was a small party of urmen, who moved aside out of deference and fear as Mathers entered the clearing, the tank waiting in the jungle shadows behind him.

Cerulean trees, their trunks ten or twenty feet in diameter, rose high above into the vaulted canopy overhead, many stripped of their bark to a height of some fifty or sixty feet. Mathers soon saw why. The dwellings clustered below within the stockade were themselves made of great curved sheets of bark. Crepuscular fingers of light sliced down through the canopy, illuminating the clearing with an almost ethereal glow. There, he found nearly a hundred urmen women and children, watching him in silence.

He threw out his arms and, almost as one, the urmen dropped to their knees.

"I offer you a blessing in the name of Skarra!"

Behind him, the tank came to a halt, cresting a mammoth tree root where it squatted like some monstrous toad. There was a muttered response from the gathered enclave, who looked afraid and uncertain.

Mathers strode forwards towards the small central group, where a man wore a headdress made from an Yrredetti facial plate. He was dressed in a mottled fur cloak over a chest plate assembled from the carapace of some dead creature, scraped clean and now inscribed with symbols.

Next to him stood a smaller, wiry man, patterns of ritual scarification obvious on his face even under the ceremonial daubings of white clay smeared across his skin. Mostly naked, he wore only a loin cloth and bands of chitinous exoskeleton, harvested from some arthropod's limbs, decorating his wrists, upper arms and ankles. The man regarded him with a sullen stare. This must be Jarak.

A group of tense and jumpy warriors stood behind them.

"I am Dranethwe of the Gilderra," said the headdress wearer. When he spoke it was with the same inflections but a more heavily accented English than any other urman Mathers had heard before. It *was* recognisable, however, if a little hard to follow at first. "My clan is honoured by your presence," the urmen went on. "We are grateful that the gods have heard us and that our offerings did not go unheeded."

"Skarra hears all," replied Mathers. Really, it was no more difficult communicating with them than with any other foreign subject of the British Empire. Learning a few words of their lingo always helped, but above all, keep it short and keep it simple. That way there would be no misunderstandings. Failing that, they always had the *Ivanhoe*. He turned back towards the tank. With great pomp, he anointed each track horn with the tip of his staff, while hissing out a command to Clegg.

"It's showtime."

* * *

ALFIE WATCHED AS the others grinned and struggled to put on their rain capes, helmets and splash masks in the confines of the tank, with all the eagerness of actors in the wings. Alfie wanted to speak out, to take one last chance to persuade them, but now wasn't the time. That time had long since passed, he realised. They were committed to a course of action, and he felt very uneasy about it.

Handing out the 'turtle shell' bruise helmets, Norman thrust Alfie's into the mechanic's chest and held it there. He leaned in close, his mouth close to Alfie's ear.

"Don't funk it. If you mess this up for us, I'll have you."

Alfie felt his face smart as if he'd been struck. As if he would. As if he'd put his crewmates in jeopardy. How could he even question that? He said nothing, but met his gaze with a sullen silence. Then, with Norman still watching, he put on his splash mask and helmet. Norman nodded, apparently satisfied, before popping something into his mouth and putting on his own splash mask.

Wally cut the engine and the tank's growling died in its throat as if pleased by the enclave's submission to its will. He lit the hurricane lamps and hung them before the driver's visors then opened the front visor hatches. The light from the lanterns flooded out as Skarra's piercing gaze lit the clearing. As quietly as possible, the crew bundled out of the hatches in the rear of the sponsons, hidden by the bulk of the *Ivanhoe*. At the rear of the tank Cecil and Reggie lit torches with a Lucifer. They fell into Indian file.

Glumly Alfie fell in with the others behind Mathers as they began intoning their version of a mock liturgical chant, but he couldn't muster any enthusiasm for it. Like Mathers', their rain capes were daubed with symbols, only less ornate. Wally and Frank were in front carrying rifles, bayonets fixed, in the *present* position, like crucifixes. Behind them came Cecil and Reggie, bearing the flaming torches. Alfie and Norman brought up the rear of the procession. Alfie knew it was so that Norman could keep an eye on him, and he resented the fact.

Jack stayed in the tank, ready with a loaded gun, should the urmen require the ultimate demonstration. Alfie felt nauseous. The Padre would be spitting feathers if he could see them now.

The first thing they did was to put the local shaman in his place with a display of superior 'magic.' After that, the others usually fell over themselves to worship them.

Behind him, under his rain cape, Norman was preparing his trick.

"I love this bit," said Cecil, the glee evident in his voice under his mask and cape. "Especially when Norman does his Great Stromboli bit. I wish he'd show me how it's done."

Reggie nudged him. "Ces, be quiet."

"I feel sorry for the poor old fool that's got to go up against us this time," hissed Norman from underneath his mask. "This is going to be my best performance yet."

"Well, I still feel dashed ridiculous."

"Should be right at home then, Reggie."

"Keep your bloody voices down and do it just as we've done before," warned Frank.

Within the whispers and flutters of the torch flames Mathers heard the voice of Skarra. He cocked his head and listened. He halted the procession before the urman chief and his medicine man. Dranethwe glanced sidelong at his white-faced shaman, who sized up the masked commander, smacking his lips, unimpressed.

"Behold the Warrior Priests of Boojum," said Mathers, indicating his crew. "We serve Skarra when he is in this world and we speak for him."

The white clay smeared shaman stepped forward, proud and defiant.

We're on his turf, thought Alfie, and he don't like it one little bit. And I can't say as I blame him, either.

"He looks like a slippery little bugger," hissed Frank.

"Oh, aye, he looks proper carny, he does. We ought to keep an eye on this one," said Wally.

Mathers thumped his staff end down on the ground, affronted. "You think you have the power to summon Skarra?

Your magics are not strong enough for that. Skarra came because he wished it. As for us, you may question our power. But you may not like the answer."

"Bloody hell, the sub's piling it on a bit thick isn't he, what's he up to?" muttered Cecil. Alfie kicked him, warning him to be quiet.

The shaman approached Mathers and performed a series of practised moves of some magical significance, flicking his tongue in and out. Was this some sort of ceremonial greeting, or was the wily old codger sizing up the opposition? Perhaps it was more of a challenge. I'll show you my juju, you show me yours. Mathers had seen the same thing in the Officer's mess, when the new blood, cocksure of themselves, goaded the old guard, feeling threatened and having something to prove. This man's ability had been called into question and they had appeared to challenge it. Best sort this now. Let this shower know who was in charge.

The shaman prised open a small leather bag hung from his waist, reached in and dug out a handful of white ashes. He began to dance around them, chanting, before throwing the ashes into the air above them. He sank down on his haunches and, with great intent, watched the ashes caught like swirling motes above them, drifting down over the crew in the shafts of sunlight, as if their motions divined some truth or intent.

"What on earth's the geezer doing now?"

"Not Dulgur," Jarak said finally.

"Is that the best he's got? We're well in here."

Mathers thumped his staff on the ground twice and the file of tank crew behind him opened out into a well-drilled rank, sticking the torches into the ground either side of the *Ivanhoe*'s track horns.

The tank squatted like a great iron idol for him, its track horns open and welcoming like beneficent arms, lit by the torches planted either side. Alfie did have to admit it looked damned impressive.

Norman slipped something into his mouth under the chainmail that draped down over the lower half of his face.

He stepped forwards and smoke and sparks began to billow through the chainmail curtain in front of his mouth.

The few simple conjuring tricks from his time on the boards had served him well at concert parties or for charming French peasant girls in the estaminets. Now, he made objects disappear and reappear and the urmen shuffled back uneasily with groans of fear. He tore up a large leaf, burnt it by breathing fire on it and brought it back, whole, to life again. To end the performance on a spectacular note, Jack fired the flare pistol from a pistol port and a bright white light arced into the vaulted forest space above.

"TRULY, YOUR MAGIC is great," declared Dranethwe for all the assembled clan to hear. He glanced at Jarak, who glared back. Defeated, the shaman slunk away to lick his wounds, which were deep. He had lost face in front of his chief and his clan. The rest of the enclave fell to their knees, lowering their foreheads to the ground before Skarra.

"Up, up," boomed Mathers. "Skarra accepts your genuflection and while Skarra may not feel the trials of life, his acolytes do. Bring food and water. Bring tribute for Skarra and his benevolence. Hurry. Do not anger him."

The clan scrambled to their feet. Dranethwe clapped his hands and the throng burst into activity, mothers snatched children into large bark dwellings, afraid the god of the underworld would take their children before their time.

Dranethwe clapped his hands again and villagers brought forth platters of fruit and meats and laid them before the masked crew. Sat between the track horns of the *Ivanhoe*, the crew fell on the food, tearing at sticky wet pulps, spitting pips and stones and ripping greasy meat from carcasses.

"Oi, manners!" said Reggie.

Frank belched loudly, provoking raucous laughter from the crew.

"At least have the decency to say Grace. We are British. We are not savages. Have you forgotten everything I've taught you?"

"Sorry, Mother," Frank said, with mock contrition.

One by one they put their food down and clasped their hands half-heartedly as Reggie said Grace, the sound of 'Amen' starting a race for the food again.

Reggie sighed. "Savages."

Mathers, still wearing his splash mask, sat with them but ate little, watching his men with a sense of beneficence.

"Sir?" said Clegg, offering a platter of meats to Mathers. "Aren't you eating?"

"Hmm? Shh. I'm listening to Skarra."

"Skarra, sir? You mean *Ivanhoe*?"

"Hmm. Yes, I suppose I do. Don't you hear it?"

"Hear what, sir? The engine is off."

"You don't hear it? No. No, of course you don't. I'm blessed, aren't I?" Mathers said, fingering his jacket collar through the neck hole of his rain cape.

Clegg looked at the two lieutenant pips winking in the firelight. "Yes, sir. I guess you are."

Sated, they sat back, picked their teeth, and wiped their mouths on their sleeves. Round the fire before *Ivanhoe,* the crew spoke in low voices.

"This isn't right," muttered Alfie.

"It's an offering. It's their way. If we didn't take it, they would be offended and what's more, they'd know we wasn't big juju men. Besides," Frank added with a grin, "the women will come along later. They always do."

"We used to be a tight-knit crew. What happened?" asked Alfie.

Frank glared at him. "*We* are. What happened to *you*, Alfie?"

"Got himself a long-haired chum is what happened."

"Leave Nellie out of this. She's got nothing to do with it. Can't you see? What we're doing, it's wrong."

Norman rolled his eyes. "Oh, listen to Uncle Joe, here."

Wally leaned forward. "Look, we could live like these fellows, grubbing an existence, of course we could. But that's no better than living in the trenches, is it? There's nothing for us back there. Here we've got a chance, a real chance to be something better."

Jack sat, whittling, not saying a word. Cecil kept glancing at him, watching him for cues, eager to jump whatever way Jack did, but Jack for the moment kept his own counsel.

NORMAN SPOKE THROUGH a mouthful of meat. "Look, we've extended our travel range a little by bringing extra petrol fruit fuel with us, but if we got each of these enclaves to distil the petrol fruit as, say, an offering to the great Skarra, then what have we got?"

Cecil looked at him blankly, stuck out his lower lip and shook his head.

Alfie could see which way this was going.

Norman waved the meat bone about. "We've got ourselves a supply line, Reggie, haven't we? Fuel dumps. We'd no longer be dependent on the camp. We'd have our own followers, our own army. We could push on and conquer more. We don't need the poor bloody infantry. They need us more than we need them."

Cecil nodded eagerly. "That's right."

Mathers, who had been silent until now, and content to listen, spoke up. "Why be soldiers, when we can be kings? Why be kings, when we can be gods?"

"Exactly, sir."

Frank warmed to the theme. "And with an army of urmen we could enslave the chatts. They love digging, can't get enough of it. But we can channel them, enslave them, and get them to dig for what we want them to dig for. This world is virgin territory, from what I've seen. Untapped wealth. We can get them to mine for gold, for silver, for rubies. Anything we want. We'd be rich."

They sat back and each contemplated, for a moment, their own private fantasy.

Dranethwe made a sign of reverence, approached and cleared

his throat. "Jarak, our shaman, he was once strong. He had the sight, but I fear he no longer has the strength to lead us in these matters. We made offerings and sought to invoke the gods. We are truly glad such strong magic has come to our aid. You have come to rid us of this torment."

The crew exchanged wary glances. This was a new one. No one had asked anything of them before. They looked to Mathers for guidance.

"You sought... aid?" he asked.

"For many radii we have been plagued by an evil. A spirit taunts our enclave and snatches our people, takes our strongest and boldest with impunity. Jarak has cast wards and spoken charms but he cannot stop it. His attempts at banishment prove fruitless. The spirit's magic is strong. You are the answer to our prayers." He cast a submissive glance toward the tank.

"This spirit you speak of, how many has it snatched?" asked Mathers.

The tank crew's gaze switched, as one, to Dranethwe.

"A dozen over the last three radii. Only the bravest of my warriors hunt now, but they cannot bring in enough game. The spirit takes from our hunting grounds, too. We are without the food we need."

Mathers sat silently, contemplating the information.

The tank crew held their breath.

"The Warrior Priests of Boojum have heard you, and will intercede with Skarra on your behalf."

Satisfied, Dranethwe backed away, bowing.

Mathers looked at his quizzical crew. "We have a tank. How hard can it be?"

They nodded and muttered in agreement.

Mathers sucked in air through his teeth and his brow furrowed briefly. The cramp in his stomach had returned, sharper and deeper than before. He suppressed a groan and eased himself up. "I'm just going into the tank. I don't want to be disturbed."

He walked unsteadily along the ironclad, one hand clutching

his gut; he used the other to support himself against the tank's side as he worked his way round the port sponson, wincing as he ducked under the gun. He clambered into the tank by the hatch at the rear of the sponson and pulled it shut behind him.

Making his way forwards to the driver's cockpit, he pulled off his helmet and splash mask, took the hip flask from inside his tunic and took a quick slug of the liquid.

He sighed with relief. It was as if a great pressure had been released. It stopped his head from banging and eased the cramps in his stomach. He rested his head back against the shell rack at the front of the sponson and took another slug.

Outside, a long, unearthly shriek cut through the night.

CHAPTER SEVEN

"We're Not Downhearted Yet..."

HIGH ABOVE THE encampment, Atkins and 1 Section, accompanied by Napoo, Chandar and Nellie Abbott, proceeded to make their way in Indian file up the valley side above the tree line. They'd make quicker time up here, and it was less dangerous skirting the forest below than going through it. They could easily pick up the tank's trail at the valley head. It wasn't going to be hard to find.

As the party climbed the trail across the face of the hillside towards the valley head, slowed by the fact that they were wearing marching order packs, Atkins paused to look back down across the encampment and at the arthropod army beyond. From this distance, they really did look like insects. It seemed hard to believe that he couldn't just crush them under his foot.

He felt disconcerted, leaving his comrades behind to face the foe. It felt like they had cut and run, leaving the battalion to their fate, but orders were orders. The chatts would run scared when they returned with the tank.

"I just hope we find it in time," said Pot Shot.

"I just hope we find it in one piece," replied Mercy.

"Better hope the crew is in one piece as well," muttered Gazette, "because I don't know how to drive one of them things."

"Shh!" said Prof. "That FANY back there is sweet on one of them."

If Nellie Abbott was sensitive about the issue, she didn't show it. "He'd better bloomin' well be alive," she called forward. "'Cause I'm going to kill 'im if he ain't."

Atkins had assigned Gutsy to be Chandar's guard, especially during this early part of the trip. They had been uneasy about having one of the Khungarrii along, so they tied the chatt's long three fingered hands in front of its body and placed a gas hood over its head to prevent it sending any scent signals to those out on the veldt.

"The thing makes my skin crawl, Only."

"Gutsy, this whole place makes my skin crawl."

Frankly, Atkins thought, he'd rather be facing the Khungarrii than whatever lay out beyond the confines of their valley. At least here, you knew who the enemy was. Out there, it was everything. It took a toll on a man's nerves, did that.

He wished he hadn't looked back, though. He felt the familiar lurch in his stomach as his heart skipped a beat. It wasn't wistfulness that did that. It was cold, gnawing fear. That small circle of Somme mud with its drifting splash of bright red poppies looked so small and insignificant from this height. What if that small circle should vanish now, going back home and leaving them behind? Feeling sick, he forced himself to turn away and carry on walking up the hillside.

Chandar had stopped to look back, too, and hissed beneath its hood. Atkins' lip curled. It seemed excited at the sight of its army below. "Do you not see it?" Chandar said in a muffled croak through the gas hood.

"See what?"

"There. Do you not see it?" Chandar touched the heels of its hands to its head beneath the mask and thorax as a sign of reverence.

Atkins squinted and stared at the Khungarrii army, frowned and shook his head irritably.

"No. What? Where?"

"There!" said Chandar. It pointed at the valley below them. "The Sky Web of Garsuleth." At the name of its god, it made the reverent sign again.

It took Atkins a moment more before he saw it. Not the Khungarrii. Chandar had been looking at the encampment. The circular trenches and the radiating communications trenches did indeed resemble a spider's web, after a fashion. Out beyond the wire weed entanglement, long paths extended out into the landscape, like anchor lines.

"So it looks like a web, what of it? Why's that so bloody important?" he snapped.

"It is a sign," said Chandar, fingering the scent-laden knots from its shoulder cloth.

"Of what, your certain victory?" asked Atkins with a sneer.

"Maybe. Yes," said Chandar. "But not here, not now." It said nothing more but its vestigial middle limbs clicked together rapidly. Like a dog wagging its tail, thought Atkins.

Gutsy pushed the chatt on up the path ahead of him. The aerial sight of the encampment had excited Chandar and beneath the gas hood, it went on chittering in its own tongue as it walked.

"Move it, y'bug-eyed Bosche," said Gutsy gruffly.

"Where are you taking this One?" it asked.

"On a pilgrimage, to meet Skarra, and if you don't behave you'll see him a lot sooner than we will."

THE RUSH OF injured and wounded had slowed to a trickle now, and in the aid post, the orderlies were preparing for the next flood of casualties.

Edith Bell stepped from the tent for a breath of fresh air. She put her hands to the small of her back and arched it to relieve the ache. God, what she wouldn't give for a nice cup of tea.

Beyond the trenches, in the aftermath of the attack, the bodies of several large battlepillars lay sprawled across the great wire weed entanglements, and might have provided bridgeheads for the besieging army if the wire weed wasn't already beginning to grow tight about their elephantine carcasses. Nearer, she could make out the occasional flashes of bayonets above the paradoses as men moved about otherwise unseen in the trenches before her, preparing for another assault.

The massed Khungarrii army had retreated perhaps half a mile or so to regroup, and sunlight glinted off a myriad iridescent carapaces until it seemed that the veldt sparkled in a dazzling rainbow display. It's almost pretty, she thought. But she'd seen them up close and knew them for what they were. She shuddered. The memory of her imprisonment in their nest was still fresh in her memory. She looked back up along the valley in the direction that her friend had left and felt a pang of emptiness. She had grown to depend on Nellie's common sense and companionship and she hoped she would see her again.

Edith only had a short rest break and hurried over to check on the shell-shocked in the Bird Cage, unsure as to what she would find. The sounds of the fighting had agitated them, and she feared many of them might not have coped at all well.

She found Oliver Hepton, the kinematographer, smoking a cigarette, staring at them through the barbed wire in a contemplative manner. From his demeanour, he might have been on a promenade looking out to sea.

"They've calmed down remarkably," he said, without looking at her. "Don't they usually, you know..." he mimed a neck spasm and twitch.

She regarded him coldly. "They can't help it."

He pulled out a partially crushed Woodbine packet from his top pocket and offered it to her. There were three battered but serviceable cigarettes left in the carton. With supplies running low she recognised the generosity of the gesture. Her father never approved of women smoking, especially in public, but that didn't stop her aunt from introducing her to the habit and, truth be told, she rather enjoyed the illicit thrill of drawing on the odd cigarette. However, his derision of the patients irked her.

"No, thank you. I don't."

He shrugged and put the packet away and Edith immediately regretted refusing.

"I hear when the battle began some ran screaming into their dugout, and some just curled up crying." The thought seemed to amuse him. He took another drag from his gasper.

The man's attitude irritated her. "Don't you have something to film?"

"I already have some battle footage, but I've only got two canisters of unexposed film left. I want to save it."

He turned to look at her.

"Those trousers don't do anything for you, you know. I can imagine you were quite pretty once."

Edith felt her hackles rise. She wasn't a suffragette, and the trousers weren't a political statement. She left that kind of thing to Nellie, who seemed to have more of a taste for it. However, if Mr Hepton found it distasteful, then right now it was a flag worth sailing under.

"They're practical, Mr Hepton, as your sex will doubtless admit. Which is more than can be said for you at this particular moment. You obviously have nothing better to do but amuse yourself by watching these poor souls."

"Oh, I dare say they'll have me running ammunition or messages or some such if the chatts charge again," he said, with an insouciant air. "Still, they do seem remarkably quiet."

Edith looked through the barbed wire fence. Almost all of the shell-shock victims had emerged from the hut or the dugout now. She had to admit, Hepton was right. They all seemed quite calm. Unusually calm, considering the state they were in earlier.

Private Jones was one of the shell-shocked in whose plight Edith had taken a special interest. He suffered from almost uncontrollable spasms, to such an extent that he found it hard to walk, eat or do anything for himself. Yet there he was, sat on an old ammunition box, as still as anything.

Her brow creased into a frown. She strode towards the gate where a soldier stood hastily to attention. She stopped and waited by the gate until he unslid the crude bolt.

She walked through, looking at the lethargic men in the compound around her as she made a beeline toward Jones, a practised smile easing onto her face. The young man looked up with eyes much older than his years.

"Hello, Private. How do you feel?"

"It's stopped," he said, holding out a hand, palm down. "See, steady as a rock."

"So I see. Can you stand for me?" She held out her arm.

He stood up in one smooth motion without taking it.

She turned the young man's head this way and that, gently, forewarning him of everything she was doing so he wouldn't become alarmed.

"It feels like such a relief."

"I can imagine," she said, holding his wrist and taking his pulse. It was slow and steady.

She felt his forehead with the back of her hand. It was slightly clammy. "A bit of a fever."

"I have a bad belly too, nurse," he said, cradling his gut. "It's started churning ever so bad."

"Have you been sick?"

He shook his head.

"What about your... bowel movements?"

"Fine," he mumbled.

Food poisoning of one form or another was a common enough hazard here, but she was puzzled. It didn't seem to be that.

Jones looked past her at the cigarette in Hepton's mouth. "Have you got a spare fag, even a nicky would do right now?" he said. "I haven't been able to hold one for ages."

Hepton shrugged. "Last one," he lied. He took a last suck at the fag as it shrivelled rapidly toward his lips, dropped the smouldering dimp to the ground and crushed it into the dirt with his boot.

"Well, as you're here, Mr Hepton, if you want to help, you can fetch Captain Lippett and Sister Fenton."

He clicked his feet together, gave her a mocking salute and turned on his heel with a wry smile.

Edith went around the compound checking other patients at random. All had a restful pulse rate. All complained of some gut pain. Most exhibited some swellings or other.

She spoke to Private Miller, his hands now bandaged.

"How do you feel?"

"Unafraid," he answered, with a smile. "For the first time in ages. How about you?"

The question caught Edith off guard. "I beg your pardon?"

Miller jerked his head towards the gate. Hepton was returning with the agitated MO and Sister Fenton bringing up the rear. "It looks like you're in trouble, Nurse Bell."

From the look on Lippett's face as he entered the compound, Miller was probably right. She knew she should have followed proper procedure and referred this to Sister Fenton first, before sending for Lippett, and knew Fenton would haul her over the coals for the breach of hospital protocol, but had thought this too urgent.

The MO looked from Edith to the shell-shock victims and back again with a bad-tempered glower. "Is this important? I haven't time for your malingerers and skrimshankers, Bell. I have other things that require my attention. What seems to be the matter?"

Edith bobbed a little curtsey, which looked odd in her part-worn serge trousers. "I don't know, sir. I wondered if you'd take a look? They don't seem to be themselves. As you can see, the hysterical tremors seem to have stopped. They all seem calm, although some are developing swellings and all are complaining of stomach pains."

"Is this what you brought me out here for, a bit of indigestion? Although if something they've eaten has eased their 'symptoms,' then we can send them back to the front line, can't we? Lieutenant Everson could use every available man right now, wouldn't you agree?"

Sister Fenton stepped up with a fierce glance of disapproval at Edith, warning of an imminent telling off. Nevertheless she covered for her nurse. "With respect, Doctor, if that is the case then we should wait and see. We wouldn't want them becoming hysterical in the trenches again. Bad for morale. And it would reflect badly on you as Medical Officer."

Lippett considered this for a moment. "Quite right, Sister." He turned to Edith. "Nurse, as you seem to have worked miracles here, do you think you could do the same with the bed pans? They need emptying."

Edith's face flushed. She had expected him to listen to her, at least. "Yes, doctor."

She hurried away, humiliated, taking a last glance at the calm, listless men behind her.

Something didn't feel right.

THE NEXT DAY, 1 Section arrived at the canyon.

"Perfect for an ambush," said Gazette after a brief recce. "But the tank definitely came this way." He looked down at the trail left by the vehicle. The wind had begun to obscure it, but there was no mistaking the parallel tracks.

"Right. This place is just one bloody big trench, so trench clearance duties. If there are any surprises in there, I want it to be us. And conserve your ammunition. Don't fire unless you have to. We may need it even more later."

Chandar was reluctant to proceed. They had taken the gas hood off it now, but its hands remain tied. Gutsy tried prodding it with his bayonet. It hunkered down defensively and hissed angrily.

Gutsy pointed his rifle at the chatt. "Don't you dare spit. Don't you dare, or I'll shoot you right here."

Chandar cocked its head to one side and gulped another mouthful of air. "No further. This is not Khungarr burri. It belongs to other Ones, the Zohtakarrii. Ones do not enter the burri of other Ones."

"Well, you were all for pushing everyone else off your territory into someone else's, so it's a little late to worry about them now," Atkins gave it a shove on the back. "Gutsy, watch it," he said. "Make sure it doesn't bolt."

"Oh, I'll make sure all right," said Gutsy. He took the length of rope around Chandar's long three fingered hands and yanked it until the arthropod began to move reluctantly.

Atkins turned to Nellie. "Miss?"

"Nellie, please," urged the FANY.

"Miss," insisted Atkins. "I want you to stay close to Porgy."

Atkins took the lead with Napoo as they entered the canyon. Mercy and Gazette came next, then Prof and Nobby. Gutsy and Chandar followed, and behind them Porgy escorted Nellie, while Chalky and Pot Shot brought up the rear.

Out of the sunlight, the early morning chill in the canyon was noticeable. The Tommies' banter had stopped now. The men were intent on their surroundings.

The walls rose straight up on either side of them. After several hundred yards, the canyon curved to the left and opened out. The shadow that encompassed the canyon walls was beginning to retreat before the sun's climbing advance on the right. High up on their sides, clusters of large blue-green blisters began to pulse in the sunlight. As they moved cautiously along the canyon floor, the shadows continued to shorten.

Napoo put a hand on Atkins' wrist, pointed along the canyon and sank down on his haunches. Atkins turned and indicated the rest of the section to do the same. Silently they sank towards the floor.

"Yrredetti," said Napoo.

Several arthropod bodies lay scattered about, which was odd. Yrredetti were lone hunters, blessed with a natural camouflage that helped them blend into their surroundings. It was one of the reasons the section had avoided the forest. These ones, though, with their mottled green carapaces, stuck out like a sore thumb against the rocks.

Atkins looked down at one of the Yrredetti bodies. Stitched across its thorax was a neat line of holes, the *Ivanhoe's* work.

"These are forest Yrredetti. Not stone. See their markings?" said Napoo, squatting and examining one with the point of his short sword. Atkins nodded. They were certainly out of place in this vegetation-free landscape, where the only growing things seemed to be the large patches of blue-green blisters that populated the walls and the rocks. "The Khungarrii attacks have driven not only the urmen from their hunting grounds, but the Yrredetti, too. They are solitary creatures but here they are working in packs to hunt. Such co-operation is almost unheard of. "

"You mean there could be more of them?" asked Nellie, hefting the unfamiliar weight of the revolver in her hand and glancing up at the scree slopes around them.

The rest of the section were eyeing the boulders and rocky clefts warily, too. A wind gusted between the rocks stirring little dust devils as it passed.

"There could be, and we're a lot more vulnerable here than a bloody tank. We'd better move on," said Atkins.

They proceeded cautiously along the canyon following the faint tank tracks. There was no sign of any living Yrredetti, forest or stone. Around another crook in the rock, the canyon widened again. Large boulders sat patiently on the scree slopes, perfect hiding places.

A landslide had slipped down to the canyon floor in a fan of scree and rocky debris, blocking their path. The tank tracks led right up to it. Atkins' stomach plummeted. The tank wasn't under there, was it?

Nobby scrambled clumsily up the landslide and stood triumphantly at the top.

"I can see tracks on the other side," he said with a grin.

"So they're not buried, then. That's something," said Chalky.

"Nobby, get down before you fall," said Prof.

"I'm the king of the castle!" yelled Nobby, spinning round, arms out, his voice full of boyish glee. "Whoooo-hoooo!" his voice echoed off the canyon walls.

"Nobby," barked Prof. "I'm not going to tell you again. Down. Now."

Nobby stopped and gave him a sullen stare. "I was only havin' a bit o' fun. There ain't no harm in that."

"There is if you bring a ton of shit down on our heads, you dozy git," said Porgy.

"Porgy! He didn't mean no harm by it," Nellie protested.

"He didn't have to."

Sulking, Nobby came clambering down. He trod awkwardly on a rock, then slipped and fell, his rifle clattering down the rocks.

"I told you..." Prof began to say.

Nobby tumbled face first into a large blue-green blister, which burst under his impact. He didn't even have time to scream. His fists beat the rock and his feet kicked feebly for a second but subsided and stopped before anyone could reach him.

"Nobby!" cried Prof.

Nobby didn't answer.

"Careful!" warned Mercy.

They turned him over to a collective gasp of horror. Atkins turned his face away.

"Jesus!"

"Poor sod!"

Nellie gasped and buried her head in Porgy's webbing. Atkins had seen many things on the Front and worse here, but this had them beat.

The front of Nobby's head and chest – his uniform, flesh, muscle, fat, cartilage, down to his sternum – had gone. It had been eaten off where he'd fallen into the thing. There was nothing but fizzing bone. Through his ribs, his internal organs continued to dissolve into a slop from the inside out where he'd breathed the stuff in.

"Nobby!"

Pot Shot held Prof back.

"He's gone, Prof," said Pot Shot. "He's gone."

"No!" Prof slumped in his arms. "I warned him. I told him a thousand times to be careful, the soft bugger." Prof's voice trailed off. He looked lost. He'd taken it upon himself to shepherd the hapless Nobby through the war. He'd got all the way through the Somme, and three months of this place and the clumsy sod trips over his own feet and dies.

With nothing else to do, they buried Nobby under stones from the scree slope. There wasn't even an identity disc to collect. The acid had seen to that. Useless, clumsy Nobby. Nobody deserved a death like that.

As THEY SAID a prayer over Nobby's grave, a flash of light caused them to shield their eyes.

"What the hell?" Atkins squinted up to find the source.

There, on the canyon wall, where the scree slope met the rock face, a large expanse of metal had been exposed by the rock fall and was catching the sunlight. It was a flat, featureless wall of dull silver metal, hidden behind the rock until it had been blasted away.

Atkins looked to Napoo, who just shrugged. Chandar let out a long wet hiss that set its mouth palps flapping.

"Holy Mary mother of God, will y'look at that."

"Blood and sand!"

"What is it?"

"I have no idea," said Porgy. "It has to be the result of some sort of manufactory, though. I mean, look at it. There is no way that's natural. Maybe whatever brought us here is inside. I'll bet this is exactly the sort of thing the Lieutenant wants us to keep a look out for."

Atkins pushed back the cap on his head and puffed out his cheeks. Hopes suddenly welled up, unbidden. It was true. There was no way this could be natural. It was artificial, made, constructed. And if that was the case, somebody must have built it. They may even still be in there. Could this be it? Could the reason they found themselves here be found in there? Maybe even a way home? Home to Flora. The thought overwhelmed almost all else. He had to know.

"Gutsy, you and the others take cover on the far side of this rock fall while me and Porgy go up and investigate. Gazette? Keep us covered. If anything goes wrong, you should be able to make it out of the canyon."

"If anything goes wrong? What the bloody hell are you planning to do, Only? We've got orders. We've got to find the tank."

"Shh!" snapped Atkins, flicking his eyes toward Chandar.

"Sorry," said Porgy sarcastically. "Skarra."

"Look, Porgy. This is the first thing we've found here that isn't built out of dirt or sticks; no offence, Napoo. Don't you want to know?"

Atkins and Porgy scrambled up the scree slope towards the metal wall. Rocks and stones slipped away beneath their feet and skittered down to the canyon floor as they clawed their way up the spoil. "Look for a door, a hatch, anything," Atkins said. "There must be a way in."

Prof turned towards him. "And what do we do if we find one? Nothing else has been too friendly lately."

"We'll cross that bridge when we come to it, eh?"

As they drew closer, he could see that the metal wall had been hidden behind a crust of rock three or four feet deep. The surface wasn't polished, but brushed; their reflections were misty shapeless hazes of khaki, like a fogged funfair mirror.

A cursory examination, however, revealed no seams or rivets, no joins of any kind. Porgy rapped on the metal with his knuckles. It was solid. Atkins unshouldered his rifle and slammed the butt into the metal, half expecting – half hoping – to hear a hollow ring. All he got was a dull, solid thud. He tried scratching it with his bayonet but the blade slid impotently across the surface patina without leaving a mark. He smacked it with the palms of his hands. "Hello! Hello? Is anyone there? Can anyone hear me? Open up!" Nothing.

He put his ear to the metal, expecting it to be cold, only to find it warm. He looked at Porgy and put a finger to his lips hoping to hear signs of life within. He heard nothing; no gentle electrical hums, no machinery and no great thrum of turbines, nothing, except the rocks shifting and clattering beneath his feet as he tried to maintain his balance. Not that that meant anything in itself. The wall could be so thick as to prevent him hearing anything. Anger and frustration welled up. Were there beings in there now, observing them, judging them?

He was contemplating his next move when there was a shout from the canyon floor. The dull crack of a rifle shot echoed briefly round the canyon walls. Atkins glanced along the scree. The Yrredetti were emerging from behind large fallen blocks of stone, and were scuttling across the slope towards the two men. They seemed to have found their nerve. That, or they were desperate.

"All right, Porgy, time to get out of here."

"No argument from me."

Porgy turned and started scrambling clumsily down the scree, half running, half trying to keep his balance, riding a small wave of rock fall as the spoil slipped from beneath his feet.

Several more shots rang out from below. Atkins took aim at an Yrredetti that was hunkered low along the scree line and fired. The creature's head exploded and the body tumbled several yards down the slope before coming to a halt. Atkins grimaced as several other Yrredetti turned their attention to it instead, and began tearing at it and cracking its carapace with rocks to get at the still warm meat within.

Porgy had almost reached the base of the scree and hands were reaching out to grab him.

Atkins was about to follow when he hesitated. "Ah, what the hell. It's worth a shot."

He pulled a Mills bomb from a pouch on his webbing and hastily set it against the base of the metal face, jamming it between two rocks. Maybe he could blast a hole in it. He took a deep breath, pulled the pin and leapt down the scree slope. He landed heavily, skidded, stumbled, and lost his footing. The world became a disorientating whirl and tumble as he careened head over heels down the slope.

Seconds later the concussion wave of the grenade blast caught him, propelling him further and showering him with dust and dirt. Small pieces of rubble rained down about him.

He felt hands pick him up and set him right, dust him off

and thrust his rifle back into his grip, even as he blinked tears from his eyes and coughed out dust. Words gradually resolved from the ringing in his ears.

"Well, Only, you scared them Yrredetti off, good and proper," Gutsy was saying. "Scuttled back under their rocks like spiders in a privy. You should have seen 'em."

Atkins doubled over and coughed again, a deep chesty cough that made his diaphragm ache, before hawking out a gobbet of dusty spit. "Good. What about the wall?"

Gutsy shrugged.

"What?" Atkins looked up. Another rock fall completely buried the metal face. He had hoped to blast a hole in the metal wall, but the bomb seemed to have had the opposite effect. "Bugger!" His shoulders slumped. Nellie came up to inspect his injuries, but he brushed her off. She had her webbing and pack all stuffed with field dressings and whatever medical supplies she could beg or steal. Atkins suspected she was almost as good a scrounger as Mercy.

"Porgy, mark it on the map. Lieutenant Everson can send another party along to investigate it."

"If we don't push on and find that tank, there might not be anybody else left to investigate it," Gazette reminded him.

Atkins was in low spirits. After Nobby's death they all were, especially Prof. For a brief moment, Atkins had hoped the mysterious metal wall hinted at a way back to Blighty. All these months, thoughts of Flora had driven him on. Now he felt he had lost her again. He lashed out and kicked a stone.

Gutsy stepped forward to comfort his mate, but Porgy shook his head.

As they headed for the mouth of the canyon, Atkins thought his spirits couldn't get any lower.

He was wrong.

CHAPTER EIGHT
"The Chances..."

DESPONDENT, 1 SECTION left the canyon and picked their way over a fan of debris down on to a great fractured plain with deep cracks and fissures crazing the landscape.

Mercy pushed his battle bowler back on his head. "Bloody hell, just when you think things might get easier."

"My wife says the same thing about our marriage," said Gutsy, slapping him on the back.

An escarpment behind them, through which the canyon ran, rose several hundred feet and stretched away on both sides into the distance. With no compass reading worth spit on this world, landmarks like this scarp were invaluable. Atkins scratched another '13/PF,' their battalion abbreviation, on a boulder by the canyon mouth to mark their trail before they moved off across the plain.

It was hard going for all, so Atkins cut Chandar's wrist bonds to help it to deal with the uneven terrain. It now scurried about, to Atkins' mind, like the insect it was.

Unable to follow the tank tracks directly across the wider gullies, they had to pick their own way. They scrambled and slid down the sides of great rocky protrusions like giant's steps, before they reached level ground. There, the gullies narrowed and the rocky terrain between levelled out.

It took them longer than anticipated to cross the plain and pick up the tank's tracks again. It was coming to mid-afternoon when they found the bodies of the jabberwock and the stone beetle on the fractured plain beyond the canyon. They could smell them on the wind before they even saw them. Nellie clapped a handkerchief over her mouth and blinked away tears.

When they came across the carcasses, they couldn't see them at first. A moving carpet of flat, woodlouse-like scavengers the size of Labradors were burrowing inside the rotting carcasses. As the section approached they slipped into the surrounding cracks and fissures with their prizes. The sight caused the party to avoid the cracks wherever possible.

The tank tracks headed towards the belt of vermillion and damson vegetation in the distance.

"Not more bloody forest. I hate forests," said Porgy. "You know, I didn't see a lick o' nature until I joined the Army. Gimme brick an' cobbles any day."

"See them tank tracks?" said Atkins conspiratorially.

"Yeah?"

"Where do they go?"

Porgy knew where this was headed. "Into the forest, Lance Corporal."

"So that is where we're bloody well going. I don't like it any more than you do, Porgy."

They followed the tracks into the jungle as it closed in about them completely. Atkins hated this. He hated what these places did to him. Every noise was a potential threat, every pair of eyes, every screeching call, a potential predator. The unrelenting tension was exhausting. Trying to breathe lightly so as to hear better only to have the rush of blood in your ears drown out the advantage. Starting at every crack and rustle around them. Napoo's presence helped little in negating that. A man's sudden death might be the only warning the rest of them got and none of them wanted it to be them. Still, thought Atkins in an all-too-brief flash of optimism, if they kept to the tracks they didn't have to worry about things like sting-a-lings, the spring-loaded barbed plants that had killed two of their section when they first arrived.

His body ached from the fall down the scree. It was a bed of bruises that had begun to bloom purple, blue and yellow. Small lacerations itched and stung beneath his heavy serge uniform. A bruise on his face swelled and stretched his skin uncomfortably, but he forced himself to ignore it.

"What are the chances we'll find the tank crew alive eh, Only?"

"Well, as I heard it told, Chalky, ain't no more than five things that can happen to a soldier: nowt, wounded – bad or cushy – prisoner, killed or doolally."

Napoo disappeared up ahead and every so often came jogging back into sight. Scouting. "Footprints. Urman footprints."

"After us?"

"No, too old. With tank. With *Ivanhoe*. Their footprints cross the beast's tracks."

"It's not a beast, Napoo."

Napoo shrugged. "I know what I know."

Atkins could never be sure whether the man was simple or mischievous. He suspected Napoo knew a great deal more than he let on.

"These tracks?"

"They were with it. Urmen were accompanying it."

"Stalking it or escorting it?"

"I cannot say."

Urmen had generally been friendly towards the Pennines, so that was good. There must be an enclave nearby. They could restock with supplies, maybe rest up. Sleeping out in the wild here was not easy, it was nigh on impossible. If the urmen had been following the tank, they might know its whereabouts, or at least which way it went. After all, it was hard to miss.

So was the totem they came across with the body of the urman lashed to it.

Gazette regarded it nonplussed, "Well, if this was them, they don't seem too friendly, like. Talk about your crucified Canadian. Fritz has got nothin' on these fellers. Jesus."

"You don't think this is what they do to captives, do you?" asked Mercy.

Chandar let forth a sound that could have been a sigh. It wandered up to the body and stretched out a chitinous arm, its long slender fingers reaching out to touch it.

Napoo stepped forward and grabbed it by the wrist.

"No."

Chandar flicked its gaze to Napoo, then back to the gutted corpse, enraptured. "This is wonderful," the chatt rasped, its fingers fidgeting, eager to touch it, but it restrained itself. "Wild urmen. I have never seen such a thing. What is its function? What is it for?"

Gutsy's lip curled in disgust as he watched the chatt enthuse over the poor sod.

"Can't we cut him down?" asked Nellie.

Napoo glanced around, examining the area around the totem without touching it. "No. It's a warning. A totem to ward off *jundurru* – bad magic. Its power is strong."

"To-tem," repeated Chandar, its fleshy mouth palps moving thoughtfully, as if committing the word to memory.

"At least somebody's happy," muttered Mercy.

They walked past it, each man intent on following the tank tracks at their feet, avoiding the hollow-eyed gaze of the totem sacrifice.

THEY HAD NOT got far beyond it when the section found themselves surrounded by urmen with spears and bark shields. Long blowpipes were aimed at them. The Tommies raised their bayonets to the guard position.

The agitated urmen were restrained only by a strong voice that barked out of the shadows. The Enfields came up and bolts cycled. It was a stand off.

Napoo stepped forwards, fingers splayed, patting the air, as he passed the Tommies. "Lower your firesticks."

The Tommies looked at Atkins. He nodded and the bayonets

were lowered. He hoped their urman guide could persuade his kin of their honest intentions and at least find out if they had any information before things went to hell. Atkins glowered and shook his head. An urman with a white-painted face stepped from the shadows. Napoo bowed. "I am Napoo, chief of the Horuk Clan. This urman is Onli of the Tohmii."

"Those aren't our real names," muttered Atkins.

"This man is a shaman," Napoo told him. "They believe given names have power. I spoke our taken names, which have less power."

"You give your name too freely, stranger." The shaman rolled his eyes upwards, scanning the canopy. "Here in the Thalpa groves, the spirits may take them. If they haven't already."

"The Tohmii are strong," replied Napoo. "Our names are still our own. We seek kin of theirs, keepers of a great beast. We have followed its spore here." He pointed at the twin tracks on the ground.

Several of the urmen muttered amongst themselves before one suddenly let out a tongue-trilling alarm. It had spotted Chandar.

"You walk with the Ones," the shaman said, his lip curled in loathing. "You are not true urmen. You are their chattel!" He gave a signal.

Atkins felt a sting and clapped his hands to his neck to find a feathered dart protruding from his skin above his collar. He plucked it out and looked at it in a quizzical way as it swam out of focus. "Bollocks," he muttered, through a suddenly drying mouth as his sense of balance went and he fell over. The skull-like visage of the shaman appeared in his tunnelling vision before all faded into blackness.

TIRED AND ACHING, *he found himself walking down a cobbled street of familiar terraced houses, the numbers on the front doors counting down as he walked. The sky above was grey, leaden, and laced with the promise of rain. The smell of hops*

*from the brewery hung heavily in the air and he breathed the
familiar aroma deeply. With every step he took, he felt the
exhilaration of a soldier on leave, nearing the end of his journey.
He sensed lace curtains twitching. He could feel the weight of
his pack on his back. An old woman shaking a tablecloth into
the breeze tutted as he passed and shut the door on him.*

*A man in a flat cap and shabby jacket passed him on the street.
"You're no better than you ought to be," he said with venom.*

*Still the numbers counted down as he walked, and there it
was. Number 12. Flora's parents' house. Flora Mullins. The
girl he had loved all his life. He dropped the pack from his back
and began running. As he approached, the door opened and
Flora stepped out. She was wearing a white blouse and long
skirt, a shawl across her shoulder, no, not a shawl, something
cradled on her shoulder in a shawl. A baby. He came to a stop
yards from her, his heart wanting to burst with joy and pride.
He smiled at her. She smiled back, and he took a step towards
her. Someone else stepped from the door behind her, a man in
shirtsleeves and braces, a man he knew well, better than any
other. His brother William, declared missing on the Somme.*

"William! You're alive. Thank God."

*His brother stepped towards him. The smile vanished from
William's face as he did, contorting into a black scowl of anger
and resentment, his hand clenching into a fist.*

*"Alive? More than I can say for you, you little shit, you
bastard, I'll kill you! I hope you rot in whatever hell you find
yourself in!"*

*He heard Flora scream as William swung at him. The fist
connected with his jaw and he went down, the world spinning
into blackness, the scream still ringing in his ears.*

THE SCREAM WENT on and pain flooded his consciousness. He
opened his eyes. He was lying on his side. He tried to move
and couldn't; his hands were tied behind his back. He strained
his neck to find the source of the screams. It was Nellie. She

was lashing out at their captors with her legs, the accuracy of her kicks hampered only by her calf-length khaki skirt, until they kept their distance, regarding her warily, and she had to settle for glaring at them. Atkins' eyes met those of Mercy. "Bastards ambushed us with blow-pipes," said the private.

Rough hands hauled Atkins to his feet. There were groans of protest around him as the others were pulled up, too. He counted all his men, Napoo, Nellie and Chandar. Their guns and equipment were piled up across the clearing, where some urmen were rifling through their haversacks.

He took in their surroundings. They were in an open space bordered on three sides by forest. On the fourth side, the land came to a stop and dropped away steeply. A gnarled narrow platform, grown out from the tree roots around it, extended out over the precipice.

Stood before the platform was the urman with the white-painted face. The shaman. His warriors stood solemnly around the clearing behind the bound soldiers.

"My name is Jarak," the shaman said. "I had a clan. I had an enclave. I had honour. Now all that has been stolen from me. I have nothing left but my power. Our chief was weak, desperate, and he found my magic wanting. Your kin came to our land with their spirit, Skarra, saying that their magic can banish the devil that has been taking our people. But why need it take my people when it can take you instead? If you are as strong as you say, then you will make worthy sacrifices to the spirits. Maybe then they will deliver us from the dulgur."

He nodded and two of the warriors started herding Porgy towards the platform, his feet digging into the tree spoil as he struggled.

"Porgy!" Atkins started forward, but two warriors restrained him.

Porgy cast him an empty glance as he passed. He'd seen the same look in men's eyes before they went over the top; the look of men without hope.

"Wait," said Atkins, standing as erect as his bonds and

aching body would allow him. His dream was still fresh in his mind, and the self-loathing it provoked still stirred within him. "My given name is Atkins, Thomas, 19644, C Company, 13th Battalion, Pennine Fusiliers."

The shaman regarded him with interest. "You are not afraid to reveal your given name?"

"No."

The shaman's eyes narrowed. He nodded at his warriors who shoved Porgy back with the others, knocking them over like skittles.

"Only, don't!"

"It's done," he said. "Make the most of it. Get out of here alive."

Atkins walked out onto the platform under his own steam, a little unsteadily, but his resolve seemed to impress the shaman. He was the NCO in charge. It was the right thing to do. It might not pay for all the wrong he'd done, but this was all he had. It would have to do. If this could buy his section time to free themselves, then all to the good. Right now, his brother's words were still fresh in his mind; never mind that they were a dream, they only served to remind him of his own thoughts. He deserved whatever fate had in store for him.

The shaman anointed Atkins' forehead with some greasy, rank smelling unguent. Atkins flinched involuntarily. He looked straight ahead at the horizon, framed on either side by the entwined and fused branches and roots that formed the living wood platform. Beyond it, the jungle tumbled headlong over the precipice, falling in a tangle of branches, roots and liana as the ground plunged away, where, hundreds of feet below, the jungle continued almost uninterrupted by the drop.

The shaman called out in his own tongue, his arms thrown wide in invocation. Warriors with spears urged Atkins to the edge of the platform out over the precipice. Around him, the boughs and roots of the platform groaned and squeaked. The wood beneath his feet had been worn smooth. How many other sacrifices had it taken over the years? How many had plunged to their deaths here? He looked straight ahead, the sense of vertigo making him stagger, but the root rails prevented him from falling. Far out across the jungle below he saw another escarpment rising on the far side. A discolouration of the jungle canopy below, marking out a long, wide, straight line, caught his eye. It didn't seem natural, but he had other things on his mind.

As the shaman continued his liturgy, Atkins' world shrank, the pleached boughs either side of him becoming revetments. He was back in the trenches, waiting for the whistle, listening to the artillery barrage and the sound of machine gun bullets zipping through the air over his head, like invisible insects. He smiled bitterly as he remembered his own personal good luck ritual; if he could still smell the perfume on Flora's last letter he would survive. His hands were tied behind his back. The letter was in the inside pocket of his tunic in his paybook. He guessed that was that, then. Time to go over the bags. He heard the shouts of the men and the loud boom and wail of an artillery shell. A second later, a plume of fire and dirt and shredded wood exploded up from the jungle below.

The urmen warriors wailed. The shaman turned, a look of puzzlement on his face. A look that transformed into one of fury as the crushing of trees and the clank and whine of heavy armour filled the clearing. The *Ivanhoe* rumbled out of the jungle and the machine guns spoke, sewing a line of dirt that vanished off over the precipice.

A band of urmen accompanying the tank spilled into the ceremonial clearing, seizing some of the shaman's warriors as others fled into the trees.

The men of 1 Section let out a rousing cheer at the sight of the landship. Chandar let out a hissing cry and sank down in supplication, fingering its silken tassels and hiding its face at the appearance of one of its gods.

"Keldoth spoke the truth," the chief bellowed across the clearing. "I had him follow you and your shaman's party, Jarak, and glad I am that I did."

The shaman, petulant and defiant, screamed incoherent

obscenities at the disturbance of his sacred ritual. "How dare you defile this sacred place? These strangers would have gone straight to the spirits as an offering to rid us of the dulgur."

"They are under the protection of Skarra," the chief said. "His priests have ordained it. I am chief. You no longer speak for the clan in these matters. Accept that or be banished." His voice softened. "You know the law, old friend."

The shaman shifted warily on the platform. "I know the law, but you have shamed me in front of these outsiders. I have known and nurtured the ways of our clan all my life. My sacrifices to the spirits have kept the dulgur at bay."

"Until now. It takes more and more. Your magic cannot stop it. Skarra's magic can. The spirits do not listen to you anymore. I must do what is best for the enclave. "

"And I have lost face. I have lost everything to these strangers but, as shaman, I tell you now, you will have no cause to thank them!"

He ran up the suspension boughs that supported the platform, vanished into the foliage above, and was gone.

Atkins slumped against the rail of roots and watched as the new urmen freed the section from their bonds. Porgy came running up, bayonet in hand, and cut his friend loose.

"It's all right, mate. You're safe. And so, thank God, are the tank crew."

Atkins cast a sullen glance over at the *Ivanhoe*. "Until I get my bloody hands on them..."

NELLIE RAN TO the tank, calling Alfie's name. Alfie, still wearing his symbol-daubed rain cape and his splash mask, stumbled out of the *Ivanhoe's* sponson hatch and caught his breath, a clean fresh breath that sluiced away the intoxicating fumes of the compartment.

"Alfie?"

He turned at the sound of his name.

"Nellie?"

He looked at her in astonishment, and then he took her by the wrist and pulled her behind the *Ivanhoe*, out of sight of the others, and took his helmet off. They embraced each other for a moment, completely uninhibited, before decorum got the better of them, and they stepped back and shuffled uncomfortably at the ease of their intimacy. She shoved him away, a business-like scowl appearing on her face.

"Where the bloomin' hell have you *been*?"

"Alfie! Quit your bloody spooning and get back in here. We can't leave without you!" barked Frank from inside.

Alfie smiled weakly and shrugged. "Better go."

ATKINS PICKED UP his equipment from the pile where the shaman and his men had dumped it, walked up to the tank and banged on the front with his rifle butt. "Lieutenant Mathers? Lieutenant Mathers, sir?"

"He ain't here," said a cockney voice from within.

"What do you mean, he isn't here? He's the tank commander. I have orders for him."

"Oh, he won't like that."

"What do you mean?"

"Orders. He won't like 'em. Doesn't do orders now." And the visor slammed shut.

Atkins stood looking at the tank, dumbfounded.

"Mathas is at the enclave. We will take you there now," said the chief.

1 Section walked behind the familiar backside and raised steering tail of the ironclad as it grumbled and slithered its way back along its own path.

Chandar hadn't said a word since the tank turned up. At first, it averted its eyes from its god, as if hardly daring to accept its presence, but as the journey progressed Atkins caught it sneaking glances at the tank. He wondered how much longer they could maintain the illusion.

Atkins didn't know whether to be mad at the tank crew or

thankful for the rescue. There was something going on here and he didn't like it. He was sure he'd like it even less once he knew what it was. And why were they so cagey about Mathers?

"What's their game, then?" Gutsy pondered.

"I don't know, but I can guess," said Atkins, darkly. "I just hope I'm wrong."

When Atkins had caught his first glimpse of the enclave, he still felt frustrated at being unable to breach that metal wall they found. That, at least, had offered the hope of some advanced civilisation. This, as strange and magnificent as it was, with its huge living bark walls, seemed like a step back, a complete lowering of expectations. His heart sank, the way it did when he first spotted the Khungarrii edifice, three months ago. There seemed little hope of finding a way back to Flora here.

They were escorted into the compound by the urmen warriors. Even Napoo seemed impressed by the scale and age of the place.

"I want to speak with Lieutenant Mathers," demanded Atkins. "Tell him I have an urgent message from Lieutenant Everson."

The chieftain smiled. "If he sees fit to grant you an audience."

Porgy leaned over. "An audience? Who the hell does he think he is?"

"A bloody officer," muttered Atkins.

The chieftain walked over to a semi-cylindrical bark hut on the far side of the compound. Smoke gently coiled up from a hole in the hut roof. It was more ornate that the other huts around the perimeter. Outside, it had torch posts decorated with some kind of animal skins. It had two small lean-tos, one on either side, constructed of thick branches and covered with overlapping leaves, in which mounds of fruits had been stored under one and meats under the other. Atkins watched as a young girl, wide-eyed and awe-struck, hurried up nervously with slices of a large red fruit and laid them under the lean-to with the other fruits. It was like a small shrine or chapel for offerings, then, thought Atkins. Great flat leaves were laid in bands on either side of the hut's length. There was something familiar –

"It's a bloody tank," said Atkins. "They're trying to copy

the tank. A lean-to either side, like sponsons? The lengths of leaves, like tracks? They've turned the hut into a mock tank."

"It's a form of sympathetic magic," said Prof. "They think they can capture the power of the tank within their enclave, make themselves strong again by doing what the tank does."

"Napoo, what do you make of this?"

The urman nodded in approval. "Strong magic. Not yet, but it will be."

"So you approve?"

"They do what is necessary for the survival of the clan."

The Chieftain appeared at the door of the hut and beckoned Atkins.

"'Ullo, you've been summonsed," said Gutsy.

Atkins strode over towards the hut. As he passed between the burning posts, he took off his cap and ran a hand over his hair.

"Mathas, high priest of Boojum, grants you audience," said the chieftain with a bright, welcoming smile.

Oh, does he indeed, thought Atkins. He ducked his head and stepped into the dark cloying space beyond. It was like stepping into a dugout. It took his eyes a moment or two to adjust to the gloom, the interior lit only by a small fire beneath a large shallow plate that held a liquid slowly vaporising with the heat. The fumes caught in the back of Atkins' throat and he coughed. He recognised the taste. Petrol fruit.

"Lieutenant Mathers, sir?"

In the dark, he heard the sound of laboured breathing. As his eyes grew used to the light, he could make out the figure of a man slumped back on a pile of furs and skins, as if on a throne. The chain links of the splash mask he wore caught the light from the flame and glittered. The guttering flame also highlighted one or two of the runes painted on the man's rain cape. Either side of him sat an attentive urman woman, but in the dim light, he could make out no more than that.

The apparition on the fur throne spoke. "What do you want?" The voice was slow, each word carefully enunciated, as if speech was an effort.

Atkins snapped a salute. "Lance Corporal Atkins. 1 Section, 2 Platoon, C Company –"

The man waved the introduction away. "Yes, yes, I know where you're from."

Atkins fished about in his jacket, pulled out a slip of folded paper, and stepped forward.

"Lieutenant Everson asked me to give you this if we found you, sir."

Mathers sighed and gestured to one of the waiting women, who leant forwards and took it from Atkins' hand. She handed it to Mathers. He opened it and held it by the incense burner. "Leave us!" he told them. The women nodded and silently left the hut.

Once they had gone, Mathers took off his leather 'turtle shell' helmet and removed his mask. "Can't see a damned thing in that." He held the paper towards the flame and squinted at the writing, drew his head back and tried to focus on it.

"Can't read it. You'll have to do the honours." He handed the paper back. As he did so, Atkins saw his face.

"Blood and sand!"

"Corporal?"

"Your eyes!"

Mathers' eyes were as black as coal with refracted iridescent rainbow swirls constantly drifting, moving lazily over their surfaces to some unknown imperative, like oil on water. Atkins was reminded of his own hallucinogenic episode shortly after they'd first arrived here. Mercy had built an illegal still and used some alien fruit to make alcohol.

"Can you see?"

Mathers learned forward, sharing a confidence. "More than you know. More than you'd want to know."

"It's the fuel isn't it, sir? The petrol fruit?"

Mathers sank back languorously into the furs. "Yes. The way it heightens one's senses. It's marvellous."

"Marvellous? It bloody near killed me and blinded several others."

Mathers sat forwards keenly. "That was you?"

"Yes, and I was bloody lucky."

"Then you'll know? You have some inkling of what I can see? The enormity of it."

"Oh, aye, and I'll tell you another thing. I never want to see it again. It's enough to send a man mad."

"Only if you can't comprehend it. But it's beginning to make sense to me." Mathers took a slug from a hip flask. A small sigh of relief escaped his lips.

"What, you're *drinking* it now?"

"It's the only way to numb the pain."

"Pain? What pain?"

"In my guts. They seem to churn more frequently now, and I long to feel the wind upon my face. In the tank, I can see the noise. I can see your words tumbling from your mouth, warm and soft and inviting but tinged with sharp reds and treacherous oranges. And your khaki uniform sounds shrill and discordant. It does not fit here."

"Sir," said Atkins, holding out the orders again. "Lieutenant Everson orders you and the *Ivanhoe* back to the encampment, effective immediately."

"No."

"Sir?"

"Holding on to your paltry trenches, the last few square yards of Earth. You're clinging to the rock as the tide comes in. Do you really think you'll ever get home? You're deluding yourself. Look to the future. This is it. Here. We were promised our reward not in this world but in the next world. This is the Next World. Can't you see? There is so much more here. What were you? Before the war, I mean?"

"Shop assistant, sir, but –"

"Shop assistant. We can be so much more here. Join me. You can be a lord, Corporal; a baron, if you wish. You've seen these people, these urmen. They can be ruled. They *want* to be ruled – by us. And those chatts. We can defeat them; enslave them as they have enslaved mankind here. They're good at digging, at building. They're insects. Ants. They can mine for us. Gold, diamonds, silver, rubies. We can stake our claims. We can all be rich as Croesus here, every last one of us. There is enough world for us all. Imagine. A British colony among the stars. A new British Empire where we can all be kings. Think of it, man."

Atkins listened to Mathers. All the riches of this world were as bitter ashes in his mouth if he couldn't be with Flora. That was all that mattered.

But the fumes began to pervade his senses, warping them gently, slowly. He had to get out of there. He shook his head, as much to clear it as to signify his rejection of the proposal before the drug seduced him.

"So you're disobeying a direct order, sir?" he asked as bluntly as he could.

"Order? I don't recognise Everson's authority here, Corporal. As Commander of the HMLS *Ivanhoe*, when we've gone dis from Battalion I have the authority to act as I see fit."

"But, sir, without the tank the battalion can only hold out for so long."

Mathers waved him away, no longer interested.

"Sir, you if you think about it, you don't have a choice."

"Is that a threat, Corporal?"

"No sir, but you will have to return to refuel. You're at the limit of your range now. Your current supply will just get you home, otherwise you're stranded."

Mathers took another swig from his flask and nodded to show he'd heard. "I will think on it overnight, but now I need to... rest. My head hurts."

Atkins' couldn't hide the disappointment and bitterness in his voice. "Sir." The word dripped with resentment. He turned on his heel and stepped out from the claustrophobic confines of the hut.

INTERLUDE THREE
Letter from Private Thomas Atkins
to Flora Mullins

19*th* *March 1917*

My Dearest Flora,

We've found the tank. The good news is that it's in one piece. I'm sure Lieutenant Everson will be pleased about that. The bad news is that the crew seem to have gone native and, as Porgy said, if you've seen the natives, that's not a good thing!

On the positive side, we've had our first proper food after a couple of days existing on emergency iron rations.

I know I didn't want Nellie Abbott to accompany us, but she really is a good sort. She's kept up with the marching and hasn't complained once, even when Gutsy got his feet out for a foot inspection. Talk about plates of meat! If those are a sample of his wares, I'll not be shopping at his shop when I get back. She packed out a haversack and webbing full of first aid stuff. I've no idea where she managed to get it all from, but I'd say Mercy has a rival in the scrounging stakes.

I think you'd like her, Flora. She has a good heart and a strong spirit.

I'm scared, though. For days now, the perfume on your last letter has been fading. I dread the day I can no longer smell it, for on that day you will have drifted just a little bit further from me and Lord knows you're far enough away already.

Tomorrow it seems we're going hunting, but given the size of some of the game here, I'm never sure that's too wise.

I hope you are well. I think of you and our baby often. Will it be a boy or a girl, do you think?

Ever yours
Thomas.

CHAPTER NINE
"Tuppence All the Way..."

As a new day dawned, the second Khungarrii attack advanced steadily on the trenches, but the Pennines were ready. The outer ring of fire trenches facing the enemy was fully manned. In the centre were the two full companies of Fusiliers fit enough for duty. Either side of them, 'Fred Karno's Army,' the companies of partially drilled and trained urmen platoons, stood armed with spears, swords, slings and longbows. They only had about a hundred longbows; still, it was enough to assess their potential. If they didn't get home first, the Pennines would have to get used to fighting with weapons like this once their ammunition ran out.

Salvaged Leach trench catapults, with a range of two hundred yards, and originally used for hurling grenades, were loaded with stones.

Over on the left flank, a copse of tall saplings had hastily been commissioned as rudimentary catapults. Bent back, ropes held the supple trunks under tension. They had been stripped of boughs, and large woven slings had been attached to their upper ends and the cups loaded with large hard-shelled segmented pods, shrapnel fruit or 'shrapples' as some of the men called them. They'd lost several men to the shard-like seeds as they exploded out from their pods. It had been Poilus's idea. In nature, if you could ever call this place natural, the parent tree would fling these rugby ball-sized seed pods away from itself and the things would burst on impact, flinging seeds and shell in a wide circle with explosive velocity in order to propagate the plant. It was crude and difficult to aim, but they didn't have to worry about accuracy. Unused to open warfare on such a scale, the chatts charged bunched up, with little cover.

Everson scanned the oncoming army through his field glasses. Assuming the chatts didn't change tactics, his plan should hold together. If it didn't he had a few surprises up his sleeves, but they were far from inexhaustible.

There had been days on the Somme when Everson had cursed having to stick to a battle plan devised days or weeks before; plans that only worked if conditions were perfect and the enemy did exactly what was expected of them, which they very rarely did. Nevertheless, the plan could not be deviated from and must be followed to the letter. Stilted thinking like that needlessly cost thousands of lives. Here, there was no immutable battle plan to which they had to stick. No pig-headed red tabs ready to march men into a maelstrom of machine gun fire, simply because that was what the original plan had said they must do, no matter what the changes of circumstance on the battlefield. He was free to respond as he saw fit, to adapt his tactics. God help him, there was a kind of exhilaration in that, especially as he watched the chatts marching towards them.

On the other hand, everything now rested on his shoulders and his shoulders alone.

It was a stroke of good fortune that somehow, the poppies seemed to disrupt their chemical communication and scent orders, confusing the chatt soldiers, and Everson had no hesitation in taking advantage of it. He would look into whys and wherefores later.

The plan involved something akin to a box barrage, boxing the enemy in, forcing them to attack the centre. That was their cone of fire. The heavy Vickers guns on the flanks would drive the chatts into the centre, where the poppy field spread out across the alien veldt. There, disorientated, unable to attack or regroup, the chatts would be in the Lewis guns' cone of fire, with the Vickers guns then able to enfilade the chatts from their flanks. It was risky, but less of a risk than letting them flank and surround the encampment.

On the right flank, soft hollow *whumps* signalled the beginning of the defence as plum puddings soared smokily into the air from trench mortar positions, exploding amid the chatt ranks, throwing whole bodies and limbs into the air.

THE FUSILIERS MANNED the fire steps, bayonets fixed.

Sergeant Hobson patrolled the fire bays, holding the line. "Look to your front. Hold your fire," he bellowed. "Look to your front. Hold your fire."

The men of Everson's old 2 Platoon stood nervously on fire steps. Behind them in the trench, Sergeant Hobson marshalled them, dispensing fatherly advice, bolstering a crumbling private here, sharing a joke to keep the spirits up there. "Make sure you keep your gas helmets handy, lads. You know what them buggers are like for spitting acid. Woodward, you keep 'em in your sights, son. Skelton, put that magazine cut-off back to its shut position. Did I give you permission to open it?"

"No, Sarn't. I just thought –"

"You don't have to think, lad. Thinking gets you into trouble."

Hobson knew they couldn't afford any nervous shooters. Every bullet that fell short or went wide was wasted and they couldn't afford to squander a single round. Soon they would have to take the enemy on hand-to-hand, he had no doubt about that. The fighting would be hard and bloody and, for some, it would be short.

"Wait 'til you see the whites of their – Well, wait 'til you can see their eyes, you can't bloody miss 'em, isn't that that right, Benton?"

"Yes Sarn't!"

* * *

THIS TIME, THE scentirrii general, Rhengar, held back its battlepillars. As the ranks of scentirrii came into range, sappers cut the lines holding the saplings and the trunks whipped up, flinging their rope slings into the air. Shrapnel fruit arced out across the wire weed entanglements. The seed segments exploded with a velocity that tore through carapaces, decapitating and shredding the chatts around the impact sites.

The first wave of chatts used the corpses of the already slain battlepillars as bridgeheads and springboards to leap across the wire weed. Slings, arrows and bullets picked them off and they fell into the waiting thickets, where the barbed tendrils pulled them down into a deadly embrace.

Once over the wire weed, they would again be in the poppy field.

"Watch your heads, lads. Fix staves!" ordered Sergeant Hobson.

Gas gongs were beaten. "Gas! Gas! Gas!"

Men fumbled at the gas bags on their chests and pulled on their gas hoods that would protect them not from gas, but the acid spit of the chatt scentirrii.

One man in every bay dropped from the fire step to fix sharpened, vertical twelve-foot staves into the sump of the trenches behind them. They had seen the scentirrii leap over their defences and into their trenches before. This time they would be ready.

Above, the aeroplane roared across the trenches and out over the chatts, its machine gun fire herding stray chatts in towards the centre and the field of poppies.

Driven into the blood-red flowers, their meticulous advance began to waver and break. Chatts stumbled blindly, trance-like, jostling each other chaotically. The rear ranks ploughed into the muddled vanguard until they, too, became bewildered and the entire advance disintegrated.

Everson's fist hammered a parapet sandbag triumphantly.

"Yes!" Now it was Lieutenant Baxter's job.

The machine guns began their deadly harvest.

A FEW ADVANCING chatts escaped the machine gun fire and leapt into the air, like grasshoppers, dropping down into the trenches from above, spitting atomised mists of acid into the defenders' faces. Some scentirrii were impaled on the waiting staves. Others shot arcs of electric fire that jumped and earthed around the trench, or through unlucky men. Others plummeted into the fire bays, their barbed spears lancing soldiers.

The Tommies' bayonets thrust up even as the chatts plummeted down. Now the fighting became dirty and vicious. Sergeant Hobson swung his trench club again and again, stoving in Khungarrii heads like clay jars.

The sounds of electrical fire whipped down the trenches, mingling with screams of Tommy and chatt as the mopping up began.

Everson watched Tulliver and his Sopwith harry the retreating chatts as it swooped down, strafing them, dropping grenades and flechettes. Several chatts had the presence of mind to turn their electric lances on the flying machine. Most of the blue arcs shot harmlessly into the sky, forking and fizzling into insignificance. One, though, hit its target, scorching a hole in the fuselage. Everson watched as the aeroplane veered off, his observer attempting to pat the flames out with a gloved hand. He vaguely wondered who was up there with Tulliver; he *had* been told. Maddocks? Maddocks, that was it.

Now Everson had repelled the first attack, he had to figure out his next move. He hadn't many more left.

SISTER FENTON DEALT with the influx of wounded to the Aid Post quickly and efficiently, deciding who needed immediate treatment and who could wait.

After the confrontation with Captain Lippett, Sister Fenton

had shared strong words with Edith. Afterwards she put her to work sorting field dressings and bandages. She wasn't too worried about the nurse's absence in the aid post. The girl had to be taught her place. Besides, the urmen had long ago proved their worth with their native salves that calmed burns, and pastes made from crushed leaves that protected wounds from infection. On the Somme, you could survive the wound but die from infection and gangrene from the smallest cut. Here, their native poultices made all the difference.

EDITH WAS FOLDING fresh bandages when Orderly Stanton popped his head into the tent.

"Edith. You ought to come and see your lot."

"They aren't 'my lot,' and I'm already in Sister's bad books."

"No, but summat strange is going on," he insisted.

Curiosity got the better of her and she scurried over to the Bird Cage. The shell-shocked patients stood about calmly. Edith went from one to the other. On each man, she saw the same blank trance-like face, each possessing a serenity that had managed to elude him in previous months.

"Townsend, Townsend, can you hear me?" She waved a hand in front of his face. There was no response. His eyes remained fixed ahead. She brought her hands up and clapped them together. Not even an involuntary blink. She took him by the shoulders and shook him, then wheeled around and strode over to another. "Hello?" she snapped her fingers in front of his nose. Nothing. It was as if they were all in a trance.

She went back to Townsend and this time took his hand in hers. He offered no resistance. She tightened her grip, squeezed and relaxed. Townsend's hand lay limply in her own. She lifted it to take his pulse. It was then that she noticed the swelling on his forearm; the skin stretched taut and hard over it, hard and round like a cyst or a ganglion, firm and resistant to her touch. She pushed his sleeve up and found another in the crook of his elbow. There was another on the back of his neck at the base of the skull. She unbuttoned his shirt and found a further eleven on Townsend's torso alone. All the others had them too, to a greater or lesser extent.

Captain Lippett would have to listen to her now. This could be contagious, some sort of disease. At least they were quarantined, she thought. She glanced back at them as she stepped through the compound gate.

She hadn't realised before, but they all stood facing the same direction. They were facing into the wind...

That alone sent a shiver down her spine.

ALL NIGHT, SKARRA had whispered to Mathers and he knew now what he must do. As the sun rose to penetrate the canopy above, he summoned Atkins to the hut.

"We will go with you on one condition," he said.

"There are no conditions, sir. It's an order," said Atkins.

Mathers regarded the belligerent corporal. "One condition."

Atkins considered for a moment, then, seeing he had no option, sighed. "Which is what, sir?"

"We have promised the Gilderra to rid them of this 'spirit' that is snatching their villagers. Doubtless, it is some wild animal, but we have given our word."

"What? Sir, we haven't got time for this. We need to get back to the encampment."

"Then the quicker we get this done, the sooner we can return. The help of you and your men will speed up the hunt."

Atkins turned and paced and turned again, caged by duty and military obedience. "I have your word, sir? Once this beast is killed we return to the encampment?"

"As an officer and a gentleman, Corporal."

MATHERS STAGGERED UNSTEADILY from the hut, his splash-mask and helmet in place, his gas-mask-topped staff in his hand. Atkins stood awkwardly by his side.

The chief, dressed in his ceremonial finery, the warriors and their families had assembled before the hut.

Mathers raised his staff; silence fell, and he addressed them. "Skarra has heard your pleas and will rid you of the evil spirit that has been plaguing your clan. The Warrior Priests of Boojum and their brethren, the Tohmii, will accompany him on his quest. But we shall return. As a sign of our bond, we leave you the Totem hut of Skarra."

Across the compound by the great bark gates, Atkins' section was waiting, webbing and backpacks on, eyeing the tank crew in their painted rain capes and splash masks with suspicion. The tension was palpable and Atkins was keen to get them separated as soon as possible. Nellie stepped forward and kissed Alfie on the cheek, which earned her a glare from Frank and Wally.

The chief accompanied them to the bark gates.

An old urman woman appeared and stood beside him. She looked at Atkins and Mathers with pitiless eyes. "Skarra will take the dulgur to his realm. I have seen it. But you, Mathas, shall not accompany it." She fixed Atkins with her gimlet-eyed gaze. "Your companion here will know such grief that might only be assuaged in the underworld. But he will have a hard choice to make."

Atkins frowned. He'd had enough grief so far. Being ripped halfway across the universe from Flora, the woman he loved, was grief enough for anyone's lifetime, but a grief so deep, so all consuming that he would kill himself over it? He didn't see it. It was the ramblings of a native woman. Superstition. He shrugged it off.

However, it seemed that Mathers took her words to heart and walked a little taller, a little more soberly.

"You see, Atkins? Mother Dreamer has told me I won't die. I won't die."

Atkins shook his head in exasperation.

The chief spoke. "The spirit haunts the thalpa groves evewards," he told them, pointing towards the direction in which the sun set.

Atkins stood close behind Mathers. Now that he had found the tank crew well and the tank operational, his anger at being dragged out on a wild goose chase needlessly festered and bordered on insolence. "All right, that's enough, sir," he hissed. "Let's go and get this thing done."

A breeze blew across the compound, rustling the huge leaves above. Mathers stood still and turned to face into the wind with a heartfelt sigh.

Frank turned to Reggie. "Give us a hand with the Sub. He'll be as right as rain once we get him into the tank."

The clan watched as the tank crew escorted Mathers to the waiting *Ivanhoe*. A great ululation rose up from a small group of young women as the tank's engine roared into life. The tank lurched off in the direction indicated by the chief and 1 Section fell in behind it.

"Why the hell are we going along with this devil hunt of theirs, Only? It's not our fight," asked Pot Shot.

"Well, it is now. For better or worse, the tankers have won these urmen over. If they don't deliver, it's our reputation on the line as well. If the story gets out that we don't protect our own, or keep our word, then the urmen will desert us; and we need allies here, so Lieutenant Everson tells me. But I'm still not sure if I bloody trust them."

AFTER SEVERAL HOURS of slow progress through the jungle they had seen nothing but trees, and the trees, to Atkins' mind, were the colour of old blood on army issue shirts, their barks blackened and rough like scabbing, but the men of 1 Section were getting tense and jumpy and eyed the armoured leviathan in front of them enviously.

Atkins, aware of Everson's order to press the chatt for information, dropped back to where Gutsy was walking along with Chandar and Napoo. Chandar's feeler stumps were waggling furiously as if trying to detect something despite its disability.

"Is something wrong?" Atkins asked it. "You seem nervous."

The Chatt gulped in a mouthful of air and indicated the jungle around them. "Zohtakarii burri. You should not be here. Khungarrii should not be here. Our scents will carry. Ones do not enter the burri of other Ones."

Napoo grunted in agreement. "It is true. If Chandar is found in Zohtakarrii burri, it will be killed. As will we."

"This just gets better," said Atkins with a sigh. "We're being attacked by the Khungarrii. These Zohtakarrii will kill us if they find us and we're off hunting something that's probably stalking us, with a tank crew that would sooner we just dropped dead." He shook his head. "The Pennines up to their necks again. So, this thing. Any ideas what we're up against. Napoo?"

"The Gilderra clan says dulgur, a bad spirit."

"Load of codswallop," Pot Shot said. "If it's taking people then it ain't no ghost, which, as I'm sure Gazette will tell you, means it can be killed."

Gazette clicked his tongue, winked, and patted the stock of his Enfield.

"Maybe Bantar," admitted the urman.

"A bantar?"

"A four armed, fur covered urman-like creature that dwells in the trees, but perhaps twice our size."

Chandar chattered, as if it disagreed.

"This One does not know, but this One fears what this dulgur might be." Chandar struggled to gulp a mouthful of air again but, as it tried to speak, nothing came out from its mouthparts but an empty belch. It tried again in its own tongue, a long sibilant sound combined with glottal stops and mandible clicks that meant nothing to Atkins but clearly meant a great deal to Chandar. The chatt seemed to shrink down on its legs into a submissive posture before swallowing more air. It regurgitated it and hastened to form words with its mouth palps. "This One means that perhaps this One was mistaken. Maybe Sirigar's prophecy of the Great Corruption was not so wrong after all," it said, looking round at the Tommies.

"What, that we're some great evil come to blight your land? Look mate, we don't even want to be here," challenged Atkins.

"Jeffries did. Jeffries was searching for something dark and forbidden. He sought knowledge of an ancient heresy. I think perhaps he may have found it."

"Found what?"

"Croatoan," it hissed.

ALFIE WIPED HIS brow. The engine shifted into the blues, and the noise tasted of tart rhubarb as he shifted his gear lever in response to Wally's hand signal.

He felt the wary, sullen gaze of young Cecil on him. The lad was staring at him with undisguised distrust. Cecil always had an unswerving loyalty to the *Ivanhoe* and its crew and had more than once got into a fight defending it against some imagined slur or slight. Alfie always knew the lad was trouble. Until they'd come here it looked like Jack had calmed him down after taking him under his wing, but maybe leopards couldn't change their spots.

"If you've got anything to say, say it!" said Alfie.

"I saw you talking with them Tommies. They want us to go back to the camp. They'll put us on a charge for mutiny. You're supposed to be one of us but that bint has turned your head. You don't know where your loyalties lie anymore!"

He launched himself at Alfie, who had nowhere to go, crammed as he was in the corner of the compartment by the shell racks. He fell back and cracked his head on the bulkhead. Cecil was on him, saliva frothing at the corners of his mouth as he screamed obscenities over the engine noise, hands at Alfie's throat, trying to choke him.

Several things happened at once.

Jack Tanner grabbed Cecil under the armpits and pulled him off. "But you all say it," protested Cecil. "You all say it about him behind his back. None of you trust him." Still snarling at Alfie, he lashed out with his foot. His boot caught Alfie on the cheek, sending his head into a shell base. Alfie slumped on the gangway planking, heaving in gulps of air down his raw, crushed throat.

Wally Clegg signalled for a right turn from the driver's cabin.

Alfie was still struggling to get up and reach the starboard track gear lever when a shuddering vibration, and a loud grating noise from under the tank, filled the compartment. It was a noise Alfie knew. The bottom of the tank had risen off the ground over some obstacle and the tracks could no longer gain traction. They had bellied. The tracks clacked and rattled impotently.

Mathers turned round in his seat. "What the hell is going on back there?"

There was a banging on the sponson door. "Hey, you're stuck. Looks like the British Land Navy has run aground. Is everything all right in there?"

Mathers looked at his crew. He fixed each of them with a stare, reserving the last and longest for Alfie. He spoke in a low, measured voice, quavering with suppressed anger. "Later. Not in front of them. Perkins, clean yourself up." Then, to make it clear that there was to be no further discussion, he called through the visor to the accompanying infantry in a cheery voice. "Spot of bother! We'll need a hand."

THE SPONSON DOOR swung open and the crew clambered out. The little bantam driver, Clegg, crouched down between the front track horns looking underneath the tank.

Atkins joined him. "What is it?"

The little man pointed under the tank. Atkins got down to have a look. An outcrop of rock had caught the low-rising tank floor and lifted the tracks from the ground.

"Is it serious?" Atkins asked, barely trying to hide his annoyance.

"Well, that depends," said the driver, standing up and rubbing the back of his neck. "We need some logs to put under the tracks."

"Well, we're in a jungle aren't we? That shouldn't be too hard," said Atkins curtly.

Alfie Perkins stumbled out of the tank.

Atkins noticed the other members of the tank crew cast him black looks. They didn't even try to disguise it.

"What's all that about?" Gutsy asked Jack.

"His fault," said Jack flatly.

Atkins accepted the explanation, figuring it wasn't any of his business. "1 Section to me," he said. "We need to find some logs to get this thing moving again, but I don't want anyone going off alone. I'll take Chandar. The rest of you, pair off. Gutsy and Porgy. Gazette and Pot Shot. Mercy and Prof. Napoo, Chalky, you stay here with Miss Abbott." He stepped in towards Chalky and added in a low voice, "and keep an eye on that lot. I don't trust 'em."

"Oi, excuse me, don't I get a say in all this?" said Nellie. "I'm quite capable of looking for logs. If you think I'm going to sit around here like a helpless gel then you got another think coming. You ought to know better than that by now. Shame on you, Only Atkins, shame on you."

Gutsy grinned at him. Atkins shot him a glance.

"Don't look at me," said Gutsy, with a look of guileless innocence. "My missus has a voice like that. If you want my advice, you'll let her have her own way. It'll be less painful in the long run."

"Fine!" agreed Atkins irritably. "Go with Napoo and Chalky. Meet back here in ten minutes. Watch out for the wire weed."

"And Jeffries," said Mercy with a grin.

"I should bloody well think so, too. Come on, Chalky!" Nellie growled as she stalked off. Flustered, Chalky ran to catch up, the jeers and catcalls of his mates ringing in his ears.

The question was, where to find logs? True, this was a jungle, but the trees were like no trees Atkins had seen before. Now that the ironclad's engine had stopped, he could hear low clicks and creaks permeating their surroundings. More than that, he could feel something reverberating through his chest, like the deep bass notes of the organ at church; felt, rather than heard. Was it an animal, or the trees themselves?

Atkins pushed on warily through groves of scab trees. Chandar kept pace with him, looking around with quick bird-like movements. It was impossible to read any expression on its chitinous white facial plate, but its chitterings had become more profuse. As the resonant note continued, he became aware of a rising nausea and, while he didn't feel sick enough to vomit, he was left feeling distinctly queasy. If the noise bothered the chatt, it was hard to tell.

"So, you really think this dulgur is this Croatoan, that's taking the urmen?" he asked, as they searched for logs big enough to suit the tank crews' purpose.

The chatt regarded him for some moments before replying. "It is a possibility," it said. "You urmen and Croatoan are inextricably linked in the lore of the Ones."

Atkins resented the remark. "Look, don't try and tar us with the same brush. We're not urmen. We're nothing like them. We don't even come from here. We don't belong here."

"No," agreed Chandar. "You migrate from burri to burri scavenging off the land granted by GarSuleth to the Ones."

Atkins shook his head in disagreement. "No, really. You don't understand. We're not like them. We're not urmen at all. We come from somewhere else."

Atkins pushed his bayonet into some coiled plants.

Chandar's middle limbs opened. "But where else is there?"

Atkins wheeled on him, annoyed by the chatt's questions. He leant in towards its face. "Up there!" he said, pointing at the sky through the forest canopy. "We came from up there. From the stars!"

The chatt craned its head for a moment, looking up at the firmament above it. Then looked at him. It stepped back on its chitinous legs, as a man might, staggered by the news. "That is the sky web of GarSuleth," it hissed, rising up on its legs in the threatening manner of the chatts and striking a defensive pose. "It is not possible. It is heresy."

Atkins was unprepared for the strength of Chandar's reaction. His goaded, off the cuff remark seemed to have struck a nerve at the very heart of its beliefs. He brought his bayonet into the guard position, ready to run the chatt through should it attack.

He had no further time to ponder the consequences of his remark as, from out of the scabrous boughs with their scaly leaves, half a dozen hissing arthropods leapt down around them, while others in red silken robes stepped from hiding, their mandibles open, spraying an atomised mist into the air about them.

PENNINE FUSILIERS

CHAPTER TEN
"To Hunt for Vermin..."

ATKINS GOT A shot off with his rifle as he sank down to the ground. Holding his breath, he struggled for the gas hood in the bag at his chest. When the atomised mist didn't burn, he knew it wasn't acid. It was the mild euphoric spray that chatts used for control, which didn't make it any less dangerous.

One of the chatt scentirrii stepped towards him, a hiss rippling its mouth parts, and swung its staff at him. He blocked it with the butt of his rifle and countered by lunging forwards with the bayonet, but as he did so, another chatt drove the end of its staff into his solar plexus, winding him. Involuntarily he gasped for air, realising too late what he'd done.

However, once he'd caught his breath, Atkins felt relieved. He relaxed and looked up at the creatures. There were nine of them. They looked like Khungarrii. From the knobs of bone on their facial plate and the dark iridescent chitinous armour, they were obviously scentirrii; so, a war party, then.

But then, what were those other ones doing there, tall and regal ivory white with a featureless facial plate, and the metal bands around their heads, the ones that had breathed on him? The burden of worries that he had carried with him lifted. Still cradling his bruised stomach, he sat back on his haunches and looked up at the creatures that surrounded him and Chandar. He smiled at them. He felt quite content to let them take over the situation. Whatever they wanted, that was fine by him.

They urged him to his feet with clicks and hisses and he obliged, not wishing to put his hosts out. The regal ones with the silken cloaks seemed to be having some sort of angry exchange with Chandar. He turned to scold Chandar for being rude towards the tall ones. After all, weren't they Chandar's people? He didn't exactly like them, but he was no longer afraid of them. In fact, for the first time in a long time he felt happy. As they ushered him along, he was able to look at the trees and plants around him and appreciate them for possibly the first time, without expecting something to leap out and kill him. It reminded him of his gun. He checked his shoulder. It wasn't there. Never mind. He didn't need his gun anymore anyway. They would protect him.

IN THE END, Alfie and the others found a fallen log large enough for the job and laid it into place just under the front track horns. Mathers stood watching, still wearing his splash mask. Alfie saw him slip an arm under his rain cape and clutch his stomach.

"Are you all right, sir?" he asked.

"Of course! Mind your own damned business," snapped the Lieutenant. "Just do your job and get the tank unditched. Hurry up." He turned away from the crew and thumped his free fist against the side of the hull.

Wally and Frank hauled clanking lengths of chains out from under the gangway floor boarding. They wound them round the log and, struggling with spanners and bolts, attached the chain to track plates. When the tank started forwards again, the log would be dragged under the tank by the movement of the tracks, lifting the tank's belly free of the obstruction. At least, that was the idea.

Alfie started at the sound of the gunshot. "Nellie!" He stood to run off after it.

Frank put a firm hand on his upper arm and pinned him with a hard stare. "Where d'you think you're going?"

Alfie shrugged his hand off. "She could be in trouble."

"Guess we know where his loyalties lie now, don't we?" said Norman brusquely.

"They're here because of us," yelled Alfie as he ran off. "If some great devil thing has got 'em, it'll be our fault!"

Wally just shrugged.

Sod 'em, thought Alfie, sweeping the undergrowth aside as he ran. They're not in danger. Nellie might be. Although the way Lieutenant Mathers had been acting this trip, maybe they all were. He was becoming unpredictable. The petrol fruit fumes seemed to be affecting him more than the others. And the way he walked round wearing that medicine man rain cape, splash mask and helmet, as if that was now more his uniform than the officer's garb beneath it, where did *his* true loyalties lie? Alfie wondered. And what was wrong with him? He didn't look well. He'd have a word with Nellie. Maybe she could give him the once over. If she wasn't –

Alfie almost collided with two Fusiliers. The tall one and his mate, Pot Shot and Gazette? They heard the others pounding in from all directions, snapping through the undergrowth, also drawn by the sound of the gunshot. As they arrived, it became clear who was missing.

Nellie came running up with Chalky and Napoo. She and Alfie exchanged looks of relief, but they didn't last long.

"We heard gunfire," she said. "What happened? Where's Only?"

"And where's the bloody chatt? You don't suppose it turned on him, do you?" suggested Mercy.

Gutsy spat. "Wouldn't put it past the sneaky bastard. Never did trust it."

Mercy found Atkins' rifle lying on the ground, He bellowed into the trees. "Only! Only! Where the hell are you? Only?" He spat on the ground in frustration. "You don't think it was that evil spirit, do you?" he asked Prof.

"I don't know. Three months ago and I'd have said it was superstitious nonsense, but here?" He shook his head. "I'm not so sure."

Alfie shuffled uncomfortably as some of the Fusiliers shot him black looks.

"What the hell are you doing here? Shouldn't you be with your mates?" sniped Porgy.

He shrugged. "I heard the rifle shot."

Mercy held them back and waited expectantly while their urman, Napoo, studied the ground. "No sign of struggle." He pointed to several sets of scattered impressions. "Ones." His fingers gently traced the shallow pad marks. "Scentirrii – heavy, others not so. These sets are deeper," he said, describing an arc with his arm. He looked up into the boughs and the broken branches overhead. "They ambushed them from above."

Nellie sniffed the air, her nose wrinkled. "I know that smell from when we were captured and taken to the Khungarrii edifice –" She sniffed again. "They breathed out something that drugged us."

Napoo tipped his head back and inhaled slowly, his nostrils dilating. He looked at Nellie and nodded in agreement. "Dhuyumirrii," he said.

"Do what?" asked Gutsy.

"Priests," explained Napoo as he softly followed the tracks for a short distance.

Gazette's eyes narrowed. "A Khungarrii rescue party?"

Napoo returned to the group. "No. This is Zohtakarrii burri. It is Zohtakarrii patrol. No Khungarrii here."

Gazette seemed relieved that they hadn't been followed. Alfie suspected he would have taken it as a personal slight if they had been pursued without his knowledge.

"What will happen to them?" asked Nellie.

Napoo's features darkened. "They will be interrogated and then killed. But the presence of the Dhuyumirrii puzzles me. They do not usually accompany normal patrols. There is something else going on here."

"Oh, great," said Pot Shot, throwing his hands in the air, "as if we didn't have enough on our hands." He glared at Alfie. "It's this bloody Hush Hush bunch that has led us to this."

Gazette patted the lanky private on the shoulder. "Yeah, but they'll bloody well help us out of it." He walked over to Alfie and poked him in the chest with a finger. "Won't you?"

Alfie clenched his fists, but restrained himself, as he caught Nellie out of the corner of his eye giving him a slight but emphatic shake of her head.

"Later, chum," said Gazette with a sneer. "We've got to find Only first."

ALFIE LED THE way back to the bellied tank. As they approached the *Ivanhoe*, the Fusiliers crowded together, like a pack.

The tank crew abandoned their task to face them. Norman slapped the spanner head against the palm of his hand.

Alfie rubbed his sweaty palms on the thighs of his coveralls and stepped forwards to defuse the situation. "One of the Fusiliers and the chatt. They've been taken."

"What, by the spirit?" blurted out Cecil, his eyes almost popping out of his head.

"No, another colony of chatts, by all accounts," Alfie informed them.

"And you lot are going to help find them," said Gutsy, daring them to contradict him.

Alfie turned to appease the soldier. "Of course we will. That goes without saying."

"No, it doesn't." Mathers appeared from round the back of the tank. "I'm in command here, Perkins. Not you."

At the sound of Mathers' voice, the Tommies squared off bullishly. Gutsy stepped forward, Mercy and Gazette either side of him, backing him up. The tank crew fell in behind their commander as he strode towards the belligerent infantrymen.

Mathers studied them. "We'll find your man," he said eventually. "Just as soon as we get the tank unditched. Now let us do our job."

"If you'd been doing your job in the first place this wouldn't have happened," said Mercy under his breath.

Mathers wheeled round. "I beg your pardon, Private?"

Mercy stood to attention. "I said, these things happen, sir."

Mathers continued to stare at Mercy before turning on his heel with a dismissive grunt. The two groups broke away from each other, the immediate tension dissipated. Whatever grudges they had with each other, they could wait.

Nellie reached for Alfie's hand. "You did good, I know that wasn't easy for you, siding against your pals," said Nellie.

Alfie raised his eyebrows and shook his head. "I'm not sure they are my pals. Sometimes lately, I don't even know who they are."

INSIDE THE TANK, Alfie, Cecil, Frank and Reggie turned the large starting handle that ran between the motor and the gearbox at the back of the compartment until the engine caught. The tank jolted as the ditching log rolled underneath it with the tracks, lifting it free of the outcrop. Wally stopped the tank before the log could damage the steering tail. Once they unchained the log, the party was able to proceed. Napoo led the way, following the trail left by Atkins' captors.

With the engine spewing out its mind-altering fumes into the compartment once more, the crew calmed down, the familiar smells and routines settling the men's fractious nerves. The news of yet more chatts seemed to galvanise them. Wally especially. In the absence of Huns, he hoped to face more chatts. He was regretting not being back at the encampment now.

The tank rumbled on through the jungle, Wally running up the engine as he ran over small trees, sending the rest of the crew grasping for hand holds to save themselves from falling against the hot engine.

"For Christ's sake, Wally, watch it, you've already ditched her once!" chided Norman.

But Wally, it seemed, was on a mission, and Mathers was inclined to give him his head.

Cecil and Reggie manned the machine guns, aware that

they were heading into trouble. The aft storage slots that held the tins of ammunition were nearly two thirds empty now, a conscious reminder to be careful with the remainder.

With a callous chuckle, Cecil mimed shooting the infantrymen that walked alongside. Alfie contemplated saying something, but his position within the crew was precarious enough. Fortunately, Jack clipped the lad round the back of the head and Cecil stopped.

The jungle landscape outside passed as every landscape did, whether picturesque French countryside or shell-pocked hell, in a series of bumps, jolts, lurches and shocks, sending kaleidoscopic patterns of colour through the compartment. In the gloom of the tank, the only beautiful landscapes were the ones that passed by smoothly, without hindrance.

Alfie longed for a road. He began to feel faint from the mounting heat. The engine was running hot, hot enough to fry bacon. The sweat began to trickle off his forehead, making his eyebrows itch, before trickling into his eyes, which began to sting. He pulled a knuckle across each of his eyelids to wipe them clean.

The compartment of the tank was beginning to waver, and seemed to expand and contract as though he were looking at it in a funfair mirror. Feeling a familiar cold flush, he flung open the sponson hatch beside him and vomited. One of the Fusiliers walking behind the tank stepped neatly to one side as he came to the splatter of puke. He looked up and grinned at Alfie, who was too intent on his own body to care. He took advantage of the open hatch to take in some untainted air before wiping his mouth on the sleeve of his coveralls and pulling the door shut, entombing himself in the iron hull again.

STILL UNDER THE influence of the euphoric mist with which they had sprayed him, Atkins felt quite content walking along beside his captors, as if he were on a Sunday afternoon walk, even though the pace was more akin to a forced march. His new companions were silent as they marched along beside him.

He wasn't chained or tied, but felt no desire to dive headlong into the undergrowth either side of him and escape. He was in more danger out there than he was here. He was more than happy to let the chatts lead him wherever it was they were going. He was beginning to feel hungry, however. He hoped there would be food soon.

"Where are you taking us?" he asked, politely.

He received no answer. He heard nothing but the deep bass groan and clicks of the jungle about them and the soft rhythmic rubbing click of chitinous armour as his captors walked on. But that was all right; they probably didn't speak English. The scentirrii he'd encountered barely knew enough to communicate to urmen in anything but the most brutal of ways. The two chatts leading the procession, though, were taller, less bulky and more regal, similar to the chatt Atkins once saw carried in a litter in Khungarr. Like Chandar, each wore a length of silk, worn thrown over the shoulder and tied around their abdomens, allowing their vestigial mid limbs to poke through, though hung with many more tassles. These were their priest class, he assumed. They looked similar to Chandar, but it was a poor broken specimen, a reject, a factory second compared to them. They carried themselves with a sense of entitlement. Their carapaces were smoother and a weathered ivory in colour, like something that crawled under rocks and stones in the dark and damp and hadn't seen the light in a long time. Atkins experienced a mild shudder of revulsion, but it passed as quickly as it came.

Atkins lost track of time as the chatts drove them on, down small tracks, switching this way and that, whether along their own or fortuitous animal tracks, he didn't know, but there was a sense of purpose to the journey. He watched their antennae moving. They were following a scent trail.

There was a crack and an agitated chittering from behind, as one of the scentirrii guards hit Chandar on the back in order to speed it up. The crippled Khungarrii was having difficulty keeping up with the speed of the group. It was cowed and walked in a submissive stoop, trying not to antagonise them.

The effects of the euphoric mist began wearing off and Atkins' thoughts slowly started to gain speed. "Where are they taking us?" he asked Chandar.

"Back to Zohtakarr? This One does not know. But this One fears," the chatt replied, through gulps and belches of air. It looked at the two red-clad chatts leading them, the priest chatts with their headbands of metal. "If those Ones are what this One thinks they are, then this One fears we have strayed too far. We should not be here. We should not be here at all."

"Why, where are we?"

Chandar looked at their guards and clicked its mandibles. "This One cannot say. This One must not say. It is Dhuyumirrii knowledge. Not for urmen."

Atkins knew that there was only one thing Chandar was afraid of talking about, an idea that petrified it. But it was also a lodestone that would swing and point to Jeffries. Croatoan.

"I've told you, we're not urmen."

Chandar hissed, its mouth palps caught in the brief spurt of air like tiny windsocks. "So you say. It does not help your case. This One would advise you not to repeat it. Scentirrii might not speak urmanii, but Dhuyumirrii may. Say no more."

Atkins couldn't let it go. "Why shouldn't we be here? What is it that we aren't allowed to know?"

"If this One's suspicions are correct, they are guarding something that does not exist. We should not have come here. No One is permitted. No urman is permitted."

"Why?"

Chandar didn't answer.

"Chandar?"

But the chatt had sunk back into silence and wouldn't be drawn.

The trail they were following broke into a glade. There, among the scab trees, the chatts broke their march. Two of the scentirrii circled the glade, their antennae waving in a frenzied manner, as if they were looking for something. Another trail? Atkins didn't know, but they seemed lost.

The Zohtakarrii chatts hissed and chattered in their own tongue and they sank down on their legs, not in submission, but tensed, ready, as if expecting an attack, gathering the three Dhuyumirrii behind them.

Atkins noticed again the loud bass sound that resounded through his chest cavity. It felt as if someone was thumping his chest – from the inside. It was very unsettling. Had this just started or had he not known or cared before now, thanks to the mist of the chatts?

Fine, white diaphanous shrouds hung from the surrounding scab trees like mouldering bridal veils. They moved and billowed in the slightest air movement. At first, Atkins thought them ghosts or spirits. Maybe even the evil spirit for which they had been searching. Passing close by one, they seemed to be only a collection of fine white filaments, like a fungus.

Beyond, the vegetation began to move and shake as though something large was lumbering through the undergrowth.

A scentirrii with a clay bioelectrical pack on its back and electric lance in its hands hissed and leapt, springing into the engulfing shadows beyond to challenge whatever lay there.

It was then, through the clearing fog of euphoria, that Atkins recalled the 'devil' of the urmen that the tank crew had been seeking, and wondered if the lurking menace ahead was the thing they sought.

Without warning, the scaly leaves of the scab trees were silhouetted against a brilliant blue-white electrical flash that died just as quickly as the high-pitched chatt squeal that pierced the leaden air.

Shreds of roiling, greasy black smoke slipped through the low bushes, easing across the ground. A chatt fired its electrical lance at it to no effect. They all fell back before the stygian cloud's advance.

The fog lapped around the legs of several scentirrii and from within it things coiled around their feet. On gaining a grip on its prey, they recoiled rapidly into the jungle, like taut rubber suddenly released, dragging their victims away with them at tremendous speed, cracking them carelessly against tree trunks as they retreated.

Atkins staggered back drunkenly as the sooty smog rolled towards him, pulling Chandar with him. There were still secrets this chatt was withholding and he didn't mean to lose it now. As they staggered back, they brushed past the ethereal shrouds, like cobwebs, tearing them before tripping over a tree root and falling to the ground. Chandar fell heavily on top of him.

The sooty cloud drifted towards them blindly. Somehow the gossamer shrouds and the greasy black smoke were connected, that much was clear. He knew enough from the past few seconds not to let it, or the things within it, touch him, but how to stop them?

Another scentirrii was snatched into the jungle with squeals and cracks as its carapace collided with trees and fallen trunks.

Atkins felt in his webbing. He still had some Mills bombs. The chatts hadn't known enough to take them from him. He dragged Chandar over a fallen scab tree.

A scentirrii grabbed at Chandar and caught it by the leg, even as another thing coiled round its limbs from within the oily black smog.

Holding onto Chandar with one hand, Atkins pulled the bomb's safety pin with his teeth and threw it into the middle of the smoky black cloud filling the glade.

The grenade exploded, blasting the cloud apart and shredding the thing within it, even as others thrashed and retreated into the jungle in alarm.

The concussion wave sent him crashing back into the undergrowth, even as it dispersed the ebony vapours and disintegrated the ghostly white veils that hung about them.

The deep bass rumble resonated through the jungle like a cry that made the very trees shudder.

Atkins, dazed and concussed, saw Chandar lying unconscious several yards away before he too sank into blackness.

* * *

IN HIS TANK, enveloped in the eternal mutterings of Skarra, Mathers felt safe. Outside of its iron embrace, he felt naked and mortal, like a hermit crab out of its shell.

It had become his cloak, his home, his bed, his temple. A cocoon, perhaps. He felt he was changing. But into what? Gone was the old Mathers, the Mathers that had stared at the tank in that Norfolk field and felt it haul up the fears and horrors from the bottom of his soul. That man had been asphyxiated with every breath of the petrol fruit fumes that had ultimately freed him. Even now, its vapours numbed the pains he felt in his abdomen, the pains that fogged his mind. In here, he could think more clearly.

Sat at his right hand, Clegg hunched forwards over the steering wheel as he peered out of the driver's open visor. Mathers watched him, single-mindedly engaged in his task, and allowed himself a beatific smile. His crew were loyal, unquestioning. Had they not all shared in the Sacrament of the Fumes, their perceptions of the world around them transformed by its Grace, the truth revealed to them all on that Pentecostal fuel day? But one of the Ironclad Temple had lost his way, lost his faith, and been seduced by life outside these armoured cloisters. The disharmony among his disciples was troublesome. He didn't need a Judas. Mathers wondered how best to deal with him. Of course, he must be given a chance to regain his faith, to repent his actions and reject the life outside. Being a member of this crew was a gift, albeit a gift that demanded sacrifice, and the others felt that Perkins wasn't sacrificing enough. Yes, Perkins should have a chance to recant and do penance. But if he didn't, Skarra told Mathers what he had to do.

He stared out of the visor of the driver's cabin. As the ruddy vegetation rolled past, he lost himself in the cacophony of the tank. The engine sang psalms, like a host of mechanical angels, each noise producing colour, shapes and smells that blended and combined in arcane forms that seemed to him to be on the verge of unveiling meaning and knowledge.

He was jolted out of it by a bright flash. There it was again. Bright blue, with an aftertaste of sour limes. He pulled on the *Ivanhoe's* brake levers and ordered Clegg to let the engine idle in neutral. He peered out through his visor in the direction the flash had come from.

It appeared the infantry had seen it too. They all held their rifles at the ready, straining to hear over the tank's chuntering.

"What's going on?" Mathers demanded.

"Flashes – looked like the chatts' electrical lances – and an explosion, possibly a Mills bomb."

There was a crashing and snapping as if something large and bulky were moving through the jungle with little regard for it, or little impedance from its vegetation. In another place, a world away, it might have been another tank crashing blinkered and uncaring through the undergrowth.

A deep, booming howl ripped the air, overlapped by a high-pitched squeal, the flavour of sarsparilla and carbolic. One of the infantrymen winced.

"That was a chatt, I've heard enough of 'em die to know it," said the tall Fusilier.

The older, bullish one with the large hands gave orders. "Mercy, Porgy, Napoo, scout forwards. See what's going on. Don't engage. Come back here and report."

Mathers watched them and their urman guide vanish into the undergrowth.

The sound of something flailing in the jungle continued for a short time. Several more high-pitched squeals punctuated the thrashing, before the sounds were lost in an explosion and diminished until the stutter of the *Ivanhoe's* engine drowned it out.

ATKINS HEARD HIS name called faintly and from far away, but he wasn't bothered. He was warm and safe. He wanted to stay here in the peaceful dark but then he remembered Flora. For a brief moment, he was content to bask in memories of her – her eyes, her smile – and then he remembered what he'd done. Shame flooded in, washing away the contentment, and he began to hurt. He deserved to be punished. He deserved pain. The more he listened to the voice and the nearer he drew to it, the more he hurt. The next time he heard his name called from afar he struck out for it, struggling for the surface, and with each wave of pain he thought only one thing: Flora.

Atkins opened his eyes and saw a female face staring down at him, lined with concern.

"Flora?"

"No. It's Nellie. Remember?" The FANY turned and looked at Gutsy, who was peering over her shoulder. "He's suffering from commotional shock."

"Things came out of the trees," Atkins croaked through dry lips, struggling to get up. "A black, oily smoke."

"Well you seem to have done a bang up job of taking care of them," said Gutsy.

"*One* of them," Atkins pointed out. "The rest took the chatts."

Gutsy shrugged. "Then I don't think they'll be back. I reckon we'll be safe here for a while."

Atkins looked around. A thin greasy black film, like an oil vapour, covered the part of the glade obscured by the smoke. "In that case, we'll make camp here for the night. Porgy, Chalky, Pot Shot. You're first on sentry duty."

Atkins looked around and saw Chandar, who was squatting close by, chittering to itself. Evidently, its carapace had protected it from the worst of the blast.

Across the way, he saw the tank, half hidden by the undergrowth like a stalking beast. The tank crew were huddled together, muttering among themselves, Mathers in his rain cape and mask, sitting in-between the front track horns, holding court. Every now and again, one or another of them would flash an acrimonious glance at the Tommies.

As they settled down to sleep, another deep bass rumble made the ground beneath them vibrate and an ululating howl, that made them all shiver and huddle closer to their fires, cut the twilight.

Above them, half glimpsed through the canopy of leaves, the alien stars came out and the Sky Web of GarSuleth began to sparkle in the dark.

INTERLUDE FOUR

Letter from Private Thomas Atkins
to Flora Mullins

20th March 1917

My Dearest Flora,

We went for a bit of a nature ramble today with the tank lads. It didn't go so well. The tank got stuck and I was attacked by insects.

Still and all, I had a happy time wandering through the woods, thinking how wonderful it would have been if you were here. Would a nature ramble agree with you in your condition, do you think? I don't expect your Aunt lets you out of the house much.

Of course, all good things must come to an end and I came to a bad one right enough, banging my noggin. Out cold, I was, but I dreamt of you, so that was a bonus. It was just a pity that I had to wake from it so soon.

I write this now by fire light as we are camping out in the wilds. Not that Gutsy notices, he can sleep anywhere. I hope that tomorrow we can return to the comfort of our dugout. There's a thing you thought you'd never hear me say. And here's another, what I wouldn't give for a pair of me mam's knitted socks. I can't darn to save me life and my last pair has got more holes than I've got toes.

Ever yours
Thomas.

CHAPTER ELEVEN
"That Wind Blowing..."

CHILL DAWN JUST tinted the pallid sky with vermillion smudges, like roughly smeared lipstick on a "lady typist's" damask cheek. A thick, low fog had settled in the early hours, sinking down into the trenches, drifting sinuously through the valley and blanketing the veldt.

Everson chewed his bottom lip and felt the old familiar mixture of thrill and fear, as he walked along the duckboards from bay to bay along the fire trench, giving encouragement to weary soldiers who had withstood two days of attack and stood it with courage and fortitude. Even though losses had been lighter than he'd expected, here and there he noticed gaps beginning to open in the front line. Another day of assaults and he might not have the men left to close them.

His thoughts turned to Lance Corporal Atkins and his mission. There was no way of knowing how they were faring. No matter how much he wanted to, he could not depend on them now. He was resigned to fighting with what he had and determined to hold out here as long as possible.

After all, there was nowhere else to go.

Every man was Stood To on the fire steps, looking over the parapets and down their rifles towards the enemy, in expectation of a dawn attack.

High above, on the hill-top on the valley side, a lone light twinkled its iddy umpty message from the observation post to the HQ below.

A runner darted through the communications trenches, calling out in a low voice, "Lieutenant Everson?" and was passed along from bay to bay by weary, hungry soldiers.

Everson heard his name. "Over here, Barnes. What is it?"

The private handed over a scruffy stub of folded paper. "Message, sir."

Everson unfolded the grubby sheet, read and reread the hastily scribbled note, and shook his head in disbelief. "It's not possible."

THE PAST COUPLE of days had meant little sleep for anyone, least of all the medical staff. Captain Lippett had worked long hours in the surgical tent ceaselessly cutting, sawing and sewing, and Sister Fenton, organising the orderlies and the urmen volunteers, seemed indomitable and tireless. Edith Bell *was* tired. The demands of the wounded were constant, from the small, frequent and easily answered requests for water or a smoke to the anguished pain-spurred appeals that only God could now fulfil. All she wanted to do was fall on her little bed and sleep, but not yet. She strode briskly through the fog, over to the compound, to check on her coterie of shell-shocked men.

"How have they been?" she asked the sagging sentry, who shivered in the dawn chill.

"Quiet as the grave, ma'am. Not a peep."

"Nothing? Nothing at all?" A hint of suspicion tinged her voice.

"Not so as I heard," he said, as he unbolted the gate to let her pass.

There were those amongst the men who couldn't tolerate any kind of confined space, not the hut or the dugout, who slept in the open as best they could with their tremors and nightmares for company. Letting a soft smile spread across her face, she went to the first pile of bedding to check on the patient. The crude mattress was unoccupied, its blanket thrown aside as if in haste. At this discovery, she merely raised a quizzical eyebrow.

As she went from one to another, she found the bedding heaps of straw-filled mattresses were all empty. That in itself was unusual. Now she was becoming perturbed. Where were their occupants? Her heart racing, she scanned the compound once more, as if to be sure of her eyes, before heading across to the hut with a rising sense of urgency. She pushed the door open. As the pale light from the doorway cut through the interior gloom, the silence that met her only increased her sense of alarm. The self-absorbed muttering, the yelps of alarm, the constant scuffling and thrashing that usually greeted her were absent. Blankets lay abandoned on the floor. The hut, like the compound, was empty.

Her mind racing, she turned and made for the dugout where some of the men huddled for comfort. In her haste, her feet slipped on the crudely constructed wooden steps and she slithered to the bottom, almost losing her balance. She recovered herself and fished in her trouser pockets for a box of Lucifers. Regretting the use, she struck one. The sulphur-bright flame flared and flickered, chasing away the chill gloom. The acrid smell of sulphur hung in the still air about her, clinging to her hair and stinging her nostrils. She held the dwindling match aloft. The dugout was as empty as Christ's tomb on Easter Sunday.

The guttering glow could shed no light on the mystery, but a shrivelled knot of fear formed in her stomach. She shuddered, dropping the match as she rushed up the steps, trying to quell the irrational panic that rose within her.

"They've gone!" she cried. "They've all gone!"

EVERSON HEADED ALONG the fire trench to the bay where Sergeant Hobson was stationed. By the time he found his old platoon sergeant, the rumours were already beginning to spread. Being a good platoon sergeant, he'd already heard them.

"Is it true, sir?" Hobson asked. Everson had known him since training and the man was a fount of practical knowledge and experience, and had been his right hand man on the Somme through the bloody summer of 1916, but he doubted if even Hobson had seen anything like this.

"Apparently. The message from Hill OP is that the Khungarrii have vanished overnight. Just melted away. Their whole army. At least, that's what it looks like."

The sergeant coughed and looked uneasy.

Everson knew the sound well enough. "Out with it, Sergeant."

"I don't like to say it sir, but isn't that exactly what happened to us? There one minute, gone the next?"

"I had the same thought, Sergeant. But it can't be that, can it?"

"The way our luck's been running recently, I wouldn't like the thought of them chatts running round the bloody Somme on our return ticket. If I allowed myself to think of that, I'd fair bloody weep with the injustice of it, sir. But one thing you can be sure of, if we've thought of it the men will have, too."

"Yes. Best keep them Stood To, Sergeant, until we can find out exactly what's happened. The last thing we need is a damned mutiny. Maybe there's some other reason, some Khungarrii high day or holy day, perhaps."

"Then again, maybe the buggers have got a trick up their sleeves, sir?"

"There is that. Either way, I don't like it, Sergeant. I'll send Tulliver up for a look-see when the light's better, but for now I need to know what's going on out there. I want you to take a patrol out, see what you can find. Take Poilus with you."

The Sergeant grunted an acknowledgement, glad to be doing something, and went along the first five bays, picking one man from each.

"Wilson, Draper, Cox, Monroe, Carter. With me."

The men fell in behind him and they worked their way to a spare bay. They pulled up lengths of duck boarding fixed with rope handles for just this eventuality. Leaning a ladder up against the revetment, Sergeant Hobson led the party out over the parapet, four of the privates carrying the duckboards. They made their way over the churned battleground towards the wire weed, hidden by the drifting mists.

Hobson stepped over the twisted, broken bodies of fallen chatts, blackened crusty ichor drying on their cracked carapaces.

The once-bright field of poppies lay trampled and crushed. Here and there, one or two had escaped the melee and still stood erect, their crimson petals unfolding defiantly like bloodied flags in the early morning sun.

The wire weed had begun moving sluggishly in the thin light, its tendrils drawn by the fallen bodies nearby. The party lay lengths of duckboard across the writhing thickets and crossed hurriedly, not wanting the grasping vines to catch them.

Even as they tottered unsteadily over it, they could make out the shapes of bodies, both chatt and human, drawn down and enveloped deep within the entanglement where the weed punctured them with its thorns to leech the nutrients from the corpses.

Beyond the wire weed, Hobson led the party past the partly-charred body of a battlepillar rising from the fog like a beached whale. Thrown catastrophically from their mount, the bodies of its riders lay broken and scattered around it. A blackened hole gaped in the side of its scorched armour, from which drifted the rank smell of partly cooked offal. Shrieking flocks of najib birds squabbled and tore at the flesh, dispersing resentfully as one of the soldiers threw a stone at them.

Hobson set off at a stooped run, using the low mist banks as cover, followed in short order by Poilus, Monroe, Carter, Draper, Cox and Wilson. They were some twenty yards beyond the wire now. He held out an arm and gestured for the men to drop down.

Where Hobson expected the tube grass to obscure their view, they found it trampled and flattened by the huge army that had occupied the veldt a day previously. Through the mist, he saw the shadows of hastily dug earthworks that the Khungarrii had been working on the day before, great heaps of spoil thrown up like breastworks. It looked as if they might have been settling in for a siege and digging their own system of trenches, or else a mine. But why abandon it, if indeed they had done? Hobson wouldn't put it past the buggers to be hiding underground ready to swarm out over them, just as the bloody Bosche did.

Carter squinted into the mist beside him. "Bloody hell, it looks like they really have done a bunk."

"You don't think they've really been whisked off to Earth, do you?" asked Monroe.

Draper shook his head. "Don't see how. It was Jeffries with his black magic got us here in the first place. Known fact, that is. Why would that bastard conjure 'em back and not us?"

"Spite? Fun? Who knows? Necromancing bastard like that. Just because he can, probably. What do you think, Sarn't?"

"I don't, son. I'm just paid to follow orders and so are you."

"Well, I haven't been paid for over three months –" Cox chirped up.

"Don't worry, lad. If I hear you grouse about pay again, I'll give you a thick lip on account," said Hobson. "That Jeffries is a blackguard of the first order, but I don't think he's responsible for this. Our job is to find out what is. How many bombs have you got?"

The men consolidated their Mills bombs. They had eight. It wasn't a lot, but they needed to check out what lay beyond the earthworks.

"Monroe, Wilson. Bombers. The rest of you on mop up. Hand them your bombs. Ready?"

There was an exchange of determined glances and curt nods. Cautiously they walked across the No Man's Land to where the chatts had been encamped. They sank down on their bellies and crawled towards the long line of crimson spoil, using the thinning fog as cover.

When they got to within thirty feet of it, Hobson tapped

Monroe and nodded. The party rushed to the earth wall and hunkered below its lip. It was about four feet high and ran for thirty or forty yards. Hobson nodded again and Monroe threw a grenade over the lip. The explosion came seconds later and they felt the wall shudder as dirt showered down on them. Nothing else happened.

With a well-honed howl of fear and rage, they leapt over the earthworks to confront whatever faced them.

They found several hastily delved round-mouthed tunnels sunk into the earth at an angle, the source of the spoil. Monroe flung in a grenade down one to clear it, should chatts be hiding down there. When the smoke, sand and debris cleared, they discovered it to be deserted.

Monroe, Draper and Cox checked out other tunnels. Some went five or ten yards before petering out, each of them empty, as if the work had been abandoned.

Scanning the misty veldt before them, they could see similar lines, the result of other delving and burrowings, all in various states of construction, but their purpose was unknown.

They found weapons lying on the ground, dropped and abandoned, among them swords and barbed spears as well as a number of the clay backpacks that charged the electric lances. Hobson made a mental note to salvage some later. They might prove useful.

Here and there, they found large crude balls of earth, six or so feet across, stacked in pyramids twenty odd foot high. Made from the spoil from the delving, Hobson had seen these things before.

"It's an important part of their burial ritual," Poilus explained. "Bodies of dead chatts are encased in clay balls to be rolled into the underworld by Skarra, their god of the dead. They have left them here for him. In the underworld they will undergo their final change into their spirit form and rise to join GarSuleth in his Sky Web."

Hobson's face gave away nothing, but Monroe shuddered. "So these are like mausoleums?"

"But there are still dead chatts lying about," Carter pointed out. "How come they didn't finish the job?"

"That is strange," said Poilus. "Never have we known the Ones come in such numbers. Had it not been for the Tohmii, we would have fled and never seen such a sight as this. That may have been the wisest thing to do."

They almost missed the chatt in the fog, standing as still as it was, tiny beads of condensation forming over its carapace in the chill morning air. The scentirrii was unarmed, but that didn't make it any less dangerous. Even unarmed, its ability to spray acid was reason enough to stay away from it.

Hobson was actually relieved. A very small part of him really had wondered if the chatts had been sucked back through the aether to Earth.

The chatt didn't move as they circled it. It should have smelled them, but it gave no indication that it had.

Carter challenged it. "Oi, chatt! Hände hoch!"

"It's not a bloody Hun," said Wilson, expecting the worst at any moment.

Carter shrugged. "Sorry, force of habit."

Even when they surrounded it and thrust their bayonet points towards it, the arthropod showed no recognition of the peril of its situation.

"What's it doing?"

"What do you think it's doing?"

"I don't bleedin' know. If I knew, I wouldn't ask."

"Fuck!" Cox fell back a step. Nictating eyelids flickered across the chatt's eyes. It was the only sign of movement, or indeed life, about the creature. "Did you see that?"

Poilus backed away. "Dulgur," he hissed. "An evil spirit. They are possessed. We should not be here."

Hobson was about to press Poilus further when there was a shout from Cox. "There's more over there, Sarn't."

Scattered through the thinning fog like stone angels in an unkempt smoggy cemetery, they found hundreds more of the disorientated chatts spread out over the trampled ground. All of them were standing aimlessly. Their passivity emboldened the soldiers who began to prod them with bayonet points. No amount of cajoling or shoving could induce a reaction.

"All right. A joke's a joke. I've 'ad enough now," said Private Wilson.

If it had been just the chatts, that would have been disturbing enough, but then they spotted Tommies stood in among them in a trance. All of them, human and alien alike, just standing. In union. Like statues. Not moving. For no apparent reason at all.

By their armbands, these were the men suffering from shell-shock.

"What the hell are they all doing?" Carter asked no one in particular.

"I don't know, but it's giving me the screaming abdabs," confided Cox, as they trod warily between the mesmerised individuals.

Private Draper recognised one of the men, an old mucking-in pal. They'd shared a dugout on the Somme. The bugger always had the cheek to complain about *his* snoring. "Townsend? Townie?"

Townsend offered no response. Draper put a hand on his shoulder and pulled him round, only to be met with a vacant stare. "Townie?" Not a flicker of recognition. As soon as he let go Townsend returned to face the direction he had been facing. Draper shuddered when he noticed a large swelling at the base of Townsend's skull.

"Let me try," said Cox, "you need to know how to treat these types." He slapped Townsend across the face. There was not a flicker of anything; not pain, not surprise, not anger, just a small trickle of blood from the mouth that the man also ignored.

"There was no need for that!"

"I was trying to snap him out of it!" said Cox.

"What are they *doing* out here?"

Draper was spooked. "You heard the urman. Evil spirits. Possession. It's Jeffries' doing. 'E's using the 'fluence, I tell you. He's coming for the rest of us!"

"Draper, shut your cake 'ole before I shuts it for you!" barked Hobson.

"They're all the shell-shocked blokes, Sarn't."

"Aye. Dixon. It seems Little Bo Peep has lost her sheep," said Hobson. "Nurse Bell won't be happy having her patients wandering about out here. She won't know where to find 'em. Carter, Cox. Go back to camp. Fetch some men to help round 'em up and take 'em back home."

"Waggin' their tails behind 'em!" said Monroe with a grin.

"Very droll, lad," said Hobson. "Very droll."

Private Wilson pushed his soft cap back on his head and rubbed his forehead, perplexed. "Here, Sarn't. How come they're all facing the same direction?"

"What's that, Wilson?"

Wilson pointed it out. "The same direction, Sarn't. Tommie. Chatt. They're all facing the same way. It's fair giving me the creeps seeing 'em doin' it all together like that. Like a drill parade."

Now Hobson could see it himself, he could feel the hair on the back of his neck bristle. He had to admit it was damned odd. None of them made a sound. They just stood there. Chatt and man, together.

"That, private, is a bloody good question and one I feel is for better heads than mine."

Private Monroe yelped with alarm. In the distance, something large rose out of a fog-enshrouded copse. It was one of the great armoured battlepillars. Ignoring them, it reared up to start languorously stripping the disc-like leaves from the treetops.

The party came across two more further on, their great mandibles crunching their way through the tube grass unperturbed by the carnage around them.

Hobson put a hand on their rifle barrels and pushed them down. "Enough. They could be right useful to us, beasts like that."

"It's all very well saying that, Sarn't, but how do we get 'em back?"

Hobson puffed out his chest, played with the end of his moustache, and pointed up at the great larva-like beast. "See that box on its back, just behind its head? That there's called a howdah. They have them in India when ridin' helephants. Same principle."

"And how do we get up there? Magic rope trick, I expect?"

"I've got me penny whistle if it helps," suggested Draper.

Hobson's eyes narrowed. "If I thought you two was taking the mick I'd have your names so fast me pencil would leave skid marks."

"Us, Sarn't? No, Sarn't. Perish the thought, Sarn't."

"Right, then. Wilson, go back and report to Lieutenant Everson. Tell him we'll need some more men out here, jildi."

HALF AN HOUR later, the sun was burning off the fog, revealing the strange, new landscape before them with its scattered pyramids of clay coffin balls, earthen banks and trampled tube grass.

Everson watched as a battlepillar lumbered towards the stronghold with a couple of Tommies sat in the howdah behind its head. The other two larval beasts fell into line and followed on behind.

The parties that went out afterwards rounded up the dazed shell-shocked Tommies, carefully avoiding the mesmerised chatts.

Other than them, the veldt was empty. It was true. The Khungarrii army had decamped, although exactly why still remained a mystery.

SERGEANT HOBSON STOOD at ease as Lieutenant Everson digested his report. Outside, he could hear ragged and muted cheers as the men celebrated their apparent victory.

"They've gone. Just like that," said Everson, shaking his head in disbelief.

"They seem to have left in a hurry, sir. Weapons have been left scattered around. There are pyramids of the dead, after their fashion and, as you can see, we have captured several abandoned battlepillars and a good many of their electric lance packs. They have been digging sir, but I couldn't say for what purpose, exactly. Mines, perhaps, to dig under our positions. And then there were the mesmerised scentirrii, sir. Sent shivers down my spine, they did. Especially when we found a number of our mob amongst them, dazed like. Like they'd been sleepwalking. None of 'em seemed to realise where they were or how they got there. Poilus claims they're possessed."

"And you, Sergeant? What's your opinion?"

"Couldn't say, sir."

"Hmm."

The report left Everson with more questions than answers. "It doesn't make sense," he muttered. "They had us. Why did they leave? And why abandon their soldiers like that?"

EDITH COUNTED THE shell-shocked patients back into the compound. She bridled when she saw them strung together with rope looped around their waists, and accosted the private escorting them.

"Is that absolutely necessary?"

"It were the only way we could get 'em, back, miss. It were like herding cats. They kept trying to wander off. But once we got 'em like this, they came quiet like," he said, somewhat abashed.

"Yes, well, they're not wandering loose now. Take the ropes off, please."

The private obliged and untied each one as they went quietly and compliantly into the compound.

"Thank you," said Edith with a curt nod, and turned to follow them in.

"Nurse Bell, a moment please!"

Sister Fenton came striding towards the compound from the hospital tents. Edith sighed with frustration. What was it this time? She turned and waited diffidently as the senior nurse approached.

"Yes, Sister?"

"These men were in your charge. How on earth did they get out?"

Edith felt her face flushing. "There was a gap in the wire, Sister. It's been dealt with."

Sister Fenton seemed to find that acceptable. "I know Captain Lippett's attitude to these men is a little harsh –"

"A little harsh?" retorted Edith.

Sister Fenton did little more than arch her eyebrow. Edith knew she'd just stepped over a line and lowered her eyes. "Sorry, sister."

"As I said," Sister Fenton reiterated for emphasis, her features softening. "I know Captain Lippett's attitude is a little harsh, but he does have a greater responsibility here. If you had concerns, you should have brought them to me. I appreciate that you have managed to care for these men in your own time and now that the fighting seems to be over, at least for the moment, I came to see if there was anything you needed for them."

Sister Fenton's show of concern caught Edith off guard. She was so used to seeing her as some dried-up old dragon, even though she could scarcely be more than ten years older than herself. Sister rarely, if ever, let that mask slip, but Edith realised that the woman was in an unenviable position. She was alone. At least Edith had got Nellie to befriend, to talk to and confide in, but Sister Fenton's station as a senior nurse, and a spinster at that, left her somewhat out on a social limb. They didn't often spare any thought for her or her plight at all. Lord knows it was hard enough for them on this world, amongst all these men, but for her? Was this her reaching out for female companionship?

"Oh. Well, I was just about to examine them. It seems they've been out all night and an extra pair of hands would be welcome, Sister."

Fenton smiled. It was a disconcerting sight. "Right, well, let's get on, shall we?" she said, rolling her sleeves up and stepping past Edith into the compound, her businesslike mask hardening into place once again.

The soldiers were meandering around aimlessly, some were whimpering quietly, some fidgeting, but it was a restless movement, not the involuntary spasms and jerks of shell-shock.

"I thought you told us that their hysterical symptoms had abated. Do they seem agitated to you?" said Sister Fenton as they walked slowly through the Bird Cage, running appraising gazes over their charges.

"Yes," Edith agreed, a frown creasing her forehead. "Yes, they do."

She found Townsend.

"Townsend. What happened? How did you get out there?"

He looked at her blankly at first, recognition only coming a few seconds later. "Nurse?"

"You were found wandering out there," she indicated the veldt.

"I don't remember," he said. "I remember wandering around out there, but I don't remember how I got there..." he looked at her in entreaty.

She didn't know how either. Avoiding his eyes, she began checking his hands and arms. There were lacerations, but from what? Barbed wire? Wire weed? She couldn't tell.

She opened his shirt. The swellings on his body had grown in number over the course of no more than a day. The growth at the back of his head had enlarged. She would have asked one of the urmen who helped out in the hospital tents if the swelling was anything they had come across, but they wouldn't come near the compound, claiming it was full of 'bad magic.'

She was distracted for a moment as a breeze picked up and blew stray stands of hair across her face. She pursed her lips to blow it away before impatiently sweeping and tucking the offending locks away behind her ear.

"Bell!" called Fenton with a note of urgency. "Bell, look!"

She looked up. The men were all turning in unison, as if performing some parade ground manoeuvre. They turned into the wind. Was it her imagination, or was there an almost audible sigh of relief, when they felt the wind on their faces as it blew in across the veldt, ruffling hair and billowing shirts?

Fenton strode from one to another. "They've all responded in the same manner. Must be some sort of mass hysteria." She shook her head. "I've never seen the like. It appears they're responding to some atmospheric change," she observed. "What might it be? Air pressure? Temperature? Humidity?" She looked at Bell, who was just as perplexed by their behaviour. "Maybe your concerns were valid after all, Bell. I think Captain Lippett should see this."

Edith stepped in front of Townsend, who now faced the oncoming wind, and waved her hand in front of his unseeing eyes. "Townsend?" There was no reaction.

She shook another man. "Miller? Miller, what are you doing?"

Miller said nothing. She tried tugging on his arm, but he stood immobile, transfixed by the wind. They seemed oddly at peace. "Miller!" She turned and faced Sister Fenton, a look of consternation on her face. "I don't understand, Sister. What's happening?"

"I don't know, Bell, but the wind seems to calm them."

Edith looked in the same direction as the men, following their gaze, out across the trenches and the wire weed, out across the veldt with its flattened tube grass, where the last shreds of mist were dispersing; where, among walls of dirt and pyramids of earthen balls, the abandoned Khungarrii also turned to face the oncoming wind.

She looked up into the blue sky, where carrion creatures shrieked and wheeled, awaiting the first warm updrafts of the day, before dropping her gaze to the horizon, towards the great grey line of clouds that hunkered there. They were moving fast, rolling across the sky towards them. Another few hours and it would be upon them.

She shivered. "The weather is turning. Looks like there's a storm on the way."

CHAPTER TWELVE
"Hallo, Hallo! Here We Are Again..."

ATKINS CURLED UP against the bole of a tree, his pack by his side and his rifle clasped to his chest. He was weary to the bone, aching and stiff, but too tired to sleep.

He was acutely aware of Mathers. It was hard not to be. He sat cross-legged atop the tank on the driver's cabin, surrounded by lighted candle stubs, still wearing his rain cape, splash mask and turtle helmet, which he never seemed to take off at all these days. He muttered to himself while the rest of his men slept fitfully below.

It was disconcerting, because he couldn't make any sense of what Mathers was saying. Sat there in the candle glow, with the small night creatures buzzing and whining around him and crawling all over him, he just looked damn unnerving.

MATHERS IGNORED THE pain. The unsettled feeling in his stomach was getting worse. The fumes from the engine seemed to be a balm for it, but the engine was off. He had already taken several slugs of distilled petrol fruit from his flask and that seemed to calm it. The problem was he was having to drink more and more of the stuff. Just inhaling the fumes was no longer enough. Now, as he sat here, small creatures of the night attracted to the flame swarmed around him. He let them crawl on him. Any one of them might have a bite that would kill him, but this was a test of faith. He could hear the voice of his god, Skarra, in their incessant buzzing. His god would protect him. All he had to do was give himself over to Skarra completely, without fear. He felt none. Even though he felt a myriad of scuttling legs, fluttering wings, stings and bites, he didn't even flinch.

AMONG THE MEN, the fragile truce between the two groups of Tommies was barely holding, each group giving the other distrustful looks, as if just waiting for an excuse.

Atkins hated being stuck on a wild goose chase with an officer whose orders he couldn't countermand. They should have been heading back to the encampment. God alone knew if it was still even there. He sat there, imagining a bloody slaughter as the chatts overran the trenches, and all because he hadn't returned with the tank in time.

He glanced over at the tank crew, bivouacked beneath a tarpaulin strung out from the starboard sponson. Alfie Perkins was in the middle of them. He was lying down, his head propped on his hand, looking across the clearing to where Nellie Abbott slept, near Napoo. After a while, one of his crewmates poked him roughly and reluctantly he lowered his head.

Chandar lay curled up on its side, almost in a ball, like a woodlouse, a length of rope tying its ankle to a tree root, a formality to mollify the others. There had been several opportunities when Chandar could have escaped but had chosen not to do so. As harmless as the old Khungarrii duffer seemed to be, it was definitely hiding something, part of which involved him, and Atkins very much wanted to know what it was.

Porgy, Chalky and Pot Shot sat on watch by the fire, and Gazette, Gutsy and Prof lay sprawled out. Gutsy was snoring loudly enough to wake the dead.

Atkins watched as Porgy got out his deck of cards. It was no ordinary deck. Each card was a small photograph of a girl he claimed he had stepped out with, which was odd because there were at least two of the music hall sensation, Marie Lloyd, in there. When quizzed, Porgy just winked and called them 'his jokers.' He started showing them to Prof, trying to engage the depressed man's interest, reeling off the stories of spooning attached to each one. Atkins grinned as Porgy slapped Prof's hand away as he tried to have a closer look at a particular card. Porgy's ambition was to collect enough to create a full deck of cards from them. Poor Porgy. He wondered how his mate would ever complete the set now.

Gazette turned over. "What's up, Only, can't sleep?"

"No, Gutsy's farted."

"Yeah, at least it'll keep the beasts at bay."

They watched the large Tommy roll over in his sleep smacking his lips contentedly, like a dog in front of a fire.

Goaded gently by the others, across the campfire, Chalky was in full flow. "The way I heard it, right," he was saying in a low voice. Pot Shot leaned forwards conspiratorially and smiled encouragingly as he continued, "Only, Everson and Ketch had cornered Jeffries, right, and he was only in the chatts' own temple planning to use it for his own black art. He had Nurse Bell tied to an altar and he was poised with a big knife, about to sacrifice her to the devil and it should have been a shoe-in 'cause Jeffries had no other weapons. So Lieutenant Everson tells Jeffries that the game's up and that he was to give himself up and come with them, his silver dagger poised above Nurse Bell's heart. But he laughs at them as he raises his hand, right? Like he was going to plunge the knife down, so the Lieutenant fires, right, and he shoots it right out of Jeffries' hand. And he curses, but not in English like you or I –"

"Or an NCO," said Porgy, winking at Gazette.

But Chalky was lost in his story now, conjuring his own retelling before the fire. "Aye, or a bloody NCO," he acknowledged before plunging on. "He curses in a foul and ancient language what no one honest and God-fearing would understand, the language of devils, and he raises his arms like he was surrendering, like, but then there were this evil red glare in his eyes and he began chanting, and suddenly bolts of green lightning blasted out of his finger tips. The first blast got Corporal Ketch and he were, like, burnt to a crisp in an instant."

Porgy nudged Prof. "Sends shivers down your spine don't it? It's like he was there."

"Oh aye, and what happened next?"

"Well, then Only – that is, Corporal Atkins – takes a shot at Jeffries, but the mad magician just waves his hand and flings the bullets back at them through the air and one gives the Lieutenant a Blighty one, right in the shoulder. An' then Jeffries starts saying as how if he can't send Nurse Bell to hell then he'll summon up summat to fetch her there. Then he starts to conjure a demon to kill them while he makes his escape and there's a horrid green glow and a smell of sulphur as something from the inner circles of Hell begins to take shape..."

"Inner circles of Hell, I like that," said Porgy, nodding with approval.

"...and Nurse Bell screams. And Only realises he has moments to act before the demon becomes as solid as you or I. So Corporal Atkins, not having no holy water or the Padre's bible, decides he has to save the lieutenant the only way he can. That's when he notices the magic circle Jeffries is stood in is made from salt, and he scuffs away the circle breaking the spell, like, before it's complete. Enraged, the demon brings down the chamber before vanishing back into the Pit he came from. Then, with the chatts' temple collapsing about him, the Corporal rescues Nurse Bell and the Lieutenant and pushes them down a shaft to safety. Then, he turns to Jeffries who is not best pleased at his evil plans being thwarted and all. The Corporal charges him with his bayonet but then Jeffries vanishes in a cloud of black smoke and a demonic laugh and Only – Corporal Atkins – vows: *By blood and sand, we'll find you and when we do we'll make, you send us home you diabolical fiend!*"

"It's true," said Porgy, wide-eyed and impressed. "He said them very words."

"Blood and sand," muttered Atkins. He hadn't caught all of it, but he'd overheard enough. "Stop encouraging him, Porgy, that's not how it happened and you know it," he growled, turning his back to them and pulling his army blanket about him. Bloody hell, every time he overhead that story it got bigger with the retelling. He was pretty sure that soon his bloody bayonet would be Excalibur itself in disguise. If Chalky knew what kind of man his corporal really was he'd be severely disappointed.

SOFTLY, ALMOST IMPERCEPTIBLY, the nocturnal noises of the jungle segued into a dawn chorus as shrieks and cries and deep bass clicks gave way to bleary hoots, whistles, trilling and whoops, alerting the men to the slow, incremental creep of daylight.

Atkins woke, stiff and aching, to see Napoo squatting on his haunches over the fire. It appeared that the urman had already been up and caught breakfast, as he was cooking several small animals on skewers over the fire.

"Right, just off for me morning ablutions," announced Gutsy, stepping into the undergrowth with his rifle.

"Keep an eye out for Jeffries!" came the usual riposte.

Atkins looked over at Mathers, still sat on top of the tank. He must have slept sitting up all night, his head lolling. Mathers' head snapped up and turned to look at him through the eye slits.

Disconcerted, Atkins started like a guilty schoolboy and averted his gaze.

Chandar was silent. It hadn't said much since their kidnapping. It was watching the tank crew pour the last of their petrol fruit fuel from the drums into the *Ivanhoe's* petrol tanks in the two front track horns. Atkins wondered if Chandar was beginning to suss them out.

"It's... an offering," he suggested.

Chandar looked at him briefly then returned its gaze to the tank. It chittered to itself, and fingered the tassels on its shoulder robe, like the Padre telled his rosaries. It seemed to Atkins that the old chatt's beliefs were being tested, though he couldn't tell how. It seemed uneasy, and that made him nervous. If it were human, Atkins would have thought it windy. Even before their attempted abduction by the Zohtakarrii, something had agitated the chatt, something it was reluctant to share. Combine that with Mathers' attitude, and Atkins felt this entire stunt was going to Hell in a handcart.

ATKINS PERFORMED HIS usual morning ritual. Every man on the Front Line had his little good luck ritual. Gutsy had his rabbit foot; Porgy had his deck of cards. Atkins had his letter. If he could still smell Flora's perfume on her last letter, then he would be safe. However, for some days now, a week perhaps, the scent had been fading almost beyond his ability to sense it. Today he couldn't smell it at all. He felt a rising panic before remembering that, back in the urmen's 'tank' hut, Mathers had been drinking the petrol fruit, and claimed it heightened his senses; maybe he could sense any faint, lingering scent. As much as he loathed humbling himself before the tank commander, the appeal might go some way to appeasing him and smooth over the rift between them. It was worth a try. Besides, he *had* to know.

He ambled over to where the officer was inspecting his tank. The words almost stuck in his craw. "Sir, I – may I ask you a favour?"

The tank commander cocked his head to one side, intrigued, and invited Atkins to continue.

"I've got a letter from my sweetheart. I – I can't smell her perfume anymore. I was wondering if you could tell me if there's any trace of it left."

"Hrm." The masked subaltern seemed to consider the request. From the tone in his voice, the idea seemed to amuse him. "Let me see it."

Reluctantly, Atkins took out the worn envelope from his tunic pocket and eased the sharply creased writing paper from it. Mathers snatched the folded note with more haste and less care than Atkins would have liked, and held it up to his chainmail and leather mask. He noticed the welts and insects bites on Mathers' hands as he held the letter. Atkins heard a quick audible sniff from beneath the chainmail. Mathers' head lolled back in a languorous manner, as he inhaled again, this time more slowly, deeper, relishing what he found there.

"Hey!" Atkins snatched the letter from his hands, scowling at the officer as if he'd just insulted the lady.

"Merely making sure, Corporal," said Mathers, his head moving as though sucking up the last faint dregs of scent, his chainmail rattling faintly.

Atkins reverently slipped the letter back into its envelope and returned it to his pocket. "Is there anything left, sir?"

Mathers appeared to be lost in a reverie.

"Sir?"

Mathers looked at him. "Yes. I can still smell it." He turned on his heel and went back to inspecting the tank.

Atkins sighed with relief. He hadn't even been aware of holding his breath. He closed his eyes, tipped back his head to the heavens and offered a muttered, but heartfelt, thank-you. He would see the day out and that, at least, gave him some little comfort.

He returned to 1 Section, who were packing their gear and getting ready to move off, and approached Nellie Abbott.

"I'm worried about Lieutenant Mathers," said Atkins. "Can you give him the once over? The last thing we need is a windy ruddy officer." Nellie looked uncomfortable with the idea. Atkins pressed the point. "Look, Alfie's life depends on this man. Do you really want that if he's funked it?"

"That's not fair, corporal."

"Maybe not, Miss Abbott, but it's true. Will you do it? If not for me, for Alfie?"

There was a stony silence and he felt himself wither under Nellie's glare. Yet another thing of which he wasn't proud. As she turned on her heel, he grabbed her earnestly by the wrist.

"He's been badly bitten by insects," he confided. She looked down at the importunate hand on her wrist, arching an eyebrow, and he released her. With a dismissive huff, she strode over to Lieutenant Mathers, who was still inspecting the tank.

"Lieutenant?"

"Yes, nurse?"

"I hear you were bitten a lot last night, I was wondering if you'd just let me look and make sure that you're all right?"

He waved her away. "There's no need."

"Mr Mathers, it's my job. It'll only take 'alf a mo'. An' if it's serious, then maybe I've got something that'll help, and if not, I'm sure Napoo could whip up one of his poultices."

"This isn't necessary."

She reached up to lift his chainmail curtain and he slapped her hand away.

"I said it isn't necessary. I'm perfectly fine."

"Mr Mathers," she said with wounded dignity. "I'll be the judge of that. Now let me help you."

Mathers turned to go, but Nellie, surprised by her own audacity, caught hold of the chainmail curtain in his mask and ripped it upwards and back, knocking off his toughened leather turtle helmet in the process. It clattered to the ground as he wheeled round and turned on the small FANY, who now held his mask in her hand.

She gasped as she saw his face. It wasn't the usual impetigo and rashes from petrol fumes that she normally saw on tank crews. Large raised red plaques covered his skin and there were swellings at his throat, but his eyes – his eyes were completely black, upon which a shifting rainbow film swirled continually, like petrol on water.

He turned those eyes upon her now. "How dare you!" he snarled, before crumpling with a groan and clutching his stomach.

"Are you all right?" asked Nellie, putting her hand on his shoulder and noticing the growth at the base of his skull. "Let me help you."

Mathers forced himself upright. "You've done enough. The fuel fumes help me all I need. They stop it spreading." He snatched back his mask from Nellie's hand and, stooping to pick up his fallen helmet, he stormed off to the tank.

"Wait, stops what spreading? Stops what, Lieutenant?"

The chunter of the tank's engine filled the clearing, drowning out the possibility of any further conversation as Clegg ran the engine up.

"Did you see?" said Nellie, still shocked.

"Yes. Yes, I did," said Atkins, thoughtfully.

"But his eyes!"

"The petrol fruit."

"Alfie doesn't have that, none of them have."

Atkins shook his head. "No, they haven't been drinking the stuff. Mathers has."

"He has some kind of infection, too. Those plaques on his face and the swellings on his neck, I've never seen anything like them."

Atkins hadn't either, but then this world was full of particularly unpleasant surprises. "I think he's drinking the petrol fruit to relieve the pain of it, but it makes him see things. Believe me, I know. I think he's mad, Miss Abbott, but he has a great influence over his men. They're fiercely loyal. If we move against him, they'll do everything they can to protect him, which will get us nowhere, and we need that tank. Lieutenant Everson needs that tank."

Napoo had a different opinion on Mathers and had no qualms about telling the rest of the section. "Someone has cursed him, and he has been possessed by an evil spirit. Who might have the power to do such a thing?"

"Jeffries," exclaimed Chalky. "Jeffries could do it, couldn't he, Only?"

Mercy clipped him round the back of his head. "Prat!" Some people just saw Jeffries everywhere.

Jeffries had sprung to Atkins' mind, too, but he dismissed the idea. Despite all the claims and the stories, his own encounter with Jeffries suggested that he was nothing more than a man. "Can you help him?"

Napoo shook his head sadly. "Those possessed by dulgur are cast out of the clan for fear of the harm or bad fortune they bring. I do not understand why the Tohmii keep theirs around."

Atkins frowned. It took him a moment to realise that he was talking about the shell-shocked. No wonder the urmen gave the Bird Cage a wide berth.

"So," said Atkins, none the wiser. "Mathers is either possessed, or mad."

"Well, that's nothing new, he's an officer," said Mercy.

1 SECTION MOVED out behind the tank as it rolled forwards, crushing a path through the undergrowth as they set off in the direction in which the smoke creatures had dragged the Zohtakarrii. The chatts had been hauled through the jungle at speed, even without the thin oily residue that coated the trees and undergrowth, the trail of snapped branches, gouged ground, and occasional chatt limb wasn't hard to follow.

Atkins dropped back and matched his stride with that of Chandar's. The chatt was silent, fidgeting with the tassels of its shoulder cloth, watching the tank closely as if still debating with itself on the matter of its divinity.

"You say the Tohmii came from the Sky Web?" it asked, unexpectedly.

"From the stars, yes."

Chandar hissed and chittered to itself and came to a decision. "Among the Khungarrii Shura there is a secret olfaction of Ones who believe, as this One does, that urmen have a greater part to play in our Osmology. Sirigar holds the old-established view; that urmen, casteless and queenless as they are, were put here by GarSuleth merely to service the needs of the Ones as they see fit. Sirigar's interpretation of the prophecy, that the Tohmii are the Great Corruption, is flawed and self-serving. That One seeks to unite wavering olfactions of the Shura behind it and consolidate its position with the defeat of the Great Corruption – the Tohmii."

"So there are some chatts that believe we are not this 'Great Corruption' then? That's heartening to know," Atkins said sardonically.

"It is an ancient prophecy, its interpretation an old debate, going back generations. The arrival of the Tohmii is but the latest. This One, however, believes the prophecy refers not to an external threat but rather an internal one; the warping and narrowing of our own beliefs to serve a baser purpose."

"Sirigar."

The chatt concentrated as it gulped down air to speak. "Yes. The only way to challenge that One is through the Supplication of Scents before the Shura. If our argument proves persuasive only the Queen can issue the necessary chemical decree, acknowledging our interpretation as the correct one, to be accepted by all." Chandar paused for another breath and bowed its head. "Our only hopes of distilling the essence of our argument lay in the Aromatic Archives of the Fragrant Libraries destroyed by Jeffries. There, too, were held the records of one of the Divine Disciplines, the recreation of the Celestial Scent, an attempt to understand its totality by alchemically capturing the Sacred Odour of GarSuleth itself. There are those, like this One, who believe that some note of the urman scent is inherent to this endeavour. Both of these sacred undertakings were dashed by Jeffries' sacrilege and the Tohmii's actions. We are diminished because of it."

"That wasn't our fault," said Atkins. "We simply wanted our people back."

"Nevertheless, the atrocity was committed," said Chandar.

Atkins was shocked. Was it really all their fault? Had they brought all this on themselves? "Why are you telling me this?"

"Your act of Kurda, saving this One, was unforeseen, unprecedented. It has cast a new anchor line into the world, a silver thread of possibilities. A web of potential not yet woven. This One would know what may be spun from it."

"You're talking in riddles."

"To you, maybe, but to this One these are signs, portents. Upon these rest the fate of your herd, make no mistake."

It was almost too much for Atkins. Internal divisions within the Khungarrii, one of which might be sympathetic to the Pennines, now powerless because of the Pennines' own actions. In one of his blacker moods, he could almost believe that God was having some cruel capricious joke at his expense. All he'd tried to do was the right thing. Almost fearing to broach the subject, he pressed on. "You said some things, yesterday. Was that smoke creature Croatoan?"

"This One does not know."

Atkins felt himself beginning to lose his temper. "Look, chatt, I'm leading my men into God knows what here. If you have any information about what we're heading into, then tell me. You once said that we had some sort of connection."

"Kurda,"

"Right. Kurda, because I saved your life. Now it's your turn. Save mine. What's going on here? What is it you're not telling me?"

Chandar fell silent, but glanced occasionally at Atkins as they walked. Perhaps, Atkins thought, the chatt was struggling with its conscience, if it had one. God help them if it didn't.

THEY HAD BEEN walking for about half an hour when Chalky stopped to relieve himself by the trackside. He screamed and stepped back, still voiding his bladder. Losing his footing, he turned round to maintain his balance, flinging out an arc of yellow drops as he went.

Mercy stepped back to avoid the spray. "Hey look out, Chalky. Bleeding hell, ladies present."

"Ruddy hell, lad! Did Shiner coming a cropper teach you nothing?" bawled Gutsy.

"There!" Chalky cried, trying to tuck himself away. "There!"

"All right, lad. Leave this to us," said Mercy, stepping past him as he, Gazette and Pot Shot approached the side of the tank's path.

Pot Shot looked down into the scrub and found he was peering into the piss-filled eye socket of a skull staring up at him through the reddish bracken.

Living on the Somme had hardened most of them to such sights. You couldn't walk ten yards without coming across a body in some state of decomposition. One trench they held had a Frenchie's arm sticking out of the trench wall. Their old sergeant, Jessop, used to hang his equipment from it.

Atkins hollered forward for Gutsy to stop the tank.

It jolted to a halt, its engine idling, splutters of black smoke coughing from the exhaust on the roof. The port sponson door opened and one of the crew, Frank, poked his sweaty face out. "What's the bloody hold up?"

"Bodies," Atkins snapped back. "Urmen."

They used entrenching tools to pull away at the tangle of bracken to expose what was left of several skeletons after the scavengers of this world had done their work. Red lichen partially covered the bones. Whatever clothing they might have once worn had completely disintegrated. There was no way of telling how they died, but this planet had a hundred and one different ways to kill you, none of them pleasant.

Mercy's clearance also uncovered the remains of some kind of wagon. There wasn't enough wood left to tell much more. It was rotten and crumbled at the touch.

These were no recent deaths. The bones had lain here for years, decades, maybe even longer.

Nellie shook her head sadly. "Poor people."

Intrigued, Chandar came over to look, its stunted claw-like mid-limbs fidgeting as it clasped its hands together. "This One never thought to witness such a sight. At Khungarr, all this One had were the artefacts scentirrii patrols brought back. To see them like this is marvellous."

Looking at the remains, Atkins thought of the old urman woman's prediction concerning his own mortality. He shuddered. All of a sudden, he felt very vulnerable to the capricious whims of this planet.

They dug a small pit and buried what they could find of the bones, the sight of which unsettled Prof, already withdrawn since Nobby's death, even further. Nevertheless, he managed to say a prayer over them before they moved on.

THE TANK LURCHED to a halt. Before them, looming out of the thinning jungle, Atkins recognised a familiar structure: a chatt edifice, or rather what was left of one. It was an overgrown and crumbling ruin, swathed in vegetation, like an old dowager decked out in the family jewels. Vines overhung the main entrance into the edifice. The top half of the structure had collapsed long ago, and creeping foliage smothered the rubble and debris strewn about the clearing. The tide of alien nature, no longer kept at bay, had flooded in to reclaim the area once more.

The Section wandered cautiously towards the once great structure. Even in its heyday, it would not have been as big as Khungarr. Nevertheless, these places were feats of engineering on a par with medieval cathedrals. They stood over many generations of constant habitation, each generation repairing and expanding the ancestral edifice to house the growing colony. What catastrophic event could have overtaken this place to leave it abandoned and in ruins? Atkins couldn't speculate.

"I have never seen such a sight," said Napoo. The spectacle of the edifice, a symbol of the urman's oppressors' might and skill, lying shattered and dashed to the ground, must have been a profound sight; an intimation of his oppressor's mortality, of their fallibility.

Pot Shot stood beside him and nodded, seeing in it the symbols of his own political beliefs. "And so shall tumble the ivory towers of all tyrants," he muttered.

There was an abrupt silence as the tank engine cut out. The silence immediately struck Atkins. The trees and the undergrowth were still and quiet. There were calls and whoops, but only far off, in the distance, as if even the jungle creatures avoided this place.

Gazette sized up the ruined edifice. "Well, if I were a man-eating evil spirit, that's where I'd set up shop, all right."

Chandar clicked and chattered and, making its sign of deference, began to back away. It seemed to know, or at least suspect something.

Gutsy clapped a heavy hand on its shoulder. "Oh, no, you don't."

Atkins rounded on it. "What is this place?"

For a moment, Chandar gabbled in its own language, its mandibles and mouth palps moving rapidly in a torrent of clicks and tuts before it remembered, caught its breath, and translated the words into something they could understand.

"It is forbidden!"

A loud clang shattered the silence as a hatch swung open on the tank and the crew emerged, blinking and disorientated in the light, coughing and wheezing.

Nellie, looking for Alfie, saw Mathers stumble out and clutch his stomach. She pointed it out to Atkins with a nudge. They watched as Mathers pulled his hip flask from under his rain cape, lifted the splash mask chainmail aside and took a slug. He straightened up. A breeze blew across the clearing and he turned into the wind for a moment, as if wistfully looking for something, half-remembered.

"Ah, here come our land navy privateers," said Prof, nudging Chalky.

"What did you say?" said Cecil, his blotchy face clouding over as he rounded on the Fusilier. "Nobody calls the crew of the *Ivanhoe* mutineers, least of all mud-sucking infantry!"

"No, what I said was –"

Prof staggered back under the lad's tackle, trying to block Cecil's furious punches.

"Oi!" shouted Jack, striding towards the pair and pulling them apart. He grabbed Cecil and yanked him back by the collar of his coveralls. "This isn't the time or place."

"But he was bad-mouthing our mob!" insisted Cecil.

1 Section gathered protectively round a stunned and shaken Prof and the two groups regarded each other with animosity.

"That's enough!" yelled Atkins. "Christ knows there are enough things out here that want to kill us without bloody doing it ourselves!"

THE ALTERCATION BARELY registered with Mathers as he strode between the two groups, scarcely acknowledging the Fusiliers. "Nesbit, that's enough. We haven't time. They are inconsequential," he said. He had other, higher matters to attend to, matters that did not require their presence. This was Hush Hush business. "Our evil spirit dwells within. So let's make it quick. I don't like being outside the tank any longer than necessary. The pain is worse out here. Grab your revolvers and weapons and follow me."

With derisive mutters and black glances at the Fusiliers, the tank crew fell in behind their commander as he strode towards the ruined edifice. He didn't need to look back at the *Ivanhoe* for reassurance, for Skarra was with him. He could hear the god's insistent ever-present whispers in his mind, directing him, encouraging him.

A SUDDEN FLUSH of fear washed over Alfie. He turned and looked back at Nellie, taking comfort in the calming, yellow glow she gave off. By comparison, the rest of the tank crew around him radiated ugly, bruised hues of suspicion and paranoia. He knew which he preferred.

Frank gave him a shove. "What are you going to do, run after your long-haired chum or stay with us?"

"Nellie can look after herself," Alfie said.

"The right choice, Alfie boy," said Frank, leaning in close. "Maybe there's hope for you yet."

*   *   *

MATHERS' SUDDEN DEPARTURE caught Atkins off guard. Why the hell should he have expected anything less from a madman? "Lieutenant, wait! Where the hell are you going? Come back, sir!"

Driven on by his own rationale, Mathers didn't even break his stride, but continued towards the ruins. "You forget, Corporal, I have a spirit to kill and when I do so, I shall become even greater than I am now. I shall add its power to my own. Skarra has promised me!"

At the mention of Skarra, Chandar hissed gently and made a sign of reverence towards the tank. Could it be that Mad Mathers was actually convincing Chandar of their deception, Atkins wondered? After all, if Mathers had started to believe it...

The tank commander had reached the overgrown, cavernous entrance and led his men into the ruined edifice.

A low, continuous moan issued from its depths.

Atkins hoped it was just the wind through the tunnels.

CHAPTER THIRTEEN
"Across the Untroubled Blue..."

OUT ON THE veldt, the ominous low rumble that accompanied the line of leaden grey clouds in the distance continued long past the point where it should have died away.

Everson made his way from the fire trench, along the sap. The disappearance of the Khungarrii was weighing heavily on his mind. What the hell were they up to? He didn't know and he didn't like it. This damn planet was full of unknowns. He seemed to spend too much time just reacting to things and trying to keep their heads above water. So far, he'd been lucky. This latest manoeuvre by the Khungarrii, vanishing like that, had unsettled him. All he could do was keep the men stood to in expectation of – of God knew what, frankly. However, they could only do that for so long and they were reaching the end of their tether already. He felt himself floundering, not knowing what to expect next.

The sap came out by the old Poulet farmhouse. Lieutenant Baxter and his machine gun section occupied the ground floor. They had set the Lewis machine gun up in a window bay, the walls reinforced by sandbags.

Baxter took him aside and, in a low voice, proceeded to question him. "Everson, any idea what the hell is going on out there? Where have the damned chatts gone to?"

"I don't know, Baxter. They seem to have abandoned the

field, but whether it's a feint or not, I just don't know. Keep your eyes peeled. I've only come here for a look-see myself. The Hill OP will keep us informed. As soon as I know anything, you will, Bernard."

He patted the officer on the shoulder and, with a shrug and apologetic smile, started up the stairs to the observation platform.

The whole of the upper level had been roughly refloored with wooden boards, and the old roof, which had been in danger of collapsing, had been removed. Most of the upper walls had been saved. Loose bricks had tumbled down and the rubble still lay scattered around the farmhouse walls. It was open to the elements but for a large tarpaulin that flapped and snapped over his head in the strengthening breeze. He stopped and sniffed. There was a pungent odour on the wind. Damp. Acrid. Rank. Animal.

"Sir!" The Corporal and two privates on watch snapped to attention as Everson arrived up the stairs. Everson found the RFC Lieutenant, Tulliver, there too, checking the weather. A makeshift windsock billowed in the breeze.

"Anything to report?" asked Everson, walking up to the empty window frame and looking out over the now desolate veldt. The heavy grey clouds sailed towards them with the threat of rain. Beyond, the rumbling persisted. "What the hell *is* that?" he muttered, half to himself.

"Sir!" snapped the Corporal, calling his attention to flashes coming from the OP up on the hillside. Everson watched them for a moment, spat out an oath, pulled out his field glasses and raised them to his eyes.

A dust cloud rolled along the veldt. Was it the Khungarrii again, hoping to catch them with their guard down? He quickly scanned the field deserted by the alien army. He spotted the immobile chatts facing the oncoming storm with an almost preternatural patience. He focused on the dust cloud. It seemed to stretch right across his field of vision, obscured only by the foothills of the valley.

"Hell and damnation! It's a bloody stampede."

"Stampede, sir?"

"Animals, Corporal, thousands of bloody animals headed this way, driven before the storm. When they pass the head of the valley I want you to fire a flare. Understood?"

"Flare. Understood, sir."

"Tulliver, get your machine off the ground, do it now before the thing gets trampled! I don't want to lose it."

"You're not the only one!" He didn't have to be told twice. He sprang down the stairs in several leaps and pelted off to the cleared take-off strip.

Everson trotted down the stairs and rushed out of the farmhouse, past the machine gun section. "Bernard," he yelled. "Bloody stampede. Best hole up there and stay under cover. They'll be here soon. Let's hope they decide to go round instead of through, eh?"

"Maybe we can help 'em decide?"

"Be obliged to you!"

Everson jumped down into the sap and ran along the jinked trench back to the outer fire trench ring. At least down in the trenches the men should be safe; well, safer. Any animals that got beyond the wire weed should just jump right over them.

At the junction with the fire trench ring, he turned right. Privates turned and looked at the sight of an officer running as he darted past, body swerving round the sandbag traverses, looking for the first NCO he could find. It was Sergeant Hobson.

"Sergeant, there's a stampede headed this way. Keep the men stood to. And for God's sake, preserve your ammunition. Don't fire unless you have to. Send runners and pass the message on. Everyone else to the dugouts. We can't guarantee their safety if they're in the open."

"Sir."

Everson ran on through several more bays and took a sharp left down Pall Mall, the first communications trench he came to. Scarcely slowing his speed for the tight confines of the trench, he wove down the zigzags, careening off revetments and almost colliding with a ration party bringing up hot soup.

"Gangway!"

"Christ, watch it you silly –"

Everson didn't wait for their mortified apologies. The soldiers in the trenches and dugouts might well weather the stampede in relative safety, but there were the tents and huts in the middle of the encampment that would be vulnerable, most of those housing the sick and the wounded and several small clans of urmen. He had to evacuate them into dugouts. He didn't want to think about the consequences if he didn't.

He collided heavily with someone running the other way, winding himself. He looked up to see the kinematographer straightening his wire-framed glasses.

"God damn it, Hepton!"

"You're in an awful hurry, Lieutenant."

"That's because there's a bloody stampede headed this way."

He caught the eager glint in Hepton's eye as he pushed past.

"Alien animal stampede? I say, that's excellent!" he heard him call back, from beyond another jink in the communications trench, as he put distance between them.

Everson shook his head as he ran on past the crossroads that connected with the support trench. The damn man was all about the sensational. Well, let him have his stampede. If he got trampled underfoot for his film, it was no skin off his nose.

He took a left turn into the support trench, the inner ring. Traffic here was heavier and he had to slow down.

"Private!"

"Sir?"

Everson jerked his head in the direction of the parados. "Give me a leg up."

"Sir?"

"Now!"

The private, nonplussed but knowing better than to ask, linked his fingers together, palms up. Everson stepped into the cradle and the private boosted him up, over the parados sandbags, to the open ground in the centre of the ring of trenches. He made his way to the hospital tent with its shabby fading red cross. He strode in, sweeping the flaps aside.

"Lippett? Where's Captain Lippett?" he demanded of the white-coated orderly.

Lippett stepped out from behind a hung blanket cordoning off a section of tent for private use – his office.

"Yes, Lieutenant, what can I do for you?"

"There's a stampede headed this way. You need to get your patients down into the dugouts."

"Stampede? But some of them can't be moved."

He had no time for this. "Now, Doctor!"

The Doctor spluttered at the impudence. Again, Everson didn't wait for a retort and heard Lippett giving orders to the orderlies and 'light duty' injured.

Most of his men were disciplined enough to follow orders, but the new urmen platoons, *Fred Karno's Army,* didn't seem to grasp the idea. Everson caught sight of several NCOs barking furiously at urmen, who weren't obeying. They should have been going down into the trenches. Instead, they were gathering portable possessions.

"Do I have to do every blasted thing myself," he muttered, as he made his way over to them. "Corporal, what the hell is going on here? Get those urmen into the trenches."

"They won't go, sir. They keep shouting something and pointing at the veldt, sir."

Everson turned on the nearest urman and threw his arms up in frustration. "What? What is it?"

The urman, now Everson looked at him, had a haunted look in his eyes, a look of barely suppressed panic restrained only by their awe of the Tohmii. He kept casting anxious glances at the horizon.

"What is it, what's out there?"

"Dapamji!" It was an urman word for death. As if the very word absolved him of any loyalty to the Tommies, he herded his family away back towards the valley, pausing only to shout the warning again. "Dapamji!"

"Sir?"

"Let them go, Corporal. It's out of our hands. Get down into the trenches."

Across the encampment, he saw Tulliver's aeroplane take to the air. That was one less thing to worry about.

A flare arced into the darkening sky with a whoosh and burst in a bright white bloom.

Everson could feel the ground begin to reverberate beneath his feet. The rumble of hooves and the snorts, whinnies and screams of animals in terror, filled the air and grew louder. There was little time left.

Sister Fenton, Nurse Bell and a couple of sentries were herding reluctant shell-shocked patients down to the dugout in the Bird Cage. Nurse Bell was attempting to round up several of the patients, but one man had other ideas. With a single-minded determination, he scrambled out through the barbed wire fencing that surrounded them, oblivious to cuts and scratches, and was now making for the front line. Nurse Bell made for the compound gate and gave chase.

"Jones! Private Jones, come back!"

Everson looked around the encampment. Most soldiers were too busy saving themselves, or their own, to notice or care about shell-shocked straggler heading *towards* the wire.

Above, caught by a gust of the steadily rising wind, the Union flag snapped and furled, briefly catching his attention. It embodied all the things he had been taught were right; King, Country, Duty. However, there were some things that he never needed to be taught. Some things were innate, tacit.

"Oh, for heaven's sake!" he said, racing after Nurse Bell and towards the oncoming stampede.

He leapt over a communication trench like a steeple chaser, almost losing his footing on the parapet, sending sandbags tumbling down into it. He pounded over a trench bridge. With his lungs burning in his chest, he headed for the barbed wire entanglements. The shell-shocked man had found the gap in it and was wading through it like a rising tide, heedless of the barbs that snatched and tore at him.

Bell clung desperately onto his arm, her weight on her front foot as she tried to use her meagre frame to halt his dogged advance.

Drawing his revolver Everson raced towards her. He could see the approaching herds now, their stench heavy on the wind. They flowed round the mausoleum mounds of the Khungarrii like a river as they met the first of the mesmerised chatts. The arthropods fell beneath them without resistance and they trampled them under foot.

He reached Bell and grabbed her arm. "Come on. We have to go. Now!"

"No, we have to save him."

"We can't. You've done enough!"

But she wouldn't give up her patient.

Everson levelled his revolver at the unwary man, who was still trying to advance despite their added weight. "God damn it, woman, if you don't let go, I'll shoot him."

"You wouldn't!"

"Watch me!" He cocked the Webley with his thumb. "It's technically desertion anyway!"

"No!" Bell let go of the man's arm, only to grab Everson's revolver and push it towards the ground.

She watched, all hope lost, as the man, suddenly free of the dead weight, surged forwards towards the wire and rushed out to meet the oncoming wall of flesh and fur.

"Jones!"

"He'll have to take his chances, though why he chose now to show some bloody gumption, I'll never know!" Everson, still gripping her wrist, began dragging her towards the trench. He leapt down on to the fire step, almost knocking a soldier off, and dragged Bell in after him. He lost his balance and ended up on his back, Bell sprawled across him and struggling to free her wrist from his grip. He relented and let her go, only for her to repay him with a sharp slap to the cheek. He guessed he deserved that. Edith scrambled to her feet, trying to recover her dignity. She stepped onto the fire step, with every intention of going out after her patients again, raised her head above the parapet, and gasped.

Everson glanced around the fire bay and, spotting a funk hole in the side of the revetment, yanked out the equipment and pulled Edith over.

"What are you doing?"

"Keeping you safe, since you seem incapable of doing it for yourself." He indicated the shallow hole, as if he were opening a door for a lady. "In."

She looked for a moment as if she might object, and knowing Bell, as he had come to over the past few months, she probably would. He shoved her into the vacant hole anyway. She looked up at him, half-annoyed and half-thankful.

"Stay there."

The rumble of hooves and feet now seemed to encompass their whole world. He returned to the fire step, risking a quick glance over the parapet. He had faced waves of charging Huns before, but nothing prepared him for the sight that met him now.

All he could see was a bow wave of dust and chaff as the solid wall of fear-driven herds bore down on what now seemed flimsy defences against such an unstoppable force. The lines of Tennyson's poem rang in Everson's head. *"Half a league, half a league, half a league on, all in the valley of death..."*

SERGEANT HOBSON STOOD in a fire bay beside Monroe, Carter and Cox, rifles loaded.

"Here they come, lads!" Hobson bellowed, taking aim. He fired five rounds rapid, bringing three beasts down short of the fire trench, but it was like Canute trying to hold back the tide.

"Bugger this!" he said, ducking. "It's like trying to swat minnies with me battle bowler. Take cover, lads. We've done all we can. Let's just try and ride this out."

They hunkered down in the trench to sit out the beastly barrage.

* * *

A GREAT WAVE of fur and bone, of blood and sinews, claws and horns, of hide and carapace rushed pell-mell towards them across the veldt. The spur of the foothills served to part the wave, funnelling stampeding animals into the adjacent valleys. It also channelled a good proportion of what was left of the panicked herds down the valley towards them.

Everson watched as the first wave of the stampede reached the wire shores of their island home, the greater parts flowing around the great circular encampment and past it, on up the valley.

Still, unrelenting waves of animals crashed and broke against the wall of wire and weed, driven headlong by some uncontrollable fear. Those behind pressed those in front ever onwards in a surge of bodies, advancing over those caught in the tightening bonds. Within moments, the tide of dead and dying had clogged the entanglements, providing purchase and passage over the wire.

The animals surged towards the front line. Everson was depending on the support and reserve trenches to take out as many animals as possible before the fire trench was overwhelmed, trying to slow or derail the stampede, to spare the centre of the camp the worst of it.

Some enterprising soldier threw a grenade into the marauding mass. It exploded in a ball of shrapnel, meat and bloody vapour, anguished animal screams piercing the heavy bass thunder.

Those animals near it tried to veer away from it, momentarily sparing the fire bay directly in front, channelling them instead towards adjacent bays. Men there, in turn, threw their grenades to avoid the onslaught. It seemed to have the desired effect, lessening the strength of the initial frontal assault, but it only worked for the first wave. It wasn't actually stopping it. They didn't have enough bombs to sustain the tactic, and the great press of creatures continued unabated, bellowing, snoring and roaring towards the trenches.

Everson could do nothing but bear witness. The sandbags shook and, through the revetment, he felt the ground tremble against his chest. The noise and the stench of musk and fear were overwhelming. He feared even the tank would not have fared well against such an onslaught of flesh.

Predators and prey ran together, their natural enmities temporarily forgotten in their headlong flight. Creatures he recognised, others he didn't, tore towards him in an unheeding rush, snapping, biting and rearing at those that got in their way. From his worm's-eye view over the parapet, Everson felt more vulnerable than ever.

Great three-legged tripodgiraffes tried to maintain their balance as they tottered headlong, striding above the packs below. Two-legged pelths, twice the size of ostriches, with sharp, hooked beaks, wove in and out of their legs, threatening to trip them, or be trampled. One tripodgiraffe did fall, its great long neck flailing as it crashed to the ground like a felled tree, to be lost, trampled under hooves.

Hell hounds bounded, snapping and snarling at each other in fear.

Large, heavy, prehensile-lipped gurduin, herbivores with great bone head-ridges, and mottled hides riddled with wart-like protrusions, thundered headlong, their brutish looks belying their usual passivity, distorted by foam-flecked mouths and white eyes rolling with terror.

"Look out," called Everson, to the men around him. "Here they come. Keep down!"

One of the gurduin stumbled, its forelegs folding beneath it. Trying to get to its feet, it was pummelled back into the ground. Others, too slow to react, and too hemmed in to manoeuvre around, barrelled into it. Some attempted to leap over, but their short legs and cumbersome bodies weren't meant for such athletic moves, and they caught their legs and tumbled over, losing their balance, to join it in the same fate, and the pile up began.

One beast, leaping the fallen, clipped the bodies beneath.

The beast's scream cut through the thunderous thrumming of the hooves around it as it tripped and fell forwards, breaking its foreleg. It crashed headlong through the sandbag parapet, its momentum and weight carrying it slithering over the edge into the narrow trough of the trench.

The soldier barely had time to scream before its huge bulk threw him off the fire step. It drove him into the duckboards, snapping planks and bones, where the beast struggled, screaming and kicking, trying to right itself, grinding the Tommy's body beneath it and smashing the revetments with its hooves. A wild kick splintered another soldier's thigh, the jagged shards of femur ripping though his khaki serge as it quickly began to stain with blood.

His mates dragged him clear of the bellowing animal, yelling for a stretcher bearer. Quickly, three bayonets were plunged into the creature, briefly increasing the thrashing and squealing. Barely had Everson stepped up and shot it in the forehead, than Bell was out of her funk hole, taking charge of the casualties, as along the front line other panicked animals leapt over the trenches, losing their footing and tumbling madly into the man-made ditches.

Choking dust sifted down from the hurtling herds above as they leapt over the trenches. The men knew enough now to keep their heads down, and huddled at the bottom, their hands over their heads, to sit it out. Some sat back against the parados revetment, their feet braced against the opposite wall, their rifles and bayonets pointed up against the prospect of a clumsy beast. Others lit up what fags they had left and smoked nonchalantly as the beasts thundered and pounded by, feet above their heads, showering them with dirt, dust, and the occasional fear-voided droppings, much to the amusement of their fellows.

Several chanced their heads and took pot-shots at the rampaging creatures from the fire steps. Caught by a stray hoof, one careless man's neck snapped back, breaking in an instant. He crumpled to the duck boards like an empty sack.

With the thunderous pounding surrounding them, dirt

raining down on them, it began to feel like an old-fashioned Bosche artillery barrage of minniewerfers and five-nines. It seemed to last forever. Everson almost laughed at the thought. Who would have thought he'd miss the good old days?

THEN, AS IT seemed the stampeding rumble would go on forever, it was over. The thunder of hooves receded, leaving only the odd squealing animal chasing after the rest.

The men waited, fearing more. It didn't come and they began to relax, laugh and chatter with the exhilaration of survival. Hobson sniffed, straightened his waxed moustache, picked up his rifle and stood up, intending to peer over the parapet, but shouts of alarm over to his right distracted him. The screams grew louder, moving along the trench towards them. Several fire bays away, he heard shots fired.

A maddened hell hound careered round the traverse, confused and panic-stricken, cornered like a boar in a run. Men leapt onto fire steps and scrambled up the parapets out of its way. Several Tommies skidded to a halt behind it in the traverse and levelled their rifles. It slewed to a halt, snarling and snapping, cornered between the traverse and Sergeant Hobson.

Hobson aimed his bayoneted rifle and pulled the trigger. The rifle jammed. Stoppage. He cursed silently but didn't back down. He gripped his rifle more firmly and dropped it into a low defensive guard. The bayonet was his weapon now.

Its way blocked, the hell hound attempted to turn in the tight space, but couldn't. Frustrated and enraged, it snapped at a man's legs on the fire step, sinking its teeth into his calf and dragging him down off the step, as the man clawed at the revetment, stretching hands that reached down, but not far enough.

It tossed its head, shaking him. Even over the man's scream, Hobson heard the man's leg snap.

Hobson let out a roar, and the beast turned its head to look at him. It opened its jaws and let the man drop. Hobson lunged forward with his fixed bayonet; the hell hound shook its head in challenge and sprung forwards to meet him. With a blood-curdling cry, Hobson thrust his rifle, plunging the bayonet deep into the creature's chest. The hell hound's attack faltered. Stuck on the bayonet, it snapped at Hobson, who held it at bay with the length of the rifle.

He glanced up at the scared men on the parapets, who looked unsure of what to do. "Well don't just bloody stand there taking bets. Fire, damn you or I'll have your names!"

Shaken from their fear, the men took aim and a fusillade of bullets slammed into the creature. Amid the cordite smoke, Hobson felt the rifle take the full weight of the hell hound as it died, and withdrew his bayonet.

Hobson looked at the firing squad on the parapet, glaring up at them from under the lip of his steel helmet. "If I find out any of you bet against me," he said. "I'll have your bloody guts for garters."

EVERSON TENTATIVELY RAISED a look-stick over the collapsing parapet and squinted through the aperture. The dust was still settling, caught as it was by wind eddies.

The bodies of beasts littered the ground: the sick, the old, the young, the unlucky, lay twisted and broken, dead or injured. The living squealed and whinnied in pain.

Satisfied that the stampede had run its course, he climbed out of the trench to survey the encampment. Around the fire trench, others climbed out, too, pushing back their helmets in bewilderment and disbelief at the devastation wreaked by the stampede.

Everson's heart sank as he turned around. Animal bodies hung from the wire entanglements, trenches had collapsed, tents had been trampled, and hutments razed. It might as well have been a bloody Hun artillery barrage.

Hobson walked up and joined him.

"All that work and we're back where we started," said Everson with a sigh.

Hobson stuck out his chest and rocked on his feet. "It'll give the men something to do, sir."

"We're going to have to strengthen the trenches, relay the entanglements, repitch the tents, rebuild the hutments..."

"Still," said Hobson, brightly. "Plenty of dung for the gunpowder experiments now, I'd say."

Everson sighed. "Thank you, Sergeant, I hadn't realised there was such a silver lining."

Hobson glanced down modestly, and shrugged. "You just have to look for it. Or in your case, sir, tread in it."

THE STAMPEDE OVER, the gas gong sounded the all-clear. Edith and Sister Fenton climbed out of the dugout. Together the nurses looked out towards the approaching storm.

Edith didn't relish the prospect of the quagmire the trenches would become under a torrential rain, and she suspected the men wouldn't either. They had grown used to the comfort of dry trenches and dugouts.

As she watched the storm shadows slide across the veldt towards them, she squinted at the voluminous roiling grey mass in the distance and shivered.

TULLIVER CIRCLED THE trenches in his Sopwith, looking for somewhere to land. The hooves of thousands of bloody animals had churned up his carefully kept strip. They'd trampled the whole landscape to buggery. There had to be somewhere to land.

His attention turned to the oncoming weather, to the great grey-blue mass rolling towards them, blotting out the achingly blue sky as it came.

Only they weren't clouds. From up here, that much was clear now. Tulliver could see what those on the ground couldn't. The danger wasn't yet over because the stampede was never the threat. It was what *caused* it that was the real threat.

PENNINE FUSILIERS

CHAPTER FOURTEEN
"Into Your Dugout and Say Your Prayers..."

EVERSON FOCUSED HIS binoculars on the storm front and felt a hoarfrost of fear creep down his spine. He adjusted the focus and blurred shadows sharpened into a moment of confusing detail. He lowered the field glasses to get context and quickly raised them again, panning across the rapidly advancing cloud front. He passed the glasses to Hobson, soliciting the Platoon Sergeant's opinion. "What do you make of it?"

With no other hint, Hobson took the glasses. "Bloody hell!" he spat, adding a hasty, "sir."

It could have been a great armada of blimps, dirigibles of enormous size, driven along by the wind. There seemed to be no source of motive power. Was this the cause of the stampede? Some kind of air force? If it was a fleet, it threatened to fill the sky.

"What are they, some kind of Zeppelins? Some sort of foreign airship?"

"Maybe, sir. No, wait, they're..."

"They are the Kreothe," said a voice, filled with horror and realisation. It was Poilus. "The great drifting sky shoals of Kreothe. Huge airborne creatures that live on the winds, never coming to earth."

"Thank God," said Everson with relief. "You had me worried there for a minute."

"And so you should be," said Poilus, looking at the approaching things in wonder. "The Kreothe may live in the air, but they feed on the ground. They come, blown by the winds, by the breath of GarSuleth. They have not passed this way in generations. I have only known them exist in tales the elders tell of older times. The last time they passed this way, our clan were still Khungarrii urmen, safe in Khungarr."

"Sir?" Hobson knocked Everson on the upper arm with the back of his hand as he held out the binoculars. "I think he's right. It's not over yet. You'd better take another look..."

Everson did.

What they had mistaken for a cloud front or a zeppelin fleet was, in fact, thousands of individual creatures, of varying sizes, floating from gas sacs, hundreds of feet in the air. Their progress was calm and measured, and above all silent. It was impossible not to be impressed by the things as they crowded the wide sky in their slow stately progress above the veldt. Air sac followed air sac in a mass of varying sizes; from huge towering majestic creatures that appeared, to Everson's imagination, like the old bulls of the shoal, to skittish flimsy little things, like younglings.

Great long thick tendrils, hundreds of feet long, hung from the creatures, dragging along the veldt, dredging for food.

Everson watched, almost spellbound, as tentacles caught animals up, lifting their catches into the air, before handing them over to the shorter fronds that clustered around the bodies protruding below the great air sacs. These, it seemed, were great prehensile tongues, that seemed to taste the creature's food before it ingested it. Everson knew many creatures on this planet were inedible or, perhaps, had defences against such predation. This was obviously the Kreothe way of countering that, testing it perhaps, before drawing it up into pulsing mouth tubes and into the belly of yet another swelling.

Everson watched, in horrified fascination, the great bull Kreothe at the head of the shoal grazing languidly, as they drifted inexorably towards the encampment. He was reminded of seeing an elephant at feeding time or, perhaps, a Portuguese Man-o'-war, as he once did as a young boy, preserved for display in a newly opened museum wing donated by his father.

He had seen enough. "So this is why the Khungarrii vanished. They didn't want to be caught out in the open under these things." He looked at Hobson. "How long have we got, do you reckon?"

Hobson pursed his lips and squinted. "Judging by the wind speed, maybe ten to fifteen minutes?"

"Here we go again," muttered Everson as he started to give orders.

There was a roar as Tulliver flew low over the trenches, waggling his wings to attract their attention. Everson looked up and saw Maddocks, the observer, pointing back towards the approaching Kreothe. A warning.

The plane circled. Everson waved to show he understood. Tulliver pointed to his machine gun, and then at the Kreothe, and headed out to meet them.

Everson grunted an acknowledgement as he turned his attention to the various runners who were now appearing, ordering all but a small defensive force into the deep dugouts. "We can't fight these things. I've no idea how. All we can do is try and warn them off. Keep any more damage to a minimum."

The translucent gas sacs of the oncoming Kreothe cast a peculiar light as the sunlight filtered through them, and the sky began to darken.

In the Bird Cage, Townsend, Miller and the other shell-shock victims stumbled out of the dugout, determined, like Jones before them, to escape their confinement again at any cost. Everson said he couldn't spare extra men to guard them. Nurse Bell, Sister Fenton and Padre Rand found themselves unequal to the task.

"What's got into them, sister?" asked the Padre, his arms wide, trying to block one man from reaching the fence, as if he were playing British Bulldogs.

"I don't know, Padre," said Sister Fenton, as she struggled to keep hold of one man. "They seemed docile and compliant until the wind changed and now, I don't know, they seem *compelled* to escape their confinement. Oh!" Flailing about, the man smacked the Sister across the face with the back of his hand, barely aware that he had done so. She recoiled in shock and he broke free and joined the surge for the fence.

The padre watched those escaping patients, already out of the compound, dash over the trench bridges towards a section of trampled barbed wire entanglement beyond.

Townsend and the others stumbled out past the mangled bodies of tripodgiraffes and gurduin.

Edith darted back past the Padre after the straying men.

"Nurse, No!" he yelled.

"Nurse Bell!" cried Sister Fenton.

"They don't know what they're doing!" she called back. "Somebody has to help them!"

QUICKLY REALISING THAT she was right, Padre Rand let out a brief growl of frustration. He could not, should not, leave them while there was still a chance. The parable of the shepherd and the lost sheep and all that.

For years, he'd told that allegory from his cold pulpit in St Chad's. They were words meant to mollify and soothe, one of many platitudes he issued daily to his congregation. The words lulled him as well, and there, in his parish, he slept. There were no great hardships for him to face, no great tests of faith. The shepherd slept as his flock wandered blithely into a new century and towards the precipice.

It was the Great War that awoke him, to find his flock in jeopardy, physically and morally, and awoke him to the meaning of the words. The true meaning. Having to live by those words he had stood by for so many years, to put himself to the test. Armed with only the small black leather-bound bible that enshrined those words, and the conviction in his heart that they must be true, he set out to steer his flock through the valley of darkness.

There, in the dark fastness of that valley, he came across evil. And there the words failed him. And he had been afraid. In Khungarr, with Jeffries, the Khungarrii put him through a ritual. It had felt like a personal test: his faith, and that of Jeffries' obscene beliefs, versus theirs. His God against theirs, and his had proved wanting. No, not his God, his faith. His faith, for one brief instance, had failed him and he was almost lost. There, he had suffered tormenting visions that challenged and tested him and found him wanting, while Jeffries had shrugged it off. Memory of the visions faded, like a bad dream he could not recall. He struggled to put it behind him, convincing himself that it was nothing more than a drug-induced delirium. Recently, the visions had tried to surface again, haunting his nights and clawing at his mind, like an itch he couldn't scratch. Every day became a battle to keep it at bay because he didn't have the courage to face it.

However, here and now, on this damned and God-forsaken world, he would screw his courage to the sticking place. Here and now, he would place his faith in his God, as Abraham had done.

He ran after Nurse Bell.

BEYOND THE FRONT trench, past the few remaining poppies that had survived the stampede, the shell-shocked now clambered over the bodies of trampled beasts, and the barbed wire, to the cat calls and jeers of the soldiers in the trenches.

Edith ran after them.

"Wait! Townsend, Miller!"

The men, neither helping one another nor hindering, each hell-bent on some personal goal, pushed forwards, free of the defences now, out into the veldt.

Edith followed, scrambling over the burst and blood-slicked carcasses of the beasts bridging the wire.

The veldt before her was a scene of ruin and devastation. The ground had been churned beneath thousands of hooves, pock-marking the surface.

The stacked pyramids of Khungarrii dead lay tumbled, and the funeral balls crushed, exposing chitinous limbs and vacant alien faces embedded in the shattered clay.

The earthworks had been toppled and yet more animals lay dead in some of the Khungarrii excavated holes.

If one squinted, it could almost be the Somme.

Here and there, a few of the mesmerised Khungarrii still survived. Most were injured, but several, that Edith could see, were remarkably unscathed. They stood motionless and patient in their enigmatic vigil.

Padre Rand caught up with her, a couple of orderlies and Sister Fenton hot on his heels.

Once clear of the entrenchments, on open ground, the shell-shocked men simply stopped, joining the surviving Khungarrii. They stood waiting as one might expect a commuter to wait, in expectation of an imminent train or motor omnibus, and with as little concern.

By now, the wind was carrying the slow stately procession of Kreothe towards them. No sound issued from the great creatures, at least any sound that she could hear. They were silent, like clouds. She heard only the abruptly terminated screams of the beasts plundered from the plain, as the huge tendrils plucked the animals into the sky. Padre Rand saw in them the false gods of this world, cold, unheeding, and uncommunicative.

There were twenty-seven men who, for whatever reason, stood waiting patiently, motivated by some unfathomable compulsion to be there. Only five people had ventured out to help them.

As the great air-shoal of the Kreothe drifted closer, the curtain of tendrils hanging below worked industriously, plucking the veldt clean, and lifting the creatures to taste them, before depositing them into their tubular maws, from where they were sucked into their huge digestive nodules. Every now and again, they rejected some creatures and let them drop the hundreds of feet to the ground, where they impacted with dull thuds and explosions of fluids and offal. It sounded, to Padre Rand, like those first big, fat, wet drops of a summer shower.

Bell, almost hysterical with desperation now, yanked at Townsend's tunic with unprofessional urgency. "Townsend!" she screamed, looking up at the great creatures gliding towards them. Their sheer size was apparent now. Getting no reaction, she slapped him across the face. For a brief moment, she thought she noticed a reaction before it faded, replaced by the emotionless mask once more. "Townsend!" she slapped him again.

His eyes flicked towards her ever so briefly.

"Help me," he said, a frail whisper barely escaping his lips. Then he was lost again, leaving only a tear sliding haltingly down his face.

She put a hand to his cheek and wiped it way with her thumb, then gave a startled yelp. A shadow moved on the back of his neck beneath his collarless shirt. The swelling pulsed briefly and she thought she saw a dark shadow, as if something moved under the taut blister of skin. She blinked. The swelling looked much as it had done over the last two days. Maybe she had imagined it.

The Kreothe were close now, almost overhead. She had to crane her neck to look up at them.

"We can't stay here!" said Stanton the orderly. "We have to go!"

"But the men!"

"We can't do anything for them."

"We can. We must!"

She took hold of Townsend's arm and pulled at him. Reluctantly he began to move with her, like a recalcitrant child.

"Stanton, take another one. Padre, help us!"

The Padre ran forwards and grabbed the nearest man.

"Come with me, my son." He met with no resistance, but no help either.

Stanton threw his man over his shoulder and staggered back towards the trenches. He got into trouble trying to negotiate the bridge of dead animals over the barbed wire. One or two men came out of the trenches and sprinted towards him to help him with his patient.

Edith ducked under Townsend's arm to take his weight. As she stood up and braced herself, she glanced back over her shoulder and regretted it.

Above them, like huge towering cumulonimbus clouds, the gas-bloated Kreothe drifted with a sedate grace while underneath the tendrils groped, picked and plucked rapaciously.

They plucked the first of the shell-shocked, a tendril wrapping around him and lifting him into the air. Edith watched with mounting horror. By some method she could not discern, the man's body proceeded to unfold like the petals of a flower, bright and wet and red, like the poppies that populated the ground below, exposing his innards as the poppy petals unfurled to expose their stamen. It was as if he were being peeled or flayed as he ascended into the sky in some otherworldly sacrament.

Others were being plucked now, like matured fruit, ascending to waiting tongue tendrils where flocks of carrion things snatched and tore at them before they were directed into the soft wet waiting maws of the mouth tubes.

Stumbling under Townsend's dead weight, Edith realised, with a sickening lurch, that they weren't going to make it.

"BELL! BELL!"

Edith looked about at the sound of her name. She saw Sister Fenton calling to her from the opening of one of the Khungarrii delvings.

"Get in quick," said Sister Fenton, holding out her hand to take Townsend. Edith pushed him down the hole and, with only a brief glance over her shoulder, followed. The delving was about twenty feet deep and sloped down at a gentle angle.

The Padre was down there with two other shell-shocked soldiers, Miller and Jones. The group huddled as far down the sloping tunnel as they could.

"Keep still," said Fenton in a low voice, as if afraid they might be heard.

One tendril dragged across the opening, throwing the burrow into darkness. Its tip probed the entrance, sending loose clods of earth and slips of soil slithering down into the hole. It began feeling its way down. Then it was gone, drawn away by the ever drifting air sacs above.

"I can't look," said Sister Fenton, turning her face from the hole. But a terrible fascination drew Edith's gaze back to the circle of sky before her, striated now by passing tendrils.

Overcome by an unquenchable desire, Townsend struggled and jerked a little and Bell tried to calm him, but he worked free of Edith's grasp, scrambling desperately for the light, and stood momentarily at the entrance, offering himself.

"Townsend!" Edith started after him.

"No!" Sister Fenton held her, and firmly forbade her from going after him. All she could do was watch as a dredging tendril found him, and after a tentative caress, caught him up and drew him into the air.

"He's gone, Nurse, but we still have two more we might save," said Fenton. Edith swallowed her grief and her anger, set her face for the practicalities of her craft, and nodded. Their job was to assist the living.

"Yes, Sister."

In bleak resignation, Edith sat huddled with the others, waiting for the ordeal to be over, the tunnel lit by stroboscopic flickers of light and shadow as the moving forest of tendrils coasted past. There, more than in the dugout, she knew something of the fear these men must have felt under constant barrages that numbed the mind and pummelled the senses, until there was nowhere a man might take refuge from the shattering conditions outside, or from himself within.

As she weakened, Padre Rand seemed to draw strength

from the trial and began muttering prayers; not meek prayers, begging to be spared from this tortuous test, but rather of strength, asking for the fortitude to bear it. It seemed to Edith as if his faith was an old, much loved, but discarded coat that he had newly rediscovered and was trying on again for size, and found it still fitted.

LIEUTENANT TULLIVER NEEDED to get his Sopwith 1½ Strutter above the shoal of Kreothe drifting implacably towards them and, given the rapidity with which they were approaching, he needed to gain height fast.

They were flying at a thousand feet, but still hadn't cleared the height of the great voluminous air sacs that kept the creatures aloft. The sun had disappeared, blocked out by the Kreothe that now filled the sky above them, and it filtered through their translucent bodies, casting a weird green twilight on everything below. It was like flying in the vaulted nave of some obscene flesh-built cathedral, the tentacles dropping down like clusters of gargantuan columns. There was nothing to do but fly through them until they could find a way up.

Several smaller Kreothe drifted by beneath them. Tulliver glanced down past his fuselage as they slipped by a hundred feet below. They looked for all the world like misshapen kite balloons, and he could deal with balloons.

First, he had to avoid the death-dealing tentacles as they found themselves weaving through a forest of the things.

Tulliver glanced up through the transparent pane in the upper wing above him. Overhead he could see the underside of the mammoth air sacs of a great Kreothe. It bulged with several huge fleshy globules and growths. One cyst-like swelling resembled a large udder from which extruded three slick, wet lipless mouths. A circle of long tongue-like members surrounded each one of them, one of which was feeding a flayed lump of raw wet flesh into an open maw. Tulliver noticed scraps of khaki serge uniform hanging from it as a flock of dark green winged creatures gathered round it, squawking and tearing at the offal, like gulls in a trawler's wake.

Filled with disgust and fury, Tulliver worked rudder and stick, threading the machine between the tentacle roots, up towards the swollen cupola above, before letting loose a prolonged burst of machine gun fire, wishing he still had burning tracer bullets left.

The winged creatures turned their attention to the Sopwith as it banked away, swooping down as one, towards the machine, with raucous harridan shrieks.

Maddocks turned the rear machine gun on them as they flew past the tumorous mouth bag.

Tulliver felt a downdraft of warm, foul-smelling air that briefly buffeted the machine as they passed beneath the maws and their writhing tonguedrils.

He had to get away from the damn things before they tore the aeroplane apart. The winged creatures seemed to keep away from the great harvesting tentacles, flocking instead around the mouth things. Perhaps they weren't immune to the juices with which those things dripped.

"Hang on," he bellowed over his shoulder at Maddocks.

Putting the machine into a spin, he went corkscrewing down around a tentacle. Maddocks peered back, to see the scavengers dropping away and returning to easier prey, and once more resuming their mouth-tube squabbles.

Tulliver levelled out, seeing a patch of bright blue sky between the huge sacs above, and put the aeroplane into a steep climb, racing to rise above a monstrous Kreothe, whose size dwarfed the tiny fragile machine.

At it passed from the green twilit world of the Kreothe's underside into the bright glare of the sun, the Strutter's shadow crossed the taut skin of the giant air sac, like a bott fly among a herd of horses – and he was going to bite. Tulliver continued climbing to gain the height he'd need for the attack. Below him now, the tops of the Kreothe were spread out in a landscape of bulbous towering sacs.

Tulliver pushed the Sopwith into a steep dive towards the Kreothe he'd targeted. He loosed a quick burst from his forward facing machine gun. The stream of bullets raked the huge billowing field of skin stretched out below them. Parts of it seemed to deflate, crumpling slowly under the withering fire of the Lewis gun, but the whole did not collapse, suggesting chambers of buoyancy.

He pulled out of his dive and flew along the Kreothe. There was nothing else they could do. They weren't going to bring one of those things down, so, instead, he pulled back on the stick and climbed, just for the sheer exhilaration of it.

The shoal of Kreothe shrank below them, the blue sky expanded to meet them and, briefly, Lieutenant Tulliver felt at home.

IN THE FIRE trench, Sergeant Hobson craned his neck and looked up at the huge translucent fleshy canopies as they passed overhead, went to the storage box and brought out a Very pistol.

"What are you going to do, Sarn't?"

"What am I going to do, Draper? I'm going to give one of those things a *very* nasty surprise."

He fired the flare pistol. The flare arced up into the sky, bursting brightly against the soft moist nodule attached to the under side of a Kreothe air sac.

An involuntary shudder ran through the tentacles that hung below it, and the nodule itself seemed to shrink and contract from the burning white light that seared through the skin.

The men watched from the trench, mesmerised.

"It's shrivelling like your balls on a wiring party, Coxy!"

"Fuck off, Draper."

The great air sac that carried the creature aloft began to burn and wither and, with its buoyancy lost, the Kreothe began to sink slowly, its now limp tentacles dragged along the ground like anchor chains, weighting it down. It descended slowly, like a holed titanic ocean liner, sinking down to its final resting place further up the valley, beyond the trenches.

The other Kreothe, if they knew or cared about the fate of their shoal member, did not react. They drifted by overhead, oblivious to the ruin they left behind, feeding off stragglers from the fleeing herds further up the valley.

THE KREOTHE HAVING drifted on, Edith, Sister Fenton and Padre Rand staggered into camp with the two soldiers, Jones and Miller, that they had managed to save. The pair were now practically comatose.

"Stretcher bearers! Stretcher bearers!" called the Padre.

Stretchers were rapidly found and the party ushered across what was left of the encampment, to the Aid Post down in the support trench.

"What have we here?" asked Captain Lippett, his concentration on a man's gashed scalp before him as he threaded a needle through the skin.

"The only two surviving neurasthenia patients, Mr Lippett. They all just walked out in the veldt and waited, waited... to be eaten by those... things," Sister Fenton informed him.

"And these two weren't, eh?"

"We dragged them into a chatt ditch."

"Quick thinking, Sister."

"It was the Padre's idea."

"Good show, Padre."

"Just looking after my flock, doctor."

Lippett looked up at Edith. "I thought that was your job, Nurse Bell. You know the men call you Little Bo Peep, do you?"

He obviously knew she didn't. The remark rankled with Edith. She had got used to being belittled and bullied and she had borne it. She knew her position. But she didn't have to like it. It was funny, but before she came to this world, she would have just taken it meekly and perhaps had a cry to herself later. Now, she felt incensed. She had tried to tell him there was something wrong with them, but he didn't listen, he wasn't interested, not in malingerers, not in cowards. She clenched her fists and felt the nails bite into her palms. She stepped forwards. Doctor or no doctor –

"Nurse!" It was Miller. He was looking in horror at Jones, who had begun fitting on his stretcher, his spine arching, his hips bucking.

"Right, get him into the aid post, we'll have to try and relieve the pressure in those cysts," said Lippett, all airs and graces vanishing in an instant. "Stanton, prepare the equipment, come on, man."

As Lippett set about his operation, Sister Fenton gave Edith a look. "A word, Nurse." She led Edith away from the Aid Post.

"Two!" said Edith through gritted teeth, doing her best to contain her anger. "Two out of twenty seven. We could have saved them if Mr Lippett had listened to me in the first place, if he had the slightest –"

"You can't know that."

"He didn't even try."

Sister Fenton fixed her with a hard stare, one that said she would brook no nonsense. "Nurse Bell. I will deal with this. I'm sure I don't have to tell you this isn't a hospital. We don't have the facilities of a hospital. We don't even have the supplies of a Casualty Clearing Station or an Ambulance train. God knows, those would seem like luxuries here. The drugs, the surgical procedures, the medicines. We are all doing the best we can. This place brings illnesses, infections, things we've never seen before, and without the benefits that modern medicine has to offer. What more could we have done?"

"But Sister," Edith protested.

"Nurse Bell!"

But Edith could no more keep quiet now than a whizz bang, or she felt she would explode. "I will not let a man like that dismiss –"

Sister Fenton interrupted. "You're letting Driver Abbott's suffrage go to your head. Mr Lippett is a qualified doctor.

You're a VAD. You've had, what, six months' basic medical training? It wasn't all that long ago you were just emptying bedpans and changing dressings. By all means, note and report your observations of your patients to me, and I will do what I can, but do not suppose to tell him what to do. Do I make myself clear?"

Edith could barely trust herself to speak. "Yes, Sister," she managed to mutter.

SOMETIME LATER, DRAINED and blood stained, Captain Lippett came out of the tent and approached the nurses. He shook his head. "He's dead, I'm afraid. Died on the table."

Edith struggled to restrain her emotions and choked back a sob. Sister Fenton remained impassive.

"If it's any comfort, the other one you brought in, Miller, is still alive." Lippett finished wiping his hands. "Though it appears you were right, Nurse Bell. They were more than just neurasthenic," he added with a trace of resentment. "Come and see." He ushered them into the tent. Edith entered, wary of what she might find. Jones' body was still on the table, covered by a bloody sheet. "They were host to some sort of parasitic infection," Lippett continued. "Fascinating things. I managed to remove some of them from the intestines."

He showed them a steel surgical tray. A thing, smaller than Edith's little finger, lay in a pool of blood. At first glance, its small delicate-looking grey body seemed ribbed, but on closer inspection, Edith realised it was corkscrewed. It looked gruesome enough as it was, but to imagine it *inside*? She suppressed a shudder. Her real horror, however, was reserved for the small head. The body tapered toward it. It was eyeless. Needle sharp hooks, as fine as fish bones, surrounded an oral sucker. As she tore her attention away from the thing she realised Lippett was still talking.

"...it's an intriguing pathology. Although most of them remained in the gut, I found a cluster of them curled round the brain stem, from where it seems they can affect the nervous system of the host," he was saying.

"Making them do things against their will?" asked Edith, her face crumpled with disgust.

"It appears so. The hosts acting against their own best interest for the parasites' benefit. It would certainly explain the patients' uncharacteristic behaviour. From the reports, I believe a number of chatts were affected, too," said Lippett, getting to grip with his subject. "I suspect that they might be the parasite's natural hosts. As hive insects, they probably have weaker individual minds. As for the neurasthenics, perhaps their weakened mental state made them more susceptible to the parasites' control. From what you've witnessed, I'd hazard a guess that the parasite's life cycle required it to be eaten by those Kreothe creatures,"

"Like tapeworms?" enquired Sister Fenton.

"Quite," said Lippett with enthusiasm. "Of course, this is only an *initial* theory. I shall continue to study the creatures – and we still have Miller."

Edith opened her mouth to say something, but was silenced by a stern glance from Sister Fenton.

"For now, our first course of action is to trace the infection back to its source," said Lippett, looking at the nurses expectantly.

"We've had no reports of strange behaviour from any of the other men," said Sister Fenton. "It must have been something specific to the neurasthenics."

Lippett nodded in agreement. "Perhaps something the men ate in the past week. It would have contained the eggs which the patients would have ingested. Once in the digestive tract, they hatched and grew into their juvenile forms. Some would have bored into the bloodstream and travelled round the body until they reached the brainstem."

Edith's face burned with shock. "Oh," she said. She was going to say more, but Sister had only just berated her for presuming too much with Doctor Lippett.

Sister Fenton raised an eyebrow as Edith turned to look at her. "Yes, Nurse Bell?"

"The stew," Edith explained.

"I beg your pardon?" said Lippett.

"The stew, Doctor. I didn't know. Honestly."

"It seems none of us did, nurse. Did anybody else eat any of it? Did you?"

Edith shook her head emphatically. "No, it was specifically for the patients. Although..."

"Yes, Nurse?"

Edith put her hand to her mouth. "Lieutenant Mathers. I remember Nellie saying he had some, a small amount I'm sure."

"Mathers?" queried Lippett.

"The Tank Commander," said Sister Fenton.

"Well, I'm sure he's in little danger. I mean it's not as if he's one of Nurse Bell's little lost sheep, is he?"

THE TWILIGHT OF the Kreothe passed and, in dribs and drabs, the soldiers climbed once more out from their dark holes into the alien sun.

Everson sighed. He stood looking at the flagpole, which was now leaning at a precarious angle, knocked by a careless Kreothe tentacle. The Union flag flapped and fluttered weakly, like an ailing dog, still wagging its tail at its master's approach.

It put Everson in mind of the leaning Madonna and Child at Albert, in France. It had stood atop the basilica there until it had been bombed. The statue survived, but leaning at an angle. It was thought that if it fell, the war would end. If only things were that simple.

Several small nearby copses had been uprooted, but in the shelter of another, the three captured battlepillars survived unharmed. Maybe, thought Everson, because the Kreothe found them unpalatable. Still, the Kreothe's loss might be their gain.

"Ever have one of those days, sir?" asked Hobson.

"Nothing but, Sergeant. Nothing bloody but."

"So, what do we do now, sir?"

"Now, Hobson?" he said, looking around at the carnage and sighing heavily. "We start again." And not for the first time, Everson's mind turned to Atkins and his black hand gang and to that damned tank. Where were they?

CHAPTER FIFTEEN
"The Better 'Ole..."

"HELL!" GROWLED ATKINS in frustration. "We'll have to go in after them."

"But they're not even our mob," objected Porgy.

Atkins looked at him. "Yes. Yes, they are. They're British Army, like us. We're all we have. We're in a hole, Porgy. If we don't stick together, if we don't look out for each other, we'll end up like those poor old sods we found back there, unknown, unmourned and forgotten, without even a decent grave. That's not a fate I intend to suffer. I intend to survive and get back home, Gutsy. I made that promise on the Somme and I'm making that promise here and, by God, I'm going to keep it. If Lieutenant Everson says we need that tank, then we need the tank – and that means we need its bloody crew, too. God knows what kind of trouble they'll get into in there, led by that madman..."

Gutsy nodded his head. "We're with you, Only." He turned round to the rest of the section. "You heard the Corporal, lads. Battle order."

The rest of 1 Section took off their packs, leaving themselves only their webbing with ammo and grenade pouches, and gas mask bags at their chest. They checked their rifle magazines and cycled the bolts so there was one in the spout, ready.

"What about me?" asked Nellie, planting herself obstinately

in front of Atkins. "They might get hurt, so I'm not staying here."

Atkins had learned his lesson where Nellie Abbott was concerned. "No, I didn't think you would," he said, with a trace of a smile. He nodded towards the Section's urman guide, who was cutting lengths of branches with his curved sword and wrapping them with some dried mossy substance to use as torches. "Stick with Napoo."

Prof and Chalky had started to make their own torches, cutting at a little grove of saplings. Saplings with a black bark with silver-grey veins. Nellie frowned. They were familiar...

"No!" she yelled, lifting her skirt and running towards them as they hacked away at the slender trunks. "No, stop. That's corpsewood. It'll kill you!"

Hearing the name, Napoo whirled round and raced across the glade, knocking the cut wood from the Tommies' hands. "She speaks true. It will drain you of your life to keep its own."

The men backed away from the saplings as if they'd been bitten – which they very nearly had.

"Ruddy hell, Chalky," joshed Mercy. "I can't turn me back on you for five minutes without you getting into some trouble or other."

Chalky shrugged sheepishly, and smiled gratefully at Nellie.

Prof shuddered. "Corpsewood?" He backed away in horror and stood in the clearing, looking round, like a spooked horse, not daring to move as if everything around might be the death of him.

"Hey, it's all right, Prof," said Nellie. "You're safe now. You scared me, is all. I'd just seen it before, what it can do."

"I don't think you're helping," said Gazette, looking up from checking his rifle one more time.

"You aren't, neither," retorted Nellie. "If I want your opinion, I'll ask the Corporal."

The rest of the section laughed and jeered. Nellie ignored them and turned her attention back to Prof. She knew that haunted look. She'd seen it in soldiers' eyes before.

"Corpsewood," Prof kept muttering to himself, shaking his head, "corpsewood."

A GENTLE DRAUGHT blew from the cavernous opening as they approached the main entrance of the edifice. Roots and boughs were woven round and embedded in the wall of the doorway until they formed a jamb, roots thrusting buttress-like into the ground, but the great bark-like doors, that would have sealed the edifice, had long since dried and shrivelled as the door plant itself had died, leaving the cavernous entrance open. Other vegetation had taken advantage of the fact, clinging to the walls and invading the fallow spaces beyond. Great hanging carpets of plum-coloured shrubbery tumbled down from cracks in the edifice wall.

As they stood on the threshold, Atkins paired the men up; one man with their rifle and bayonet at the ready, accompanied by one holding a torch. Gazette walked with Pot Shot, Porgy with Chalky, Mercy with Prof. Gutsy, gun shouldered, held Little Bertha, his meat cleaver, in his hand, the flames of the torches reflecting off its polished surface. Napoo and Nellie Abbott brought up the rear. Atkins kept an eye on Chandar.

The chatt sank down on its legs and moved reluctantly. Atkins had half expected it to make a break for it and run. It could have fled, but something kept it with them; against its better judgement, as far as he could tell.

"So, what is this place," he asked. "It's an edifice, right? Made by your people?"

Chandar craned its neck, looked up at the outer wall of the ruined edifice towering above them and hissed. "It is a colony of lost Ones."

Atkins' eyes narrowed. "You knew about this place?"

"Not exactly," rasped Chandar. "Of places like this."

"So, what is it, some mythical missing colony?"

"No, you misunderstand. It happens that once every so often a new queen hatches, while one still rules. It is a time of great regret.

Usually the colony's current queen and her nursery entourage kill them, but some survive to attract followers from among the Dhuyumirrii, scentirrii and Djamirrii. We have had such divisions at Khungarr, though many generations ago. If they are strong enough they can replace the old queen, but more often than not, they are killed or driven from the colony and must attempt to start a new one if they are to survive. The difficulty lies in where they can do this, for the ancient scent texts tell us that GarSuleth divided the world between all his children. The world is spoken for. Judging from the size of this edifice it was a small one and could not sustain itself. It also sits within the Zohtakarrii burri."

"The chatts that attacked us?"

"Yes. Because of this One's injuries, they thought that this One was outcast from Khungarr. This One let them think that. If they had known that this One was not, then we would have been killed. They seemed to show very great interest in you."

"As I recall, so did you lot."

"Agreed."

"How *did* you get your injuries?" asked Atkins, his curiosity piqued.

"This One once tried to challenge Sirigar in open ceremonial debate and paid for it, as you can see." Chandar opened its arms, inviting Atkins to study its body.

Atkins looked at the chatt with its hobbled gait and broken antennae. "Sirigar did this to you?"

"Sirigar's followers did, before this One had a chance to challenge Sirigar, no doubt under that One's instructions."

Atkins let the matter drop, he had more pressing problems right now. "So this place is nothing special."

"No, it is merely a failed colony."

Atkins regarded Chandar with suspicion. "So, if this place doesn't worry you, what does? You mentioned these Zohtakarrii guarding something that isn't there. It obviously isn't this because it's quite clearly here. I can see it. What is it you're not telling me, Chandar? Do you know what that thing is in there, this evil spirit? Is it Croatoan?"

Chandar hissed at the mention of the name. "No, by GarSuleth's Breath, this One does not know. This One merely feared what it *might* be."

This was getting him nowhere. Atkins waved the others on, and they walked into the cool cavernous gloom of the derelict, rubble-strewn antechamber.

"Here would have been the work area," Chandar said. "Here the djamirrii, the workers, would have brought and sorted their harvest before taking it to storage chambers or the fungus farms." The chatt looked around at the desolate place it had become. "All colony life was here."

Their feet stirred the dust and debris that had fallen from the chamber roof. The once smooth walls were now home to invasive creepers that poured in round the opening. A shaft of sunlight falling inside the main door cast a suffuse reflective glow across the rest of the chamber. Here and there, they saw the brittle, dried up husks of long dead chatt bodies, their outlines softened by decades of drifting dust, as if overcome by some long-forgotten catastrophe.

Atkins pushed on into the gloom beyond the penumbra of sunlight, at least knowing that the end of this mission was in sight. All they had to do was kill the creature that had gone to ground here and they could return to the encampment. They had rifles, Mills bombs; they even had a couple of flares. If that lot failed, they had the tank. They could blow this entire ruin sky high if they had to. Either way, it ended today. After that, Mathers was Lieutenant Everson's problem.

There were several tunnels leading off the antechamber. Napoo knelt and examined the dust on the floor, while Nellie held the torch for him. It was easy to spot the footprints left by the tank crew. "This way," he said, leading them across the dusty floor. The party fell in behind him, bayonets at the ready. Atkins looked back at the bright entrance, the hard outlines softened by translucent hanging fronds and back-lit by the sun, and turned back to face the dark. He shuddered. He hated these places.

The tunnel they entered sloped up perceptibly. Roots and creepers had slithered on in advance of them long ago, affixing themselves to the floor and walls, and they had to watch their footing. Eventually the tunnel began to level out. Their torch flames guttered in a soft breeze.

In places, the luminescent lichen, that Chandar told them used to sit in niches lighting the passages, had grown wild and unkempt, giving an opalescent glow to the tunnels.

Here though, the trail was lost. Something had swept along these tunnels so frequently there was no dust trail left to follow. It must be the creature, Atkins realised. There was a hardened black sheen to the walls here, as if the oily residue it left behind had dried. There was no way of telling which of the branching passages the tank crew had taken.

They moved cautiously along a passage. The further they went without incident, the more anxious Atkins became.

Openings yawned in the passage walls. They all had to be checked out. Some were adjoining tunnels, others chambers, empty and bare.

Porgy thrust his torch into another room as they passed, while Chalky lunged forwards in an "on guard" stance with his bayonet. Holding the torch high, lighting the gloom with a flickering orange glow, Porgy cast a glance around the small chamber. There was another passage exiting on the far side. He edged across the room and along the short passage beyond, holding out his torch to illuminate a second chamber.

"Jesus, Mary and Joseph! Only, you'd better come and take a look at this!"

THE TANK CREW had no idea where they were, but they followed Mathers, who seemed to know which way he was going. They didn't need torches. They could see well enough, thanks to the synesthetic petrol fruit fumes that now flooded their bloodstreams. Their footsteps produced colours and flavours that rippled down the chatt-made circular tunnels.

Mathers led them deeper into the labyrinthine tunnels of the ruin, taking switches and junctions without a second's pause until, deep in the ruined edifice, they came to an empty chamber. Alfie could not see anything remarkable about the chamber, there was nothing to indicate why they might have stopped here.

"This will do," said Mathers. "We don't want any interruptions."

The crew turned to Alfie. Their looks were not pleasant.

Alfie edged back towards the chamber entrance, but the others surrounded him. "What's all this in aid of?" he croaked. "I thought we were going to kill this evil spirit, this devil."

"We are, but first we have some business to attend to," said Mathers. "You."

"Me, sir?"

Alfie felt a surge of fear drive into his limbs, ready for flight. Too late. Frank and Norman seized him by the arms and held them out at his sides, as if he were being crucified. He struggled but they held him fast.

"Sorry, old bean," said Reggie, with a weak, apologetic smile. "It's for the best."

"I don't understand, sir. What have I done? What have I done to any of you? I've followed your orders, sir. I've helped keep the tank running. I've kept your secrets."

Mathers shook his head in disappointment. His voice was calm. "True. You are with us, as you have been since Elveden. Your mind, however, is... elsewhere."

Without effort, Alfie's thoughts turned to Nellie. Was that it? Was that what all this was about?

Mathers stepped towards him. Bruise-coloured auras rose from his mates on the convection currents of their own body heat, and collected gently in the dome of the chamber above their heads.

He looked up at Mathers, who now stood over him in his rain cape, the leather and chainmail mask inscrutable. "Sir, what're you doing?"

Mathers nodded. Frank and Norman forced Alfie to his knees, still holding his arms out straight at his sides. "I'm offering you a chance to recant, Perkins, a chance to rejoin the fold, as it were."

"But I never left, sir."

"You're forgetting, Perkins. I can *see* you. You're confused, afraid. You have to let go."

Mathers nodded at Wally.

The cockney stood behind Alfie and pulled his head back with a hand on his forehead.

Alfie continue to struggle, but to no avail. "No! Whatever you're doing, sir... don't!"

Mathers reached under his rain cape and retrieved his hip flask. He took the top off. Alfie felt Wally's calloused fingers on his nose and briefly smelled the cigarette-stained tips before they pinched his nostrils shut. Alfie struggled, refusing to open his mouth. Mathers stood and waited patiently. The moment Alfie opened his mouth to gasp for air he poured the petrol fruit down his throat.

"Receive the Sacrament of Skarra," he said, in reverent tones.

Alfie coughed and spluttered, but Wally clamped his hand over his mouth until he swallowed. He felt the spirit burn down the back of his throat, bringing tears to his eyes.

Then his world exploded.

Frank and Norman let go of Alfie, and the gearsman slumped back on his heels. Briefly, the world was afire, all his senses screaming. The chamber was a shifting kaleidoscope of unnameable colours, bringing vertigo and nausea. Unfathomable shapes of sound danced at the periphery of his vision. He paused, dry-retching. He took deep breaths, one hand braced against the floor, until the vertigo passed. Like a newly struck Lucifer, the initial flare of sensation died down and the world settled, more or less, but brighter and keener than before, as the undiluted petrol fruit coursed through his system.

"You *see* the world the way I do," he heard Mathers say, or was that smell? "Transubstantiated by the grace of Skarra."

He looked towards the taste of Mathers' voice as he stood over him holding out a hand. Alfie reached out, took it, and found himself hauled to his feet through a dizzying wave of vertigo. It took a moment for his new world to reorient itself.

Alfie looked round and *saw* Mathers. And he saw the things *within* Mathers. The Lieutenant put a finger to his chainmail, where his lips were. The meaning was clear. *Shhh.*

WITHOUT A TORCH, Atkins edged cautiously down the dark passage, towards Porgy's light, emerging into another, larger chamber.

He drew an involuntary gasp at the tableau he found there. Around the chamber were four mummified human corpses; dry, taut skin stretched thinly over bone, brittle hair still attached to the skulls, perfectly preserved in the arid atmosphere of the edifice. It was clear from their sizes that they might be a family. Two small bodies, children, lay in a crude moss-stuffed mattress on the floor, clinging to each other, as if in their sleep. One was a boy, dressed in a nightshirt, the other, a girl, in a dress. The body of a man, sat on a rough chair, slumped over a makeshift table constructed of rough-hewn planks. He was dressed in a shirt and trousers, with braces. The remains of a once full and bushy beard now straggled wispily from his chin. On the table was an oil lamp. The body of a woman lay sprawled on the floor, as if trying to drag herself towards the children. Her hair was tied in a bun at the back of her scalp and she wore an ankle-length skirt and a blouse. The skirt and dirty white underskirt had ridden up to expose the shrunken and desiccated legs and feet still laced in worn leather boots.

A dark and terrifying thought began to uncoil in Atkins' mind. His mouth went dry, and he suddenly found it hard to breathe, as if all the air in the chamber had been sucked away. It felt as if he were standing on the edge of a vertiginous black chasm.

Porgy came back from a brief exploration of further

chambers beyond that one. "There are three more chambers like this one. Bodies in each of 'em."

"Like these?" Atkins said in a hoarse croak, his mouth dry with fear.

"Yes, poor buggers."

He felt his stomach screwed into a knot, as tight as that he felt when about to go over the top. A cold sweat broke out all over his body, chilling him. He shivered as he numbly followed Porgy into the next chamber; he could hear the pulse of blood in his ears, and his heart beat loudly in his chest, straining to burst out of his ribcage.

Beyond them, in the next chamber, Mercy held the torch high so he could see. Here was another group of people. On one side of the chamber were two bodies laid out and covered with sacking sheets. They had obviously died before the others and been laid out with the respect due to the dead. The other body had not. It belonged to a woman wearing a small white cap on her head, wisps of ginger hair escaping from underneath it over her brown, parchment-like skin. The body was sat slumped against a wall on another mattress, a tartan blanket covering her legs. Shadows cast by the torch danced in her sockets and her lips were drawn back, exposing rotten teeth. Her skeletal fingers were covered with a translucent film of skin, and they lay over a black object that sat on the blanket in her lap.

Atkins squatted down, his hands trembling, as he gently tried to pull the object from her hands. He winced as a finger snapped off, but retrieved the object. Covered in black leather, it was a book; embossed in gold on the front were the words *Holy Bible*. He opened it up. There was writing on the fly page in a neat copperplate hand. *"This gift is of Ichabod Wallace to his beloved daughter Eliza on the occasion of her marriage to James Edwin Bleeker, April 1832."*

These were no urmen. These were humans, from Earth.

Atkins staggered back to the first chamber in a daze. Unlike him, the others hadn't quite grasped the significance yet.

"The poor little things," Nellie said, as she draped a blanket over their small frames.

"Blimey, even you couldn't get much meat off this lot, Gutsy," Gazette said.

"Maybe not," he replied, "But my wife would damn well try and sell 'em if she could. Don't let a scrap go to waste, she don't."

Gazette took in the butcher's ample frame. "So, every little bit gets used, does it?" he asked, with a wink, indicating Gutsy's trousers.

"Get away!" said Mercy. "You know what they say about butchers' wives, only the best cuts for them, am I right, Gutsy?"

Gutsy replied with a lecherous grin and a wink, "Oh, aye, lad."

Nellie gave a discreet, lady-like cough. It had more power than a dozen barking NCOs and resulted in a muttered chorus of embarrassed apologies.

Chandar was in its element. To the chatt, this was a treasure trove of urmen artefacts. It hardly knew where to start. It had learnt, though, not to touch the bodies, however much it might desire to.

"Here," said Porgy sombrely. "This was on the table."

It was a journal. Atkins leafed through the diary, taking in snatches of information like a hungry man tearing at bread.

They were a party of pioneers from Oak Springs, Illinois in the United States, emigrants under the captaincy of Edwin Bleeker, travelling west on the California Trail looking for a new life in California. It seemed that they, like the British Empire, felt they had a 'manifest destiny.' There were eighty-six people in the party and fifty-four wagons pulled by oxen and horses. They had made it to the frontier and Independence, Missouri, where, in March 1846, they started the two thousand mile trek that would take them north towards the Great Salt Lake along the California Trail.

Atkins didn't understand the geography, but at some point, there had been an argument as to which way the overlanders should proceed. Oh, there were names he recognised from old *Western Adventure* story magazines – Chimney Rock, Fort

Laramie – but the rest meant nothing. Having made it to the Rock Independence in late June 1846, where the travellers had carved their names, they set off again. More names: Fort Bridger, Sheep Rock, Devil's Gate, Salt Lake.

A guide they had picked along the way, one Barnaby Witger, advocated a short cut, the Campbell Cut-off through the Wasatch Mountains, and across the Great Salt desert towards the Humbolt River.

From the earliest diary entries, it was clear it wasn't an easy journey, between exhausted oxen, broken axels, and deaths from cholera.

Right now, though, the events on Earth were of little importance to him. His hands shook as he looked for entries telling of their arrival here, in this place, on this world.

He flicked forwards until he found it. August 14th 1846. He skimmed through from there.

August 14th. Today a fog descended as we made our way. We lit lamps but we could barely see the wagon in front of us. It was decided we would stop and wait for the fog to lift before we continued, but we were afflicted with a violent nausea and many of our party began bleeding from ears, nose and mouth...

A violent vertigo drove our oxen to their knees...

Louisa May Franklin fell from the wagon and under the wheels...

Lukas Bergen's compass no longer works. We cannot tell North from South.

...when the fog did clear the sight that met our eyes was not one we expected. Some say we must have taken a wrong turning and that we should turn back and retrace our steps, but we can find no landmarks.

...the night sky is passing strange and affords no familiarity...

He read on...

August 16th. Foul demonic beasts descended on our wagons, mauling and killing most of our oxen, dragging them away. They overturned the Marchants' wagon, breaking William Marchant's leg...

August 17th. This place is a hell. Hourly we cursed Campbell and Witger's names. The Campbell Cut-off has cost us dearly. Today we lost three dear children, stolen away by winged creatures...

August 24th. William Marchant died today of an ungodly infection to his leg. We made a coffin and buried him.

September 3rd. We have found shelter, an abandoned ruin in the woods. It is better than the wagons, which we had to abandon. We could not get them through the trees...

September 9th. Isaiah Walker led a party of twelve to find help.

Dear God, the people lasted barely three months in this place. He turned the page and turned back again. There were pages missing, torn out; over an entire month, gone. He turned to the last entries, a panic rising in his chest.

October 13th. We ate the last of our surviving oxen today...

November 19th. Last night, my dear George passed away of a terrible fever. He was delirious and did not know me. The Hollands died yesterday in fearful agony. I fear that if Isaiah Walker does not return soon he will come too late. May the Almighty preserve us and see our souls safely to Paradise.

Atkins closed the book. Feeling light-headed, he shoved the diary at Mercy and staggered from the chamber. Mercy said something, but he didn't hear it. The world had shrunk, pressing in on him, constricting him. He shoved his way past the damn chatt, which was clicking at him. He needed air. He stumbled out into the dark of the passage and felt some small relief from the cool breeze that blew along it.

The Pennines were not the first humans to find themselves here. But after what they had just found, the thought brought little or no comfort to Atkins now. Those people had *died* here. They died *here*. There was no way home. It was a one-way trip. Everything he had clung to had been washed away. He felt bereft, adrift.

Gutsy called out from back up the passage, "Only, are you okay? It's just that Mercy said you seemed a bit windy."

"A bit windy?" said Atkins, with a sardonic laugh. "Ha, that's a good one." He wiped away the tears with the coarse serge sleeve of his tunic. He welcomed the rasping pain on his eyelids and cheeks. "I bloody well funked it, Gutsy. I funked it."

"It happens to the best, Only, you know that," said Gutsy, walking towards him. "What matters is you pick yourself up, get yourself back on the fire step."

"Yes, because that worked so bloody well for Ginger, didn't it?"

"Ginger had mates. So do you."

"There's no point, no bloody point. There's no way home, Gutsy. I promised I'd look after Flora, but you saw yourself, there *is* no way home."

"Flora? Your brother's fiancé? Very noble sentiment, is that. You're to be commended."

"No, you don't understand."

"Oh, for God's sake, Only. You're not the only person to have lost people! We all have family and loved ones back in Blighty. Do you think you're the only one who doesn't feel sick looking up at the stars? Do you think you're the only one who doesn't wake with a start in the middle of the night with their name on your lips? Do you? D'you think you're the only one whose heart breaks with every dawn we see here? We're all in the same hole here, Only. If you know of a better one, go to it!" Gutsy sighed, shook his head sympathetically and softened his tone. "Look, whatever's going on in your head, you need to sort it. Box it up, put it away. If your head's not here, you're going to get yourself killed. You're going to get *us* killed. And I'm not going to die because *you've* got a broken heart."

Atkins looked at him and nodded. There was nothing more to be said. Together, they walked back to the chambers.

When they got there, Mercy had the diary open in his hands. Atkins could tell from the stunned, downcast faces of the men around him that they had all heard the contents of the journal. Even Chandar seemed aware that something had happened, even if it wasn't sure what. Atkins looked at each of the men in turn. "We can tell no one of this. We must keep this secret. Can you imagine what would happen to morale if the rest of the battalion find out? It would tear it apart."

The rest of the section shuffled uncomfortably. They knew, right enough.

"No," said Atkins decisively. "We keep this a secret between ourselves for now." He looked at Nellie. "Not even the tank crew are to know. We tell Lieutenant Everson and no one else, and he can decide what to do with this information. Is that understood?"

There was a muttered agreement.

"Good. Now let's do right by these folk."

Salvaging only the family bible and the journal, they used a grenade and blew the entrance to seal the chamber, burying the families within and burying, in their own hearts, a little of the hopes each of them had nurtured of getting home again.

INTERLUDE FIVE
Letter from Private Thomas Atkins
to Flora Mullins

21ˢᵗ March 1917

Dearest Flora,

Today has been a black day. Today I fear I have lost you for good. I will never see you again, never hold you in my arms, and never hear your laughter again. The scent on your last letter has faded now and is lost to me forever. Perhaps it was an omen.

For all the months I have been here, I have held onto the fact that one day, one day soon, I will return to you. If I can't do that, I

CHAPTER SIXTEEN
"All the Sunshine Turns to Gloom..."

As THE MEN of 1 Section continued their search for the tank crew, the mood that seized them was a sombre one, akin to those moments before the whistle blew and they went over the top. Under the burden of the new secret they carried, each man was momentarily adrift, alone on a sea of his own thoughts. If they had lucky charms they sought them out now in the privacy of the semi-dark catacombs.

"Oh, Christ, we're really stuck here. We're never going to get home," moaned Chalky.

"And we're stuck here with you, but you don't hear us moan about it," said Porgy.

Prof, who could usually be counted on to chivvy Chalky along, had sunk into a morose silence.

Nellie tried to cheer the young lad up. For all that these men were soldiers, some were little more than boys. "Shhh. Don't say that. You don't know that."

Atkins chalked another wall to mark their way and turned to the sweating butcher by his side. "Chalky's right, Gutsy."

"Maybe he is and maybe he isn't, but there's no need to say it. How many times has a man thought that in the trenches? And what good has it ever done him?"

"Aye, but there, home was only a Blighty one away, Gutsy. Now..." he left the sentence hanging.

How did Lieutenant Everson do it, wondered Atkins? How did he marshal his own fears, which must have been the same as any man's, and yet be able to go down the line and dispense encouragement and fortitude?

Atkins felt he had nothing left to give. He was empty. Empty of zeal, empty of heart. Empty of hope. Yet again, this world had ripped the wind from his sails. He was completely sapped. It was like wading though a quagmire of Somme mud, when concentrating on putting one foot in front of the other was almost too much, and some men allowed themselves to be sucked under and drowned, rather than fight against it to take another step.

Maybe he deserved this. What if this was his punishment? Had his indiscretion with Flora finally reached the ears of God? For a moment, self-loathing rose up within him. This place was now his purgatory, and on some level he welcomed it, embraced it. Whatever it threw at him he would endure, the penitent Fusilier.

They moved on through a honeycomb of passages, threading their way through tunnels, traversing chambers and inclines where ancient, inhuman passages branched and branched again, leading to dead ends and roof falls. Piles of rubble and debris made some corridors impassable; thick infestations of plants, weeds and roots choked others. There was, however, still no sign of either the tank men, or whatever haunted these earthen halls. Only the odd, discordant piping notes from the few air vents not choked with weeds broke the silence.

"Mathers!" Atkins called at intervals, hoping for a reply. "Mathers!" The place was a labyrinth. Even supposing they heard him, they might never find him.

Chandar wandered alongside, ostensibly as a guide, but scent-blind as it was, it seemed just as lost and disorientated as the men and just as unwilling to be there. Atkins regarded the chatt with repugnance. Its featureless ivory white face plate and rasping monotone voice revealed nothing of its own feelings. It toyed with the tasselled knots of its shoulder throw, its stunted middle limbs clicking together lightly. Nerves? Impatience? Who knew? Atkins pressed on, deliberately trying to ignore it. He hated the fact that this creature was somehow drawn to him, that this Kurda thing had somehow bound them together in its eyes. Well, not this soldier, no sir. He wasn't beholden to this creature.

The incline levelled out and they came upon a small rubble-strewn concourse that once might have been a major thoroughfare. Various passages and chambers ran off it. Haphazard shafts of sunlight punctured the gloom from collapsed roof sections above, the holes draped lazily with questing vines and roots.

Atkins spotted a doorway, ornately inscribed with chatt hieroglyphs round the entrance. He'd seen one like it in Khungarr.

"The chambers of their Anointed Ones," Chandar said, making its deferential gesture, touching the tips of its long fingers to its forehead and thorax.

It was their temple. He nodded to Gutsy, who ordered the section to cover the other entrances to the concourse. Gazette, Pot Shot and Prof took up positions using what rubble there was as cover. They didn't want to be caught out by whatever haunted this place.

"Hold this position, Gutsy. I'll check this out. Porgy, Chalky, Mercy, with me. The rest of you stay here. Napoo, stay out here with Miss Abbott."

Atkins and Porgy entered first, Chalky just behind, holding the torch high above his head. The great domed chamber was twenty yards across, but in comparison to the great one at Khungarr, this was a country chapel. Several openings led off the main chamber and Porgy and Chalky covered them with their rifles as Atkins and Mercy slowly circled the room, checking each of them in turn.

The first went several yards before a roof fall blocked it. The second curved round the outer wall of the chamber, at a steep incline, before debris blocked it, too.

"Well, Mathers didn't come this way," said Mercy.

They retraced their steps back down to the sacred chamber. Chalky held up his torch. Above, on the domed ceiling, Atkins caught sight of a broken pattern of lines and dots, the remains of a painted fresco, the rest of which had crumbled from the ceiling. From the patches left, it looked like a night-time sky marked with constellations.

"The sky web of GarSuleth," hissed Chandar. The chatt grabbed Atkins' arm and pulled him back. Chunks of the ceiling had fallen down. They lay on the floor under a sifting of dust that crunched under his feet. "Watch where you walk," it chattered, after its asthmatic fashion. "The representation of the sky web is still sacred, whether on the ceiling or in pieces on the floor. Stepping on it is blasphemy."

Around the walls of the circular chamber, there were niches that looked as if they might have held statues. Each was empty but for hieroglyphs that covered the surfaces in whorls and spirals, some separate, some interlinked.

The chatt hobbled eagerly over to the alcoves, avoiding the fallen chunks of fresco. Stepping into one and facing the wall, its long fingers traced the inscriptions with light, rapid touches, before moving to the next.

"Well?" asked Atkins with impatience.

"If it's anything like our trenches it'll be rude jibes about the last mob," observed Porgy.

"The niches contain sacred texts for contemplation and prayer. The glyphs on the wall between seem to be a history of this colony. They called themselves the Nazarrii. This One was aware of such splinter colonies, but never thought to see one. They did not act in Kurda. If a false queen and her retinue escaped, all mention of them would be expunged from the colony's records. It would be as if they had never existed. They were outcast. Even among Khungarr's aromatic annals there were but the vaguest references to such dishonourable incidents and then only in far gone spira."

"He's actually happy about this," Gutsy commented.

"Well, he's about the only bleedin' one," said Mercy. "The place fair gives me the willies, it does."

It was true. The incessant piping tone from the air vents soon began to grate on their nerves, like the whistling of whizz bangs.

Chandar moved to a section of wall between niches. "At first, all went well, but the Queen fell prey to a grave sickness. Large numbers of eggs were laid to become workers but they were born malformed." It paused and clicked its mandibles. "Such a sickness also affects the Queens of Khungarr."

"Tell me about it. We saw some of those things in the Khungarr nursery. Ugly buggers. Haunted my dreams for bloody weeks, those things did," said Mercy, with an affected shudder.

"This One thought Khungarr alone in suffering such a curse," hissed Chandar, moving to the next section. "The Nazarrii began to fail within the first few generations. There were not enough healthy workers hatched to sustain the colony's growth and expansion."

"So the place was doomed?"

"Without workers, it could not succeed."

"I thought your mob used urmen slaves."

"It is true. GarSuleth provided."

"Well, that's one way of looking at it," said Porgy.

"But it seemed that it was GarSuleth's will that this colony fail." Chandar bowed his head towards the wall, and its antennae stumps waved in a wistful fashion. "Here, the script ends. The colony was failing, that is beyond doubt. Even the Nazarrii recognised the fact." It turned to face Atkins. "But something else happened here."

"What?" asked Atkins uneasily.

"The glyphs do not say. Some catastrophe befell the edifice, causing them to abandon the place."

"Or be killed."

"Perhaps the coming of the evil spirit that now dwells here?" Chalky offered.

"Perhaps, yes. There may be so much more here, but so much more information that is lost to this One." Chandar lifted a finger to touch its antennae stumps. "Why would any Ones abandon their edifice? This One does not know. This One cannot read the scent text."

"I can," said a voice from the gloom.

THE MEN OF the section wheeled round, their rifles raised and bolts ratcheted, training their weapons on the opening even as the clipped voice reverberated around the chamber.

Mathers stepped from the shadows, with his crew behind him grinning like jackals.

"Lower your weapons," said Atkins, with a scowl.

"I can read your scent texts," repeated Mathers.

"You, sir?" asked Atkins, barely trying to suppress his sarcasm.

"Yes, Corporal. I am open to so many things, now." He gestured expansively at the darkened vault above them. "I see things. The air here is full of them. My senses are flooded."

"Well, he's flooded with something all right," muttered one of the Fusiliers. "I wouldn't bloody trust him if I were you."

Mathers beckoned. "Perkins will agree with me, won't you, Perkins?"

Alfie Perkins stepped unsteadily out of the gloom, held upright by the big boxer, Tanner, and Atkins saw his eyes; black like oil slicks.

Atkins shook his head. "Not, you, too?" He turned to Mathers. "What have you done?"

The bantam driver sneered. "Oh, he's with us, now, good an' proper."

Reggie smiled apologetically. "Well, he always was. He just didn't know it. Our own doubting Thomas, if you will, until the Sub granted him his own personal Pentecost."

Mathers stepped past Atkins to the wall Chandar had been examining.

Atkins gripped the officer's upper arm. "Why should we trust you, sir?"

Mathers looked down at Atkins' hand, his contemptuous look lost behind his splash mask. His voice was cold and measured. "Let go, *Lance* Corporal. Or I'll have you for striking an officer."

Atkins held his grip long enough for it to border on insubordination and for the pair of them to know it. "How do we know you can do what you say?"

Beneath his mask, Mathers smiled. "Lily of the Valley," he whispered.

Atkins frowned. "What?"

"That was your sweetheart's perfume, wasn't it? On the letter? Lily of the Valley. How else could I know?" He let that sink in for a moment. "Do you trust me now, Corporal?"

Dumbfounded, Atkins released his arm.

"Hm," Mathers added with a satisfied grunt, tugging his tunic sleeve straight as he stepped past Atkins.

He looked at Chandar, the chatt's visage as blank as his own masked features. "You say there are scents here? That's the way you things communicate, isn't it?"

"It is so," said Chandar, watching him carefully, "but urmen cannot read them."

Mathers paused, fished out his hip flask, took a slug, and emptied it. Damn. He upended it and shook the last drops from the rim, through the chainmail into his mouth, then proceeded to do what the chatt thought impossible.

He turned his attention to the wall. He could see the glyphs and the blank, unfilled space. He stood before it and concentrated. He inhaled, slowly and deeply. As he did, faint colours began to permeate the surface of the vacant space, like an after image. There was something here; a scent message impregnated into the wall. With each purposeful breath, the colours grew stronger, and began to take on form in the space between him and the wall, hovering before his eyes, taking a shape he had come to recognise, a base note, on which the whole composition was built, pungent and overwhelming, one of the first words he had learnt in his synesthetic vocabulary.

"Fear," croaked Mathers. "Something is coming." He reeled back as the next aromatic note almost overwhelmed him. "Here!" he gasped. Another stringent note subsumed and washed this one away; a lingering top note that persisted after the others had faded. "Fear. Flee."

"What the hell is that, some kind of warning?" asked Atkins.

Chandar stepped forwards, its mandibles ticking together as it forced the urman words out through its mouth palps. "No, you misunderstand. It is merely history, a few scraps of scent from the past." It turned to Mathers, its clawed middle limbs open, its antennae stumps jerking. "How is this possible? Urmen are scent-blind. How is it that you can decipher the chemical commentaries of the Ones? This is unforeseen, this is beyond wonder."

Mathers threw his arms wide. "It is a gift from Skarra, the gift of tongues."

Chandar let out a long low hiss, but its eyes fell on the empty hip flask in Mathers' hand and it fell silent, lost in thought.

Mathers felt the overwhelming scent of fear from the message rousing him to panic. He felt the urge to flee, and might well have done had not a spasm in his stomach sent him doubling over as ripples of pain washed though him. He rode each agonising wave until they subsided and, with them, the feeling of fear.

"Something, I don't know what, was coming. It arrived. They fled," he said, still panting though the pain.

"That's it?" said Atkins, unimpressed.

Mathers stood, steadying himself against the wall as he pulled himself to his full height. "Can you do better, Corporal?"

"No sir. But we already know about the dulgur."

"*If* that is what they were talking about, Corporal."

A SHOT ECHOED around the chamber. It came from the concourse. "Gutsy, Mercy, stay here. Keep an eye on that lot."

Atkins ran to the opening and peered round, ready for anything. Anything but what he found.

He was greeted by Pot Shot with an anguished looked on his face. "It's Prof."

Prof? Atkins couldn't see with the others gathered around but, as he approached, they parted. Between them he could see a large pile of rubble, and protruding from behind it he could make out a bare right foot. That was all he needed to see.

"Oh, Prof." Atkins groaned. "You stupid sod."

Prof lay slumped against a pile of debris. He had discarded his puttee, boot and sock to one side, his bayonet to the other. The top half of his skull had been blown away and his brains splattered over the rubble behind him. His rifle lay along his chest. Nellie knelt by him, but there was nothing she could do.

"He was sobbing quietly for a while. I thought it best to leave him, then I heard him say 'sorry,'" said Pot Shot. "I never thought –"

Suicide. Not always easy for a soldier. Some just stuck their heads above the parapet and waited for a German sniper. Others, well. The barrel of the Enfield was too long. You couldn't just stick the muzzle in your mouth and use your finger to pull the trigger. You had to take your boot and sock off, then use your big toe instead.

For some of the Tommies, the only thing that kept them going was the fact that they might find a way home. There had been a flurry of suicides when they'd first arrived, and every so often they found another poor bugger who'd found he couldn't take it anymore, in a trench or a dugout. With the discovery of the Bleeker Party came the realisation that that there was no way home, that they were stranded on this hell world. It was just too much.

"You know the routine, Porgy," said Atkins quietly. "Paybook and disc. Redistribute his bombs, rations and ammunition."

Nellie shook her head slowly in disbelief. "Why would he do that?"

Gutsy put a big fatherly arm round her and steered her away from the sight. "He'd just had enough, love. He hasn't been quite the same since Nobby died. I think perhaps finding them emigrants was the last straw. It takes something like that, when you're a long way from home."

Although there was no love lost between them, the tank crew hung back, and gave 1 Section the space to briefly mourn their dead comrade.

It was then Nellie caught sight of Alfie. Her mouth formed a silent 'o' of shock when she saw his eyes, but he shook his head to dissuade her from any action. She relented, reluctantly, and only for the moment.

They piled blocks of rubble and debris over the body, burying Prof where he lay. Chalky muttered a hurried prayer before they moved on.

Atkins was angry now. If it hadn't been for Mathers and his blasted quest, Prof might still be alive. But he had his orders. If they were going to get Mathers and the tank back, they had to kill this blasted creature. Atkins turned to the masked Tank Commander. "Right, let's get this done. Which way, Lieutenant?"

Mathers paused for a moment, considering the options, then pointed to one of the passages leading off the concourse. "That way."

ATKINS AND 1 Section fell in behind him. Mathers nodded, and the tank crew brought up the rear as they began to descend into the edifice's subterranean levels.

Nellie fell back, snatching a chance to talk to Alfie.

"What have they done to you?" she hissed angrily.

"Not here," he begged her. In the dark, his fingers found hers. He squeezed her hand to placate her. "It's all right, it will pass."

She glanced at him with suspicion.

"It'll pass," he reassured her.

Frank gave Alfie a shove from behind. "No fraternising with the enemy."

He let go of her hand, taking comfort in her soft golden glow, as she returned to Napoo's side. She glanced back, searching for reassurance. He offered a smile for her sake.

Small galleries and chambers led off the curved passage at regular intervals. They searched each set. Atkins barely noticed. None of it mattered. It was all dry as dust, and dead, just as they would be. All he could think about was Flora, how he would never see her again. Never smell her perfume again, or see their child growing up. His child. He imagined the life he had lost, married, with the child, little William. He could feel his weight in his arms and smell its hair. See his smile as he recognised him. Gone, all gone.

Atkins became aware that someone was talking to him.

"Only," Gazette was saying. "Chalky's found something. I think you ought to see it."

Atkins looked at Chalky. "Show me."

Emboldened, Chalky took the lead and showed him a tunnel running off the main passage. Chandar accompanied him. Chalky pointed to the far wall of the chamber. "It were down here. I was just checking and saw it glinting in the torch light. There."

Atkins saw the glint on the floor by the wall. He walked over, sank down on his haunches, and picked it up.

"What is it?" asked Chandar.

Attached to a small scrap of bloodstained khaki cloth was a brass button. Atkins examined it, rubbing it clean with the pad of his thumb. There upon the button, in relief, was a bomb, fuse aflame, with crossed rifles and a crown, all cradled in a wreath. It was the crest of the Pennine Fusiliers.

He blinked and looked up at Gazette. "Check your uniform buttons," he said, his voice imbued with a sense of urgency.

After a little fumbling, it became clear that they all had the requisite number.

"It's not from any of us," reported Gutsy.

Atkins hardly dared think it. There was only one man who might have made it this far. One man.

Gutsy stared at him. "Christ, you don't think –"

Atkins nodded. "Jeffries. Who the hell else could it be?"

SKARRA CONTINUED TO mutter in Mathers' head. In the confines of the edifice, his heightened awareness was flooded with new sensory details. The information was pressing in on him and he was powerless to stop it.

"I can see him," said Mathers, taking the bloodstained scrap and staring fixedly at it.

"Who?" asked Atkins.

Mathers waved the button at him. "Jeffries."

The corporal stared at him. "What do you mean?"

"I can *see* him, his scent on it. I should be able to track his scent trail if there is any left to follow."

"You can do that?"

Mathers looked at the chatt. "Skarra tells me I can."

He was aware of the chatt watching him intently as he concentrated on the scrap of cloth. Using the shapes, sounds and textures that danced around it, Mathers was able, with some effort, to draw Jeffries' scent out of the surrounding kaleidoscopic mists. He watched as vaporous tones of purples and reds coalesced and evaporated rapidly around each other, trying to confuse and deceive. They shifted and changed, into blues and yellows, like a snake shedding skin after skin, as it sought to slip beyond even his heightened perception, but he held it fast in his attention. Under the haze of stale, sour human aromas, he had his base note now; that part of a man that was immutable, unchangeable, distinctive. It resolved itself into a thin green thread of scent that he could follow.

He had no doubt that others in his crew, Clegg or Perkins even, who had received such a concentrated dose of petrol fruit juice recently, might see something of what he saw, but they lacked the education, the intuition, to make the connections he was now experiencing.

Fascinated, he began to walk haltingly, following the fragile drifting airborne trail, constantly checking it with the control scent of the khaki scrap. The others followed at a distance. Slowly, he became attuned to it, to the dancing particles of scent, sweat and blood. At first, it was nothing more than a scent echo, a faint trail hanging in the air, then it began to take on a phantasmagorical shape. Indistinct at first, it coalesced into the faint, ethereal figure of an infantry officer. Hardly daring to breathe, he followed the redolent wraith as it continued its journey. It entered a series of chambers. He watched as it crossed to a wall and crouched down, inspecting something there.

Mathers stepped closer to see.

As if sensing him, the wraith turned. Mathers recognised it as Jeffries. It looked directly at him. A disdainful smile spread across its face as it stepped towards him. With the guilty start of an eavesdropper caught red-handed, Mathers cried out and lurched back, out of reach of the apparition as it advanced on him, and lost his concentration.

In that moment, it seemed to him that Jeffries gesticulated and, upon that gesticulation, proceeded to evaporate until there was nothing left of his incorporeal form but a faint drifting trail suspended in the air.

Mathers reeled from the chamber. "He was here. He was reading... something on the wall."

A wave of pain rippled out from his abdomen, through his torso, up his spine and down through his limbs, causing him to double over. He'd been away from the tank for too long. He fumbled for his hip flask. He'd forgotten it was empty. He grunted with frustration and pain, pulling his splash mask and helmet from his head, and sucking in great lungfuls of air. The plaques on his face were now red and livid and his eyes, iridescent swirls on black, seemed unfocused and inhuman.

"Easy sir, I've got you," said Jack Tanner.

Following her instincts, the FANY approached the group, her eyes catching Alfie's as she passed. "Let me help," she said.

Cecil stood up, held out his arm, and refused to let her pass.

"It's all right, miss," he said belligerently. "We've got him. He don't need nobody else."

"She can help, sir," Alfie insisted.

Mathers turned his head and looked at him through the slits of his splash mask.

"No, Perkins, you know she can't."

LEAVING MATHERS TO the care of his crew, Atkins took a torch and pushed past them with impatience into the chamber. Holding it high, he could see the markings on the wall. They were not like the chatt glyphs. With a swell of frustration, he realised they weren't in a language he could read either. He couldn't make any sense of it. But it *was* familiar. He brushed his hand briefly over the scratched graffiti with curiosity. It looked like the coded script he had seen in Jeffries' journal, the one Lieutenant Everson pored over obsessively. Then he saw something he did recognise. His brow furrowed. He fished in his top pocket and pulled out a folded piece of tattered paper. The leader of every patrol had one, Everson insisted upon it. He unfolded it to reveal a carefully copied symbol. He compared the two now. There was no doubt.

It was the Sigil of Croatoan from Jeffries' journal.

Atkins' mind was a flurry of thoughts, like a shaken snow globe. He found an ember of hope in the ashes of his world.

Jeffries had been here. It couldn't have been by chance. He had a map. Had he expected to find this place? What was its significance? What information did the coded writing contain? What did it all *mean*?

He had no answers. One thing he did know was that Jeffries was his only lifeline, and his mind seized on it and wouldn't let go. If Jeffries wanted the information, so did he. Somehow, Jeffries was the key. Maybe his boast back in Khungarr, that he was their only way back, wasn't just a desperate tactic to buy himself time to escape. One way or another, Atkins wanted to know the truth. Taking a pencil stub from his pocket, he laboriously copied the symbols on the back of the piece of paper.

With his mind consumed with thoughts of Jeffries, he exited the chamber. He turned to the tank commander, who had recovered his composure and replaced his mask and helmet, once again hiding the ravaged face and the unnerving eyes that, Atkins now knew, saw things beyond the reach of normal human senses.

"Sir, you said you could follow Jeffries' scent trail. Lieutenant Everson expressly ordered that any leads on Jefferies' whereabouts be reported. I need to know which way he went from here. Can you do that much?"

Mathers looked up at him. Around him, his crew glared at Atkins with undisguised suspicion. The young lad, Cecil, watched Atkins like a hawk, his fists balled by his sides. Mathers put a hand on the boy's shoulder and he relaxed slightly.

"Once I have killed this spirit and taken its power, and not before."

As THE PARTY readied to move off again, Atkins led the way, eager to pick up whatever kind of trail Jeffries had left, clambering over a low mound of rubble partially blocking the passage. As he held out the torch into the stygian space beyond, an arm reached out of the darkness and pulled him off balance. A hard, calloused hand, that smelled of dirt and sweat, clamped over his mouth and Atkins felt a blade bite into his throat, under his Adam's apple, as he struggled to catch his breath...

CHAPTER SEVENTEEN
"The Far Gone Dead..."

THE TORCH FELL from Atkins' hand as he grabbed the wrist holding the blade to his neck.

"Be still," said an insistent voice at his ear, "or you will die here."

He recognised it. It was Jarak, the ousted shaman from the urmen's forest enclave.

The shaman swung him around as a shield between himself and the soldiers. Atkins saw his mates bring their rifles up. The tunnel, however, was too narrow for them to flank or get a bead on his assailant without hitting him, too.

The shaman adjusted his grip, dropping his free arm across Atkins' chest to grab his webbing, the knife still at his throat.

"Go on, kill me," Atkins growled at him. "But the moment I drop, they'll shoot."

Jarak ignored him. "Where is your shaman?" he barked at the soldiers.

Mathers stepped forwards.

"You shamed me before my people," the shaman said, the fury in his voice barely under control. "You took my place."

"You could have stayed and served me," said Mathers.

Napoo shook his head. "No, he could not. He has but two paths to regaining his place with the clan now. Banishing the dulgur, or killing his usurper."

Jarak sneered at Napoo and jerked his chin towards Chandar, half hidden behind the soldiers, and snarled. "You consort with the Ones, yet do not wear their mark. What trickery is this?"

"No trickery. The One is our prisoner. The Tohmii are free urmen, like you, like me. They are a powerful clan. They have fought the Ones and triumphed."

"Now I know you lie."

"You have seen their power for yourself."

"The urman speaks the truth," Chandar chittered.

Napoo turned his attention to the shaman. "And where is the rest of your party?"

"The shaman's party is dead," said Jarak bitterly. "The dulgur took them; the dancers, the dreamers, the warriors. What use is a shaman without his party, without his apprentices? Who will safeguard the clan now? You?" he snapped at Mathers. "Your crawling god is mighty, but I have seen you. You are in thrall to it and it will drag you with it into the underworld. You are not long for this place, and what will the clan do then?"

Atkins might have felt for the shaman; he, too, had lost everything. He, too, was between a rock and hard place, no thanks to Mad Mathers, but the pressure of the blade on his throat cancelled out any sympathy he might have had.

"And you," he growled into Atkins' ear. "Your sacrifice at the precipice would have saved my enclave then. Perhaps it might do as much now. If you are such a powerful clan, then maybe your sacrifice may be acceptable to the dulgur, and it will leave my enclave alone, and I shall regain my place among my people. I will return to them in glory having banished the spirit by my own deeds, or else revenged upon my usurper."

The blade rocked against Atkins' throat as the urman shifted his weight and began to drag him back down the passage.

"Stop!" shouted Mercy, but Jarak wasn't listening.

Atkins missed his footing and the blade bit into his skin as he struggled to keep his balance. He glanced down and saw the passage was coated with a thin layer of black deposit.

There was a warm, foetid breeze from the depths of the passage behind Atkins, as if something large and fast were pushing the air before it, causing the flames from the torches to gutter wildly in the dark.

"GarSuleth preserve this One!" hissed Chandar, sinking as low as it could.

The rasp rapidly became a slick sucking sound, and the shadows around Atkins grew darker as an oily cloud billowed round their feet. He scrambled to maintain a footing on the slick residue.

The sound stopped. For a heartbeat there was silence.

The shaman screamed as he was ripped away from Atkins, his knife raking across Atkins' neck. As the great black tide retreated into the darkness, the shaman was dragged with it and his cries were swiftly smothered, like those of a drowning man.

Atkins dropped to the floor, his hand clasping his throat. Above him a hail of gunfire roared out, muzzle flashes bursting in the darkness, one or two bullets whining off the tunnel walls.

As the fusillade died away, Nellie burst from the pack, pushed past Mathers and dropped down by Atkins.

He coughed and spluttered, gasping for breath, and she gently, but firmly, prised his hand away from his neck. It came away slick and hot. She worked to wipe away the blood and sighed with relief. "You're lucky, Corporal. It's not as bad as it looks. This will sting," she said, as she applied an urman poultice to the wound from a pouch at her waist.

Atkins sucked in air through his teeth against the pain. "Funny, I don't feel bloody lucky."

She took off Atkins' tunic, removed his braces and undid his shirt. She pulled a field bandage pack from the bag at her hip and tore open the paper wrapping, all with a practised ease. "Hold that," she said, placing his hand on it. Nellie wrapped and rewrapped a length of bandage round his chest and shoulder to keep the neck dressing in place. "What the hell was that thing?"

"The dulgur," said a grim-faced Napoo.

Mathers wandered past them, staring down the sloping passage into the dark, looking at something nobody else could see.

"Curious. That creature doesn't belong here," he said, to nobody in particular. "I *see* it. It is not of this place. It should not exist here. It was brought forth from... elsewhere."

Chandar clicked its mandibles together rapidly. "It is true. It is an abomination."

Chalky crossed himself. "Jesus, Mary and Joseph, I knew it. It's a demon from the depths of Hell, isn't it? Summoned by Jeffries to do his bidding. Oh, Lord and his saints preserve us."

"Don't talk daft. A demon? How is that even possible?" asked Gazette.

Porgy intervened. "*We're* here. How is *that* possible?"

"Man has a point," admitted Pot Shot.

With the attack of the creature, the place had gone from labyrinth to lair.

Atkins got to his feet. "We need to get out of here. That thing, whatever it is, knows we're here now, and I don't want to get caught in these tunnels again."

Mathers cocked his head. "What?" he said.

"I said we need to get out of here, sir."

"Quiet, Corporal. I wasn't talking to you," Mathers snapped, listening to whatever phantom voices were enticing him. "Yes, of course," he answered.

He turned back to Atkins. "We're headed this way, Corporal." He began walking down the tunnel in the direction the thing had taken.

"Sir?" queried Atkins, but he received no reply. He pressed the point. "Sir, you're not well. It's not safe," but the officer ignored him.

The tank crew shoved through the Fusiliers, to fall in behind their commander, with an insolence that made the Fusiliers bristle.

As he passed Nellie, Alfie didn't dare look at her. He didn't need to. Her shining aura was all he needed to see. Nevertheless, he contrived to walk by her and his fingers found hers briefly.

"Mad Mathers is going to get us all killed," Porgy objected in a low voice.

"Quite possibly," said Atkins, his voice laced with resentment. "But he is an officer and, as our orders are to bring the tank back, we can't very well leave here without him, can we?"

Chalky broke his step to try to stay alongside Atkins for moment. "It's all right, Only. I'm not afraid. I know you can kill the demon."

Atkins rolled his eyes and swore under his breath.

"Boy sees you as role model," said Gutsy, wrily.

"Oh, believe me, I'm nobody's bloody role model." The thought of Flora burned brightly in his mind.

"Maybe not, but apparently you have a reputation. Poor Chalky's probably expecting you to magic up Saint George himself right about now."

"Well, you'd know about that."

"Eh?"

"Saint George. You're the one married to the bloody dragon by all accounts."

"Now *that's* the Only I know and love," said Gutsy, with a guffaw, slapping him on the shoulder. "Good to have you back."

MATHERS PUSHED FORWARD, trusting to his new abilities. He could see the scent trail of the creature, the spirit, now – a thin, tenuous vapour trail, so delicate that any movement tore it and it dissipated on the air current. "This way," he declared, indicating the right hand fork without a second's hesitation. The bantam driver, Wally, was at his right hand, as ever. Frank and Norman were flanking the stupefied Alfie, while Cecil, Jack and Reggie trailed in their wake. Atkins and 1 Section followed on behind as rearguard.

* * *

ATKINS HEARD A sound in the tunnel behind him, like a tide sucking on shingle, as something rushed along the tunnel walls towards them. "Run!" he yelled.

Ahead of him, after a moment's confusion, the tank crew took him at his word, herding Mathers before them.

Atkins turned and knelt and, with Gutsy, held the tunnel as the rest of the section raced swiftly past. They felt the wash of foetid air, and in the darkness something moved, bearing down on them like a train. Gutsy pulled off his bayonet, slipped it back into its sheath at his waist, and fitted the wooden baton of a rifle grenade into his Enfield barrel. He pulled the trigger and the pair ran up the tunnel to where Mercy and Porgy were holding the second line.

The grenade exploded, the shock wave almost blowing Atkins off his feet as he raced past Mercy. Porgy fired three rounds rapid into the dying fireball and the pair joined Atkins and Gutsy in the retreat. They reached a gallery at the junction of five tunnels, where the others had taken shelter from the funnelled blasts.

No sooner had the noise of the grenade died than they heard a low rumbling howl, not from behind them where the creature had taken the brunt of the attack, but from below, the dread sound funnelled up from the depths via the surrounding tunnels.

"Bloody Nora, don't say there's more of them!" groaned Mercy.

Atkins jerked his head at the tunnel openings. "Pot Shot, Gazette, find one that goes back up to the surface." His gaze met Mathers' inscrutable mask, almost daring the officer to countermand his orders, but he didn't. He was clutching his stomach and holding onto the small driver.

"This way, Only!" called Gazette, at the mouth of a tunnel. The section and tank crew retreated into it, alert, their rifles sweeping the tunnel mouths around them.

Not taking his eyes from the direction they had come, Atkins ordered Gazette and Mercy to scout the tunnel. "And hurry!"

he said, hearing the tidal rush of things moving up through the adjoining tunnels towards them from the darkness below.

"I want two volunteers," yelled Atkins.

"I'll stay," said Mercy.

"Me too," said Chalky, although he seemed less certain than Mercy.

Atkins shook his head. "Go up with the rest, Chalky."

Chalky stuck his chin out, like a stubborn child, and clasped his rifle until the whites of his knuckles showed, as if he expected Atkins to take it off him. "No. I'm staying. I know you'll protect us, Only, the way you did Lieutenant Everson."

Atkins nodded and waved the others off.

With Mathers' indomitable will crumbling, as he lost his fight with whatever was ailing him, the tank crew took it upon themselves to protect their precious bloody commander. They took off up the tunnel, Wally and Alfie supporting Mathers between them, the rest of 1 Section herding them along. Napoo grasped Nellie's hand and raced up the tunnel with her, even as she drew her revolver.

Atkins, Mercy and Chalky held the tunnel mouth at the gallery. A foul breeze blew around it, and the dust on the floor began to swirl in eddies, as things rushed up from the depths towards them.

Chalky began muttering the Lord's Prayer.

"Cover me," Atkins said, as he raced around the gallery, tossing a grenade down into each of the four tunnels. He heard them land, rattling off into the darkness, and he dived back for cover between Mercy and Chalky. They crouched down as the grenades went off one after the other, like a barrage, bringing down the tunnels. Dust and debris billowed into the gallery, filling it with a gritty, choking cloud.

From deep below came a low awful sound, that reverberated in his chest and made his very bones ache. He could hear rubble and debris clinking as something with weight and speed rammed against the tunnel collapse, attempting to drive its way through.

"Go!" he cried.

Mercy needed no telling. Chalky hesitated until Mercy grabbed his arm. "Run, you daft bugger!"

ALFIE FOUND HIMSELF leaving the gallery behind and herded up the passage, under the insistent barking of the Fusiliers. The initial barrage of hallucinations from his 'baptism' were wearing off. If that was the world Mathers wanted him so badly to inhabit, then he could keep it. It was as if Mathers needed him for his own shaman's party. The others may have bought into it, but Alfie wouldn't. He struggled against the horrifying new world invading his senses. The comparatively gentle side effect of the fuel fumes he could put up with, but this enforced ingestion was a brutal assault on the senses. It terrified him, but what terrified him more was the fact that Lieutenant Mathers wasn't scared at all.

Alfie fought against it, as hard as it was to cling to the mundane when your world was ablaze with wonders and horrors. Nellie's presence helped. Without her, he feared he would be as lost as the others.

"The Lieutenant needs to rest," panted Clegg, under the subaltern's weight. "He can't carry on."

To their right the tunnel wall had partially crumbled away to reveal a void beyond.

"This'll have to do," said Jack, stamping his boot into it several times. The edges of the hole collapsed, creating an opening big enough to enter. He thrust a torch through to reveal an empty space, which would provide some protection against the concussions. "Get in, hurry!" He directed the tank crew and Fusiliers into the space beyond.

They found themselves in another round chamber. One of the Fusiliers held a torch high to illuminate the place.

"Jesus!" exclaimed Alfie.

The bodies of several chatts lay on the floor of the chamber: Scentirrii, judging by the heavy carapace casings. They were covered with fine dust or ash, which had hardened over them, softening their outlines. With them were the bodies of two more chatts, priests. Alfie knew them by their featureless faces and the mouldering tasselled silk sashes. They lay on the ground under a covering of calcified dust, as though they had died peacefully, resigned to their fate. They had seen others like them, but not this far down.

Across the chamber, as though unfit to die with them, were the bodies of three worker chatts. These, however, had died violent deaths, their carapaces broken open.

Chandar stepped reverently around them, chittering to itself softly, its stunted middle limb restless. But it wasn't the bodies that agitated the chatt. It was what had been entombed with them; a motley collection of jars, amphorae, and pots of varying sizes, hastily gathered and stacked on shelves in niches and on the floor.

Smirking, Norman picked up a sealed stone jar. "Here, lads. SRD rum rations, and about bloody time!" He made to smash the neck against the wall. Chandar rounded on him, reared up on its legs and advanced towards him, its mandibles open as it hissed.

ATKINS GAVE MERCY and Chalky five seconds. He slung his rifle over his shoulder, then took two grenades in one hand and pulled the pins. He dropped the grenades into the middle of the gallery, on the floor at the mouth of the tunnel, and sprinted up the incline. Five second fuses. How far could he get in five seconds?

Four thousand. He heard something ploughing through the rubble below him.

Three thousand. He felt his stomach churn as another low howl reverberated through his body.

Two thousand. An arm reached out of an opening to his left, grabbed his webbing, and yanked him into a passing niche.

One thousand. The bomb went off. A blast of dirt roared past the opening.

Coughing, Atkins looked up to see Mercy and Chalky grinning at him.

They waited for almost a minute, but heard no further sounds of pursuit from below. They allowed themselves to breathe again. The three dust-covered men grinned at each other with the elation of survival.

"I could murder a bloody fag," said Mercy, patting his pockets. "But I'm right out."

"Blood and sand," said Atkins. "If *you're* all out, things are a lot worse than I thought."

THE LIGHT OF a torch, filtered by the still settling dust, bobbed back down the passage towards Atkins, Mercy and Chalky. "Only!" It was Pot Shot, speaking in a low, urgent hiss. "Only? The chatt's turning nasty. You'd better come and sort it out or Gutsy says he might have to kill it."

"Bloody hell!" Atkins' jubilation melted away and his face set again as he, Chalky and Mercy followed the lanky private up the gently rising passage until they could hear Chandar hissing and spitting.

By the time Atkins arrived, the unsealed chamber was the scene of a tense stand-off. Mathers had slumped to the ground, a couple of his crew clustered around him. The big one, Jack, was holding back Norman, who looked as if he wanted to bash the chatt's brains out. The others were squaring off against Chandar. 1 Section had leapt to the chatt's defence. Napoo had stepped in front of Nellie, his sword drawn, watching the proceedings warily.

Atkins was stunned. He turned his back for five minutes and they were at each others' throats! "What the hell's going on? There's a thing – things – out there that are trying to kill us and you lot want to do this? Now?"

"That's your problem!" Frank said with a snarl, jabbing his revolver towards Chandar. "Bleedin' chatt freak. Norman picked up one o' them old jars and it got all cut up about it."

Porgy butted in. "Lieutenant Mathers was looking a bit ropey so we ducked in here to rest. We saw these chatt bodies and jars and stuff, and Chandar gets all excited until that tanker starts clowning around with 'em."

Chandar raised itself up on its legs, in Norman's direction, and hissed, slicing its mandibles. Cowed, Norman slunk back.

Atkins stepped between the Hush Hush crowd and the chatt, his bayoneted rifle pointed at it. "What's going on, Chandar?"

The chatt turned to him, but did not relax its defensive stance. "These receptacles, they contain many sacred texts. To treat them like that is disrespectful."

Atkins glanced at the shattered vessels. "All right. He won't do it again. Now calm down. What's so important about them anyway?"

"There are copies of scentopedia, holy books, here, that were destroyed in Khungarr by Jeffries. There are aromatomes, even older. This one" – it indicated a jar – "this one was declared heretical in Khungarr many spira ago. Some of these are older than Khungarr itself. Do you not realise? This is a find of incalculable importance. The Ones here sealed themselves in with them in order to protect them from whatever befell the edifice. They gave their lives to guard them. There are scent texts here of great significance and antiquity, and that urman almost destroyed one – on a whim."

"I don't understand, why didn't they dig themselves out?"

"Because these Ones were commanded not to, or commanded to await rescue when it was safe. This one cannot say. But with these, Khungarr can begin to replace the scent scriptures we lost, that you cost us. Some may even provide the scriptural proof we need to finally move against Sirigar and his olfaction. But if these ignorant urmen proceed to destroy them, then this One will never know and the Tomhii Clan may yet be doomed. They must be salvaged and taken back to Khungarr. You must aid this One. It is Kurda. If this One had not accompanied you to this place, then these would have been lost or destroyed forever. Their discovery is the will of GarSuleth, and so is their retrieval."

"What, so we're working for chatts now?" said Mercy, with disdain.

Atkins knew from Chandar's interrogation by Everson, and his own conversations with the thing, that there were bigger matters at stake here. He didn't quite understand, but he knew this scent library was important. They had the tank. They could transport all these things back. It wasn't going to be a popular decision, but it was the right thing to do.

"It's not good enough they've got urmen slaves to do their dirty work for them, now you want us to help them?"

"It's not that simple." Atkins lowered his voice briefly so the tank crew couldn't hear. "You saw those American pioneers. They're dead. They couldn't survive on this world by themselves. Besides, *we* have urmen flocking to *us* for help, and protection, too. Tell them, Napoo."

The wily old guide nodded. "The Tohmii are powerful, like the Ones."

"But the chatts use chemicals to keep the urmen docile!" said Nellie. "I've experienced it."

"I said it's not that simple," said Atkins, remembering his recent experience with the Zohtakarrii. "Those urmen work for them in return for food, shelter and protection. How is that different from you, Gazette, at the mill, or you, Mercy, at the Brewery, or your uncle down the pits, Pot Shot?"

Pot Shot shrugged, as if pained to admit it. "The man's right, we may not use chemical decrees to keep our workers in place but we use money to the same ends. It's not that much different. Still, doesn't make it right, though."

"But the chatts are attacking our trenches right now and you want us to help them?"

"Chandar's part of a movement that can stop that, and these jars can help. We have orders to return to the encampment with the tank anyway, so we might as well take these back with us."

Gazette spoke up. "Only has a point. Whatever way you look at it these jars are valuable. It gives us an advantage. We have something they want. We can hold them to ransom."

He looked round the chamber, meeting everyone's eyes with a challenging glare.

There was a murmur of agreement, even among the tank crew.

Chandar began pointing out the most important jars to salvage. Atkins' section took off their packs and began filling them.

Reggie and Norman slipped off their coveralls from over their service dress, tied knots in the arms and legs to create makeshift bags and began to load them up under Chandar's direction.

In their haste, one of the tank crew, Reggie, let an amphora slip from his fingers.

"Dash it!"

It shattered against the earthen floor, its thick oily contents permeating the chamber as its contents splashed into the dirt. A pungent odour rose from the spreading pool.

"Be careful!"

There was a loud clicking from Chandar as it picked over the shards of stoneware jar. It hissed and clicked rapidly as it turned one over, marked with chatt glyphs.

"What is it?" Atkins asked, recognising the sounds of agitation.

"A heretical unguent, prepared from the living bodies of Ones. Used to aid prophecy. The prophecies that arise from it are said to be dire and inescapable. No One has dared use it for spira, beyond counting. Perhaps it is just as well it is gone." Chandar sank down on its legs.

Gutsy tapped Atkins on the shoulder. "Then again, maybe it hasn't." He nodded towards Mathers, who had begun to clutch his stomach in pain and pushed off his splash mask and helmet.

MATHERS JERKED, HIS back arching as though he were having a fit. He took a deep gasping breath, inhaling the vapours that coiled and entwined as they rose from the smashed jar.

In the air around him, expanding with the vapours, an alien

world of shape, sound and colour, translated from the scent, began to take shape, drowning out all else.

The soldiers and crew around him faded like ghosts, as he railed against the synesthetic visions that overwhelmed his mind. The pain in his stomach dulled to a vague throb.

A spot burned on his retina. It grew larger, and Mathers realised he was witnessing events long ago.

The world was as it should be. GarSuleth watched over its children from its great sky web, beads of dew glistening on it in the night sky. The Nazarrii, already failing, pleaded for GarSuleth's intercession to save them.

The spot burned in the sky, bringing with it fear. The horror mounted, as its cursed name spread on the Breath of GarSuleth, from colony to colony. Mathers could taste the acrid tang of the sky usurper's name on his tongue. It tasted of blood and iron and bile. Croatoan.

The light grew brighter and brighter, outshining all the other dew-bedecked spots that shimmered and shone in the great Sky Web. It grew brighter still, seeking to outshine GarSuleth itself and tear the web asunder.

A mighty struggle ensued and burned across the vault of sky for days and nights, as GarSuleth fought the interloper before making the fatal bite, defeating the usurper and casting it from the sky web.

It took days for the defeated deity to fall. The false god tumbled from the sky web that spanned the heavens. It fell in fire, and as the usurper fell, the Nazarrii took this as a sign from GarSuleth and forsook the edifice, but too late. The sky giant fell not far from ill-fated Nazarr.

The world shook with its impact. The edifice felt the full wrath of the usurper's death throes as its final breath tore across the land, blasting all that stood in its path, and fire followed fast on its heels.

It was bound and imprisoned by GarSuleth's brother, Skarra, god of the dead, god of the underworld, to dwell in eternal punishment.

The middle notes told how some were selected to entomb themselves, to protect their most sacred scents against the death throes of the usurper.

As those middle notes died away the full horror of the top note became apparent. Buried alive, the priest chatts, abandoned by their god, harvested and prepared the unguents necessary to make one final horrific prophecy from the very bodies of the worker chatts that remained sealed in with them. And now that cannibalised chrism flooded Mathers' mind.

He gasped for breath. His voice became a hoarse whisper as he began to prophesy. *"As the breath of GarSuleth leaves us, so do these Ones leave this scent of prophecy. Our trail has led to this place at this time. Heed, then, the final inescapable prophecy of the Nazarrii that yours may not. In the spira when the Breath of GarSuleth grows foul, the false dhuyumirrii shall follow its own scent along a trail not travelled, to a place that does not exist. Other Ones will travel with the Breath of GarSuleth, the Kreothe, made, not tamed. Then shall Skarra, with open mandibles, welcome the dark scentirrii. There shall emerge a colony without precedent. The children of GarSuleth will fall. They shall not forsake the sky web. The anchor line breaks."*

The final notes of the scent, hastily distilled from the dead chatt workers, died away, leaving Mathers' mind entombed with them in the dark. A dark he knew. And feared.

He screamed.

CHAPTER EIGHTEEN
"The Lonesome Dark..."

MATHERS COLLAPSED AS his mind returned to this world. As he did so, the men about him solidified and the pain in his stomach returned.

Atkins stared at him. "What the hell was all that about?"

"It is a prophecy," said Napoo, in awe.

Mercy dismissed the idea. "Mumbo jumbo more like. It don't mean anything. The man funked it a long time back."

"Oi!" snarled Norman.

Mercy flashed a sheepish smile, and held up his hands apologetically, before turning back to his mates and tapping his temple.

Chandar chattered as the prophecy-inducing liquid soaked into the dry earthen-packed floor where it could do no more harm. "This does not augur well. It would have been better if this liquid had been destroyed than used to make a heretical prophecy. But it is too late, the words have been spoken. The deed is done."

"You can't believe that stuff?" said Atkins.

"Things will be as GarSuleth wills them."

Nellie sank down beside Mathers. "Let me see him?" With reluctance, the tank crew let Nellie minister to their commander, who sat slumped against the chamber wall, saliva dribbling from his mouth, his face an ugly patchwork of livid red lesions. She unbuttoned his collar to find the swellings at his neck had now spread down over his torso. She felt for the pulse at his wrist. It was racing.

She looked up at Reggie. "His condition is worse. I don't know what to do about it. I certainly can't do anything here."

Reggie nodded in agreement. "We got to get him back to the *Ivanhoe*. It always goes better for him when he's in it, Miss."

Nellie frowned. "The fumes, yes. Well, first things first, we must get him out of here."

Atkins could hear the sound of something below repeatedly ramming roof falls. One of the creatures was attempting to clear its way through the rubble of the collapsed tunnels. "Then, Miss Abbott, you go with them. Hurry."

"Are you sure, Corporal?"

"Yes. Keep an eye on Lieutenant Mathers. Napoo, go with her." The urman was reluctant to accompany one he considered possessed, but Atkins had gambled that his loyalty to them would extend to Nellie. The urman nodded.

Atkins resented the fact that they had come all the way for the tankers, and now had to put their lives on the line for them again. However, when he spoke, the tone was matter-of-fact. "We'll buy you time. Keep going up. If we're not out in an hour, use the tank to bring this place down and kill these things, then get back to the encampment, toot suite. Go."

The big boxer, Jack, nodded his thanks and, supporting the semi-conscious Mathers between them, Jack and Frank led off up the passage. Alfie followed, cocked revolver in one hand, torch in the other. Nellie and Napoo fell in behind them. Reggie and Norman carried their makeshift coverall bags, with Cecil and Wally, which tapped and clinked as they walked.

Atkins watched them go as the light from their torches receded up the slope and the tunnel faded into blackness again.

Below them, the sounds became more urgent, as the repeated clinker and clatter of tumbling debris told them that the creature was breaking through.

"Stand to!" Atkins ordered. He knelt with Chalky and Pot

Shot in the tunnel. In a rank behind him stood Gutsy, Gazette, Porgy and Mercy, their packs and webbing bulging with stone jars. Despite the number that the men were carrying, Chandar looked despondently at the containers they had to leave behind. "So many, so much... knowledge..."

The intermittent smash of rubble became constant as the creature found enough momentum to push through the barricade, ploughing a wave of rubble as it raced up the tunnel incline towards them.

"Fire!" ordered Atkins.

A fusillade blasted into the darkness. The onrushing wave of rubble didn't slow.

"Fall back!" yelled Atkins. "Fall back!"

THE SOUND OF gunfire behind them spurred Nellie, Napoo and the tank crew on, passing through several galleries, taking any upward tunnel, the jars clanking together as they tried to pick up their pace without breaking any.

"We'd get out of here faster if we didn't have to carry these bloody things," Wally groused. "Why can't we just dump 'em?"

"Because, like the infantryman said, these things can hit the chatts where it hurts, wherever the hell that is. And I'm all for that," said Norman.

"Just imagine you're on ration party and quit griping," said Reggie.

Mathers stirred. "Sir. Are you all right?" asked Jack.

He shook off his crewmen's help. "Never better, Tanner, never better," he said, breathing deeply. The pain in his stomach was fading fast. Mathers felt calmer than he had done in days. It was as if whatever fever he had been suffering from had broken.

He felt an insistent need to feel the wind on his face. He stopped, confused. There, a faint cooling air current from a branching tunnel to the left. He turned towards it, not a doubt in his mind. The draft in his face drew him on and he gave in to the impulse.

Behind him, his crew called after him, perplexed, "Sir! Sir!"

"Stay there!" he commanded. He did not need them now. He walked on down the tunnel, and the breeze grew stronger. He luxuriated in the feel of it upon his skin. He heard the sound of something rushing up the tunnel towards him, but he wasn't afraid. He smiled to himself, content. He saw a slick, black bulk that filled the tunnel bearing down on him, and he stopped and welcomed it with open arms.

ATKINS AND THE others, meanwhile, raced up the tunnel and took a fork, which led to another gallery. Passages and chambers led off in several directions, up and down. The discordant whistling from the choked ventilation system seemed amplified here, making the men, tense and edgy already, feel even more windy. Chalky had started to fret and whimper.

In the centre of the gallery, they found recently dead chatt bodies. Atkins recognised the scentirrii and the priests. "Zohtakarrii," he said, as he passed them. Something had deposited them here. The Section spread out and scouted the gallery.

Gutsy pointed at another pile. "Urmen. Must be that shaman's bunch."

"The chatts were killed outside. Why have they been left here?" wondered Atkins.

A hard translucent substance plugged several adjoining chamber entrances, sealing them. Atkins cupped his hands to one and tried to peer through. For a moment, he couldn't make anything out. Something moved, slapping against the translucent barrier, something with the texture of tripe. The pressure from within grew. The whole of the barrier began to click and snap under the pressure. Cracks raced across the surface. The plug began to splinter.

"I think that's why!" said Atkins as he stumbled back with the others, retreating to the centre of the gallery, as the seals on the other chambers began to creak under the strain from within.

Chandar sank down on its legs and hissed.

Chalky whimpered, a wet stain spreading down his khaki trousers. Poor sod. Atkins reckoned it was as much from the unsettling sound of the whistling, that reverberated unpleasantly in the bowels, as from fear.

"Stick with me," he said, patting the lad on the shoulder. Chalky looked at him through the tears he was trying to fight back. "I'll see you, right, lad."

"I don't think it's a good time to be here," said Mercy.

The seal shattered and something began uncoiling from within. Two shapeless black creatures, the size of motor cars, slopped out of their foetal chambers on a tide of thick fluid that sluiced across the gallery floor, washing up against the piles of bodies and depositing the creatures on the chamber floor. The glistening creatures lay like great excised viscera. They seemed totally without skeletal support, with no discernable head, limbs or features of any sort. Then after a moment their shapeless bodies began to contract and flow, drawing themselves in; whether as a defensive reflex or like the first awkward attempts at movement by a newborn calf struggling to stand, it was hard to say. At the same time, orifices formed, gaping black lipless holes that began to suckle blindly at the air.

Gazette nudged Pot Shot. "Better hope it goes for the dead ones first."

"Would you go for Machonochies when there's steak?" asked Gutsy.

"Fair point."

The heaving black bulks extruded tendrils, which quested blindly towards the waiting bodies and, finding them, began to drawn them towards their open maws.

A third creature was expelled from its chamber like afterbirth and, unable to reach the food thanks to its birthmates, it sent tendrils out after the Tommies.

"And for my next trick," Gazette announced, "pick a tunnel, any tunnel."

Atkins picked one and they ran, the stone pots and jars chinking and clattering as they did.

*   *   *

THE TANK CREW, abandoned in the passage by Mathers, began to turn on themselves.

"We'd better go after him," said Frank.

Norman shook his head. "He told us to stay here."

Reggie stepped forwards. "He's ill, even if he won't admit it himself."

Norman glared at him. "Well, there's no point us all going. Send him." He jerked his thumb at Alfie. "*If* he's got the balls. I want to see him put himself on the line for the Sub."

"No!" Nellie protested.

"It's all right, Nellie," said Alfie. "I'll fetch him. I'm not afraid."

"Alfie, don't!"

Alfie smiled shyly and gave her a wink that exuded more confidence than he felt. "I won't be long. Back in two shakes of a lamb's tail. The Lieutenant can't have gone far."

"And why the hell should we trust you?" snarled Cecil, stepping into his path. "You've never understood the Lieutenant's plans. He's a genius, he's got it all sorted out, up here," he said, tapping his forehead. "He's a man of vision. He has plans for this world and he's taking us with him. But oh, no, you don't want to go. You know better. You'd rather be with your bint, here."

"'Ere, you watch your lip!" snapped Nellie.

"Or what," Cecil jeered, "your beau will swing for me?"

Nellie's eyes narrowed, full of focused fury. "He won't bloody have to, I'll do it myself."

Alfie sighed. He didn't want to do this. Not here, not now. "You can't see it, can you? Any of you! It's the fumes talking, all of this. This isn't the crew I knew back in Norfolk. You lot have been riding my back about my loyalty. I've done as much to keep the *Ivanhoe* going as any of you, and we're standing here arguing about it while the Lieutenant could be in danger. He's not himself." Cecil didn't back down. "Fine. In return,

I'm trusting you. With her!" he pointed at Nellie, knowing that he didn't have to trust them. The urman, Napoo, would keep her safe, and she had her revolver.

"Seems like a fair deal," conceded Reggie, arching an eyebrow. "Cecil?"

The sullen loader muttered under his breath, but let Alfie pass.

"Look after her," called Alfie, holding up his torch, "and if we're not back in five, get the hell out of here."

"Alfie!"

It was hard leaving her, but he had to do this. He had to regain their trust. Mad or not, Mathers was still the tank commander and, despite what the others may think, he wasn't himself. He was the only other one who knew about the things inside Mathers, the things Mathers had been fighting. Holding the torch high, he turned and gave Nellie a bright smile and an airy wave and, with a deep breath, plunged into the waiting dark.

DRIVEN ON BY hunger, the black mass of the freshly hatched creature propelled itself after the Tommies. Atkins and the others raced along the tunnel, desperate to stay ahead of it. Chandar bounded alongside them, its legs showing a power and spring it had kept well hidden. Around a slight curve in the tunnel came a faint glow of light.

"Lads, daylight! We've made it!" yelled Porgy.

Atkins grabbed the flagging Chalky by his webbing and dragged him on. They pelted up the curving inclined passage as it led upwards for several hundred yards. The light grew brighter until, used to the gloom of the labyrinth, their eyes ached. They could see a round opening now, draped with foliage.

The low susurrating sound of pursuit still harried them, closer now.

"Run!" shouted Atkins. He gave Chalky another shove and felt one of the chatt pots in the lad's pack break. A green sticky stain spread over the canvas. He hoped it wasn't anything important.

Mercy and Gazette came to an abrupt halt at the mouth of the opening. Gutsy barrelled into them, almost sending Porgy sprawling, but Mercy caught his webbing. Chalky came staggering up.

Atkins glanced over his shoulder. The creature was gaining. "Get out, get out!" he bellowed, closing the last few yards between him and the rest of the section.

"Not this way, we can't," said Mercy, sounding grim.

"What do you mean?" said Atkins, pushing through them to where the foliage draped across the opening. He parted it with an impatient sweep of his arm.

The ground fell away. The tunnel opened onto empty space. A hundred or so feet below, he saw the canopy of the jungle spread out before him.

"Eh, up!" said Mercy, grabbing Atkins' webbing as he flailed to keep his balance.

The tunnel came out on the side of the precipice. Only it wasn't just a precipice. Looking out across the top of a jungle canopy below, he could make out the far side of the valley with its rising cliff face, the one he'd seen before, when Jarak tried to sacrifice him. He saw now that it wasn't a rift valley as he previously thought. From here, he could see that the cliffs curved round and met, the sides of a vast crater hundreds of feet deep and filled with jungle. Over to his right he could see the mysterious discoloured line of vegetation in the crater that he'd noticed before.

None of which helped them now. They were trapped, and the creature was rushing towards them.

ALFIE SHUFFLED CAUTIOUSLY down the passage, holding the torch high, and peered into the gloom. From somewhere up ahead he could hear a constant muttering.

"Sir?" he called. "Lieutenant Mathers, sir!"

At the very edge of the torch glow, he caught sight of the scarecrow figure of the tank commander in his shamanistic rain cape.

"Perkins? Don't move. Stay there."

Beyond Mathers, something filled the tunnel space, writhing. Alfie held his breath. The creature waited, small tendrils waving tentatively in the air around Mathers, apparently mollified by the Lieutenant's muttering. The tentacles retreated into the body of the creature, and Alfie watched it withdraw back down the tunnel with a sucking sound, the way it came.

Alfie edged forwards, uncertain as to whether the thing had truly gone. "How?" he began.

"I wondered that myself," said Mathers, unperturbed. "But you've seen them."

"What, sir?"

"These things inside me. I think it could sense them. I don't think it likes them."

Alfie remembered the glimpse he got after being forced to drink the petrol fruit. He didn't like them either.

Mathers turned to the Gearsman. "I need to get back to the tank, Perkins. I can't fight them any longer. I was ready to give myself to them just then. I can feel them interfering with my mind. They want me, *need* me to die, for some reason. The fumes seem to subdue them somehow, but I can't hold them back by myself for much longer."

"We'll get you back, sir."

"Don't tell them, Perkins. Don't tell them about the things inside me. They don't need to know."

Alfie thought they did. He didn't want to be a confidant. He didn't want to be burdened with secrets, but he bit his tongue. "My lips are sealed, sir," he said, guiding the weakened officer along. Mathers offered no resistance.

Alfie saw the bloom of torchlight ahead. "We're here," he called. The light moved along the passage towards him, highlighting Jack and Frank below it, as they approached.

Mathers had lapsed from lucidity again and, vacant-eyed, muttered to himself.

"We need to get him back to the *Ivanhoe*," said Alfie, as Frank and Jack took Mathers from him.

"Alfie!" Nellie rushed forwards to hug him but stopped herself, the fleeting moment of impropriety before the others embarrassing her. Alfie was amused to find the tank men averting their gaze and shuffling awkwardly.

"We must carry on," Napoo reminded them.

The crew picked up their jar-stuffed coveralls and let the urman take the lead, thinking to blame him if they remained lost. They pushed on, the tunnel spiralling upwards at a gentle gradient.

Mathers was delirious. He revived briefly when they felt the fresh air blowing down the tunnel. The tank crew stumbled towards it, finding a breach in the wall. They pushed through the tangled mass of creepers and vines obscuring their view, and caught sight of the tank across the clearing.

"Yes!" A weary cheer went up. Even Alfie was relieved to see the great iron beast again. It was like coming home. Inside that, they would be safe.

MATHERS ROUSED SLIGHTLY, his brow furrowed as he listened intently. He couldn't hear it anymore, the constant whisper of Skarra. It had gone and he didn't know if it would ever return. He felt an unassailable grief so profound he wanted to howl. Then he felt the wind on his face. For a fleeting moment, he caught sight of the faint scent spectre of Jeffries, a supercilious smile on his face, as he turned and waved before walking away from the edifice and dispersing on the breeze.

As the breeze blew, all his cares blew away on it. He forgot Jeffries. He remembered a vague feeling of sorrow, but not why. A moment later, he no longer even remembered that. All he knew was the wind. He turned to face it and waited.

THE COLUMN OF air pushed ahead of the creature and ruffled the curtain of foliage behind them.

Chalky was whimpering with fear. Gutsy muttered to him in calm tones.

"We've got bombs. We can kill it," suggested Pot Shot.

"If we don't bring the tunnel down with it, it's still going to block our way back," said Atkins. "No, we're going to have to lure it out of the opening." He peered out of the gaping hole at the surrounding rock. Above, there was a large overhang, that looked impassable. The top of the cliff was seventy or eighty feet above them, but seemed too sheer to climb. Around the opening, however, were small trees with spreading root systems, holding them to the cliff face, that might hold a man? There was only one thing for it.

Atkins swung back in. "There's a small ledge to the right, and creepers that should hold our weight."

"Should?"

"Best I can do."

Gazette shook his head. "I'm not bloody going out there."

"Well, that creature is headed this way whether we like it or not. Jump or be pushed."

"Let's do it," said Gutsy, reaching out and grabbing a root. The plant creaked, but held, as he stretched out for another further along. "Well, if it'll hold me... You follow me, lad," he called to Chalky, "and just follow the advice of me missus when she's getting undressed – don't look down. Many's the time I wished I'd followed her advice, son, believe me. Brr." He shook his head vigorously until his jowls wobbled.

Gazette edged out. "I hate heights."

Pot Shot, Porgy and Mercy scrambled out over the other side.

"You too," Atkins told Chandar.

"But what about you?" the chatt asked.

"Oh, I'll be joining you shortly, don't you worry."

The chatt scuttled out with a cockroach-like speed that startled Atkins as he watched it use the invading roots to scurry up the passage wall and out of the tunnel mouth. He shuddered, then checked that his men were out of the way.

He ran back down the passage a short distance, intending to bait the creature. He fired a couple of rounds, not imagining that he'd stop it, but just to goad it. The bullets buried themselves in the oncoming flesh with sucking *thwups*. "Come on, then, you ugly bugger. Come and get me."

He turned and ran. The great glossy wet bulk, spraying its lubricating oily mist to ease its way, barrelled towards him. He could see the opening ahead. It wasn't far, but it was further than he wanted it to be. He had grossly underestimated the speed of the thing, and its blind, instinctive need for food. It began to put forth thin tendrils that flailed blindly, closing the distance between them.

As he raced towards the end of the tunnel, he saw Mercy's face and arm silhouetted against the light. "Run!" he yelled.

How the hell did he think that was going to help? Of course he was bloody running.

As he pounded the last few yards, Atkins felt a tendril wrap round his puttee. No! He was so damn close. A couple of yards shy of the tunnel mouth, he took a deep breath and bellowed his rage and fear, putting everything he had into one last, desperate lunge. He leapt through the curtain of foliage.

For less than the space of a heartbeat, he hung in the air. He saw the blue sky ahead and glimpsed the awful fall to the jungle below, before strong hands grabbed his webbing and swung him aside.

Another heartbeat. He crashed into the cliff wall with a force that winded him; one of Chandar's precious amphora shattered in its pouch. He saw Mercy's sweaty, grinning face and grabbed instinctively for the roots in front of him.

A heartbeat later the newly birthed creature, oiling the tunnel as it came with its greasy black vapour, shot out, arcing into space, glands on its body spraying Atkins with the disgusting stuff as it passed.

The limbless thing tumbled down through the air to the jungle canopy below, losing the slug-like shape forced upon it by the constraints of the passage. Freshly extruded tendrils writhed helplessly in mid-air.

Atkins breathed a sigh of relief. "Blood and sand, that was too close by –"

He felt a tug on his leg, and then a wrench that almost pulled him from the cliff. The creature still had a tendril wrapped round his leg as it fell, threatening to drag him down with it. He could feel the root he held tear from its anchorage. Wide with horror, his eyes met those of Mercy.

Mercy made a desperate grab for Atkins' wrist, but his hand was as sweaty as Atkins' own. Atkins slithered from his grasp.

"Only!" roared Gutsy, fumbling to free Little Bertha.

He could feel his wet clammy fingers slipping from the root. His eyes still locked on Mercy's as he shook his head, absolving him of any blame. There was nothing more to be done.

The coarse texture of the root began to slip away under his fingertips.

With a rapidity of movement none had seen from it before today, Chandar scuttled, face-down, over Atkins' back. The chatt's mandibles scythed through the tendril holding his ankle, and the creature crashed down through the canopy below and was lost from sight. Atkins felt Chandar's vestigial claws bite deep into his tunic, gripping him long enough for hands to reach down and haul him back up.

They clambered back into the tunnel and the shocked party caught their breath.

Gutsy looked at Chandar and shook his head in wonder. "Jesus, Mary and Joseph, I didn't know they could do that. Did you know they could do that?"

Slumped against the tunnel wall, Atkins looked up at his saviour. "Thank you."

The chatt sucked in a chestful of air. "It was Kurda," it lisped.

Atkins nodded, still catching his breath. He regarded the chatt for a moment. "What is that place?" he asked, waving a hand at the crater beyond the tunnel mouth.

Chandar hissed and sank down on its legs. "Forbidden. That place does not exist."

"Well, it clearly bloody does exist. It damn near killed me!"

"It is forbidden to the Ones."

"I like the sound of that," said Gutsy. "Anywhere the chatts can't go has got to be good."

Mercy snorted. "I wouldn't be too sure. This world would kill you at every turn. If you ask me, there's probably a bloody good reason why they don't want to go there."

Atkins got up and stepped towards the chatt. "You've been windy since we came across the Gilderra enclave. When the Zohtakarrii captured us, you knew then where we were, didn't you? You knew about that place down there, that crater."

"It is forbidden, forbidden to speak about. It does not exist for us. Other Ones, like the Zohtakarrii, whose territory borders it, patrol to make sure no One goes in and nothing comes out. It has been that way for spira upon spira."

Atkins stared hard at the chatt, but its facial plate gave nothing away. It had no expression to read. He had no choice but to take what it said at face value. For now.

"Let's get moving before another of those things decides to corner us here again."

In the birthing gallery, two creatures were cracking the dead chatts' chitinous shells. Another freshly-birthed horror had fallen upon the urmen bodies, gripping them with extruded tendrils, and sucking the meat from them, leaving nothing but ichor-covered skin and bone, like discarded greasy chicken carcasses. Such was their voracious appetite that they paid no attention to the Tommies.

Atkins tapped the air with a finger, pointing towards a passage on the opposite side that seemed to run upwards. They skirted the repulsive, shapeless things and, once the section was safely in the tunnel mouth, Atkins ordered Pot Shot and Mercy to throw a brace of Mills bombs into the centre. The creatures exploded in balls of flame and silent thrashing tendrils that shrivelled in the heat.

They followed the passage as it curved upwards, until Atkins felt sure they had climbed more than the hundred or so feet that would bring them back to ground level. Light blossomed in the distance, filtered through hanging foliage. With the point of his bayonet, Atkins parted the curtain of leaves and vines. "Blood and sand, not again!"

Wherever the passage may once have led, it now looked down on a large overgrown amphitheatre formed by the collapse of the entire central core of the edifice, the once raw and jagged violence of the edifice's destruction now softened by alien nature's reclamation, overgrown with tangles of creepers, fighting for dominance. Tree-like things clung to the shattered walls. Around them, on the now exposed and weathered walls, they could see other tunnels and runs, at various levels and angles, opening just as abruptly out into the central space.

It reminded Atkins of when he and his brother William dug up woodland ants' nests as boys, breaking open the mound to reveal the network of tunnels within, Flora protesting as the disturbed ants swarmed around their feet.

Looking down into the ruined bowl beneath them, it became clear that the great creatures that had pursued them through the chatt-built tunnels, that had come out to the jungle to search for prey, were not many creatures at all, but a single many-tentacled one. The small ones they killed were merely hatching young.

In the basin of ruined tunnels and collapsed chambers, something huge and shapeless heaved and pulsed. They could see no eyes or mouth, in fact no organs or limbs of any kind other than the tendrils that fed into open tunnels like roots.

Atkins had no doubt that Jeffries could well have summoned what he saw from some demonic circle of hell. Its existence stirred a deep revulsion, not just in him, but the whole section, and this from men who had seen bloated corpses move and writhe obscenely in the Somme mud, infested by feeding corpse rats burrowed into their putrefying innards.

This was the evil spirit that had been stealing urmen. This was what they had come to kill.

CHAPTER NINETEEN
"You Have Only Once To Die..."

THE THING SQUATTED in a large ruined central chamber. The roof had collapsed around it, leaving its back, if that's what it was, half-exposed to the elements. It was a great black mass larger than several zeppelins. The black, feathered tripe-like flesh bore a cross-hatching of scars, old and new. It had tentacles sunk into lower tunnels, like roots. Others were constantly dipping into seemingly random passage openings around it, even as others withdrew. It seemed rooted to the spot. That would explain the absence of animals around the edifice. It had exhausted its local food supply. Forced to stretch its tentacles further to find food, it had encroached on the enclave's hunting grounds to snatch urmen.

The thing throbbed as it withdrew a tentacle from a tunnel below where the Tommies stood. It was wrapped delicately around the remains of one of its young. Following some primitive instinct, it dangled the sloppy, burnt, shapeless mess before it, shaking it gently, trying to revive it. It created other, more delicate, tendrils to prod and probe it. After a cursory examination, they retreated into the mass. Then it drew the tendril, holding the dead creature, back into its body, and its offspring along with it.

"It doesn't look happy," said Mercy.

Gutsy peered down. "You wouldn't be, either, if someone had killed your baby."

"It just *ate* its dead baby, so I hardly think it's that bothered," Porgy declared.

"What the hell is it?" Atkins asked Chandar.

"This One does not know," it wheezed, forcing out the words. "It – it is not mentioned in any aromapedias. It is not GarSuleth-made."

"Whatever it is, I think we're going to need the damn tank to take it out," said Gazette, unfazed, his mind never straying from the job.

"Hell, no!" Porgy slapped Atkins on the back. "Only here can do it single-handed, can't you, Only?" He grinned at his mate. "Come on, Chalky's told us all the tales."

"Aye," said Mercy with a grin. "Seven at one blow!"

Atkins curled his lip. "Piss off. How many bombs do we have left?"

Gazette did a quick tally. "Six."

Atkins leant forward to get a better look at the thing, doubting that they would be enough. He stepped back sharply as the edge of the lip crumbled away beneath his feet. Several large chunks skittered down the exposed walls before hitting an outcrop, and bouncing off over the lower slopes, where some were ensnared by thickets of creepers. The rest bounded down in ever increasing arcs, before landing on the creature's back in a shower of thuds.

A stream of tendrils exploded upwards towards them from around the fallen rubble.

"No, it's definitely not happy," said Mercy.

"Back!" ordered Atkins, but the section was one step ahead of him. Chandar, though, hesitated, mesmerised by the sight, until Atkins put a hand on its carapace and pulled it away.

He took a last look over his shoulder as thin black tendrils appeared over the lip of the truncated tunnel. Some had already begun searching the gaping hole where they had stood. As they explored the tunnel further, they began to entwine and merge into one, growing in bulk, thickening and expanding until one single tentacle filled the space, blocking out the light.

Rushing down the tunnel, it expanded further until the walls began to crack and shudder under the pressure of its passing.

Atkins ran for his life.

THE GREAT IRON hulk of the *Ivanhoe* sat where they had left it, hunkered in the clearing, waiting patiently like a faithful beast.

Exhausted, the tank crew staggered towards the waiting behemoth.

Norman, Reggie, Cecil and Wally set down their coverall loads of chatt jars and stretched. In the daylight, Mathers' swollen face looked much worse than they had imagined.

"And I thought impetigo from petrol fumes was bad," Norman remarked.

"How comes he's the only one that's got it, though?" asked Cecil.

"Officer in't 'e? They've got more sensitive skin than us lot. Known fact, is that."

"The sooner I'm back in the *Ivanhoe*, the better I'll feel," said Wally.

"Best get the tank started up, then, I reckon," said Jack.

Nellie patted Napoo on the forearm. "Thank you."

With a faint smile, the urman gave a grunt of acknowledgement and nodded as she left his side.

He squatted down on his haunches, looking decidedly uncomfortable. He was wary of the Lieutenant, but just as cautious about the tank. Although aware that men operated it, he was convinced that there was sorcery involved. Alfie approached the urman, "Thanks for looking out for Nellie – I mean, Miss Abbott."

Napoo looked up at him. "She is a good woman." It was a threat as much as a statement of fact.

"Yes. Yes, she is," replied Alfie, sensing that he had outstayed his welcome. He made for the tank. His path took him past Nellie, who was splashing water from her canteen on the back of her neck. She was relieved to see that Alfie's eyes had almost returned to normal. He wanted to tell her about the thing inside Mathers, but changed his mind. "Will you check the Lieutenant out, again? He doesn't look too clever."

"Do I tell you how to tune your precious engine?" she remarked.

"Yes, actually."

She beamed as she made her way over to check on Mathers, who seemed to be enjoying the soothing wind on his face. "Then I'm much too good for you, Mr Perkins."

Norman saw her examining the Lieutenant. "We just need to get the engine started up, is all, Miss. Once the Sub can take a drag on the fumes he'll be top o' the bill again," he insisted.

"Top o' the bill?" said Nellie. "He's had so many turns he's a regular Marie Lloyd. It's not those blessed fumes he needs, it's rest and proper medical attention."

Frank intercepted Alfie on the way to the tank. "Where do you think you're going?"

"To start the engine, if three of you lazy buggers'll lend a hand."

Frank shook his head. "I don't think so, Alfie." He leaned in. "You may have won the Lieutenant over, but he's not quite himself at the moment. Me and the lads? We ain't decided on you yet, you and your sweetheart. You see, we was all cushy 'til she and them Tommies showed up. The Sub's scheme has all gone to pot since then. You was never for it, was you? I reckon you've been sabotaging us all along. You stay there, with your lady friend."

"What the hell's got into you, Frank?"

Frank crossed to the tank and noticed an oily stain on the grass under the sponson. "Bloody hell. Perkins. I knew it. Look like something has been leaking here!" He went to open the sponson hatch. His forehead creased with disbelief as he tugged at the handle. "It's stuck." He pulled at the handle again.

"Put some oomph into it!" jeered Cecil.

The door resisted, then came free with a sticky, sucking sound. He toppled backwards onto his arse, causing a ripple of belly laughs across the clearing.

Frank's brow buckled under the weight of incomprehension as he sat staring up at the open hatchway.

Something slick and black filled the tank compartment. Something with the texture of tripe.

Tendrils whipped out from the mass, wrapped around Frank's head, and yanked him into the tank. He didn't even have time to scream.

1 SECTION RAN hell-for-leather down the narrow sloping tunnel, almost stumbling down the incline. Cracks and rumbles accompanied the sound of tide-sucked shingle behind them, as the creature's extruded limb ploughed after them, shattering the walls as it went. All the while, the passages resounded to the ultra-low keening rumble that made Atkins want to loose his bowels.

Ahead, the tunnel wall exploded in a choking cloud of debris and dust, as a second tendril smashed through the wall at right angles, cutting off their escape, before punching out through the opposite wall. With the thing approaching from behind, they were cornered.

The men collided to a halt as the tentacle passed in front of them.

Atkins pointed behind them. "Gazette, Gutsy. Watch our backs."

Porgy groaned. "Jesus, what're you going to do now?"

"Quit your griping. What's the worst that can happen?"

"You'll get us all killed?"

"You're not afraid of that, are you, Porgy?" said Mercy.

"What? Of course I bloody am, I don't want to die – when you die they stop your pay."

Atkins grinned and snatched a Mills bomb from Chalky's webbing pouch. If he set it off here, the tunnel would channel the explosion. They had no cover. At this distance, the concussion wave would render them senseless. The shrapnel blast would shred them. Standing inches from the passing tentacle, he pulled the pin with his teeth and held down the safety lever.

"Chalky, stab the damn thing with your bayonet," he yelled.

Chalky hesitated.

"Chalky, for fuck's sake – *Now*!"

The lad's training took over. He charged the still passing tentacle in front of them, as if the Sergeant Major was standing right behind him, and let out a battle roar before thrusting his bayonet deep into the dark, otherworldly flesh. As the tentacle moved past, the blade opened up a slit along its surface. Thick black ichor sprayed out.

Like gutting a fish, Atkins thought. He took a deep breath and, hoping to God this worked, thrust the grenade into the gash as it raced by, flinching away from the stabbing bayonet, taking the bomb with it.

"Down!"

Every man in the section dropped to the ground and covered their head, smashing another couple of amphora in the process. Gutsy pulled Chandar to the floor and pressed its head to the ground. Somewhere beyond the tunnel wall, the grenade exploded, precipitating more showers of dust and rubble.

The tentacle before them reared back sharply from the pain in a reflex action, withdrawing back across the tunnel; a ragged, torn stump leaking a trail of thick, black liquor. Within seconds, it was gone.

"You did it! You banished Jeffries' demon!" Chalky cried in jubilation. "Thank the Lord. I knew the Corp would kill the fiend. Didn't I say? Didn't I?"

Mercy reached out, patting him on the shoulder. "Steady on, lad. We don't want it going to his head."

Gutsy rolled his eyes and grinned. "Hear that, Only? Everson won't know whether to mention you in his dispatches or his prayers, now."

Behind them came the rumble of a roof fall. The tentacle thrashed about as the creature reacted in shock to its injury, bringing the tunnel crashing down. A great cloud of dirt and dust billowed towards them, overtook them and left them gagging and coughing.

"Go!" ordered Atkins, picking himself up.

The Tommies scrambled to their feet and rushed on. All but one torch had been extinguished. It was enough to light the way, but not bright enough to give them much warning of anything else in the deep dark of the tunnels.

They passed an earlier scrawled 13/PF chalk mark with some relief, and took a broader, descending passage.

As they ran, they could hear muffled thuds and thumps from all around, some too far away to be of concern, some too close for comfort.

It put Atkins in mind of the interminable Hun artillery barrages they suffered when the minniewerfers and five-nines would pummel the front lines for hours or days. The nerve-shredding pounding continued around them, accompanied more and more often by the long, slow rush of tunnel collapses.

"What's going on?" cried Chalky, flinching at every crash.

The demon creature was thrashing about, trying to find them, Atkins guessed. It was no longer content to use the chatt-built tunnels and passages to hunt them, but was tearing down galleries and punching through chambers, searching for the bugs that were tormenting it.

"I think the damn thing's reading its shirt, looking for us."

"You mean it's chatting us?" Porgy came back.

"You could say that, aye."

"Bloody cheek!" said Porgy, affronted. "No offence," he added, nodding an apology at Chandar as it raced alongside with its hopping gait.

They wound their way down through tunnels and galleries, threading their way back through the labyrinth as best they could, avoiding the many tentacles now ploughing through the tunnels in search of them.

The passage roof in front of them bowed and buckled, as cracks appeared. Slivers of silver daylight drove down into the dark confined space, slicing through the dust motes before the roof caved in. A tentacle punched down through the tunnel, and on through the floor, with a force that almost threw them off their feet. They darted to the right, down a smaller tunnel. Further down, daylight streamed in from some kind of window or breach. They were against an exterior wall. Atkins wondered how far they were above ground.

"Frank!"

Frank did not respond.

Jack darted towards the tank in the vain hope of rescuing him.

The tank came alive. Black tentacles burst from the drivers' visors, from the pistol ports around the tank, and from the hatches, all thrashing wildly.

Jack ducked and danced, as light on his feet now as he had been in the carnival boxing ring before the war. He edged towards the open sponson through which Frank had been pulled, but was driven back as the tendrils lashed out at him.

Napoo drew his sword and pulled Nellie behind him. "Alfie, stay back!" she screamed, as he joined the others, trying to find a way past the pseudopodia as they whipped through the air.

They took pot shots with their revolvers, aiming for the pistol ports or at the portion of the writhing black mass that presented itself through the sponson hatch. Alfie shouted at them to stop. "You might damage the *Ivanhoe*!"

Nellie peered round Napoo in horror. "What on earth is it?"

Distracted, Mathers looked towards the tank. He seemed clear and lucid, for the moment. "It is the spawn of the thing that inhabits the ruins. It is not of this place," he declaimed.

Reggie started towards him, concern etched on his face. "Sir?"

Mathers turned to him and spoke as if he might have been discussing the finer points of cricket over cucumber sandwiches on a summer's evening. "Didn't you realise?" He gestured vaguely towards the ruined edifice. "It has no protection of its own against the predations of this world. Its sire found its way inside the ruins for shelter. This one found its way inside the tank. Don't you see? It's using it as a shell, as a hermit crab does, to armour itself."

"But Frank. What about Frank, sir?"

"Frank?" Mathers stared blankly at the tank, unconcerned. "Frank's gone."

Norman tried to follow the Lieutenant's logic. "So you're saying all we have to do is winkle it out? Then we're going to need a bloody big pin, if you don't mind my saying so, sir."

"A bayonet!" suggested Cecil.

"Going to need something bigger than a pig sticker, son," said Jack.

Nellie frowned. "I know just what we need to lance this boil." She ran over to the undergrowth, to the little copse of black-barked, silver-veined saplings she had spotted when they arrived at the edifice. "Napoo, help me."

Napoo joined her. He arched an eyebrow as he realised what she was looking at. "Corpsewood?"

"Will it work, do you think?"

"What is it?" asked Alfie.

"It's a scavenger plant. It usually feeds on dead or rotting flesh, but eats living things if it can, hence the name, so be careful."

"It... might work," said Napoo, with caution. "But it must be handled with great care. We have never used it in such a way."

Alfie was insistent. "We need the tank back. If this is the only way, then let's do it."

Since the creature in the ruins had frightened off anything that the corpsewood might feed on, pickings were thin. The wood had grown up around the bodies of small creatures, their bones embedded it its trunk and protruding from the black bark.

The tank crew watched, fascinated, from a safe distance, distracted occasionally by the creature within the tank as its tentacles whipped and thrashed hungrily.

Wrapping his hands in bandages from Nellie's webbing pouches, Napoo set to work, cutting down the stand of black corpsewood saplings. Thin and reedy specimens, eager for sustenance, the silver vein-like creeper stems around them unwound and inclined towards Napoo's hands, like a plant following the sun. He threw them aside too quickly for them to latch on. With deft strokes of his sword, he stripped them of their spiny branches and fashioned their tips into sharp points. He bound part of the shafts with a lengths of split vine to give some protection against the corpsewood for the wielder. Within fifteen minutes, Napoo had a brace of crude corpsewood spears.

Alfie watched in awe as Napoo threw the makeshift spears with confidence. Lashing tentacles knocked some aside to clatter harmlessly off the iron plating, but he targeted the open sponson hatch, and the corpsewood spear buried itself in the exposed black flesh. It puckered and shrivelled around the wound as the silver grey creepers wormed their way slowly into the creature. It was enough to prove that the idea worked, but not enough to rid them of the thing.

"We can't get close enough," said Norman, as he and the others tried to target the creature while avoiding its tendrils.

Mathers walked up and hefted one of the corpsewood spears experimentally. "I can," he said, exchanging a look with Alfie. He picked up a bunch of the spears and walked towards the tank. Reggie and Norman tried to stop him, but he waved them back.

The tendrils whipped and lashed wildly, but he pressed on, showing no fear, for he had none left to show. The things inside him saw to that, he was sure of it. He was within the reach of the flailing tendrils, but they wavered uncertainly, and then retreated before his advance, as if loath to touch him. Its sire could sense the things within him, and so, too, could its spawn. He was an anathema to them. By the time he was in striking distance of the tank, the creature had completely retreated inside it.

He thrust the corpsewood spears through the drivers' visors, the pistol ports, and through the view slits in the gun shield. Trapped inside the ironclad, the creature recoiled from the pain as the corpsewood sought to burrow into it.

Mathers climbed onto the top of the tank, threw open the manhole in the roof and thrust another spear down into the compartment, driving the creature down. In desperation, the thing began to squeeze itself out of the port sponson hatch. He dropped down into the tank to push his advantage, herding the shapeless creature back out of the tank with his last spear.

The heaving bulk flopped gracelessly from the ironclad and it grew tendrils to help drag itself away. However, the creature's back half was dead, atrophying beneath the corpsewood. Starved for so long, the many spears had sent their vein-like silver creepers deep into the creature's body, and had begun to leech its life from it. Weakening, the creature's tentacles could no longer keep the men at bay.

Once they realised it was dying, the tank crew fell on it in a fury, using sticks, wrenches and chains to take out their fear and anger.

"That's for Frank!"

"Do that to our *Ivanhoe*, will you?" bellowed Cecil, stamping on a weakly twitching tendril.

Wally, incoherent with rage, thrashed his chain down, over and over again. His face turned red, and spittle flew from his lips, as he took out the frustrations he realised he could no longer take out on the Hun.

Alfie held back, fretting. "Stop!" he cried, "stop!" But they weren't listening. Alfie grabbed Norman's arm as he raised it to land another blow. "Stop it! Look," he said. "Look!"

Amid the now beaten, shapeless bulk, its wounds running with thick viscous fluid, they could make out a shadow in the depths of the creature that looked vaguely human in shape. Because it had been.

"Oh Jesus. Frank!"

Norman dropped the wrench, drained. The others too, sobered up, their chests heaving.

Mathers clambered unsteadily from the sponson, a tin of grease in his hand. He tipped it over the creature as the roots of the corpsewood spread further into it. He lit a Lucifer and dropped it on the thick lubricant. It ignited with a bright indigo flame. The tentacles writhed feebly in the flames before shrivelling. As the grease melted with the heat, it ran, spreading out, coating the rest of the creature, basting it. The flames followed, consuming it, the corpsewood, and Frank.

Jack pulled Cecil back from the monstrous pyre. Reggie made the sign of the cross and muttered a prayer.

"Get the tank started," Mathers ordered, quietly.

Alfie, Cecil, Reggie and Norman squeezed in through the small sponson hatches, one after the other. Wally followed. Mathers paused in the sponson hatchway. He heard the grind of the giant starting handle. The engine caught and the *Ivanhoe* awoke from its slumber with a growl.

A breeze caught the burning creature, fanning the flames, causing the corpsewood embers to burn brighter, and the flesh to char and crackle in the heat.

Mathers turned into the wind, a hand on his belly as if it pained him. He felt weary, too weary to worry, too tired to care, and too exhausted to fight it anymore.

"Now it comes," he said, almost with relief, before climbing into the tank.

THE TOMMIES RACED down the sloping tunnel and burst out into the giant space of the ancient antechamber. It echoed with the continual pounding of the creature around them, unseen.

Exhilaration mixed with fear as, across the open, rubble-strewn space, they caught sight of the withered bark gates that once guarded the main entrance to the edifice.

The ground shuddered beneath their feet as something pummelled away beneath them, making it hard to keep their balance. Great chunks of hardened earth, compacted to rock-like density, plummeted from the domed ceiling high above, like a barrage, exploding around them in rocky shrapnel.

It was just like going over the top into No Man's Land, Atkins thought, as they sheltered in the mouth of the tunnel, only here there was no officer's whistle to set them off. It was down to him. Another time, another place, they had done this before. Atkins checked his rifle. "Mercy, Gutsy, you're with me. The rest of you, wait for my signal. Leapfrog us. We'll hold the middle ground while you make for the door. Cover us from there."

His section returned almost imperceptible nods. He took a deep breath and darted out in the domed space, amid the pounding and crashing rubble, Mercy and Gutsy at his heels.

They made a stooped run to the middle of the chamber, weaving between the crashing debris. They threw themselves down by a large chunk of rubble, sweeping the other openings for pursuing tentacles, as the pounding continued around them, reverberating through the chamber. "Come on!" hollered Atkins, beckoning the others.

Gazette, Chalky, Pot Shot, Porgy and Chandar raced across the open space, dodging masses of falling masonry that sent showers of dirt and rocky shrapnel into the air.

"Bleedin' hell, it's just like old times!" yelled Porgy, flinching as chips and shards of rock whistled past them.

"Yeah, what price your soft caps now, eh?" said a cocky Pot Shot, patting the steel battle bowler on his head.

A huge chunk of masonry plunged to the floor and shattered close by. A lump sheered off, smashing the lanky Fusilier in the back of the head. He dropped to the floor like a bag of bones.

Gazette had gone a few paces before he realised his mate wasn't by his side. He turned and saw the gangly figure lying on the ground like a broken marionette. "Pot Shot!"

Gazette ran back to him. He knelt, gathered in the lanky man's limp limbs, and turned him over. He lifted Pot Shot's head. His hand came away covered with blood.

Mercy crouched at his side. "Come on, mate, let's get him out of here." He gathered up Pot Shot's rifle, and slung it over his shoulder, and together the pair of them dragged their fallen comrade to the shelter of the rubble.

The walls shuddered under the continual impacts. From around them, in the ruins of the edifice, came the sound of collapsing tunnels, crumbling passageways and the awful *thud, thud, thud* of pounding tentacles. The whole place was coming down.

Atkins ducked as a piece of roof, the size of a gun limber, smashed down a dozen feet away. They couldn't stay here. Atkins gave the order. "Make for the door!"

Gazette and Porgy carried Pot Shot, staggering under his weight and the juddering impacts from under the floor. Chalky stuck with Chandar as they weaved drunkenly towards the opening.

Cracks crazed across the walls, racing them to the entrance. The mouth of one of the tunnels began to flake and crumble. A tentacle burst from it, flailing blindly.

Porgy opened fire, five rounds rapid, driving it back.

"Did you see the size of that?" he grinned.

The floor bucked beneath their feet. Great blocks of floor split and lifted. The broken slabs tilted violently. Another pounding sent them spinning up into the air.

"That?" said Gutsy. "Pff. That was a tiddler. Now that," he said, as a huge tentacle erupted through the floor, "is something worth worrying about."

"Don't like the look of yours much!" Atkins yelled to Gutsy, as they ran, stumbling over the debris towards the door.

Lumps of roof rained down around them, exploding into dust, adding to the clouds of dirt that already hung in the air.

Smaller tentacles sprouted violently from the weakened floor about them. They swerved to avoid them, Gutsy taking a swipe at one with Little Bertha.

Reaching the entrance with Chandar, Chalky gave covering fire, sniping at the tentacles until his ammunition ran out.

Mercy and Gazette, with Pot Shot between them, stumbled into the sunlight cutting into the chamber. Atkins, Gutsy and Mercy followed close on their heels.

"Good, shooting, Chalky," said Atkins, patting the lad on the shoulder. Chalky beamed with pride.

Under cover of the dust cloud that billowed from the edifice, an oily black mist drifted out of the entrance and something caught Chalky's ankle. It yanked his feet out from under him. Chandar hissed in alarm.

"Atkins! Dear God, Only, save me!" he shrieked, his fingers scrabbling at the dirt, leaving brief, bloodied gouges in the earth, as he was dragged feet first back into the waiting darkness.

Porgy grabbed his wrist, but found himself dragged along too, until his shoulder crashed into a boulder. He screamed and let go.

Gazette fired three rounds rapid at the tentacle before his magazine emptied, but it wouldn't release Chalky.

As the tentacle pulled Chalky into the edifice, he looked pleadingly at Atkins to save him one way or another.

Gazette spoke urgently. "Only, he's being dragged into hell. You can save him from that at least."

Atkins blinked away the stinging tear in his eye, raised his Enfield, gritted his teeth and fired. Chalky went limp as his now lifeless body was reeled back into the collapsing edifice.

1 SECTION WAS racing from the shadow of the crumbling building and running towards the tank, shouting. Mathers, peering out of the sponson, couldn't make out what they were saying over the sound of *Ivanhoe's* engine, the ground trembling under a relentless pounding, and the roaring of rubble slides, as parts of the ruined edifice toppled and collapsed.

Gauging from their urgent waving, however, it meant trouble. Best to be safe. He clambered into the tank, the fug of petrol fruit fumes embracing him as he entered. The engine ran up. The tank made a jerky turn to face the edifice, then lurched towards the retreating soldiers, black smoke belching from its back.

Tentacles writhed out of the edifice now.

The soldiers ran past, carrying one of theirs between them, the chatt scurrying alongside. The tank clattered and clanked towards the edifice to face the large writhing tentacles of the creature. This was no job for infantry now. This was a job for the Machine Gun Corps Heavy Section.

Cecil was loading a shell into the breech of Jack's starboard six pounder when a huge tentacle unfurled from the disintegrating ruins. It seized the *Ivanhoe* and began to drag it, slowly, inexorably, towards the edifice.

PENNINE FUSILIERS

CHAPTER TWENTY
"There's a Silver Lining in the Sky-ee..."

EXHAUST FUMES BELCHING from its back, its engine growling, the *Ivanhoe* clawed doggedly at the ground as it hauled against the tentacle clutching it, like a determined hound worrying a rope. It made some ground, its track plates pawing at the earth, pulling away from the tentacle until it began to lose its grip on the tank, but the creature was unwilling to let its prey go. More tentacles whipped out, lashing themselves around the ironclad, drawing it back again, foot by foot towards the collapsing ruins.

In a tug of war for its life, the tank fought back valiantly. Bursts of machine gun fire tore through the tentacles. The port gun spoke, demolishing a section of the edifice, bringing it down on yet more tentacles.

The *Ivanhoe's* engine began to whine under the strain. The tracks slipped, losing traction against the slow, insistent pull of the tentacles. Gradually, but certainly, it was being drawn into the edifice. The tank's tracks scored great long furrows in the ground as the tentacles dragged it towards the gaping entrance.

Inside the *Ivanhoe,* the compartment began to fill with black smoke from burning oil and grease. The track wheels clanked and whined, trying to keep purchase on the iron track plates as they slipped.

"Oh hell, don't let us throw a track now, please God," said Reggie, crossing himself as he passed Norman a shell for the port gun. Before returning to his gear station, he let off a short burst from the belt-fed Hotchkiss machine gun, the bullets chewing through another tentacle.

"It's no use, I can't get a shot!" Norman bellowed over the engine noise.

From his seat at the front, Mathers indicated that Reggie and Alfie should use the track gears to try to swing the tank to starboard and get him a better shot.

Reggie put his track into second as Alfie, cursing under his breath, shifted his into neutral. The tank began to swing round to the right. Alfie could feel the gears beginning to judder through the gear lever.

As THE IRONCLAD occupied the creature's attention, Atkins, Mercy, Gutsy and the others dragged Pot Shot to safety across the clearing. A little distance away, a foul smelling fire was still burning itself out.

Lying discarded on the ground nearby were the two tank crew coveralls, stuffed with stone jars and sacred scents. Chandar chattered and insisted they carry them to safety, too. They picked them up as they passed, dragging them along.

"Over here!" Nellie waved from the edge of the clearing. "Where's Chalky?"

Mercy shook his head.

"Oh."

As soon as they laid Pot Shot down, Nellie, thankful for the opportunity to do something other than watch the tank struggle with the creature, fell to her knees and set to work examining him.

"Is he going to be all right?" Gazette asked, fearful of the answer.

With as much care as a battlefield would allow, she gently slipped Pot Shot's steel helmet off. In some cases she'd seen, that had been all that was holding the skull together, or the brains in.

Delicately Nellie felt his skull, feeling for fractures or breaks.

"Is he – ?"

She let out a small sigh. "No. Thank God. It's only a scalp wound. He's suffering from concussion. His helmet probably saved him. He'll live."

Atkins turned his attention to the tank. All he had to do was bring the tank back. One simple order. One simple *bloody* order. It should have been a piece of cake. His heart sank as he saw it losing its struggle against the creature. The engine whined and the tracks churned up the ground. Despite its weight and power, it seemed to be fighting a losing battle, but at least it was still fighting. "Let's see if we can't convince that thing to let go!" Atkins said.

They moved as close as they dared, took up position and fired at the sinuous tentacles gripping the ironclad. Bullets tore through flesh; others struck the iron hide, sparking as they did so.

Inside the *Ivanhoe*, splashes of molten metal, caused by the impact of the bullets, flew around the compartment.

Cecil shrieked as one hit his cheek, "Jesus, now our own side are trying to kill us too! Why the hell are they shooting at us? Oh, God. Frank said Mathers would get us killed, he did!"

Jack turned and with a warning glance at Mathers' back in the driving seat, bellowed into Cecil's ear. "Button your lip!" Not that Mathers could have heard him over the noise of the engine.

Across the clearing, Gutsy pulled out a rifle grenade. "Last one," he said. He dropped it into the barrel of his rifle, braced the shoulder stock on the ground, and fired. The grenade arced through the air, landing near the entrance. It exploded, shredding a tentacle and releasing the tank, even as others sought to take its place.

The *Ivanhoe* lurched backwards as its tracks, running in reverse against the pull of the edifice creature, engaged with the ground. Once it had ripped free of the smaller tentacles, Mathers slammed on the brakes. "There's your shot," he yelled over the engine.

"Thank you, sir!" shouted Norman ecstatically as he manhandled the portside gun round. He fired. Through the gunner's vertical viewing slit in the gun shield, he saw the shell explode and a section of huge, black tentacle vaporise in a plume of atomised flesh and ichor. "Yes!"

Seconds later, Jack fired the starboard gun. That, too, hit home. The creature thrashed in pain, its tentacles demolishing the edifice, sending rubble crashing down on the Ivanhoe. The tank jerked into motion, reversing clear of the tumbling debris.

The *Ivanhoe's* guns fired again, bringing down more of the decaying structure. The tentacles wavered uncertainly, and then, by degrees, retreated into the ruins with a long, low rumble of pain.

WATCHING THE ROUT of the creature, as the shelling of the ironclad drove it back underground, the Fusiliers cheered in jubilation. It was short lived.

Cutting through the rumble of the edifice and growl of the tank, came the crashing sound of trees creaking and falling and the high-pitched jabbers and squeals of animal fear.

Atkins' eyes narrowed. Where the hell had they come from? The dulgur had hunted the area clean of game, hadn't it? He noticed the queer cast of light across the clearing, a strange kind of pre-storm twilight. It was as if the sun were being filtered through dirty glass.

"What now?" He looked up, irritated.

An immense bank of drifting clouds was obscuring the sky. No, not clouds; creatures, with vast snake-like members hundreds of feet long, hanging beneath them, tearing up trees, lifting them into the sky, plucking animals from the canopy as though they were grazing.

The ruined edifice and the clearing around it fell under a twilight shadow as they drifted across the sky, eclipsing the sun overhead.

Atkins watched in horror as the animals were flayed, as they rose to where yet more tendrils grasped the things and fed them into great wet mouth tubes. Underneath the tubes, swarms of black things danced like flies around dung.

Mercy gaped up at the sight. "Holy Mary, Mother of God!"

"Get under cover!" yelled Akins. Not that anyone needed telling. They ran for the shelter of the trees. They all saw what was happening to beasts snatched up by the shoal of airborne leviathans overhead. None of them wanted to be next.

The great sky-borne creatures filling the sky drifted over, oblivious to their presence. The light strained through the massive translucent gas sacs that kept them aloft, like huge living zeppelins.

"What the hell are they?" Atkins yelled above the cacophony.

Chandar chittered and shrunk down on it legs, almost as if it were trying to curl itself into a ball. "GarSuleth protect us!"

"Kreothe!" said Napoo, craning his neck and watching them in fear.

"That's bad, then, is it?" Mercy remarked as he looked up to watch the stately procession of creatures across the sky. Most had their long limbs curled up under their gas sacs. Only a few of the bigger ones fed as they drifted lazily over the jungle, dragging their long snake-like limbs, dredging the ground for food.

There was a terrible sound, a long low bass cry from the edifice, accompanied by the sound of collapsing walls crushing vegetation as they fell.

A huge Kreothe floated sedately over it, its long harvesting tendrils draped below it, into the ruins. Although the creature was hidden by the ruins, Atkins could see its black tentacles lashing and wrestling with the trailing tendrils of the Kreothe, wrapping themselves around them, trying to pull the sky leviathan down.

The two great beasts grappled tentacle-to-tendril, appendages slipping and sliding through and round and over as they each tried to gain an advantage.

The Kreothe's vast gas sacs inflated and it rose up, accompanied by the sound of crashing as walls collapsed. There was a terrible cry, a deep bass groan that shook the ground around them and a deep sickening tearing as the

Kreothe ripped the creature from its setting amid the ruins, uprooting it, and drawing it up into the air.

As the Kreothe drifted over the section, it worked to haul in its slippery catch. Long harvesting tendrils firmly gripped the black, shapeless creature. Where they gripped it, great wounds opened, as if it were being flayed. Now seen whole, the creature looked to Atkins like a shellfish plucked from its shell, slick, wet and raw.

In retaliation, the creature threw up tentacles around the Kreothe's feeding tendrils, while lashing down at the spindly scab trees below, trying to anchor itself, but they, too, were torn from the ground.

The black shapeless mass writhed and shifted, extruding new tentacles to thrash against the gas sacs of the Kreothe. Locked in a life or death struggle, the two creatures each fought to dominate and subdue the other, tentacles wrapping, enfolding, and choking.

The flock of scavenger things began to swarm about the shapeless creature, pecking and tearing.

The creature had now gained a purchase on the sky beast's gas sac and pulled itself up, allowing its form to change and flow, trying to engulf and swallow its opponent.

They drifted off over the crater, the slow silent battle shifting first one way and then the other. It seemed that the epic sky duel would continue until one lost out to sheer exhaustion.

"Only!"

Atkins' attention returned to the ground. A smaller Kreothe had latched onto the tank and was trying to haul the *Ivanhoe* up, but the sheer weight of the ironclad resisted its efforts. It lowered several more harvesting tendrils in an effort to increase its grasp on the vehicle.

It proved too heavy for the Kreothe to lift, yet it was unwilling to let go of its prize and, as the wind drove the enormous creature on, it dragged the *Ivanhoe* backwards with it across the clearing, almost, but not quite, lifting it clear of the ground.

The tank couldn't get enough traction on the ground to

drive in the opposite direction and break free. Occasionally, the tracks would bite into the earth and it would make some small, defiant gain of ground, only to be lifted off again. Atkins could see its guns trying to target the Kreothe above, but they couldn't get enough elevation.

"Damn! Come on!" said Atkins. "Napoo, stay there with Nellie and Pot Shot, don't let anything happen to them."

The section moved off quickly, staying in the shelter of the trees to take cover from the great dredging sky limbs. Chandar lagged behind, hesitant.

"Oh, no, you don't," said Gutsy, dropping back and waving the chatt on with his rifle. "We're not losing you as well."

Chandar snapped his mandibles together aggressively, but complied with great reluctance.

The Kreothe was slowed down by having to drag its dead twenty-eight ton weight through trees. The section raced ahead of it. The thinning jungle gave way to hardy shrub for several hundred of yards. Beyond that yawned the great crater, the land that, according to Chandar, did not exist.

Already, those Kreothe at the head of the shoal were drifting majestically out over it.

INSIDE THE TANK, the crew were thrown about as the *Ivanhoe* was dragged, crashing through a small grove of scab trees. Much to Reggie's disapproval, they were shouting and cursing, peering through pistol ports to see what the hell was going on.

All except Mathers. The officer was calm almost to the point of indolence, and seemed heedless to the danger, just when his crew needed him the most.

For all Alfie's efforts, the engine was beginning to show the strain. His petrol fruit-filtered vision was returning to full strength now as the engine fumes flooded his body. He could see from the deep blues and indigos emanating from the engine that it was at the limits of its capacity. The track gears were engaged in second forward speed but it wasn't making a blind bit of difference. They were still being dragged backwards.

Cecil opened the sponson door, hung out looking up at the underside of the Kreothe, with its tongue tendrils and mouth tubes, and fired his revolver up at it. They didn't have any effect. "Bleedin' 'ell!" you ought to see the size of this bugger! It's bigger than any bloody Zeppelin."

"Get back in, you daft sod!" yelled Jack.

Cecil ducked back in. "Like a giant bleedin' jellyfish it is!" He reached out to close the sponson door and stared in horror. "Fuck! There's a cliff coming up!" he yelled.

The petrol fruit fumes building inside the iron hull worked on Mathers, helping him break free of the ennui exerted over him by the things he carried inside him.

Jack heaved on the shoulder stock of the gun and howled in frustration. "I can't get enough elevation on the gun to hit it, sir, if I could hit it, we'd have a chance."

"Get out," said Mathers. "Abandon the tank."

"We won't leave you, sir."

"You don't have a choice, I'm ordering you out. If the *Ivanhoe's* done for, then there's no point in you all dying."

"But, sir..."

"That's an order, Clegg. And... Wally? Some good has to come out of all this. Tell the Corporal, tell... Atkins, I've seen it, Jeffries' trail. It leads to the crater. It leads there for a reason. It's the blank on the map the chatts fear, the place that doesn't exist. The name they will not admit to. Make sure he knows that. It's more than chatt myth. I suspect it'll be of some importance to him."

"Sir." Wally slipped from his driver's seat and joined Jack in the starboard gangway.

Cecil opened the hatch again. He could see the precipice approaching fast. Above, he saw the great long tendrils reaching up towards the underside of the Kreothe as it dragged the *Ivanhoe* along.

"Time to go, lad," Jack said. He pushed Cecil out of the sponson hatch before the lad could object, and then followed him.

Wally braced himself on the hatch jamb, looked across at

Alfie, still at his gear station, and nodded before launching himself from the tank, rolling clear of the tracks.

Over on the other side, Reggie and Norman jumped from the port sponson hatch. "And you, sir?" called Alfie.

Mathers turned and looked at him. "We've both seen these things in me. I'm dead already, Perkins."

"But not yet, sir. And neither is the *Ivanhoe*. I'm not leaving, sir."

Neither knew if the Kreothe could bear the weight of the tank without the ground to support it. If the Kreothe could carry its weight then it would sail out hundreds of feet over the crater, where it still might drop to destruction. On the other hand, its weight might just drag the thing right out of the air.

The tank, in one last effort to avoid it fate, roared its defiance as its metal tracks grated and clawed at the ground, raising a cloud of dust that momentarily obscured it, until updrafts from the crater snatched it away.

For a moment, the *Ivanhoe* held its own against the great sky creature, anchoring it as others drifted on past. The Kreothe's long harvesting tendrils stretched taut, like an anchor chain against the pull of the tide.

Snorting like an obdurate old bull, the *Ivanhoe* inched forwards away from the precipice. The men cheered the ironclad on. It seemed beyond all belief that the intrepid machine could take on the weight of the vast creature above. Slowly, however, its little gain was lost and it lurched back towards the edge of the crater, its back end sliding perilously close to the rim. Then, with a lurch, the rear steering tail toppled over the edge.

The track wheels clanked and squealed, trying to gain traction, but as they churned, they ate away at the very ground supporting the ironclad. Its nose rising up off the ground, the tank began to tilt over the edge.

Mathers smiled though the pain. "You've made your choice after all, Perkins. You could have left with the others, been reunited with your sweetheart."

Alfie ignored him. "We've got one chance, sir. We're tipping. We just need a few more degrees to get the gun elevation we need to hit that thing. I need you to be ready."

The tank lurched, tilting sharply. The sponson door swung open, banging against the bulkhead. Alfie reached out to grab it, catching a vertiginous glimpse of a steep rocky cliff below them, bevelling out to a shrub-covered slope descending into a canopy of thick jungle below.

A spanner skittered down the gangplank, hit the rim of the hatch with a clang and pinwheeled out into the void.

Blanching, he reached out, pulled the hatch shut, and secured it. He didn't want to lose his balance and topple out.

"This is it, sir!" He lurched unsteadily towards the loaded gun. Grunting with effort, he gripped the shoulder stock under his armpit and heaved the gun barrel up as far as it would go and fired.

The *Ivanhoe's* gun pounded. Above it, the shell exploded against the Kreothe. The concussion wave sent ripples round the gas sac, before tearing out of the upper side. The blast shrivelled the smaller tendrils beneath it and, with raucous shrieks of alarm, the flock of scavengers that swarmed beneath it scattered. The harvesting tendrils holding the tank whipped back up, like cords cut under tension, and the *Ivanhoe's* front track horns crashed back down onto solid ground.

FROM THE SHELTER of the trees, Jack and Cecil burst out in a jubilant chorus and Reggie, Norman and Wally joined in.

"The Sub did it! He bloody did it!"

"The Sub *and* Alfie," Jack reminded them.

Atkins puffed out his cheeks and exhaled. Jesus, that was close. A slow, burning anger overwhelmed his relief. From now on, he was bloody well in charge. He had orders to get the tank back to camp and, now, that was exactly what he was going to do. It helped matters that the tank would have to return with them to refuel. All of a sudden, he was eager to start back.

*   *   *

INSIDE THE *IVANHOE*, Alfie, dazed, picked himself up from the gangway and saw Mathers slumped in the commander's seat. The visor plates had slammed shut with the impact and nothing but a flickering festoon light lit his plaque-ridden face. Alfie clambered forwards into the driver's seat to check on him.

Mathers' chin rested on his chest. Alfie gently lifted the officer's head to check for injuries. His eyes snapped open. "I can feel it, Perkins, a pressure inside my head, in my belly."

"We need to get out, sir."

"No."

"Sir, we're on the edge of the cliff."

"You go, Perkins."

"Come with me, sir."

"If I go out now, I'll die. Whatever's inside me, they're making me want to go out there. They need me to go out there. They want me to offer myself to those *things*. But I won't. I refuse. *I absolutely bloody well refuse*. I am clothed in iron and armed with cordite. I will not go like this!"

Alfie's eyes met Mathers', but the iridescent swirls that looped and whorled within them disconcerted him. "Then just drive forward, sir. Away from the cliff edge."

Mathers shook his head. "The track gears are jammed."

Jammed? Perkins frowned and glanced back down the compartment, over the top of the engine. "Then I'll go back and see if I can free them. You hang on, sir." The gearsman stepped down onto the gangway and edged his way to the back of the compartment.

Mathers continued talking, raising his voice over the engine. "It's a bloody good machine, Perkins. How you've kept it running these past few months is beyond me. A bloody miracle. I was... wrong about you."

Alfie shrugged it off. Now wasn't the time for recriminations, least of all against an officer. "You weren't yourself, sir."

"Did you know I had shell-shock, Perkins, before I joined

the Heavy Section?"

Alfie didn't know what to say, but felt that the moment called for honesty. "There... there were rumours, sir," he called back.

The tank groaned and creaked under him as he edged his way past the gun and Hotchkiss towards the starboard gear panel.

"I was buried in a dugout for four hours, couldn't move a muscle. Dead man lying of top of me. Bugger probably saved my life. Funny how fate catches up with you." He waved his hand, indicating the interior of the tank. "Here I am, entombed again. No matter how far you run, there you are. It's a rum old world."

Something in the tone of Mathers' voice made Alfie glance back. Mathers was raising his revolver to his temple. "I wonder if Skarra will be waiting..."

Alfie lunged up the gangway. "Sir, no!"

There was a grinding crunch and sudden lurch. The tank tilted, slipping backwards, sending Alfie reeling back down against his gear station. The weight of the hydraulic steering tail, ironically designed to be used as a counterbalance when crossing wide trenches, was now having the opposite effect and was dragging them over the edge to destruction. He felt the tank pitch steeply as it slipped backwards.

Alfie could almost imagine the scene outside, as if he were back at Elveden, watching one of the tank trials. In his mind's eye, he saw the rim of the crater, weakened by the grinding of the tracks and the weight of the ironclad, begin to splinter and crumble. Boulders tumbled away, drawing with them steady streams of soil.

He tried to reach for the manhole above him, but lost his footing as the *Ivanhoe* tilted further and he fell back against the gear station.

The ground beneath the tank slipped away like sand through an hourglass, crumbling under its weight in a gentle but inevitable landslide of rock, soil and roots. The *Ivanhoe's* front track horns reared into the air, like a startled stallion, its angle becoming more unstable until, like a sinking ship, it slipped from sight.

A gunshot reverberated loudly inside the iron hull.

Stores broke free and tools tumbled loose, ammo boxes crashed out of their slots. A Pyrene fire extinguisher slipped from its fixings and span toward Alfie. He screamed.

The ironclad went over the edge.

SHOCKED, THE FUSILIERS and surviving tank crew watched as the tank toppled over the rim. From the crater came the sound of tortured metal and rock. Seconds later, there was a loud crashing, an eruption of animal calls and flocks of green-skinned bird-like raptors took to the air in panic from the crater jungle below.

Atkins ran to the edge, Gutsy, Mercy and Porgy hard on his heels. Nellie came running up, in time to see the tank go over the edge. She screamed. Gazette wrapped his arms around her, not so much for comfort as restraint.

Atkins stopped, feet from the lip, and cautiously stuck his head out over the edge. A few loose rocks broke away and tumbled down. "Oh, bloody Nora!"

"Jesus!"

"Buggerin' hell!"

The drop wasn't sheer but it was a very steep camber. They could see the twin furrows gouged down the escarpment as if the *Ivanhoe* had been dragged down into hell, fighting all the way. It was possible to track its path down the crater-side, where it had torn trees and plants from their roots before it crashed down through the canopy hundreds of feet below, to be swallowed by the jungle beneath.

Atkins felt sick and lighted-headed. His whole body sagged.

The tank was gone.

Above, the last of the Kreothe drifted sedately over the crater, and the sun began to peer out from behind them, a gleam of sunlight reflecting off the edge of its translucent gas sac.

INTERLUDE SIX

Letter from Private Thomas Atkins
to Flora Mullins

21ˢᵗ March 1917

Dearest Flora,

For a while today, I thought I had lost you forever, but the great big world keeps turning and showed me there is always hope. Sometimes in our darkest moments, that is hard to remember. It's funny how the smallest and most insignificant of things can give you hope. Today I found it in a lost button.

And for the rest of the day, we tried to winkle something from its shell, had our fortunes told and were stung by some jellyfish. It sounds like a day at the seaside and I wish it had been. I bet I'd look pretty dapper in a blazer, straw boater and you on my arm as we stroll along the pier.

Having said we'd found the tank, we lost it again. I don't think Lieutenant Everson is going to be very pleased. Nothing to do now but go and face the music, if there's any music left to face.

I don't even know what I'll find when I get back to camp. I have never been so far from it. The thought that it might have vanished and left me here tortures me.

All of us live in daily fear of that, whether we speak about it or not. But then, I suppose that's selfish. Folks back home live in fear of their worlds vanishing, too. In many cases, theirs have. Too many good men have not returned from the trenches. I vow to you now, Flora, I will not be one of them.

Ever yours,
Thomas

CHAPTER TWENTY-ONE
"Each Night, After a Fight..."

ATKINS FELT NUMB.

He stared down into the crater, not sure what to do next, hardly able to believe that the tank had gone at all. Cecil, Norman and Nellie all tried calling out, for Mathers, for Alfie, hoping for some reply, some sign of life. They shouted until their voices were hoarse. There was no reply but the sound of the jungle.

The tank crew had an urgent whispered discussion, and finally pushed a reticent Reggie towards the Fusiliers. He straightened himself up, cleared his throat and marched over to Atkins. "We've had a talk and we've agreed, we have to get down there," he informed him.

"How?" said Atkins, with a shrug. "We have little rope, certainly not enough to reach the bottom. And even if you do get to the bottom, what are you going to do? You can't get the tank back up here again. There nothing we can do."

Nellie strode up to him. "It's not just a tank, there are people down there who might be alive, or had you forgotten?"

"No. Have you forgotten we've lost three of our mates for this bloody mob? Have you? Because I haven't."

Her face clouded over. "But you *know* yours are dead, Corporal. You saw them. We haven't. Have you any idea what it's like to have someone listed as 'missing'?"

Her rebuke stung. Atkins thought of his brother, William, lost since the Big Push back in June. He thought of his mam and Flora and how they felt and his cheeks briefly flushed for shame. He tried again, in a more conciliatory tone. "I'm sorry, but it doesn't change anything. We were sent to bring the tank back for a reason. I have my orders. I have to report back to Lieutenant Everson, if he's still there to report to." He cast a meaningful glance at Chandar, who hung well back from the crater's edge, chittering to itself, and fiddling with its damn tassels.

"Oh well, orders!" Nellie gave up, threw her arms up in disgust and walked away.

Reggie coughed. "We're staying here. There must be some way to help the Sub and Alfie. We were wrong about him. Stayed trying to save the Sub and the tank. More than any of us did."

Atkins placed a hand on Reggie's upper arm, an awkward gesture of comfort. "We'll return with help. We'll bring teams of sappers. If we can salvage the *Ivanhoe*, we will."

"Then I'm staying here, too." said Nellie belligerently. "Alfie could still be alive. They could be injured."

Atkins was torn. He would do the same if it were his pals. Still, he had to get back to the trenches if he were to return with help. "Napoo, stay here with her. We'll go back to the encampment, if it's still there, and get what help we can. We can leave you a couple of rifles and a little ammo. Don't do anything stupid while we're gone."

Hesitantly, Jack came over to Atkins. "Before you go, the Sub asked me to give you a message."

Atkins looked at him blankly. "Message?"

"He saw Jeffries' trail. Said it led to the crater. Said something about a place that doesn't exist, that chatts is feared of? It didn't make much sense to me, but he said you'd know what he meant."

Atkins looked at the chatt again. This whole journey the damn thing had been talking in riddles. He went over to

Chandar. "What is that place?" he demanded, waving an arm airily in the direction of the crater.

Chandar looked at him, its mouth parts knitting the words. "It is forbidden. It does not exist."

He rounded on the chatt. "Yes, so you keep bloody saying, but *why* do you keep saying it? What is it you're not telling me? Why is it forbidden? Answer me!"

Chandar hissed, torn between postures of threat and submission. "It... it is Nazhkadarr, the Scentless Place. The place that should not be. The Burri of the Fallen..."

Atkins shook his head slowly, his anger now a slow burning fuse. "Talk sense! For God's sake, talk sense, just for once!" The discussion was attracting attention now; Gutsy moved in.

"It is the Crater of... Croatoan," it hissed quietly. "That is why. That is why it is forbidden to us. It is heresy, a blasphemous stain on the world GarSuleth wove for his children. It should not exist."

"Why the hell didn't you tell us?"

Chandar reared up on its legs, its mandibles scissoring. "Because the last time an urmen of the Tohmii asked about the fallen one, half of Khungarr was laid waste." It noticed Gazette pointing his rifle at it and sank back down again. "Your capture of me was no accident. I was sent to seek out the intentions of the Tohmii." Stung by the revelation, Atkins listened as Chandar carried on. "Your acts of Kurda have cast an anchor line of fate. Between this One and you something is being woven. The question remains, what?"

Atkins looked out across the vast jungle-choked depression. "The Croatoan Crater?" No wonder Jeffries had come this way. "What's down there?"

Chandar became meek and evasive again. "Nothing must enter the crater, nothing must leave. That is the will of GarSuleth."

Atkins could feel the short fuse of his anger burning down. He balled his fists. "Gutsy, get this... thing away from me until it decides to talk some bloody sense!"

Chandar turned as Gutsy escorted it away. "Nothing must enter, nothing must leave!"

"Yes, well it's a bit bloody late for that!" snapped Atkins as he looked at the crumbled lip and the track marks left by the tank.

Mercy steered Atkins away. "We're all a little tense, mate. I think we should just go. The sooner we leave, the sooner we can come back with help."

Atkins' eyes never left the chatt while Mercy spoke, but he nodded in agreement.

1 SECTION WAS ready to depart. They had made a litter and were carrying all the jars and amphorae of sacred scents they had managed to salvage from Nazarr before its collapse. There were more than they thought and less than Chandar would have liked. He fussed over them, adding torn crushed leaves to the roughly woven wattle frame that Napoo had constructed, as packing to prevent them from breaking on the long journey back. Atkins, still angry, avoided Chandar, although the chatt was coming back with them. Everson ought to hear what it had to say.

Atkins went over to where Jack and the other tank crew, Reggie, Cecil, Norman and Wally, waited with Napoo and Nellie. Atkins held out his hand. Jack took it. "We'll be back as soon as we can. Napoo's a good man. Look after Nellie."

Jack nodded. "We'll be here."

He stepped over to Nellie. "Look, I'm sorry. But we have to do this. We'll be back in four or five days."

Nellie nodded. "Tell Edith I'm fine."

Atkins and the remains of his section set off. Pot Shot, his head swathed in bandages under his now-lucky battle bowler, insisted on making the journey with them, even though Nellie was just as adamant he should stay and rest. "I'm hard-headed," he said, tapping his bandaged skull. "My place is with these reprobates. You don't know the trouble they'd get into without me."

They followed the paths through the jungle, bypassing the Gilderra enclave.

"Shouldn't think they'd be too pleased to see us," said Mercy.

"We got rid of the evil spirit, didn't we?" said Porgy.

"And the tankers cost 'em one shaman and got their replacement killed. I expect Napoo would have something to say about that," Pot Shot informed them.

"Oh, aye," said Porgy. "No doubt."

Atkins had plenty of time to mull over all that had happened in the past few days, and figure out how he was going to tell Lieutenant Everson.

He worried about the awful truth behind the Bleeker Party. It was a terrible secret he was asking his men to keep and he wondered what kind of price it would exact, not just on 1 Section, but also on the rest of the Battalion. That burden would soon belong to Lieutenant Everson.

But there was hope, too. Well, hope of a kind. He felt the button in his pocket, rubbed his thumb over the raised casting. Atkins had to believe there was a way back to Flora – and his child. He had to put that right, even though it might cost him everything else.

Right now, though, the fear of not knowing what he'd find back at camp drove Atkins on, and he kept the pace up. They had done forced marches before and nobody complained this time. They all wanted to get back, even though none of them knew what was waiting for them.

EDITH BELL WAS in the Bird Cage with Stanton, the orderly. They were gathering up the personal possessions of all those killed by the parasitic infection, the patients she had nursed for the past three months. The place was vacant, depressing and forlorn now. Blankets and discarded mess kits littered the ground. The emptiness was heartbreaking.

She saw Captain Lippett making his way across the parade ground towards the compound. He was the last person she wanted to see right now. She put another blanket on the pile and pretended not to notice him.

He approached and looked at her in that brusque surgeon's matter-of-fact manner. "I thought you ought to know, Nurse, Miller died less than an hour ago."

Edith replied in a similarly sterile manner. "Thank you, Doctor." Edith had steeled herself for the news since she had brought him in, but you always hoped. Thinking that was it, she returned to her task.

However, Lippett had more to say. "I couldn't have operated without killing him. We have no anaesthetic. I'm reduced to the level of a Crimean butcher here, which is a wholly unsatisfactory state of affairs, as I'm sure you'll admit. And even if I could have removed those parasites from his bowels, I doubt whether I could have done the same to those attached to his nervous system without inflicting great damage and pain."

"I understand that, doctor."

Lippett opened his arms. "I'm not an ogre, Nurse. Being stranded here, trying to be everything to everyone... I wanted to be a surgeon, not an army butcher. I can't do everything and I realise I need staff who can think for themselves, who see things I can't. Fenton tells me I have such a woman in you, should I but care to listen."

His openness took Edith aback. Her reaction must have shown on her face.

He coughed to cover his discomfort. "This is a new situation for all of us, Nurse Bell, and something we're going to have to learn to cope with."

She wasn't sure whether he was talking about their general circumstances, here on the planet, or more specifically, his having to listen to a nurse for once. Either way, she gracefully accepted the compliment.

"On another note, Nurse, if you're right, and this neurasthenia is the result of emotional shock, then we shall doubtless have more of these cases as men fail to cope. The war may no longer affect them, but this hell of a world may, and we can't send them down the line for convalescence so there is no relief from it. If you want more responsibility, I'd like you to set up a special ward for them. None of this barbed wire, eh? At least that way they won't come back to you more injured than when they left if they escape." Lippett smiled stiffly. He was clearly uncomfortable with the situation. "Now if you'll excuse me, I must go and report my findings to Lieutenant Everson."

Edith curtseyed. "Yes, Doctor."

Despite her grief, she walked away taller and straighter, with a renewed vitality she hadn't felt in a long time. She took a deep breath and smiled. She already had ideas.

WALKING ACROSS THE fractured plain, back towards the canyon, Atkins and 1 Section saw the unmistakable shape of Tulliver's aeroplane above, no doubt searching for them. Atkins frowned. Everson must be anxious if he allowed Tulliver up in the air. The pilot waggled his wings in response to their frantic hat waving and headed home. It was a cheering sight. If nothing else, it meant the encampment was still there. It hadn't vanished back to Earth without them.

On the other hand, it dismayed Atkins. Everson would know now that they didn't have the tank with them and that failure ate away at him.

Atkins and the others were shocked when they came over the valley head and looked down into the encampment. He had to be honest, he wasn't quite sure what to expect, but to see the churned and trampled ground below them was quite a blow. Even Chandar let out long low hiss at the sight of the devastated trenches.

At first, Atkins thought it was the result of the battle with the Khungarrii, and then he saw the burning pyres of animal corpses and the body of the dead Kreothe, splayed along the valley like a washed up jellyfish at low tide. The veldt beyond, what they could see of it, had fared little better. However, there was no sign of the chatt army that had occupied it scant days ago. He shook his head in disbelief. Myriad questions tumbled through his mind and he was eager for answers.

As they made their way down the hillside and along the valley towards the encampment, Atkins saw fatigue parties at work, repairing trenches and wire.

"Eh, up. It's King Arthur returned from his latest quest," jeered one working party NCO. "Found the Holy Grail then, have you lad?"

"One of your admirers?" asked Porgy.

SERGEANT HOBSON MET Atkins and escorted him straight to Battalion HQ. "Good to have you back, lad."

"Glad to be back, Sarn't. What happened here?"

"What hasn't happened, more like. I'm sure the Lieutenant will tell you all about it. He's anxious to hear your report."

Atkins avoided Hobson's eyes. "I expect Tulliver has told him."

"Maybe, but he's waiting to hear it from you."

Atkins knocked on the doorjamb to the battalion HQ dugout.

"Come!"

He stepped inside and stood to attention before the Lieutenant's desk. Everson was writing in the Battalion War Journal; he'd have a lot more to write once Atkins had given his report. "At ease, Corporal." He finished writing, and then looked up. "Where's my tank, Atkins?" Everson could tell from the Corporal's face that it wasn't good news. He sighed. "You'd better tell me everything."

Atkins did. He told him about the canyon and the mysterious metal wall. He explained about the Gilderra enclave and the evil spirit, but kept back Mathers' worst excesses.

Everson nodded and waved them away. "It's all right. I can't say I'm surprised. Mathers always struck me as a bit windy. Hid it well, though."

Atkins frowned. "Sir?"

"We had an infection here. Some sort of parasite, the MO says. It affected the shell-shocked; their weakened minds were apparently more suggestible to the parasites. The infected act as if they're possessed. I suppose they were. They're all dead, now, the shell-shocked. Seems this parasite needs its hosts to be eaten by the those Kreothe things in order to 'continue its life cycle' or some such," Everson paused and let out a sigh. "Lippett thinks the parasites' main host is probably the chatts and *they* wouldn't have been infected if they hadn't marched here to fight us, foraging for food on the way.

Atkins felt he was in some bizarre estaminet bad news contest. He told Everson about the ruined edifice of the Nazarrii and the tentacled creature, and their Kreothe. They both assumed it must have been the same shoal. Everson countered with the stampede.

Then Atkins produced the Bleeker Party's bible and the journal from his haversack. Everson flicked through them with a wonder that transmuted to fear as the ramifications set in.

"Dear God," he said. "We weren't the first?"

"It doesn't look like it, sir."

"And they all died here?"

"As far as I can tell, yes, sir. They didn't find a way back."

Everson looked at him in alarm. "You've told your men to keep this a secret?"

"Yes, sir. And Miss Abbott. I thought you'd best know what to do with the information, sir."

Everson ran his fingers across the battered journal, as if to make sure it was real. He was silent for a while, and then he looked up. "You did the right thing, Atkins. Leave this with me. At the moment, things round here are a powder keg. I'm not sure how the men might take the news. I'd prefer to have something positive to say to them. Anything positive, really."

Finally, Atkins told him about the *Ivanhoe*.

"So it's lost, then," said Everson.

"No, sir. We know exactly where it is, we just can't reach it. I believe the technical word is ditched, sir."

"And where is it?" asked Everson. "Exactly."

Atkins took a deep breath and dealt his trump card. "The Croatoan Crater, sir."

Everson felt as if he had physically had the wind knocked from him. He sat back in his chair. "The *Croatoan* Crater?" He hardly dared voice his next thought. In the end, he didn't have to.

Atkins fished about in his tunic top pocket and pulled out a blood-stained scrap of khaki. He tossed it onto the desk. Everson looked down at the button attached to it, and then up at Atkins, for an explanation. "We believe it belonged to Jeffries, sir. I believe he was at the Nazarrii edifice on his way to the crater. For what reason, we can only guess. But to my mind the name is a big clue. Along with this." He produced the tattered paper with the Croatoan symbol and placed it face down, revealing the hastily copied symbols from the edifice.

"I've seen this before, or something like it," said Everson, leafing through Jeffries' coded journal. "Aha." He stabbed a finger on a page and placed the book down next to the paper. The arrangement of symbols was identical.

"What do they mean?" asked Atkins.

Everson's shoulders sagged. "I have no idea." He looked up at Atkins in earnest. "But the chatt, Corporal, this Chandar. Did you find out anything more from *that*?"

Atkins exhaled heavily. Where to start? "Half truths, prophecies and riddles, sir, but it seems there are factions who don't agree with Sirigar's urman culling policy, Chandar among them. Factions that might look on us favourably, especially since we've come back with some holy scent texts from Nazarr. Chandar seems very keen to return with them to Khungarr. Thinks they might start a revolution, sir."

"In the meantime they're ours, are they?"

"Yes, sir."

"Right, well, let's get them somewhere safe; keep them under guard until I find out what best to do with them." Everson got up from his chair and began to escort Atkins to the dugout door. "Thank you, Atkins. It can't have been easy, especially losing the tank. It wasn't your fault."

"About the tank, sir. We've left the tank crew, Miss Abbott and Napoo out there, trying to do what they can."

"We'll organise a salvage party and, while we're at it, we'll take a patrol to check out this mystery wall."

"But how are we going to raise the tank, sir, even it is in one piece?"

Everson smiled. "Don't worry about that, Atkins. We've got something that'll do the job, believe me. Now go and get yourself some food and a rest. You and your men have earned it."

Everson sat back in his chair, feeling strangely pleased with their new situation. Since they'd been here, they had done nothing but react to things. Now he had enough information to act, to do something here. The question was, what?

IN THE JUNGLE of the Croatoan Crater, half-buried by the torn and shredded undergrowth that caught and halted its headlong rush to destruction, the great ironclad ticked and creaked, like a wounded beast gone to ground, its monstrous roar, for the moment, silenced.

THE END

The Pennine Fusiliers will return in
The Alleyman

GLOSSARY

Battalion: Infantry Battalions at full strength might be around a thousand men. Generally consisted of four *companies*.

Black Hand Gang: slang for party put together for a dangerous and hazardous mission, like a raiding party. Such was the nature of the tasks, it was chosen from volunteers, where possible.

Blighty: England, home. From the Hindustani *Bilaiti* meaning foreign land.

Blighty One: A wound bad enough to have you sent back to England.

Boojums: Nickname for tanks, also a Wibble Wobble, a Land Creeper, a Willie.

Bosche: Slang for German, generally used by officers.

Breastworks: Temporary, quickly-built fortifications, consisting of low earth walls usually about chest height.

Canteen: A water bottle.

Chatt: Parasitic lice that infested the clothing and were almost impossible to avoid while living in the trenches. Living in warm, moist clothing and laying eggs along the seams, they induced itching and skin complaints.

Chatting: De-lousing, either by running a fingernail along the seams and cracking the lice and eggs or else running a lighted candle along them to much the same effect.

Commotional Shock: Contemporary medical term referring

to the physical short-term concussive effects or 'shell-shock,' from a shell blast and viewed as a physical injury, which qualified soldiers for 'wound stripes,' possible discharge from the army and a pension.

Communication Trench: Trench that ran perpendicularly to the *fire trench*, enabling movement of troops, supplies and messages to and from the Front Line, from the parallel support and reserve lines to the rear.

Company: One quarter of an infantry battalion, 227 men at full strength divided into four platoons.

Emotional Shock: Suffering from 'nerves.' Unlike *commotional shock,* those suffering from mental stress were merely seen as sick and not entitled to a 'wound stripe.'

Enfilade: Flanking fire along the length of a trench as opposed to across it.

Estaminet: A French place of entertainment in villages and small towns frequented by soldiers; part bar, part cafe, part restaurant, generally run by women.

FANY: First Aid Nursing Yeomanry. The only service in which women could enlist and wear khaki, they drove ambulances, ran soup kitchens, mobile baths, etc. in forward areas.

Fire Bay: Part of a manned fire trench facing the enemy. Bays were usually separated by *traverses*.

Firestep: The floor of the trench was usually deep enough for soldiers to move about without being seen by the enemy. A firestep was a raised step that ran along the forward face of the fire trench from which soldiers could fire or keep watch.

Fire Trench: Forward trench facing the enemy that formed part of the Front Line.

Flechettes: From the French, meaning 'little arrow.' Used early on in the war, they were large pointed darts that were dropped from an aeroplane over trenches and were capable of piercing helmets.

Fritz: Slang term for a German.

Funk: State of nerves or depression, more harshly a slang word for cowardice.

Funk Hole: Generally, any dugout or shelter, but often referred to niches or holes big enough to shelter one or two men scraped into the front wall of a trench.

Gazetted: All military promotions and gallantry awards were officially announced *The London Gazette*. To be the subject of such an announcement was to be gazetted.

Gone Dis: Short for 'gone disconnected.' Originally used by Signallers to mean a telephone line was down, usually from shelling, and that they were out of communication.

Hush Hush Crowd: Nickname for the Machine Gun Corp Heavy Section, or Tank Section, owing to the secrecy that surrounded their development.

Iddy Umpty: Slang for Morse Code and, by extension, the Signallers who used it.

Jildi: From the Hindi – get a move on, quick, hurry.

Kite Balloon: An observation balloon, carrying a basket for an observer but attached to the ground by a winch.

Land Ship: A tank.

Lewis Machine Gun: Air cooled, using a circular magazine cartridge holding 48 rounds each. Lighter and more portable than the Vickers.

Linseed Lancer: Slang for a stretcher bearer of the *RAMC*.

Look Stick: Slang for a trench periscope.

Maconachie: Brand of tinned vegetable stew. Made a change from endless Bully Beef, though not by much.

Mills Bomb: Pineapple-shaped British hand grenade, armed by pulling a pin and releasing the trigger lever.

Minniewerfer: German trench mortar shell.

MO: Medical Officer.

Mongey Wallahs: Cooks or chefs, from the French *manger*, to eat.

NCO: Non-Commissioned Officer; used for Sergeants Major, Sergeants or Corporals.

Neurasthenia: Contemporary medical term to describe emotional shell-shock, less charitably seen as a 'weakness of the nerves.'

No Man's Land: Area of land between the two opposing Front Lines.

OP: Observation Post.

Parados: Raised defensive wall of earth or sandbags along the rear of the trench to help disperse explosions behind the line.

Parapet: Raised defence of earth or sandbags at the front of a trench to provide cover for those on the *firestep*.

Part-worn: Clothing previously worn by another soldier, either deceased, ill or otherwise having no further use for it.

PH Helmet: Phenate-Hexamine Helmet. Early type of full gas mask. Not so much a helmet as a flannel hood soaked in neutralising chemicals, and a mouth tube and distinctive red rubber valve for exhalation.

Platoon: A quarter of an infantry company, commanded by a Subaltern. Consisting of 48 men divide into four sections.

Plum Pudding: Nickname for a type of British trench mortar round.

Port: The left side of a vessel or ship.

Puttee: Khaki cloth band wound round the calf from the knee to the ankle.

RAMC: Royal Army Medical Corp, often summoned with the well-worn cry, "stretcher bearer!" Uncharitably also said to stand for Rob All My Comrades.

Reading Your Shirt: The act of Chatting.

Red Tabs: Slang for Staff Officers, after the red tabs worn on the collars of their tunics.

Revetment: Any material used to strengthen a trench wall against collapse; wooden planking, brushwood wattling, corrugated iron, etc.

RFC: Royal Flying Corps of the British Army.

Sally Port: Small, hidden passage out under the parapet of a fire trench used for sorties into No Man's Land.

Section: A quarter of a platoon, usually consisting of 12 men in the charge of an NCO.

SRD: Supply Reserve Depot. The initials were stamped on official army issue stone rum jars issued to platoons, although the initials soon came to stand for other things like Service Rum Diluted, Soon Runs Dry or Seldom Reaches Destination.

Starboard: The right side of a vessel or ship.

Subaltern: Or Sub; a commissioned officer under the rank of captain; first or second lieutenant.

Tankodrome: A tank park and workshops behind the lines where maintenance and repairs can be carried out.

Traverse: Thick sandbag partition built in trenches to prevent enfilading enemy fire and to limit the effect of any explosions. In fire trenches they were used to create fire bays. Also; purposely-built changes in angle of direction in any trench to achieve the same effect.

Sap: A communications trench that runs out from an already existing trench to an emplacement, kitchen, latrine or stores.

Sappers: Generally, a private in the Royal Engineers. But in this case, a small dedicated unit formed by Everson from those men with a trade – bricklaying, carpentry, etc. – to perform a similar function.

Scran: A general term for food.

Sponson: The side-mounted gun turret of a tank, taken from the naval term. The Mark I 'male' tank had no central-mounted roof turret, like later tanks, but two side mounted sponsons, one on either side. Each sponson was armed with a six pounder gun and a Hotchkiss machine gun.

Stand To: Stand to Arms. Highest state of alert when all men should be ready for immediate action, weapons at the ready. Occurred regularly in the trenches at dawn and dusk to repel any attempted attacks.

Star Shell: An artillery shell consisting of a large magnesium flare and a parachute. Used for illuminating battlefields at night.

VAD: Voluntary Aid Detachment, women volunteers providing auxiliary nursing assistance to the Red Cross and registered nurses.

Vickers Machine gun: Water-cooled, belt-fed, machine gun. Heavy and bulky, but more accurate than the Lewis.

Whizz-Bang: A German 77mm high velocity shell.

Windy: Or *to have the wind-up;* apprehensive or anxious about a situation.

Pat Kelleher is a freelance writer. He has written for magazines, animation and radio. He served his time writing for a wide variety of TV licensed characters, translating them into audio books, novels and comics. Yes, he's written for that. And that. And even, you know, them. He has several non-fiction books to his credit and his educational strips and stories for the RSPB currently form the mainstays of their Youth publications. Somehow he has steadfastly managed to avoid all those careers and part-time jobs that look so good on a dust jacket.

NO MAN'S WORLD

BLACK HAND GANG

PAT KELLEHER

UK ISBN: 978 1 906735 35 7 • US ISBN: 978 1 906735 84 5 • £9.99/$12.99

On November 1st, 1916, nine-hundred men of the 13th Battalion of The Pennine Fusiliers vanished without trace from the battlefield, only to find themselves stranded on an alien planet. There they must learn to survive in a frightening and hostile environment, forced to rely on dwindling supplies of ammo and rations as the natives of this strange new world begin to take an interest. However, the aliens amongst them are only the first of their worries, as a sinister and arcane threat begins to take hold from within their own ranks!